The Light in the Hallway

OTHER BOOKS BY AMANDA PROWSE

The Girl in The Corner

The Coordinates of Loss

Anna

Theo

How to Fall in Love Again: Kitty's Story

The Art of Hiding

The Idea of You

Poppy Day

What Have I Done?

Clover's Child

A Little Love

Christmas for One

Will You Remember Me?

A Mother's Story

Perfect Daughter

Three-and-a-Half Heartbeats (exclusive to Amazon Kindle)

The Second Chance Café (originally published as *The Christmas Café*)

Another Love

My Husband's Wife

I Won't Be Home for Christmas

The Food of Love

OTHER NOVELLAS BY AMANDA PROWSE

The Game

Something Quite Beautiful

A Christmas Wish

Ten Pound Ticket

Imogen's Baby

Miss Potterton's Birthday Tea

PRAISE FOR AMANDA PROWSE

'Amanda Prowse is the queen of contemporary family drama.'

Daily Mail

'A tragic story of loss and love.'

Lorraine Kelly, *Sun*

'Captivating, heartbreaking and superbly written.'

Closer

'A deeply emotional, unputdownable read.'

Red

'Uplifting and positive, but you may still need a box of tissues.'

Cosmopolitan

'You'll fall in love with this.'

Cosmopolitan

'Warning: you will need tissues.'

Sun on Sunday

'Handles her explosive subject with delicate care.'

Daily Mail

'Deeply moving and eye-opening.'

Heat

'A perfect marriage morphs into harrowing territory . . . a real tear-jerker.'

Sunday Mirror

'Powerful and emotional drama that packs a real punch.'

Heat

'Warmly accessible but subtle . . . moving and inspiring.'

Daily Mail

'A powerful and emotional work of fiction with a unique twist – a practical lesson in how to spot a fatal, but often treatable disease.'

Piers Morgan, CNN presenter

'A truly amazing piece of drama about a condition that could affect any one of us in a heartbeat. Every mother should read this book.'

Danielle Lineker, actor

'A powerful and emotional page-turner that teaches people with no medical training how to recognise sepsis and save lives.'

Dr Ranj Singh, paediatric doctor and BBC presenter

'A powerful and moving story with a real purpose. It brings home the dreadful nature of this deadly condition.'

Mark Austin, ITN presenter

'A festive treat . . . if you love Jojo Moyes and Freya North, you'll love this.'

Closer

'Magical.'

Now

'Nobody writes contemporary family dramas as well as Amanda Prowse.'

Daily Mail

The Light in the Hallway

AMANDA PROWSE

Text copyright © 2019 by Lionhead Media Ltd
All rights reserved.

Published by Lake Union Publishing, Seattle

www.apub.com

Amazon, the Amazon logo, and Lake Union Publishing are trademarks of Amazon.com, Inc., or its affiliates.

ISBN-13: 9781542041171
ISBN-10: 1542041171

Cover design by Rose Cooper

Printed in the United States of America

The Light in the Hallway

1992

'I asked my mum. She said no. And not just a regular no, but a no with her hand up.' He pictured her serious face and pose, like a policeman stopping traffic. 'That means a forever no and not an "I'll think about it" no, which usually turns into a yes, eventually.'

Ten-year-old Nick sat on the kerb outside his house and kicked his scuffed trainers at the softening tarmac floor warmed by the hot sun, huffing at the injustice of it all.

'She said she had asked my dad and he said he wasn't about to go into debt just so I could have a bike.' Nick had heard his father before on the topic; it made his face red and his nostrils flare. *Debt provides the right level of worry to send a working man to an early grave. I saw it rip my parents apart and it's a state in which I will never live. Better to go without than go into debt. Mark my words . . .*

Nick wasn't sure he agreed with this, figuring that to have a bike would be the best thing in the whole wide world, early grave or not.

Alex, his classmate, folded his arms across his faded *Alvin and the Chipmunks* T-shirt and bounced his small rubber ball repeatedly on the same spot, catching it with one hand. The sound was both captivating and irritating.

'Well, my mum said if we could afford things like bikes then she wouldn't be pulling extra shifts at the Co-op and stacking shelves when she'd rather be at home with a cup of tea and her feet up, watching *Corrie*.'

Eric, the third member of this esteemed yet nameless gang, whose Yorkshire twang was the strongest, sighed and looked from Alex to Nick. 'My mum said, "Get out of the sodding kitchen, you little bas'tad," and then she threw a potato at me.' He let this sink in as their snickers burbled. 'I'm taking it as a maybe.'

As ever, Eric, their sharp-witted friend, was able to turn the upset of having asked and been denied the one thing they truly wanted – bikes – into something hilarious. Nick was in awe of how his lanky mate trotted out swear words and funny responses, unafraid to answer back at a particular volume from the side of his mouth, which meant adults didn't always hear but he and Alex always did, making it a battle to keep those giggles in and their faces straight until they were able to explode. This was one of Eric's skills. This and his enormous capacity for food; they called him the 'Human Dustbin', and how much he ate was mightily impressive. It was the norm that Eric would quickly finish what he was eating, whether it be a bag of crisps, a school lunch or a biscuit, and then stare at him and Alex in the way a family dog might, watching with wide eyes and a mouth that quivered at the possibility of a share in the food Nick or Alex was eating. It was usually out of kindness or guilt that Nick would hand over at least a bite to Eric, who would be so happy, his reaction so grateful, it far outweighed the discarded morsel he had been cast.

Nick was stumped. With a flat-out 'no' from all parents, how were they going to get bikes so they could roam the moors, get from A to B with haste and, more important, circle the market square, looking casual while showing off to anyone who might be loitering? This particular mode of transport was, in Nick's opinion, the one thing that shouted out, LOOK AT ME! I'M A KID WHO IS GOING PLACES!

He clamped his top teeth over his bottom lip, as he did when he had to try to figure something out.

It wasn't fair. Life wasn't fair! He hadn't asked to be born in this small, rubbish town in the middle of nowhere where there was only one rubbish cinema, one rubbish shop, no ice rink – something he had seen on television and was very keen to try – and no motocross club (ditto). In fact, the only places to hang out were the garage at his parents' house, the Rec, Market Square and the Old Dairy Shed on the outskirts of town – a rather dilapidated steel-framed barn, long abandoned and where the older lads and lasses went to snog. This he knew for a fact because he and his friends would sneak up from the east side and climb on an old crate to peer in on the shenanigans from the little window in the side where the glass had long been pelted away by forcefully chucked stones. There the three would stand and gawp, fascinated, offended and delighted by the moans, squeals and fumblings that took place on the cold concrete floor of the Old Dairy Shed, which was scattered with pigeon shit, discarded cigarette butts and old chip wrappers. On one occasion they had observed fumblings taking place up against the steel girder in the middle of the echoey space. Nick had loped home in silence, more than a little unnerved by this athletic feat. It didn't seem right standing up. Not that it seemed very right lying down either.

The other place they liked to congregate was the long green-painted iron bench in Market Square. The bench, with its worn brass plaque to Albert Digby, the son of a farming family who had lost his life serving his country, carried a fiercely adhered to 'hierarchy of occupancy' code. It was quite simple. Grown-ups took precedence. After them, if you were in upper school the bench was yours, followed by junior school attendees and then primary school. But then there were caveats: boys who played football for the school team could oust just about anyone; the footie team players really were like mini celebrities. Then there were the groups of girls who took ownership of the bench by dint of the fact that no one wanted to intervene, get too close or talk to the huddle.

They were intimidating – a seething mass of flicked hair, cheap perfume and loud, loud laughter. Nick and his mates thought these huddles were glorious. Contained within were all the mysteries of the universe and the only two things they coveted and admired as much if not more than the racing bikes which eluded them: boobs. They found boobs fascinating and hilarious in equal measure. The sight of boobs was enough to transfix them, and hearing the word 'boobs' enough to send them into paroxysms of laughter.

'So, if our parents aren't going to buy us bikes' – Nick continued to ponder the dilemma in hand – 'how are we going to get them? There has to be a way.'

'We could rob some!' Eric suggested enthusiastically.

'Who could we rob bikes from?' This seemed to be Alex's concern, rather than the illegality and immorality of the suggested act.

'Dunno.' Eric chewed his thumbnail. 'Ooh!' he shouted, jumping up in a lightbulb moment. 'The postman. He has a bike!'

'That big red one with the rack on the front where he rests his postbag?' Alex hinted at the rather distinct nature of the man's standard-issue bike, the only one in the town. 'I think people might notice if it went missing and we were doing wheelies on one very similar in the street!'

There was a beat of silence.

Nick stared at his mate. 'Anyway, isn't the postman your uncle John who lives next door to you?'

'He's not next door,' Eric fired back. 'He's next door but one.' As if this might be all the difference needed to give his idea the possibility of success.

Nick and Alex exchanged a look.

'You're such a div, Eric!'

'And you're a knobhead!'

And so it went, the trading of various insults that covered everything from mental impairment, physical defects and sexuality, all standard fare in these exchanges.

'You've got a girl's foo-foo instead of a willy!'

'You've got a girl's foo-foo, no willy and you wear frilly knickers!' Eric retorted.

The boys shouted ridiculously and raucously, as if volume were a big weapon in the war of words. Nick shook his head. Their verbal jousting might be funny but it wasn't helping him figure out how they could get bikes. He sighed again.

Life was not fair.

ONE

'So, are you going to come with me, Oliver?' Nick hated the hesitancy to his tone, torn between wanting to keep the question casual and not alarm the boy, but at the same time feeling the pressing need to leave, knowing this was it. The sole reason for his return home was to try to encourage his son, give him the opportunity to be part of this. Thinking ahead and trying, as he had over the last few months, to eliminate any future regrets. Not only was this easier said than done, but he was now wasting precious time. He hovered in the bedroom doorway, certain Oliver had heard the question despite the dire electronic music that blared from the laptop. This was the second time he had asked in as many seconds. The fact he felt the need to repeat it suggested he was hoping for a different response the second time around.

Oliver shook his head, his expression neutral but his jaw tense, gripped as ever by whatever game now flashed on the screen, the bright colours, pings, beeps and whistles, the modern-day equivalent to a pin-ball machine, the mastery of which was always infinitely more urgent than anything Nick might have to say.

Even today.

'I know you're *saying* no, it's just that . . .' he began, not knowing how to finish.

His son looked up briefly from the laptop balanced on his bony knees which held him captive and to which he returned his gaze, almost daring his dad to speak again.

'The thing is, Olly,' Nick tried again, and again the words ran out. The roof of his mouth was dry and his tongue stuck there. He had never fully understood the phrase 'paddling like a duck beneath the water', but in that moment he did. He looked calm, his voice was level and yet inside he was screaming.

'I'm not going. I don't want to.'

'But they said—'

'I'm not going, Dad! That's it.' Oliver's tone was a little more forceful now.

Nick took a deep breath and tried to recall the words Peter, the counsellor, had said during their last chat.

'Try to remember that there is no right or wrong way to behave . . . Don't force or coerce, because that's the road to conflict and neither of you need that on top of everything else . . . Remember that she is not only your wife, she's Olly's mum too. Tread gently. Leave doors open, encourage, listen and try to understand that this is everyone's personal journey and everyone takes a different route. Be ready to prop him up when he most needs it, and if it's at a time when you most need propping up, that's when it can seem hardest . . .'

'Okay.' He nodded, tapping his wedding ring on the door frame. 'Okay, son. But if you change your mind, I'll be leaving in a few minutes.'

'I won't change my mind.' Oliver worked his fingers on the keys at double speed and bit his bottom lip.

Nick left the bedroom door ajar and, having neglected to do so that morning in a mad rush to leave the house, he cleaned his teeth quickly in the sparse green-tiled bathroom at the top of the stairs. He popped his blue toothbrush in the pot next to his wife's lilac one and splashed his face with cold water, patting it dry on the hand towel that felt a little stiff to the touch and had a vague smell of mould about it. Laundry, yet another task, an aspect of ordinary life that had fallen by the wayside in the shadow of the tidal wave from which he was running. Although with his energy levels sapped, it would be fair to say it was now more of a crawl than a run. He balled the towel and threw it into the plastic laundry basket which lived in the corner by the sink.

He took his time, though aware of the urgency, opening the kitchen window, inviting a breeze into the stuffy room where the sun beat against the misty window for the best part of the day. He put the milk back in the fridge and located his car keys, giving the boy a chance to change his mind.

Hoping . . .

He carried a weird sensation, empty with a hollow thump to his gut, which felt a lot like hunger, and yet he was simultaneously wired, full, as if on high alert.

With one last opportunity looming, his eye on the clock and his heart racing, he ran back up the stairs and walked purposefully into Oliver's room. His son had slipped down on the pillows and pulled the duvet cover up to his chin. The sight of him curled up like this reminded Nick so much of when his boy was five, six, seven – hiding from the monsters that might lurk under the bed – and his heart tore a little. The actual quilt had been discarded in a heap on the bedroom floor – no need of the fibre-filled warmth on this balmy summer evening – and yet he felt an unwelcome chill to his limbs.

'Olly.'

Oliver stayed silent.

'Olly, this is the last chance—'

'I know. Just go! Go then! I've already said!' he shouted, and Nick knew this newly ignited row was more than either of them could cope with.

'Okay, son. Okay.'

He ran back down the stairs, his pace urgent now, and out of the door, to sit in the driver's seat, letting the engine run and rubbing and flexing his hands, as if this might remove their tremor. He revved the accelerator with a desperate desire to see Oliver launch himself from the front door at the last minute and jump in beside him, like he might do if this were a movie, when with the clock ticking and the risk of getting trapped or left behind was at its highest, the hero would buckle up, safe. Enabling the audience to breathe a huge sigh of relief . . .

He didn't.

It was as if he heard the clock on the dashboard tick as the big hand jumped forward. Nick reversed at speed down the steep slope of the narrow driveway and travelled the route towards Thirsk that was now so familiar he often arrived at either end of the journey with little memory of driving it.

He thought he would feel more, but his numbness, an emotional anaesthesia of sorts, was not wholly unwelcome. It had been an odd day. A day he had tried to predict many times in the preceding months, attempting to play it out in his mind, imagine what it might be like, but to no avail. He had been with Kerry since he was sixteen years of age and yet this was the last day – the last day for her and the last day for them. It was surreal. In his ponderings there was higher drama, background tension and a swell of emotion that he figured would carry him along in its wake, but so far everything, up until this point, had felt rather ordinary. A little flat even and, for that, disappointing. He had been into work for an hour that morning, sorted his shift pattern for the next month, explained to Mr Siddley, Julian Siddley, that his routine might be in turmoil for a while as things had taken a sudden but not unexpected turn.

'It's my wife . . .'

And then he went to sit with her. Like he did every day after work, before work if she'd had a particularly bad night, and all day at weekends.

Beverly and the rest of the girls in the back office had been tearful and sweet and wanted to hug him or squeeze his arm knowingly, which only made him feel uncomfortable. It was such an odd thing to do to a colleague who you were only on nodding terms with across the canteen, when the conversation was usually of the jovial or jokey variety, but he knew they meant well. The small market town of Burstonbridge on the North York Moors was a bump of a settlement with one main road that ran right through it. There were no tall buildings, no districts, no high-street-branded stores, and everyone who stayed past school age worked either in farming, the small businesses that supported the farms or at Siddley's.

Travellers taking the scenic route between Helmsley and Guisborough stumbled across the place, pausing to photograph the pretty war memorial, the sloping, higgledy-piggledy cobbled streets and the solid Norman church as they stopped at Mackie and Sons garage for fuel and plastic-wrapped sandwiches or to potter around the gift shops in Market Square, which sold overpriced rubbish to tourists alone. It was a close community; most people who worked at Siddley's did so like their parents before them. Aunts and uncles recommended nieces and nephews, and mums and dads took great pride in seeing their offspring march through the door, wet behind the ears, to take up the mantle of picking, packing and shipping out imported party lights, festoon lights, outdoor lighting rigs and spotlights for big events. It might not be the most glamorous of places or one with a corporate ladder Burston folk could climb, but they arrived at work happy, certain in the knowledge they would be leaving with a wage at the end of the week.

Siddley's was a family company, and a Siddley had been at the helm since it started in 1946. It was Mr Douglas Siddley who had started it, a local man who came back from the Front and recognised that post-war Britain wanted nothing more than to put up bunting and strings of festoon lights along its pub and shop frontages, rear gardens, bandstands and schools. Siddley's brought welcome light to places that had been dulled by war. This frippery, along with eating bananas, oranges and other food denied to them during the years of austerity, was proof that the dark days were over. And folk celebrated whilst dancing without guilt to new music, hand in hand with the beaus they had tearfully waved off to war, those who had returned. Yes, it was Douglas who got the firm up and running, but it was his son, Joseph, who had seized the opportunity for export and expansion and hadn't looked back.

Mr Aubrey Siddley, Julian's father and Joseph's son, had sent word via Caitlyn, his daughter-in-law. She said he sent his best regards and to shout if Nick needed anything. It made him smile, knowing that with the size of the Siddley house – Alston Bank up at Drayfield Moor, with its long sweep of a driveway and parkland on either side – he'd have to shout bloody loudly. Nick pictured a child's bike abandoned on that driveway with the back wheel spinning and even now it made his hackles rise.

What Nick had really wanted to do when he left the depot that morning was jump on an aeroplane and go as far away as he could, all alone. Just pack a bag and go anywhere – anywhere in sight of the sea and where he could walk barefoot on sand. He'd take his five hundred pounds savings out of the bank and run . . . But then he thought about Oliver, who might pretend to be a big man but was just a scared, gangly eighteen-year-old who was at a crossroads, waiting for his 'A' level results, which would be in his hands in five days' time. Nick thought about the house and his job and his mum and his mother-in-law and felt the weight of responsibility sit heavily on his shoulders. Despite his daydream of escape, there was no beach in the world far enough away for him to outrun his responsibilities.

It wasn't the first time he had felt this way – *How . . . How are we in debt, Kerry? How has this happened?* – but today was not the time to think about that.

He parked the car in the car park and took a minute to steel himself, thinking about Peter's words of advice earlier.

'I think you should go home, Nick . . . and maybe see if Oliver wants to come in.' It was the pause that spoke loudest of all, all that the counsellor didn't say.

'I did call him earlier and offered to go and pick him up, but he said he didn't want me to.'

'I know, but I think you should go home and maybe see if he *does* want to come in . . .' Peter had repeated, his tone a little more forceful. And Nick had listened to the man who had more experience of this than him and whose thoughts were not fogged by the enormity of the situation.

'Okay.' He had nodded and Peter laid his hand on his shoulder, as if this were the right answer.

He had been home no more than ten minutes when the call came in, not long enough to make a cup of tea, the milk for which he had grabbed from the fridge while he went to knock on Oliver's bedroom door.

'I think . . . I think you should come back, Nick. Don't rush, drive safely, but get here as soon as you can . . .'

He had known this time would come, and yet nothing over the last few months could have really prepared him for it. He slammed the car door and walked briskly inside, raising a hand to Mary on reception, who he had learnt over recent months liked knitting, holidays in Lanzarote and roast lamb. She had six grandchildren and was allergic to penicillin and cats, liked one daughter-in-law, hated the other. It was funny the rubbish you picked up when you had all the time in the world to hang about and chat. And he liked chatting to Mary, whether she knew it or not. Talking to the old lady who volunteered to greet visitors was one of the highlights of his day, a very welcome distraction when he needed a little air or a change of scenery. Nick knew he would miss her, because if there was no chatting to Mary that meant there was no need to visit St Vincent's, and if there was no need to visit St Vincent's then it meant the worst had happened.

And here he was.

He pushed on the door of the ground-floor bedroom that had been his haven and his prison for more hours than he cared to think about. A room where a minute could last an hour. He knew every inch of the pale pink walls and the window that looked out over the car park. He knew the rust spot on the metal window frame, the missing handle on the top drawer of the bedside cabinet and the small damp stain in the corner of the ceiling that, depending on his mood, looked like the Isle of Wight or a fried egg. He knew that the air conditioning worked well at night, but was a bit hit and miss during the day. He knew that water drunk from the sink in the bathroom tasted of iron and that the space between the loo and the shower was just a little too small to accommodate a woman who fell and wanted to stay put, without the energy or inclination to rise again. He closed the door behind him and entered.

The atmosphere was uncomfortably close and he wished he could throw open a door and let the cooler night air in. Her breathing had changed. The atmosphere had changed. Sharon, the nurse, stood up from the chair by the side of the bed. She placed her hand briefly on his arm.

'You know to just press if you need anything, Nick.'

He nodded. He knew the drill.

'Olly not with you?' She looked over his shoulder, as if the boy might appear, and he turned to follow her stare, feeling a leap of joy at the thought that his son might have somehow made it here after all.

'No. He didn't want to come.' He swallowed. 'I tried.'

She gave a tight-lipped smile of understanding.

'Is there anything, anything we need to . . .' He looked to the bed and away again, unsure of what he was asking, but feeling that he should be asking something.

'There's nothing more we need to do, Nick.' This time her smile was wide and comforting. The smile of someone who was in control, and this reassured him, he who was new to this experience. Sharon was not. 'You know where we are.'

He nodded again and took the seat Sharon had only just vacated.

He ran his fingertips up his wife's arm as she lay in the bed. She looked different than when he had last seen her an hour or so ago. She was a little grey, and a slow, foul rattle accompanied each breath.

'Cor, I was gasping for a cup of tea.' He laughed, the loud noise an intrusion that ricocheted off the walls. 'Nearly managed to grab one too before the phone rang.' He reached for her fingers and thumbed the skin on the back of her hand. She didn't move or open her eyes or grip his fingers in return, although he imagined she did. 'I think they've given you something to help you sleep, haven't they? Well, you just sleep, lass. You just sleep and I'll sit right here by your side.'

He stared at her head tipped back on the pillow, eyes sunken, lashes sticky and her thin face pinched, skin like waxed paper. Her eyes closed, mouth open and that awful rattle . . .

'It's still warm out, but they said the temperature is going to drop tonight, not that I mind. You know what I'm like, can't sleep if it's too warm. I think I'll put the heating on boost, just in case it gets very cold. I know you don't like the kitchen floor to be icy on your bare feet or to have to walk into a chilly bathroom in the night. Yes, I'll do that.' He coughed again. Her lack of response was almost deafening. 'I was thinking earlier about how lovely it would be to have a holiday. Maybe sit in front of the sea and walk on a beach. Do you remember all our lovely holidays at Filey? That B&B with the squeaky bed and Oliver when he was younger in the little room next door, and you were so worried about making a noise that if we fancied a cuddle we had to pull the duvet on to the floor and be as quiet as church mice.' He laughed. 'Those were the days, eh, love?'

He closed his eyes briefly. The sentiment he wanted to express was not something that came easily, but this was the time. 'I love you, Kerry.

I love you, my mate.' He pinched the top of his nose to stop the emotion that threatened to cloud this moment. 'I think about the first time I took you out and I was so nervous I could hardly speak. Just kids, both of us, weren't we? You thought I had a stutter; I was so worried about saying the right thing and making you like me. God, I was *desperate* for you to like me. Well, I must have done something right, nearly nineteen years next May. Nineteen years . . .' He kissed the back of her hand. 'I know people say it all the time, but it really does feel like yesterday. Where did that time go, eh?' He bent forward and rested his face on the pillow next to hers and whispered, 'I know it's not all been perfect, and that maybe we have . . . drifted. But I wouldn't swap a single second of it, Kerry. Not one. I love you. I will do my best with Olly, I promise you that. And I will miss you every single day. You're my girl. You'll always be my girl. But you go now, my darling. You don't have to be brave. You don't have to hang on. You can rest and you can have peace, go to sleep, knowing you're loved . . .'

He felt the slip of tears across his cheek and over his nose and after some minutes, he couldn't say with accuracy how many, he became aware of the quiet. And it was surprising, shocking almost, and unexpected, even though he had been waiting for it. Waiting for it for six months or more, truth be told. Gone was the rattle; gone was the weak pulse of life that an ailing body gave. Her mouth had fallen open and her face was now somehow softer. He sat up, eyes wide, a slight sense of panic in his chest and a terrible aching void of nothingness in his gut, topped with exhaustion.

'Kerry? Kerry?' he said softly. Bending low, he kissed her face. 'Sweet dreams, lass. Sweet dreams.'

Instantly he felt his muscles soften with relief at the realisation that their nightmare was finally over and they were both free.

Guilt swooped in and punched him in the throat, leaving him breathless. *Relief? She is dead, Nick! Dead! How dare you?*

Reaching for the red cord, he pulled it and sat back in the chair. In the seconds while he waited for Sharon and Dr Ned to come in he felt the warmth leave the room.

'Are you okay, Nick?' Dr Ned asked, his voice a little echoey.

He looked up at the face of the man who had cared for his wife. 'I don't know,' he answered truthfully.

◆　◆　◆

Nick pulled up on to the steep driveway and looked at the house, which sat shaded forlornly in the soft bruise of darkness. He pictured his son, no doubt still lying on his bed, cloistered in the dark, alone with his own version of sadness. His eyes were drawn to the small rectangular window above the front door, from which Kerry would always ensure a light shone. Regardless of the season, as soon as night pulled its blind on the day, she would flick the switch next to the stairs, ensuring that Oliver coming home from school, he returning from work or any casual visitor could easily find their way to the front door. The light in the hallway was, however, more than just an aid to ensure a stumble-free trip up the path; it was a beacon, a sign of the life that lay behind the door, the promise of a warm welcome, a cup of tea, company, home.

Nick looked to the right at John and Liz's front room next door, noting the haze of light that filtered from the sitting room out over the lawn. He felt a stab of something a lot like jealousy, misplaced he knew, but how come their lives got to carry on happily, while his whole world had fallen through the big black hole left by cancer? It wasn't fair. Why them? He remembered saying as much to Kerry when her results came through.

'Why us? Why you?'

And she had smiled at him in the way she did, as if she knew the answer and he was still trying to catch up, and said, 'Why not us? Why not me? Life throws curveballs; you've got to either catch them and throw them back or dodge them. That's it.'

He closed the front door quietly, wary of waking Oliver if he was asleep and in truth hoping he was, a chance to delay the appalling conversation they were going to have. He clicked on the hallway light and slipped off his shoes, before putting them in the bottom of the cupboard in the hallway, trying not to look up at Kerry's shopping bag hanging on the hook on the back of the door, or her wellington boots that she slipped into to take Treacle for her morning and evening walks. Treacle the beagle-cross who had tumbled into their lives a couple of years ago, something for Kerry to concentrate on during her treatment, a beloved distraction who was currently being cared for by his mum and sister across town, one less thing for him and Oliver to have to think about. Although right now he missed the little pup, knowing the soft whine of welcome and the feel of the warm coat under his palm would have brought some small measure of comfort.

He heard the squeak of the hinge on Oliver's bedroom door and took a deep breath, looking up at his skinny boy, who stood in his plaid pyjama bottoms and loose T-shirt, gripping the banister.

'Come down, Olly.' His words sounded sticky from a dry mouth as he made his way into the neat rectangular lounge where the floral cushions, strategically placed, softened the burgundy leather sofas and sank down into the chair in front of the telly.

'Look at you in your throne. Remote control in one hand, cup of tea in the other! You look like the king of the castle. I love you, Mr Bairstow. This is a proper posh three-piece suite. I'm a bit scared to sit on it. I feel very grand.'

'Nothing could be too grand for you. And if I'm the king then you're the queen, so sit back and enjoy your new settee. Might as well, the novelty will have worn off by the time we finish paying for it!'

He didn't put the light on, preferring the dimly lit space, far better suited for this worst of moments.

Oliver sat in the corner of the sofa, coiling his legs beneath him. He grabbed a cushion, which he placed over his chest, as if this feather-filled shield might offer a little protection from the verbal blows about to be delivered.

'It was very peaceful.' Nick's voice carried the croak of someone containing distress. 'She just went to sleep, but as I say, it was peaceful and I think at the end of the day, Olly, that's the best thing we could ever hope for the people we love.'

'Can I go now?'

'What?' The boy's words were unexpected and Nick felt the shameful glide of relief over his bones that there was not going to be the storm of emotion, the tears and anger that he had imagined for so long.

'I said, can I go now?'

'Of course, but if you want to talk to me, if you want—'

Oliver leapt up, cutting short his dad's speech as he walked briskly from the room. He heard the heavy footfall of his steps as his son ran up the stairs, back to the solace of his bed, no doubt. Nick sat back, taking in the room, which looked appropriately drab and cold in the half-light and where a thin layer of dust had settled on the surfaces. He thought about the conversation with Kerry's mum, Dora, who had arrived quickly after Kerry had passed. He stood in the corridor, loosely holding the small woman, who sobbed into her soggy handkerchief, while her friend Maureen and her other daughter, Diane, looked on.

'She's . . . She's with her dad now, isn't she?'

Dora looked up at him with red-rimmed eyes wide with hope. And he had nodded, not sure what he believed, but knowing that the kindest thing to do at that moment was to offer a crumb of hope that the woman who had unimaginably lost her younger daughter might hold in her palm when the night felt like it would never end. Diane, Kerry's sister, had sobbed noisily as she walked her mum to the car, her arm across her shoulders, with Maureen propping her up on the other side, their walk slow and meandering.

He stood from the chair and made his way up the stairs, a quick glance at the bottom of Oliver's door telling him that he had turned the lamp off. He hoped his boy might sleep, wishing at some level that he could turn the clock back to when Oliver was small and Nick would sit on the edge of the bed, take him in his arms and rock him gently, telling him everything was going to be just fine . . . This followed by the sharp tip of realisation that if Oliver were small again, then Kerry would be by his side, young and fit and healthy, and there would be no need for the comfort offered over this terrible, terrible event.

He locked the bathroom door and stared at her lilac toothbrush sitting next to his in the pot. He took it in his hands and cradled it to his chest. This little plastic bristled stick that she had abandoned many weeks before had been a symbol of normality, of their life together, where night upon night they would stand side by side and clean their teeth before bedtime, elbows clashing in the narrow space between the bath and wall, smiling at their reflections in the mirrored medicine cabinet because all was good in their world. Happy with their lot.

A toothbrush – such an intimate object and one now without use because Kerry was gone. He pictured her smiling mouth and that slight shake of the head that told him not to be so silly. It was just a toothbrush. He wanted so badly at that moment to hold her, to feel her warm skin beneath his fingertips, that the ache hit his gut like a punch. Nick slipped down on to the cork-tiled floor, where his tears broke their banks and his chest heaved with the heavy weight of loss. His tears came so thick and fast it was hard to catch a breath. His distress took the last of his energy and, weak with exhaustion, he crumpled, crawling across the landing to the airing cupboard. With tears sliding silently down his face he kept his promise; hauling himself up, he switched the central heating on to give the house a boost of warmth. He knew how she hated to walk into the bathroom with chilly toes.

He woke the next day, as dawn broke. He had slept fitfully, waking often with a headache that made his thoughts cloudy. He felt odd; his brain raced ahead, mentally sorting his schedule for the day.

Must get up, have a shower and get to St Vincent's early, don't want her sitting on her own . . . before grief slammed the brakes on his plans and the realisation that he didn't have to go to the hospice, in fact would not have to go there ever again, left him feeling a little lost, now that his routine and his main preoccupation had been removed.

He was desperate for a cup of tea, but was distracted from the task by the mess that littered the work surfaces. He stumbled around the kitchen with the gait and concentration of a drunk. Slowly, he stacked dirty dishes and the cold, tea-stained mugs into the sink before abandoning the task halfway through. He opened the back door of the kitchen to catch the morning breeze.

'*That's it, Nick, let the day in . . .*' He heard her words as plainly as if she were standing behind him.

Fatigue and forgetfulness lulled him into the armchair in front of the television. The dishes could wait. Everything could wait. He kept the curtains drawn, not wanting the prying eyes of well-meaning neighbours who he was in no doubt would already know that Kerry had passed. Burstonbridge – or Burston, as locals knew it – had one school, one post office, one supermarket, two churches and seven pubs, and was a place where everyone knew someone you knew. He and Kerry had grown up here and their wider families spilled into every street and cul-de-sac in the immediate surroundings. Word would have got around very quickly. He pushed his fingertips into his closed eyes, trying to ease the soreness born of crying hard until he had fallen asleep. As he sat like this, in thought, he heard the flap of the letter box bang shut.

And so it began.

No more than an hour or so later there was a stack of envelopes forming a cushion on the welcome mat. He smiled inwardly at the thought that if Treacle had been home she would have loved it, nuzzling the slender paper gifts containing heartfelt words that had sat poised on the nibs of pens and the tips of tongues since that final diagnosis nearly four months ago: *spread . . . metastasise . . . three months, tops . . .*

'It'll be all right, love. Either way, it'll all be all right. We have to make the best of it.'

'How will it be all right, Kerry? How can we make the best of it?'

'We have to, love, because we have no choice . . .'

'Dad?'

'Yes?' He sat forward with a jolt, so lost in the memory of their conversation that it took him a second to realise Oliver's voice was real and coming from the doorway.

'We've run out of milk.'

'Milk?' He tried to catch up.

'Yes, there's no milk.'

'But there was half a bottle in the fridge when I left last night.'

'I had some cereal.' Oliver kicked his bare foot at the bottom of the door.

'I'll go and get some.'

Nick stood and waited, looking at the boy, hoping this interaction might be the precursor of something more, a revelation of sorts, questions even, but no. Nothing. He watched his son trudge back up the stairs, noting the dirty soles of his feet. Kerry would no doubt tell him to go and bathe. He grabbed his house key from the little wooden shelf above the radiator, stopping to gather the cards, which he scooped into a pile and plopped on the bottom stair.

The front door was only half open when he saw his mum walking towards him in her pyjama bottoms and an oversized T-shirt. Her eyes were red and swollen from crying, and Treacle strained on the leash. He took a deep breath, not knowing if he was ready to face either of them, not that he had any choice.

'Oh, Nicky!' she sobbed. The only person still to call him this, and a name he disliked but didn't have the heart to tell her so.

22

'We are okay, Mum.'

'No, you are not!' She trod the step and wrapped him uncomfortably in a short, tight hug. 'You're not okay, and you're still my lad, no matter how old you get. Did you get my texts? I didn't know whether to come over last night or whether to leave you with Olly to talk things through. I couldn't sleep. I sat in the chair all night with Treacle on my lap and I've cried a river. It's so unfair, Nicky, so bloody unfair!'

'It is.' He unhooked Treacle's collar and hung her leash on the back of the cupboard door.

'But a happy release, son, a happy release from all her suffering.' Again her tears sprang. 'Where's Olly?' She looked over his shoulder and then up the stairs.

'In his room.'

'Shall I go up?' she asked, grasping at the neck of her T-shirt, flustered. 'He might like to talk to his nan or just want a big old cuddle.'

'I think just leave him, actually, Mum. He'll know you're here and he'll come down if he wants some company.'

'Poor little lamb. My heart is breaking for him,' she murmured. 'How was Dora? Was Diane with her?'

'Dora was . . .' He struggled to find the words to adequately describe his mother-in-law's sense of loss, certain only that it was similar to his own. 'She was as you'd expect, and, yes, Di was with her.'

'Poor woman. Poor, poor woman.' She shook her head. 'It's every mother's worst nightmare. I've written to her and will pop the letter through her door.' She mopped her tears.

He felt ill equipped to deal with his mum's woe, barely knowing how to handle his own. He pointed out of the front door.

'I'm just going to get milk, actually. We've run out.'

'Milk? Don't be daft! You can't go out for milk!' His mum stood back, shocked.

'Why can't I?'

'Because you have to stay *in*. You have to stay in quietly and sit with the curtains drawn.'

He felt the inappropriate burble of laughter leave his mouth. 'I have to stay in?'

'Yes, Nicky! Your wife has just passed away.'

You don't need to tell me that! I know it! I know it! I know it!

His mum continued. 'And you don't want to be seen gallivanting up to the shop as if nothing is amiss. What would everyone think?'

'Christ, Mum, I wasn't planning on gallivanting anywhere, and secondly, my whole world is amiss and it has been for the last few months.'

'I know that, love, I know,' she whispered.

He sat back down on the bottom stair and ran his hand over the stack of envelopes. The truth was he had been grieving for Kerry for a long time. This might be the first terrible shock to the community, and all those who heard the news whispered at the bus stop, canteen or corner shop this morning, but to him it was, in fact, the last.

It was the end of a horrible chapter that had drained him of all energy and happiness. He had over the past weeks managed to haul himself to the shop on many a day, dropped Oliver at school or had taken Treacle for a wee, whilst barely able to put one foot in front of the other with exhaustion, digging deep to find a smile and a nod for his neighbours, who wanted to pass the time of day, talking about football or the weather while his nerves and heart were shredded. And right now all he wanted was a cup of bloody tea.

'*I'll* go and get the milk.' Without further discussion his mum bustled out, shutting the front door firmly behind her. Treacle trotted over the laminate floor and paced back and forth, as she had over the last few weeks, looking for the woman who always had a treat, a kind word and a soft palm held out in readiness to pet her.

The dog barked and then whined. Nick clicked his fingers and pulled her close to him, running the flat of his hand over her flank. 'I know, girl, I know.'

'Is Nan here?' Oliver asked as he came down the stairs.

'She's just gone for milk.'

'Hello, Treacle, hello, girl!' Oliver stepped over him and dropped down into the hallway, holding their family pet close to his chest and bending with his head close to hers. Nick had smelled the whiff of a teenage body in want of a good wash with soap, but was again unsure of the right thing to do or say, whether to nag him over something as irrelevant as personal hygiene when his mum had just passed was a step too far. There were lots of things he didn't know, and the only person he would be comfortable asking was Kerry.

'I was going to go to the shop, but Nan said I had to stay inside.' He pulled a face.

'Why do you have to stay inside?' Oliver looked up briefly.

'I don't rightly know.' He ran his hand over his stubbled chin. 'I think she thought it was not the done thing to go out today.'

'As long as I can go out next Thursday – my results are coming out.'

'I know.' He looked at the boy and wondered how it was that he had not mentioned his mum, not once. Should he start the conversation?

Don't force it, love. He'll talk when he's good and ready . . .

He heard her voice in his ear loud and clear and even gave a small nod to show he understood.

'How are you feeling about your results?' He hoped this was a safe topic.

Oliver shrugged. 'Don't know, really. Not much I can do about them now, is there?'

'Guess not.'

'Just hope I've done enough to get into Birmingham.'

'Birmingham sounds like a long way away.' He felt the flare of emotion at the prospect of being here in the house without Kerry and without Oliver.

'Everywhere is a long way away from Burston.' He continued to stroke Treacle.

'Good point. And you know, if you don't like it there, you can always come home.'

'I've got to get in first, Dad. Business Studies is a popular course, so I need the grades.'

'I know, but I'm just saying, university is all well and good, but it isn't the only way to make a life for yourself,' Nick lied, hoping his words might provide the salve to his son's hurt should he not make the grades, for he fervently believed that higher education, the thing which circumstances had denied him, was indeed the way to make a wonderful life.

Oliver nodded, and his next words when they came, so matter-of-factly spoken, took the breath from Nick's throat and left him a little winded.

'When will the funeral be, d'you think?'

The funeral . . . the funeral . . . any old funeral, not 'my mum's funeral'. How can you ask so casually when the very idea of it cuts me in two!

'Well' – Nick swallowed – 'I need to go and see Wainwright's today and sort it all out, but I think it'll be next week.'

'Next week.' Oliver nodded calmly. 'The same people who did Grandad's?'

'Yes, same people who do everyone's around here.'

Oliver stood. 'And you went to school with Michael Wainwright?'

'Yes, he was in our class. He knew your mum and that helped when we went to see him, before' – he coughed – 'a while before. She made plans to make sure it was as easy as possible for us now.'

He had done it, mentioned her, made it real. It felt akin to dipping his toe in the pool of grief, and it felt cold.

Oliver took a breath and looked up at the glass panel of the front door as his nan made her way up the path with a bottle of milk under one arm and a four-pack of toilet tissue under the other.

Nick let her in and watched as his mother made a beeline for her grandson.

'Oh, there he is! Oh, Olly! My little darlin'!' She dumped the purchases into her son's arms and enveloped Oliver in a restrictive hug. Nick saw the comedy in the moment as his son rolled his eyes over her shoulder and stuck out his tongue, fighting for breath and a little space as his nan almost garrotted him with the ferocity of her loving hold.

And this was how it was, the two of them passing the days, largely in separate rooms, coming together occasionally to calmly and quietly pour cereal or to greet the steady stream of visitors who pitched up, crying, clutching damp tissues and more often than not with a home-made cake, a meat pie or a batch of biscuits in their hands.

He and Oliver would exchange a knowing look and give assurances in the way that was becoming familiar: they were fine, needed nothing and they were grateful for the time the callers had taken to come and see them. Nick fell into bed each night in a state of near collapse. He was bone tired, too exhausted even to worry about his son's lack of emotional display or to dread the funeral, which was now planned. The George, the pub closest to the church, had been booked for the wake and Nick confirmed that Kerry wanted the same hymns they had had at their wedding; it seemed fitting. One of his last thoughts before falling asleep was what it would be like in the church if no one sang. On their wedding day Kerry had given a rousing rendition of 'Give Me Joy In My Heart', as Nick had neither the voice nor the confidence to sing out loud. He hoped someone would pick up the mantle, help him out, now dreading the idea of them all standing in an awkward silence.

You looked so beautiful . . .
You looked so handsome . . .
I felt like the luckiest man in the world . . .
And I the luckiest girl . . .

Nick looked at the clock on the mantelpiece and sat forward on the edge of the sofa, waiting for Oliver to come home. This was it. Two years of hard work and all that they had been through; the results of his efforts would be judged in three letters, single grades printed on a slip of paper. Nick's palms were a little clammy and he took a deep breath.

It doesn't matter, nothing does . . . you did your best, son, you can be so proud of that, and you had so much to contend with, more than most people have to face in a lifetime . . . don't beat yourself up about it, a path will reveal itself to you; it always does . . . we can go with plan B . . . He practised the words of comfort and commiseration. 'Oh, God,' he muttered under his breath. 'I don't think we have a plan B.'

He stood and tried again, in vain, to arrange the cushions the way Kerry had done them. They still defeated him, these pointless floral squares of feathers that sat like unwanted passengers on the sofa and chair, taking up space. He loathed them and yet couldn't bring himself to throw them away, not when they had been carefully chosen by her hand and had felt the touch of her cheek as she lay on the sofa to watch *Strictly* with her feet on his lap.

He sat back in the seat and folded his arms across his stomach, his head tipped back, imagining as he often did that Kerry was in the kitchen busying away, as she liked to do, and that all was right in his world . . .

He must have fallen asleep, as the front door crashing open and hitting the shelf above the radiator in the hallway woke him. He sat upright, remembering instantly the reason for Oliver's urgency, and his heart raced accordingly.

'Mum! Dad! I did it! I did it!' the boy called from the hallway. 'I got three . . .'

And then a bang as if something had hit the floor.

And then silence.

Nick had heard the words loud and clear, so naturally, so comfortably called that it took a second or two for the universe to catch up. He looked towards the door, expecting his son to walk in. After a couple of seconds, he stood and went to investigate the silence. He put his head around the door and knew that he would never forget the sight that greeted him.

Oliver was sitting on the welcome mat, coiled into a ball like a small child with his chin on his chest and his knees raised. His arms were clamped around his shins and his whole body shook.

Nick sank down to join him on the floor, and that was where they sat on the bristly welcome mat that felt anything but. Oliver raised his head and the sight of his distress caused Nick's own tears to pool.

'She's not here, Dad! She's not here, is she?'

'No, son. She's not here,' he managed through his own distress, hating to extinguish the faint look of hope in his son's eyes.

'Oh nooooooo! No!' Oliver's wail was loud, deep and drawn from deep within. He banged the floor with his hand. 'I wanted to say goodbye to her! I wanted to . . . to tell her things and I wanted to say goodbye!' He sobbed noisily. 'I didn't want her to leave me, Dad! I want her here. I want her here with us! And now she's gone and I didn't have the chance to tell her . . .'

'She knew, she knew, love. She knew what you wanted to say to her, she did!' Nick almost shouted through a mouth twisted with distress.

'You don't know that! You don't know anything!' Oliver kicked his leg out and smashed it into the wall.

'I do! I do, son. I was with her when she went. I was there, sat by her side, holding her hand, and I know what her last words were and they were for you!'

He put his arm around his son as his crying subsided a little. 'They . . . They were?' He looked up with an expression that was heart-wrenching in its desperate need.

Nick nodded.

'Yes.' He ran through the lie in his head, knowing Kerry would understand. Hoping Kerry would understand.

'What . . . What did she say, Dad?' Oliver gripped his forearm like a small child wary of separation.

Nick coughed to clear his throat; he ran his palm over his face before speaking slowly and steadily. 'She said; tell Olly I love him and I know that he loves me.'

Oliver wiped his eyes with the back of his hand, sniffing. 'She did?'

'Yes. She did. That's what she said.'

Oliver smiled briefly through his tears and let out a long, slow breath that sounded a lot like relief. 'I was worried that she didn't know . . . didn't know that I loved her. And that I will miss her.' He cried again.

'Oh, she knew, she knew, Olly, and she wanted me to tell you that she knew.'

Again the boy smiled through his distress.

'Was she in any pain? At the end? I keep thinking of her hurting and it makes me cry.'

'No.' He shook his head. 'Not at all. They had given her a lot of drugs and she spoke softly to me and she was calm, not in pain, just sleepy – you know, the way she looked and sounded just before she dozed off on the sofa. Then she just closed her eyes and went to sleep. It was peaceful and quiet and lovely, really.'

Forgive me, Kerry. I'm not a liar, but I don't know what to do . . .

You're doing fine. Just fine, my love . . .

Oliver nodded and took his time digesting this. He took another deep breath and sat up straight, sniffing once more and swiping at his eyes. 'I got two As and a B, Dad. Enough for my place at Birmingham.'

Nick felt the swell of relief and pride in his veins. He had done it. Oliver had bloody done it! 'I'm proud of you. And I know your mum is too. She always was.'

'Do you think she knows I got in?' Oliver now studied the slip of paper in the palm of his hand.

Nick nodded; words were impossible, stoppered by the lump of raw emotion that rose up in his throat.

1992

'Finish your tea, lad. I've got something for you.' His dad stood at the back door in his work boots and shorts with his shirtsleeves rolled high and tight above his elbows. Nick looked up from the kitchen table where he ate fish fingers cut into squares and dipped into a mountain of tomato ketchup.

'What is it?' A gift from his dad was rare, but Nick allowed himself only the smallest stirring of excitement, picturing some of the things his dad had given him before. A pocket watch that used to belong to his great-grandad now shoved in his drawer.

Boring.

The General Encyclopaedia, volume P-Q-R, which had obviously made a break for freedom from the other volumes, presumably where important information on all things concerning the other twenty-three letters lurked. Nick skim-read it on the loo, learning briefly about Pandas, Pendulums, Queens of England, Quebec, Rotor blades and Rio de Janeiro. This too he consigned to the drawer.

Boring.

'Well, you'll have to come out and see.' His dad grinned and Nick felt the flutter of something in his stomach. Maybe, just maybe, this wasn't a rubbish gift after all – maybe it was something absolutely brilliant.

He let his fork clatter to the plate. Fish fingers could wait! His thoughts raced, quite literally, as he pictured the one thing other than boobs that was all his heart desired: a bike! Could it be that his subtle hints, mild nagging and expressions of desire had been listened to? He allowed himself to picture a shiny ice-blue racer with chrome spoke wheels, a leather saddle and dropped ram-horn handlebars and him, astride the thing like a warrior on horseback, a mighty colossus to be admired and envied as he circled the bench in Market Square where the girls and older lads gathered.

What, this old thing? Yeah, it's my bike . . .

Scooting his chair away from the table, abandoning his fish fingers, he ran out into the back garden and there, propped against the shed, was . . . half a bike.

Nick felt his gut drop and tears of injustice gather. He sniffed, embarrassed, disappointed and trying to hide his feelings from the big man with hands like shovels that worked so hard. His dad, misconstruing them as tears of joy, ruffled his hair in an uncharacteristic display of affection. He was a Yorkshireman, after all.

'What d'you reckon?' His dad beamed, rubbing his hands with enthusiasm for the tubular frame made of aluminium where white paint once graced the surface, but now sat in patches and, where it wasn't worn away, was scratched. There were no handlebars, dropped, ram horn or otherwise, no seat and, most crucially of all, no wheels. The cogs, chain and pedals, however, were complete. Nick tried and failed to focus on them.

'Where's the rest of it?' he asked with as much enthusiasm and as big a smile as he could muster.

'Well, that's the beauty of it, son.' His dad walked over to the offending frame and ran his hand over its pitted surface. 'Not only is it the bike you have been nagging us about, but it's also a project. And it's good to have a project in the summer holidays. You and those two vagabond mates of yours are going to have to use your wits, find the bits you need to finish the job and build a bike.'

'I don't think we know how to build a bike,' Nick whispered, picturing Eric, who had the patience of a gnat and the dexterity of an elephant. Plus, they had no money to buy the bits they needed, even if they had had the knowledge.

'You will never know what you're capable of until you try, lad. The trying is good for you and the rewards great if you take the chance. But mark my words: by the end of the summer, Nicky, lad, you will have a bike. You will succeed, if you want it badly enough.'

He watched as his dad reached into his back pocket and pulled out a small brown leather case.

'What's that?' This object lying in his dad's palm with a sturdy zip containing something precious enough to be cased in leather – a grown-up thing! Now, *this* had his interest, going a long way to ease his disappointment.

His dad drew a slow breath and took his time in handing over the case, as if a little reluctant to part with it.

'In this little pouch is everything you need to build and maintain a bike.' He nodded, and again came the hair ruffle, which Nick gratefully received, tilting his head a little like a happy dog whose owner has found just the spot.

Nick licked the blob of ketchup from the side of his thumb and carefully undid the zip. Inside the case was a steel tool, rectangular in shape, but with hexagonal holes cut out of it at various points, a U shaped indent and a sticky-out key shape with two mini prongs on the end.

His dad leant close and blocked out the light. Nick could smell his workingman's smell of sweat, the glue they used up at Siddley's and a scent he didn't yet recognise. It was the faint tang of fear that hung over the man in a cloud, common to all who worked for the wage that helped them ride the wave from one month to the next but were fully aware that one dry spell, one bump in the road, and the whole family would sink. It was the smell of a man trapped on the hamster wheel of life.

'My dad gave this to me. It's a Raleigh multi-tool or multi-spanner and it has seen some use, I can tell you.' He smiled, as if recounting some of the use it might have had, and judging by the smile on his face, Nick guessed they were good memories.

'What y'doing'?' his sister, Jen, hung out of the back door and shouted.

'Nothing for you to stick your beak into, lass,' his dad responded, and Nick liked the way his comment isolated his sister. This was between him and his dad.

'Good, because I couldn't care less anyway!' Jen shouted, but the quiver to her bottom lip and her shrill tone suggested otherwise.

'It's man's stuff.' His dad chuckled and Nick smiled.

He felt invincible and excited.

'Yeah, man's stuff,' he echoed over his shoulder.

'Shut up, you dweeb!' Jen yelled before running back inside.

Nick turned his attention back to the spanner; not even his sister's jibe could dampen his joy.

His dad pointed at the tool. 'These holes fit over the nuts and bolts to loosen and tighten them, and the big scoop is for removing pedals. The little prongs will tighten and loosen the brakes. You take good care of it,' he added sternly, his tone enough for Nick to feel the full weight of his responsibility as custodian of the tool. *Man's stuff*... It went some way towards lessening the completely gutting dissatisfaction he felt at being given half a bike.

'I will, Dad.' He nodded at the big man. 'I will.'

With fish fingers no longer on his mind, Nick ran to Eric's house and the two of them went to call on Alex.

'What's up?' Alex asked as he slipped from the front door, stopping on the path to shove his index finger into the back of his trodden-down sneakers and pull them up his heel.

'Wait and see.' Nick built the tension.

'Do *you* know, Eric?' Alex was intrigued as the three made their way back to Nick's parents' garage.

'Nope.' Eric frowned, dragging a stick along the wall. 'He won't tell me what the big secret is.' He shook his head, but had a spring in his step that suggested he too was excited.

'You'll see in a minute.' Nick liked this powerful position in which he found himself, especially having the little leather case nestling in his pocket.

'You're not the only one with a secret,' Eric piped up.

'What's your secret, then?' Alex asked.

Eric looked up and down the road and without the need for further coaxing, confident that he was not being overheard, he beckoned his mates closer. 'My mum has got a secret new job.' He beamed.

'Is she a spy?' Alex asked, wide eyed.

Nick didn't know much about spying, but even he thought it might be a stretch for Mrs Pickard to go from working shifts in the care home in Thirsk, where she looked after old people who were really old, like forty, to spying.

'No,' Eric laughed, 'not a spy, but a secret job that I can't tell my dad about.'

'What kind of secret job?' Nick was curious.

'A job with Dave the Milk.'

The boys all knew the local milkman, Dave.

'Why's it a secret?' Alex asked the question for them both.

'Because it's a surprise – she's earning extra and I mustn't spoil it,' Eric explained, 'but Dave the Milk comes over on a Thursday night while my dad is at billiards and I'm not allowed in the house.'

'In case you see their secret work?' Alex asked.

'Yep.' Eric nodded, still dragging the stick over each and every surface. 'I bet she's saving up to get my dad a stereo for his car; he's always banging on about one and I think that's the secret.'

'What are you supposed to do when they are working?' Nick couldn't imagine being barred from his home for any period of time, especially of an evening when, in the winter, it would be dark and cold; he swallowed the fear this conjured.

Eric shrugged. 'Don't know. Go up the Rec, come to yours . . .'

Nick nodded, as if both of these sounded reasonable.

With the Bairstows' garage in sight, the three boys broke into a run, as if the anticipation were more than they could stand. They let themselves in via the side door and immediately switched on the lamp on the workbench and sat on the green canvas camping stools his dad had given them to use on the condition they did not leave the garage.

'Okay,' Nick began, as his two friends stared at him. Carefully he reached into his pocket and pulled out the leather case.

'What's that?' Eric, impatient as ever, leant in.

'Is it a nail scissor set?' Alex guessed.

'He'd better not have dragged me all the way over here for a chuffin' nail scissor set!' Eric scoffed.

Nick and Alex laughed, not only at his anger but the fact that they knew there was nowhere else Eric needed to be and that he would tramp all the way over for a lot less than that.

'It's a Raleigh multi-tool, also called a multi-spanner.' He liked demonstrating his knowledge.

'Can I hold it?'

Nick nodded and passed it to Alex, who wiggled his fingers inside the little holes and turned it gently over in his palm.

'What's it for?' Eric asked, while balling up a sheet of newspaper and trying to throw it up over the steel beam that ran the length of the garage.

'It's the tool for our project.'

'What project?' Eric sneered; Nick had made it sound dangerously like work, and the summer holidays were for anything but.

Nick stood and marched them to the garden, confident his friends would follow.

'This!' He pointed at the frame still propped against the shed.

'Where's the rest of it?' Eric asked with typical candour.

'That's the best bit.' Nick drew on the enthusiasm he was starting to feel. 'We have to finish it, build it, and then we get a bike!'

Alex ran his hand over the frame and nodded, as if he knew what he was looking for and approved.

'We need to find the parts and the bits we need and then figure out how to fix it all together.' Nick hoped he made the task sound less Herculean than it felt.

'So hang on a minute.' Eric wiped his nose with his fingers. 'We find all the bits and parts and we build it together . . .'

'Yes,' Nick confirmed.

'So who will own the bike at the end of it?'

Nick pondered this.

'We could all own a piece of it,' Alex suggested, fair-minded as ever.

'Well, it's my frame, *technically*, and I've got the tool.' Nick banged it against his palm. 'Plus, we'll be doing it in my garage, so I think I should have half and you can each have half of a half.' His maths wasn't that great.

'So a half of a half each for us and a whole half for you?' Alex clarified. Nick nodded; it didn't occur to any of them at that point that only one person could ride the bike and so *technically* they would each have one hundred per cent of the bike when they were on it.

'Let's shake on it,' Eric suggested, and the three put their grubby hands into the middle and clasped what they could, heaving up and down with force.

'Anyone want a cookie and some juice?' his mum called from the kitchen window.

Eric ran inside quicker than Nick could suggest they should name their bike-building gang . . .

Alex looped his fingers under one of the brake wires and joggled it back and forth, shaking his head. 'That bike tool is *really* cool.'

'It is, isn't it?' Nick turned the coveted object over in his palm.

'I don't want to put anyone off, but it might be harder than we think to build a bike. I tried to build an Airfix kit my Auntie Natalie got me for my birthday, but I couldn't finish it. It's still in the box under my bed.'

'The way I see it' – Nick drew breath – 'we will never know what we are capable of until we try. The trying will be good for us and the rewards great . . . At the end of it we'll get a bike!'

Alex stared up at him. 'You sound like your dad.'

Nick smiled, unsure as to whether he was pleased or offended.

'You ladies comin' in for snacks or what?' Eric yelled through the back door with a mouthful of Custard Cream.

TWO

Nick manoeuvred into the spot in the car park, pulled on the handbrake and took a deep breath.

'Flippin' 'eck, I thought the whole idea of living in halls of residence is that everything is provided for you.'

He looked up through the windscreen at the vast blue-and-yellow Ikea warehouse and felt the ball of dread in his stomach. Shopping was his least favourite activity. He always found his attention wandering and a mild sense of claustrophobia setting in after a few minutes. And whilst a quick scoot around B&Q with knowledge of exactly what he needed was just about bearable, shopping for soft furnishings and homeware was his most dreaded thing.

'I don't know what we need from here.'

'Dad.' Oliver sounded a little exasperated and a lot more like the adult out of the two. 'It said online that in my room there will be a bed and a desk and a chair and a noticeboard, that's it. I need to get a duvet and pillows, duvet cover, wall stuff, fairy lights.'

'Wall stuff? Fairy lights? What on earth?'

'Dad! Everyone has fairy lights in their room. It's a thing.'

'It's not a thing in Burston. Crikey, when I was a lad people thought you were posh if you bothered with a lampshade on the big light.' He laughed. 'And besides, can you imagine what Eric and the like would say if they knew you were buying lights from Ikea! They'd say, "What's wrong with Siddley lights? Are we not good enough for you now you've got a place at a fancy university?"' He smiled at the half-truth.

'Okay, can I just say, don't start any conversation with anyone you meet at Uni with the words, "When I was a lad" or "Flippin' 'eck!"'

'Olly, you haven't even finished your degree and you're already ashamed of me. This must be the great social divide everyone speaks about.'

'That's right. And I am ashamed of you. I don't want Siddley lights, I want Ikea lights, and while we are on the subject, don't try to make a joke with anyone. Your jokes aren't funny, which makes them more like weird statements.' Oliver jumped from the passenger seat and shut the door, laughing.

'My jokes *are* funny,' Nick huffed.

'They're not, Dad. It's just that no one has the heart to tell you.'

'Well, you're certainly all heart today, son.'

Nick followed him. This was a good day. Not one he had been look-ing forward to. Dropping his only child in a city he had never visited was a fearful prospect, but packing up the car to leave that morning, chatting en route, stopping at the service station for a gargantuan break-fast and, even here, in this soulless car park, as their light-hearted jibes flew back and forth, it felt as if a weight had been lifted, distracted as they were from the business of grief by this momentous day.

Oliver grabbed a trolley and Nick felt an uncomfortable shiver at just how much money might be spent. They had only been financially straight for a year or so, and since Kerry had been ill he had worked his set hours and no more, which meant no bonus and no spare cash. Not that he would have changed a thing; spending as much time as possible with her had of course been his priority, and neither did he want to restrict his son in any way or put a dampener on this day, but all that aside, with money tight, it was always at the forefront of his mind. His five-hundred-pound nest egg was more quail-sized than ostrich. They wandered into the store and found themselves in the 'marketplace'.

'What on earth are these?' Nick picked up the flat square rubber trays that were stacked in a myriad of colours, running his fingers over the jigsaw-shaped indents.

'They are novelty ice-cube makers.' Oliver held his gaze, clearly waiting for the retort.

'Of course they are. Who buys this stuff?' Nick could see no sense in spending good money just to have your ice in the shape of a jigsaw piece or a ball, and who bothered with ice anyway?

'Everyone apart from us, Dad, that's who.'

Nick laughed heartily. 'Now that's funny. I remember you coming home from school and telling me you needed a BMX because everyone had one apart from you, but you were seven. I thought you might have grown up enough to think of a more convincing argument.'

'It was true, *everyone* had a BMX apart from me!'

'Everyone?' Nick raised his eyebrows.

'Well, all of my mates, and so it felt like everyone.'

'When I was not much older than seven, my dad—'

'I know. I know.' Oliver raised his palm. 'He made you build a bike and it taught you a lesson, blah-di-blah-di-blah! I really don't need to hear the bike story again, but while we are on the subject, everyone *did* have a BMX apart from me.'

'Okay, Olly, you win. I shall get you a BMX, for Christmas.'

'I don't want one now! But a new car would be nice.'

Nick lobbed the ice-cube tray back on to the pile and walked on with the cart.

New car would be nice! Don't I bloody know it . . .

He pictured the shiny new silver Jaguar with a hefty price tag sitting on the forecourt at Mackie's, which Nick had admired while having his own car serviced.

'She's a beauty, eh?' Bob had whistled and let his eyes sweep her sleek silver curves.

'Really is. Bit out of my league, I'm afraid,' Nick had joked, swallowing the bitter tang of jealousy that flared on his tongue. What wouldn't he give to drive a car like that? How did you get to be a bloke who could afford that kind of car?

'Right, back to your heap of shite,' Bob had joked, turning his attention to Nick's motor.

Nick had nodded his understanding that the brake discs were on the cusp and the front left tyre a mere millimetre away from a failure, and he had promised, hand on heart, to get the work done. And he would, when funds allowed.

'Oh, and Gina said to say hello.'

Nick had coughed and left the garage a little quicker than was polite. Better that than run into Gina Mackie.

He and Oliver navigated the vast interior of the store, where studio sets were laid out in a way that made him feel that every room, in fact every facet of their home, was dated and in serious need of an upgrade. This he could apparently achieve with the addition of fancy potted plants, sofas with matching footstools and bookshelves crammed with everything from cacti to candlesticks and quirky photo frames, but no actual books.

'Here we are: bedroom stuff.' Oliver rushed ahead and Nick caught him up. The two stared at the racks filled with bundles of cream-coloured quilted things, labelled with long and complicated Swedish names peppered with 'O's and 'A's carrying dots and circles above.

'Flippin' 'eck!' Nick exclaimed and stared at the array.

'That's the second "flippin' 'eck" moment you've had today.'

'I know, but where do we start with this lot?' He stared at the bewildering display. 'All you need is a basic double duvet and a cover. I wish your mum was here.'

And just like that, his words sucked the joy from the moment, firmly bringing down the shutter of reality on this fun-packed day. It was the truth; Nick wished it were Kerry trawling the shelves, confident that she would know exactly what size and tog 'Hönsbör', 'Myskgräs' or 'Tilkört' to go for.

Oliver grabbed a plastic-wrapped duvet, stuffed inside its wrapping to form a cylindrical shape.

'This one?'

'I reckon so.' Nick nodded as Oliver lobbed it in the trolley, quickly followed by a pack of two flattened pillows.

Nick cursed the solemn mood he had created, but was not about to start censoring the mention of his wife; that would be the very worst thing. It was, as his mum had reminded him only that very morning, early days.

And it was. Seven weeks . . . Less than two months since he had walked into that room at St Vincent's and watched her pale, grey face rattle its last breath. Seven weeks that felt simultaneously like seven hours, or seven minutes. He wondered if this feeling, this sense of shock, would ever pass.

'I said which one?' Oliver said firmly, holding two packets up to chest level, while Nick mentally caught up.

'That one.' He pointed to a grey-and-white-striped duvet cover, which he chose at random.

There seemed to be a swell of people around the till area and Nick bit the inside of his cheek and drummed his fingers on his thighs in a bid to focus on something other than his growing desire to run for the exit.

Finally, with their goods squeezed into the gaps around the suitcases on the back seat, they set off for the University of Birmingham.

'Are you excited?' Nick asked, as the car pulled in behind a queue of others, waiting for the smiling, fresh-faced student in the green luminescent T-shirt and holding a clipboard to direct them to the right place.

'Nervous.' His leg bounced up and down.

'No need, Olly. Everyone here feels exactly the same.'

'I guess so.'

'I'd be excited.' Nick spoke the truth, able only to imagine what it might have meant to him to be in his son's position, starting a degree at university and walking into a world where opportunity and chance would be at his feet. He thought briefly of the fancy Jaguar on Mackie's forecourt and wished for his son the kind of career, the kind of life, that might make owning a car like that possible.

It could have been his imagination or his oversensitivity in light of recent events, but everywhere Nick looked he saw students with their mums – often their dads too, but it was the mothers who caught his attention. Some were quietly holding bags to carry up the stairs with a mournful look; others organised and doled out boxes, lifted from the boot of their car. He was overly aware of their presence and again felt the absence of his wife keenly.

Oliver's room in the low-rise block was smaller than Nick had imagined, with barely enough space to walk between the bed and the desk, but that aside it was clean and warm.

'At least you'll be able to turn off your lamp, open the window and water your cactus thingy without having to leave the bed.' He smiled at his son.

Oliver shook his head, still apparently not in the mood for his dad's humour or commentary.

'Knock knock.'

They both turned towards the long-haired girl in the oversized black glasses and baggy plaid shirt who stood in the doorway a little awkwardly.

'Hello, neighbour. I'm next door.' She pointed towards her left.

Nick said nothing, as nerves meant the only phrases that floated into his mind were *Flippin' 'eck! These rooms are small, aren't they?* and *When I was a lad I'm sure it would have been lads in one building and lasses in another!* but having had both these phrases and all attempts at humour banned by his son, he stayed schtum.

'Hi.' Oliver raised his hand in a manner Nick was sure was meant to be cool, but was in his opinion a little surly. He smiled broadly at the girl, as if his friendliness might make up for his son's rather aloof manner.

'I'm Tasha.' She swallowed, touching her finger to her chest in a kooky way. 'And I guess I'll see you later!' Her eyes, he noted, lingered for a second on his boy and he realised how out of the loop he was on what was considered attractive by youngsters nowadays. Maybe Oliver with his standoffish demeanour and the slightly greasy lick to his sticky-up fringe was what smart girls like Tasha were interested in. That and a whole bunch of fancy fairy lights, which were apparently 'a thing'.

'What?' Oliver asked. Nick was unaware he'd been staring at his son.

'Nothing.'

'She's just a friend.' Oliver whined.

'Is that the first time you've met her?'

'Yeah.'

'Oh, well, good that you're planning a friendship; she seems nice.' He smiled.

Oliver ignored his comment and bit a small hole in the plastic wrapping of the duvet. He shook the quilt out vigorously over his bed and stood back. Both men stared at the narrow strip of duvet that sat in the middle of the double bed.

'We got a single.'

'I figured as much, son. Put the cover on it and no one will notice.'

'*I'm* going to notice; it'll be freezing!' the boy tutted.

'Olly, this is a centrally heated room the size of a shoebox and it's a rather warm September, plus you have thick pyjamas and socks. Order another one online or whatever; it'll turn up in no time.'

'We are rubbish at this, Dad.'

He watched the boy struggle to remove the duvet cover from the packaging, and two pillowcases fell on the floor.

'I know.'

'Anyway, you can go now. There's no need to hang around, you've got a long drive back and I'm good,' Oliver said brightly. It felt a lot like a dismissal.

Nick pulled his son into an awkward hug. 'Remember, if you're not happy with anything or you feel homesick or you just want to chat, call any time, or jump on a coach or I'll come and get you. You just need to say the word.'

'I'm fine, Dad.'

'I know you're fine now, but I'm just saying that if at any point you're not fine, then that's okay, and you're welcome home any time. You and me against the world, the Bairstow Boys! Just call.'

'Are . . . Are *you* going to be okay?'

He wouldn't forget the way Oliver looked at him with the pinched brows of someone who was worrying in reciprocation. Nick laughed out loud.

'Oh yes, don't you worry about me. I can't wait to have the remote control all to myself and to sit in peace without that boom-boom music that judders through the floorboards. I'll be right as rain. Plus, I've got Treacle.'

'Bye then, Dad.'

Nick hugged him once more, tighter this time, letting his hand press the boy's narrow back into his chest and hoping that he got the message where words failed him. *You're going to be fine, Olly. I love you. I'm proud of you . . . We both are.* He walked away briskly, out of the room and down the stairs without looking back, cursing the thickening of emotion in his throat.

He pulled into the traffic jam on the M1 and wound down the window, trying to ignore the pang of guilt that Oliver might be less than comfortable on his first night away from home.

'Bloody single quilt.' He sighed, picturing the moment the cashier in Ikea had asked for the grand total of one hundred and sixteen pounds – *one hundred and sixteen pounds*! How was that even possible when everything they had bought cost no more than a few quid? He had bitten his lip and handed over his credit card, thinking ahead to how he could save a few bob over the coming months and pay it off.

He hoped Oliver would make more effort with Tasha, who seemed like a nice girl. Nick figured it must have taken courage for her to come and introduce herself. He knew he'd be happier once the boy had made friends. He laughed at how similar this was to Olly's first day at school; only then he knew his son would be home in time for tea and a bedtime story. He felt kindly towards the girl, the way she had looked at Oliver . . .

Dating had been so much easier for him and Kerry, who courted in a time without the pressure of social media, when the only phone most people owned was the one your family might have in the hallway on a little tile-topped table inside of the front door, the use of which was closely monitored by their parents. He couldn't imagine how hard it might be to appear cool and confident while comparing yourself with the images of perfection beamed into these youngsters' hands at every second of every day. Almost instinctively he ran his hand over the bulge of his gut, which sat over the waistband of his jeans, the result of giving up his nightly run to sit with Kerry – that and an over-reliance on the chip shop when pushed for time and without the inclination to cook. Yes, he smiled at the thought of how very different it had been in his day.

Kerry Forrest had for years been nothing more than a name in the school register, one of a pack of girls who were indistinguishable to him and who hung out in a cloud of perfume and giggles, often to be found sitting in a huddle on the bench in Market Square. They were to him and his mates alien and unattainable. But then on one particular day in the summer term, at the age of sixteen, he walked into afternoon class, scanning the seats, looking for Alex and Eric, and he saw her sitting alone on the other side of the classroom. Having only been vaguely aware of her for most of his school life, it was as if he saw her for the first time. She stood out like something shiny in the gloom. He couldn't take his eyes off her and, along with the quickening of his heartbeat and a dull ache of longing in his gut, he felt the leap of excitement in his chest. This girl, *this girl!* She had been under his nose all this time and yet here she was, calling to him like something new and golden. He noticed the bloom on her cheek and chest as she slipped from child to woman and then, as if drawn, she looked up and he had no choice but to swallow his fear and speak. Actually speak to this goddess! It took every ounce of his courage.

'All right.' He nodded at her, keeping the smile from his face and adding just enough of a sneer to preserve his exploding heart, should rejection or humiliation be forthcoming.

'All right,' she answered quickly, before turning her attention to the textbook in front of her. He looked back in her direction as she too lifted her eyes, and for a second they looked at each other, this time with the beginnings of a smile on their mouths and the crinkle of laughter around their eyes.

And that, as they say, had been that.

The following fourteen weekends were spent hand in hand, often just walking and talking. They ventured up on to Drayfield Moor, where the wind lifted their hair and mud clung to their boots. He had picked and handed her a sprig of purple heather, which she pressed and kept in her little christening Bible in her bedside cabinet. Another day they followed the meandering path along the trickle of river that bisected the town, stopping to kiss on the narrow footbridge before sitting arm in arm with flushed cheeks on the bench in Market Square in front of the war memorial. One memorable evening was spent at the local travelling fair which had docked on the outside of town. Here they squealed on the bumper cars and gorged on popcorn. Next came a weekend trip to Filey on the bus, the travelling to and from with thighs touching and fingers entwined just as glorious as walking on the sand, and before he knew it, at the tender age of seventeen Nick had excitedly and keenly proposed marriage to this girl who had captured his heart.

His parents threw a party, his mum happy and his dad quiet, as guests crammed into the small house where relatives, his and hers, took up seats on the sofa and his mates occupied the back garden, swigging from shared cans of lager and taking the piss out of the boy about to be married, while taking it in turns on the rickety swing. When he and his bride waltzed up the aisle, a winter wedding with snow on the ground and a roaring fire in the pub after, Oliver had already and unexpectedly taken up residence in her willing womb and the newly married Mr and Mrs Bairstow were all set. Set for life, that's what he had thought, standing at the altar of St Michael's and speaking the words sincerely: 'till death do us part . . .'

Nick thought about that day now and knew that he could have never in a thousand years have imagined that their parting would come so soon. He felt cheated. He looked at the empty seat next to him.

'Single bloody duvet. Only us, eh? His room seems nice, though, cosy.'

You did great today, really great, came his wife's imagined reply.

'I'm going to miss him. I'm not even home yet and I already wish I'd spent more time with him before he went. I feel like everything has come around very quickly.'

It's what we always said, Nick; we'll raise him right and let him fly . . .

'Aye, we did. But I didn't think it would be this hard to watch him go.' He swallowed. 'I miss you too. So much.' He cursed the tears that gathered.

You're doing great, love. It'll get easier. You'll see . . .

◆ ◆ ◆

Darkness had begun to bite on the day as Nick pulled up the steep driveway. His mum must have dropped Treacle off, as he heard her barking at the sound of the car arriving home.

He put the key in the lock and was in truth glad of the dog's welcome; walking into the echoing silence might have been more than he could cope with today. He put the kettle on and let Treacle out into the small back garden for a run. He watched the steam rise from the kettle and plopped a teabag into his mug, looking forward to the restorative brew. The front doorbell rang. Nick sighed, feeling an instant flush of guilt at the dread he felt. The prospect of having to entertain his mum or Kerry's mum, Dora, regaling them with each and every detail of Oliver's arrival at Uni, was not something he wanted to do, not tonight, when tiredness left him feeling a little frayed and now missing Kerry too, so much. He wanted nothing more than to be left alone to mourn.

He flicked on the hallway light and opened the front door.

'Oh!' He took a step back, surprised to see Beverly from work on the doorstep. Odd to see her out of context and in casual gear.

'All right?' She pushed her hands into the pocket of her jeans.

He nodded.

'We're going to the pub' – she nodded in the direction of the Blue Anchor – 'a few of us from work, and thought you might fancy a pint?'

'Oh!' he uttered for the second time in as many seconds. This was unexpected. He and Kerry had not been the 'going to the pub' type and he couldn't remember the last time he had done anything social.

'You coming, then?' Beverly pointed down the lane and took a step backward along the path.

Nick pictured his teabag in its mug on the countertop. 'D'you know, I think I'll give it a miss tonight, but thanks for asking, Bev.'

'Next time, then,' she said casually, turning and walking back out into the darkness.

'Yep, cheers.'

He settled Treacle into her basket and climbed the stairs with his mug, letting his eyes run over the neatly made bed, the floral bedlinen chosen by his wife, and again he hoped Oliver was warm enough, comfortable enough, or failing this, having too good a time to care about the discomfort of a single duvet. He again pictured Tasha with her large specs and goofy smile.

Beverly's knock on the door had unnerved him a little. He was grateful, of course, for everyone's concern, but at the same time felt her arrival to be a slight invasion of his privacy. He couldn't remember a time when he hadn't known Beverly, but there was a big difference between knowing her to chat to at work and going as part of her gang to the pub; one thing to receive her condolences across the warehouse floor as she passed through with a clipboard but quite another to have her turn up at his home. She and Kerry had been a year apart at school and, whilst not mates, they were acquaintances.

With his tea drunk and his teeth cleaned, Nick undressed and bundled his clothes into the wicker laundry basket by the door. He wondered why she had thought to ask him. The last thing he wanted was an invite to the pub out of pity. He wondered if his mum or Dora had put her up to it, or maybe his sister, Jen. They were friends. It was his last thought before falling asleep; it had been quite a day. He flung his arm over Kerry's pillow, as he had done every night since she had gone in to St Vincent's, and it helped a little, the feel of something beneath his arm. A poor substitution, of course, and the vague scent of her that had lingered on the cotton was now sadly gone.

'Night, night, love,' he whispered.

Night, night, my love, sweet dreams . . .

1992

The boys had fallen into a routine more rigorous, time consuming and exhausting than school, but none of them seemed to notice that. And apart from Alex's one week in a caravan in Blackpool with his nan and grandad, the three had no plans that might get in the way of their project. They saw the six-week summer holiday stretch out in front of them like an eternity. Eric, always up first and seemingly keen to be out of the house, would call for Alex en route and the two would arrive bright and early at Nick's house, rain or shine. In shorts and T-shirts, the boys paid no heed to the weather but dressed for the date, and August was certainly the month for shorts. Nick's mum would make Eric a breakfast of egg on toast, which he would wolf down. His dad would shake his head. 'Slow down, lad! No one's going to take it away from you.'

Nick was getting dressed in his bedroom when he heard the boys thunder up the stairs.

'Nick!' Alex called with urgency.

He slipped his *Batman Returns* T-shirt over his head and stared at the door as his friends burst in.

'Look!' Eric beamed as he lifted the beautiful Y-shaped object in his hands. 'Handlebars!' he screeched. 'And not just any handlebars, really wide ones!'

The three jumped up and down on the floor until his mum yelled up the stairs, 'For the love of God, stop the jumping! Sounds like you're coming through the ceiling!'

The boys stopped jumping and each held a piece of the unwieldy metal tube, staring at it as if it were the gift of gold.

'Wow!' Alex spoke for them all.

'Where d'you get it?' Nick couldn't believe that this glorious bit of kit had fallen into their grasp. They had spent the best part of the last week, after careful instruction from his dad, rubbing off the old and knackered paint from the frame with wet and dry paper and painting it with primer, ready for a new coat of paint, the colour of which they were yet to decide on and over which there was much debate. Then they had carefully taken the chain apart and cleaned and oiled each link, delicately putting it back together. A fiddly job, especially with slippery fingers and an overwillingness to use the tool that actually made the job a lot harder, but that didn't matter, not when to hold it in their hands and do *man's stuff* felt so brilliant! They had made a good job of working on the bits they had, but they knew the time was drawing close when they had to start looking for other parts. Truth was, Nick felt more than a little nervous. Working on the half a bike in the garage within reach of a cold glass of squash and the biscuit barrel was one thing, but to go hunting all over Burston for specific parts without a bean in their pockets felt like quite another.

'Dave the Milk got it for me!' Eric admired the handlebars with a look of self-congratulation. 'And I thought it was only milk he delivered,' he quipped.

'Where did he get it?' Alex shared Nick's curiosity.

Eric shrugged. 'Don't know. I told him we were building Half Bike' – he unwittingly and officially named their creation – 'and said we needed bits and he pitched up last night with these in his hand. Aren't they brilliant?'

'They are!' Nick confirmed.

'Is your mum still doing her job with him?' Alex wondered.

'Yep.'

'How do we fit them on?' Alex stared at the rather sharp ends.

'We use the tool and figure it out.' Nick grabbed his trusty leather case from the bedside table.

'Nick, do you think, erm ' – Alex hesitated – 'do you think . . . I mean . . . Could I . . .'

'Spit it out, Wendy!' Eric shouted. They didn't know why, but Eric often gave them both random girls' names, and if you weren't on the receiving end of such a moniker, there was nothing funnier.

Nick giggled.

Alex continued unabashed. 'Can I take the multi-tool home one night? I promise I'd look after it and I'd bring it straight back in the morning.'

Nick shook his head and put the gadget in his pocket. 'No, Alex,' he said firmly. 'It's too valuable to let out of the house. It used to be my dad's and it's got its own leather case.' He stressed this important factor. Not that he didn't understand Alex's desire, because to have this thing in his own possession was empowering and gave him confidence. Nick often fell asleep thinking of how he might tackle an intruder; with the multi-tool in his hand, he would jump from the bed, lunging the little pronged end at the baddy's throat – not dissimilar to a Batman move – and just knowing this little weapon was within reach meant he slept soundly.

In the garage, Nick and Alex straddled the frame and held it firmly in place, with muscles flexing unnecessarily and sweat forming on their smooth top lips. Eric stood with the handlebars raised and, with his tongue poking out of the side of his mouth, manoeuvred the longest pole until it was lined up with the corresponding opening at the top front of the frame. He pushed until they heard a satisfying thunk.

'It fits!' Eric yelled, taking a step back to admire his handiwork.

Alex rested his end of the frame on the floor and ran to the front of the bike, where he dropped to his knees and, with the multi-tool in his hand and at the ready, used it to tighten the bolt at the top of the bars that sat snugly inside the frame.

Eric sat forward in the spot where the saddle would live and gripped the bullhorn handlebars.

'This feels great! When I grow up I'm going to get a Harley Davidson and ride all the way across America! And I'll stop every time I see a hot-dog shop and get a hot dog with onions and mustard and ketchup, then I'll have an ice cream and set off again.'

Alex shoved him to one side and took up the same position. 'When I grow up, *I'm* going to get a Harley Davidson and ride around Market Square really loudly!'

Nick laughed. 'Well, I don't want a Harley Davidson.'

'Why not, Shirley?' Eric interrupted, and it was Alex's turn to giggle.

Nick looked at his dad's tools all neatly tacked to the shadow board on the garage wall behind his workbench and drawn around with a marker pen so he always knew exactly where to put them after use.

'I want to get a nice car and drive to work in an office, and I want to have a ham-and-cheese sandwich for my lunch and live in a big house, and I want to press a button on my desk and someone will bring me an orange Fanta whenever I want one.'

'Well, my dad says if you want to work in an office you have to go to college or university,' Alex added.

'I think I might go to university,' Nick said softly, surprised that there was not more ribbing.

'Is there a university near here?' Eric asked, his voice a little raspy.

'There's one in York. Jen's ballet teacher went there,' Nick said with authority.

'You could go to university,' Alex said. 'You're clever, Nick.'

'I'm as clever as Nick!' Eric yelled.

'It was Nick that got the frame for Half Bike and he's the one with the multi-tool,' Alex pointed out.

'That doesn't make him clever!' Eric spat. 'It makes him lucky.'

Nick stared at his friend, who looked like he might cry, and he didn't know what to do.

'What would you learn at university, Nick?' Alex eased the moment with his question.

Nick shrugged. He hadn't thought that far ahead.

'He'd do ballet, like Jen's teacher, wouldn't you, Shirley?'

Nick laughed – they all did.

And just like that, Eric wiped at his eyes and was back in the room.

THREE

'Can you say it again, Olly?'

Wearing his hi-vis orange vest over his company polo shirt, Nick stood in the middle of the yard, surrounded by pallets of sealed, taped boxes waiting to be loaded on to the trucks. He shoved his finger into his free ear to try to dampen the noise coming from the packing floor and beyond. The whir and beep of forklift trucks, the drone of the packing machine, the ringing of bells and timers, the rumble of the conveyor belt and the chitter-chatter of the workforce, interspersed with their raucous laughter, made it hard for him to hear what his son was saying.

'Olly, say that again? I didn't quite hear you!' He walked briskly to the wire perimeter fence and faced the white metal wall of the warehouse opposite, an ugly structure Aubrey Siddley had put up in the 1990s, blocking the once beautiful sight of the wide sweep of the moors that had been his father's view when he was a packer at Siddley's.

'I said I want to come home! I hate it here, Dad. I don't want to go to university. I've changed my mind. I don't like it! I'm not staying here. I don't want to do it. You said to just call you if I wanted to come home, and so I am.'

'Okay, okay, son. Just take a deep breath.' Nick closed his eyes and placed his hand on his brow, trying to think of the right thing to say, the right thing to do. It wasn't as if it was a call from nursery to say his son had a slight temperature and Kerry could pack up at the café early and go fetch him home; this was grown-up stuff. Nick had read with a sense of alarm articles on teenage kids at university committing suicide. Peter, the counsellor at the hospice, had warned him that depression was not uncommon among families, especially youngsters, who had to deal with losing a parent, and even more so if the loss was preceded by a prolonged illness, often with the full effects being felt after the parent had passed away. All these thoughts now raced around his head. And they scared him.

'What's happened? You sounded happy the last time we spoke.'

'I don't know! Nothing's happened, nothing I want to talk about over the phone. I just don't want to be here, Dad, I really don't. I want to come home!'

He was aware of the swell of panic in his son's voice, matched by a hike in his own heart rate. He heard Kerry's words in his head: *Actually, Nick, this might be grown-up stuff, but it really is just as straightforward as a call from nursery – whether three or eighteen, you need to pack up and go fetch him home . . .*

He took stock and mentally planned the conversation he would have to have with Julian Siddley, explaining why he needed to abandon his shift and hotfoot it down to Birmingham, whilst also wondering if he had enough fuel to make the trip.

'Just calm down, Olly. Take deep breaths. It's okay. I'm on my way. I'll be with you in a few hours, as quick as I can, and we can talk it through—'

'I don't need to talk it through, Dad! I just want to come home. I'm not staying here. Please just come and get me, or I can jump on a coach and we can come back and pick up my stuff later?'

'No, don't do that.' Nick knew he had made a promise and also figured that if his son was quitting it'd be better to make one trip and shove all of his belongings into the back of the car. 'I'll be there as soon as I can. Just sit tight, okay?'

'Okay. Thank you, Dad.'

Oliver sounded a little calmer now, and so young. To hear the faint echoes of distress and then the relief in his tone made Nick's heart flex.

'I'm on my way. And if you need to talk before I get there, send a text and I'll pull over and call you straight back. Don't do anything stupid.'

'What do you mean, don't do anything stupid? Like what?'

Like take tablets . . . cut your wrists . . . jump off a building . . . I don't know!

'Like panic. Don't panic. Just sit tight and I'll be there soon.'

'Okay. Thanks, Dad.' There it was again, that little voice that pulled at Nick's heartstrings.

He knocked on his boss's open door and walked in.

'Everything all right, Nick?' Julian looked away from the computer screen and sat back in the red leather captain's chair that had been part of the office for as long as Nick could remember, present when he visited his dad at the factory as a boy aged ten and had stood in front of Mr Aubrey Siddley.

'Nick!' The man had smiled. 'The rogue explorer of Drayton Moor! Seen any pumas lately?'

He and his dad had laughed before Mr Siddley gave him a sticky handful of mint imperials from a large glass jar which sat on the wonky green filing cabinet behind his desk. Nick had shoved them in his trouser pocket and was disappointed to retrieve them when he got home and find them moist, fluff-coated and only good as bin fodder.

'Yes, everything's fine.' Nick held Julian's gaze, disliking the fact that he stood in front of the desk while Julian sat; his stance implied he held his boss in a regard his sentiments did not echo. 'Well, I should say, nothing to worry about workwise, but I just had a call from my Oliver—'

'At Birmingham, isn't he? How's he getting on? Business Studies, isn't it?'

Nick picked up the slightest note of derision in the man's voice, but that might have been his imagination, knowing he could be a little oversensitive when it came to Julian Siddley.

'Yes, that's right, and I thought he was getting on great.' This was life in Burstonbridge, life at Siddley's, where everyone had half an interest in everyone else's life. It was often a comfort, but sometimes the lack of privacy left him feeling like he wanted to scream.

He remembered when Kerry got her first set of test results from the GP, insisting she didn't want him to take time off to come with her.

What difference does it make whether I'm there with you or Diane? It won't change what's said. Don't be daft, Nick – go to work, don't worry and I'll see you when you get home . . .

Kerry had left the doctor's appointment with her arm looped through her sister's and only two hours later, as he walked out of the factory gates to make his way home, he was aware of the tight-lipped, sincere nods of awareness from his colleagues and the slow blink and smile of the woman closing up the bread shop . . . News travelled fast here, faster than he could get home to hear it first-hand.

'Oh dear, it sounds like there is a but.' His boss comically took a deep breath through gritted teeth and it irritated Nick more than it should.

'Yes, well, he has just called and' – he paused, not wanting to admit to his boss that Oliver might be about to abandon the course of which Nick had felt so proud – 'he's having a bit of a wobble and wants me to go down. I wouldn't ask ordinarily, but what with it only being a short time since we lost his mum, I feel I should go down and check things out, bring him home if need be.'

'Nick, of course.' The man tapped his fingers on the jotter in front of him, as he did when he was thinking. 'Do what you need to do. You know the score, just make sure Dennis has the loading schedule and that everything is handed over, but of course, go. Don't worry about things here.' He flapped his hand, indicating that no lorry load of lighting could be considered nearly as important as Oliver's well-being. Nick knew he was right and felt both relieved and angered that Julian had given him permission. He gave a tight smile, knowing it was easy for Siddley junior to say, very easy when you had family wealth behind you and a large, shiny Range Rover sitting in your private parking space. But it was quite another thing for Nick when the bills came rolling in at the end of the month and suddenly that shift he might miss became very important indeed.

He recalled with a shiver picking up the brown envelope from the welcome mat about six years ago now, intrigued by the unfamiliar logo. Ripping the sheet from its confines as the breath caught in his throat and his knees went weak. It had to be a mistake. There was no way . . . but there it was in red ink. Mrs Kerry Bairstow owed the sum of seven thousand pounds. *Seven thousand pounds!* It was as he leant on the banister and scanned the sheet, looking at the long list of purchases, that Kerry trod the stairs with an armful of laundry and they locked eyes. Her face fell and her lips looked bloodless and he knew . . . he knew it was no mistake.

'Thanks, Julian. I really appreciate it.'

The man restored his glasses to indicate the conversation was over and turned his attention back to the wide computer screen that almost filled his desk. Nick considered himself dismissed.

'Oh, I see. Half day, is it?' Eric called from the loading bay as Nick climbed into the car.

'Something like that.' He looked up at his friend.

'Well, you missed a good night last night in the pub, a proper laugh, and we got chips on the way home.'

'Sounds like a belter – chips, eh?' He laughed. 'Didn't realise you were there.'

'Yes, whole crowd of us, it was good.'

Nick felt a flicker of relief that it hadn't just been Beverly who was after his company; that whole idea had left him feeling a little uncomfortable.

'So where you off to?' Eric pulled him from the thought.

'Just had a call from Olly. He wants to come home; says he wants to quit university. He's had a change of heart.'

'Wants to come home? You're kidding me? He's only been there five minutes!'

'I know, but he's saying he wants to leave university, doesn't like it.' Nick levelled with his best friend.

'But he's such a smart lad. What's happened? I thought he was right as rain?'

'Me too, and he seemed to be – I got a text to say he'd settled and everything. Now I don't know what's happening, but he sounded anxious.' Nick ran his hand over his face.

Eric nodded, his smile gone. Having lived each step of Kerry's illness with Nick and Oliver, staying over at the house so Nick didn't have to rush back from St Vincent's on a school night, making sure Oliver was fed on the days when Nick was preoccupied with Kerry and providing an ear when Nick needed to talk, Eric knew better than most that the two were fragile.

Nick had knocked on his best friend's door and fallen to his knees right there in his narrow hallway on the night he left Kerry at St Vincent's for the first time.

'It's all right, mate, it'll all be okay.' Eric had sat by his side and extended his index finger and the one next to it, placing the two fingers on his friend's shoulder and pushing them gently into his skin.

'It won't be all right! She's not coming home again, Eric! She'll not come home! That's what they said, more or less. This is it! It's not like when she went in and out of hospital; this is the start of the end, I know it is, and I can't stand it! I can't cope! I don't know what to do!' His tears had come thick and fast, the only time he had ever cried this way in front of his pal. 'I don't want her to leave me!'

Eric now called down from the forklift, 'Do you want me to come with you?'

'No, mate, but thanks.'

'Well, look, shout if you need anything. Want me to take Treacle out for a walk later?'

'Oh, Treacle.' He had nearly forgotten her. 'Yes, that'd be great. Grab the house keys off me mum.'

'Will do. Is Jen in?' He waggled his eyebrows.

Nick laughed. It didn't matter that his mate was in his thirties; he was still trying to get a date with Nick's sister, as he had been since he was ten or so years of age. Eric had been the only one in the community to greet the news of her divorce and return to the family home a couple of years back with an air punch. 'That's the best news, mate! She's free again!'

'Yes, but free or not, she doesn't want to go out with you,' Nick had pointed out.

'Ah, but she did once and will again, you'll see. It's a waiting game.' Eric had beamed.

'Just how long are you prepared to wait?' Nick was curious.

'As long as it takes, lad.' Eric had winked at him. 'As long as it takes.'

Nick and Kerry had both always admired his tenacity, for wait he did.

It was mid-afternoon and the motorway wasn't too busy. Nick stayed in top gear and sat in the slow lane, trying to keep to a steady sixty miles an hour. It was a compromise between controlling his urgent desire to get to Oliver in the shortest possible time and preserving precious fuel. Nick felt confused and concerned, having believed when he had dropped his son in Birmingham only six days before that in all likelihood he would not be seeing him until Christmas.

And yet here he was.

His first thought was that he wanted Oliver to be happy, that above all else, of course. And yet still the hammer of despair thudded loud and heavy in his head when he thought of the chance his son was giving up. Eric was right: Oliver was a smart lad, and with a degree under his belt he could choose his path. Nick had watched him work so hard for his 'A' levels, battling in the atmosphere of home, heavy with his mum's illness, treatments and side effects. Their whole schedule had been punctuated by her bouts of sickness, hospital appointments and tiptoeing around the house while she slept. But Oliver had managed it and was the first person on either side of the family to get to university, let alone a prestigious one like Birmingham. Apart from Julian Siddley, Nick didn't know anyone who had a degree, and yet Oliver appeared to be on the point of giving it up. It hurt him to see a place so hard won thrown away and he feared his son might regret it. His job, he knew, was to point this out in the most tactful, supportive way possible without applying any pressure. He exhaled through bloated cheeks, nervous at the prospect. The situation was tempered by the fact that this grief, still fresh, was an unpredictable thing, and if Oliver wasn't coping then it was also Nick's job to help put him back on an even keel.

'I wonder if he could take some time off? Start again later in the term, or even next year? I don't know how it works, and I don't know who to ask.' He said this aloud, tilting his head towards the passenger seat, which Kerry used to occupy, as the junction for Birmingham loomed ahead.

When he arrived he parked and made his way across the communal courtyard to Oliver's halls of residence, feeling a little out of place among the student population in his steel-toe-capped work boots, padded-knee trousers and with the Siddley logo on the chest of his polo shirt. He suspected that most of these students had parents who wore suits and felt the flush of inadequacy as he walked the pathway in the uniform of the maintenance staff. Another reason for Oliver to achieve more – so he might never know what this felt like. Nick wanted him to sit behind a big desk one day like Julian Siddley and not stand in front of it, nervous about asking for an afternoon off. He looked around at all the kids, loping around in twos or bigger packs, some wearing University of Birmingham T-shirts and all laughing, chatting, holding files or with backpacks slung over their shoulder, lest anyone be in any doubt they were esteemed scholars. And he more than understood their pride and the confidence they exuded. These were kids with the whole world at their feet. And he made no secret of the fact that he wanted Oliver to be one of them.

'I'm not going to university, Dad. I'm getting married. Kerry's pregnant . . . Dad . . . Dad? Say something!'

He made his way along the corridor, which now had a very different atmosphere from when he had experienced it on drop-off day. Then it had been quiet, a little subdued, gloomy almost, with the nerves of all newcomers and their parents bouncing off the bare magnolia-painted walls. Now music wafted from under doors, he spied posters stuck to walls, laughter filled the communal kitchens and the whole place felt a lot more personalised, more like a home and less like an institution, and one where a party was about to break out.

He knocked on Oliver's door and stood back, swallowing a flutter of nerves and wondering how his son might appear. He pictured the pale-skinned, red-eyed distress; the haunted look that had been his son's mask during Kerry's funeral. Nick braced himself for whatever Oliver's emotional needs might be, remembering the boy's breakdown on the day of his results, when the grief he had tried to keep at bay finally caught up and overwhelmed him. He would never, ever forget the sight of his son crumpled and coiled on the welcome mat by the front door, so entirely broken, hurting more than he ever had and lost to his grief. Even the memory of it brought a lump to Nick's throat. He offered up a silent prayer that his son's meltdown today was not on the same scale, not only because he doubted his own ability to cope right now, but mainly because he did not want to see him go through anything close to that again. And again Peter's words came to mind.

'Grief is not a linear journey. Sadness is not a sequential thing. Your thoughts and feelings will dart this way and that, like a jagged rollercoaster that can drop you to the lowest low and raise you up to the highest high, and you have to almost sink back into it, submit, go with it and not judge it. In the beginning you will live at its will, but then, as time progresses, if you're lucky, the tide changes and you will find you're gradually taking back control. Your grief will be a little more under your own control, and that really is the start of true recovery, when you can set the pace and choose your moments . . .'

It was a second or two before Oliver opened the door, and the greeting was not what Nick had been expecting. In fact, it was in such contrast to the image he had painted that it shocked him.

'Hi, Dad.' The boy beamed and stepped back, holding the door open, almost with a flourish to his hand, to allow him entry. 'Come in!'

Nick exhaled, realising only then that he had been holding his breath.

'Are you okay?' He looked him up and down, searching for visible signs of distress or harm, and found none. In fact, with a slight flush to his cheeks and his eyes bright, Oliver, if anything, looked positively chirpy.

'I am now,' Oliver offered with an undercurrent of laughter. 'But I had a bit of a wobble this morning. Sit down.' He pointed to the chair at the desk, on which he had placed a rather flat, garish cushion with a cactus print on it.

Nick sat. It felt odd to be in his son's environment. A guest. He felt his pulse settle, lulled by the atmosphere in the room and his son's demeanour.

'So, let me get this straight.' He was struggling to get a handle on the situation, which only hours earlier had sounded like the most extreme emergency, and yet now, judging from Oliver's manner and smile, felt like nothing of the sort. 'You said you wanted to leave university?'

Oliver sat down on the bed and rested against the wall, where more bright cushions lined up along the wall had turned it into a sofa of sorts. It was highly creative and a surprise that his son, who was happy for his bedroom at home to resemble the local dump, piled high with dirty clothes, empty cups and the contents of discarded folders, had this flair.

'I had a bit of a panic.' Oliver sighed, rubbing his palms together.

You had a bit of a panic? Me too after I took that bloody call! He kept these thoughts to himself. 'Right.' Nick felt the stir of frustration in his veins; he had cut his shift. Driven over a hundred and fifty miles and had sat with a twist in his gut for most of the journey, over a bit of a panic. 'What was it made you panic, son?' he asked, trying to keep his tone level.

'I got my reading list this morning.'

'Your reading list?' He wasn't sure what that was and again felt a flash of ignorance.

'Yes, all the books we have to get and study for our first year, and it's a big list, Dad. Not only the textbooks we need to have, but recommended reading as well. I guess I freaked out.'

Nick took a breath. 'So you called me over a list of books you have to read?'

Oliver nodded. 'I felt a bit overwhelmed.'

He stared at the boy and ran his thumb over his stubbly chin. 'You know, Olly, I don't know whether to laugh or cry. I've driven for the last few hours with my heart in my mouth. I didn't know what was waiting for me. *A bit overwhelmed . . .*' he repeated, shaking his head. 'Your mum has died, her treatment was rough on all of us, we didn't have a proper Christmas last year when things were too bad, we've lived off rubbish food' – he laid his hand on the small pouch of stomach that sat over the waistband of his trousers – 'we've stayed up all night on too many occasions because she was too sick to lie down, the Hoover caught fire on your birthday, Treacle ate part of your "A" level project, we haven't had so much as a day trip out let alone a holiday for more years than I care to remember, we got through that soul-crushing funeral, and yet you nearly lose the plot over being given a list of *books* to read?'

'Yes.' Oliver blinked.

'I see.' Nick took a deep breath. 'But just to clarify, you're feeling okay now?'

'Yes.'

'Well, that's good,' he offered, with a hint of sarcasm that he hadn't intended. Nick suddenly felt very tired, realising that adrenaline and anticipation had been his fuel for the last few hours. He couldn't remember when he had last eaten.

Oliver sat forward. 'I spoke to a couple of the guys here, and Tasha, and they all said I needed to look at it logically. I mean, it's not like I have to read the *whole* list, and even if I did, then I get to do it over a long period of time.'

'That's true.' Nick sighed again. 'I suppose the answer is when things like that floor you, try not to get in a flap about it. Go for a walk, do something different and get your head straight. Your friends are right: put it into perspective and take it one day at a time.'

Oliver nodded and Nick felt relieved that his son's degree course was still on track. It made him realise just how much it meant to him for Oliver to have a ticket out of Burston, if that was what he chose. Higher education would give him options he and Kerry had never had.

'Do you want a cup of tea, Dad?'

'I'd love one.' He smiled at the novelty of his son offering him refreshment and, as was the norm, felt the familiar flicker of regret that Kerry was neither here to experience it nor waiting at home for him to share the moment with upon his return. He knew it would have made her chuckle.

'Be right back!' Oliver jumped up from the bed and disappeared from the room.

'Honestly, Kerry, he offered me tea. Like a proper grown-up! He was so excited to have his own mugs and access to a little kitchen.'

'Ah, bless him! And to think he can't even bring his dirty cups down from his bedroom or put his pants in the dirty laundry when he's home!'

'I know it, and I just sat there like a plum while he disappeared . . .'

'Love him, Nick, he's growing up.'

'He is, love, he's growing up fast . . .'

Nick looked around and took in the detail that meant his son had settled physically, at least. The pinboard with his York City FC poster on it, a half-filled water glass on the desk by his bedside, his colour-coded files neatly stacked on the deep windowsill and his single duvet nestling inside the voluminous cover with a quilted throw folded over the end of the bed.

Oliver returned with two mugs, which contained a passable, dark enough tea, and a packet of gingersnap biscuits, from which Nick took three. The diet would have to start tomorrow.

'Yorkshire teabags,' Oliver informed him with pride as he handed Nick the mug.

'Of course.' He chuckled. Nick took a sip and was glad of the restorative brew. 'Now my heart rate has settled and I can see it's not a matter of life and death . . .' He winced a little at the phrase, which leapt from his mouth with ease, as if he had forgotten that life and death had been their preoccupation and sadness for so long now. Oliver didn't flinch and Nick continued. 'I have to say I'm a bit relieved that you're not giving up on your degree.'

Oliver's leg jumped, his heel tapping out a nervous rhythm on the Indian rag rug beneath his foot.

'Not that I'm saying you *have* to finish; there is no pressure on you either way' – he tried to grease the path for whatever Oliver might decide – 'but I think you have this amazing opportunity that a lot of people would give their left nut for.'

'Would you?'

'Would I what, son?'

'Would you have liked to have gone to university?'

'Erm.' The question took him by surprise. He took his time framing his answer, taking a sip of his tea.

I thought I could have it all. I thought I could do the right thing by Kerry, be a good father to you, set the best example, please my own dad and make a good life. But it turns out I was wrong; you can't have it all. University was going to be my ticket; I wanted the car, the house, a big desk and someone on call to bring me orange Fanta . . . I gave up the dream to work at Siddley's. It was all about getting through the week, earning enough to keep food on the table and you in nappies. I thought it would be temporary, thought I'd figure something out and find a way, but here I am. Stuck. And as for your mum and me? We were kids, playing at being grown-ups, and by the time I realised we were playing at it I was a grown-up, a grown-up with responsibilities, and that was that. Would I go back and trade it all for a place at a university like this? Would I let Kerry listen to her sister? No. No, a thousand times no, because the truth is I did love her . . . even though we had our issues – who doesn't? And you, Oliver, you're the greatest thing I have ever done. I pass the mantle to you and you will live the life I could only have dreamed of, my boy . . .

'I guess I would have liked to have been smart enough to get a place at university.' He hoped they might leave it at that.

'Come off it, Dad, you're plenty smart!'

The vote of confidence was a welcome boost to his flagging self-esteem. He recalled being sixteen with the fire of self-assurance in his belly that made him feel invincible. When he was the first to get married he felt like an adventurer, a ground-breaker. This before some of the boys in his year packed up to leave Burston, ready to study at Sheffield, and one even went to London, and Nick was left behind and suddenly he didn't feel that clever or that confident. Not any more.

'Oh, I don't know about that.'

'Yes, you are! Grandad always said you could have been anything, had you and Mum not had me so young and you having to take the job at Siddley's.'

Nick remembered the day he walked through the factory gates by his dad's side. His old man had always been so proud to walk him around the place, introducing him to anyone and everyone with his hands gripping his shoulders.

This is my boy, Nicholas . . .

Have you met my lad?

This is Nicky, top of his class at Burstonbridge Comp, aren't you, son?

And Nick had always felt ten feet tall walking in by his side, and yet on that day, with Kerry nearly five months pregnant and the rent on the one-bedroomed flat above the off licence due, things felt very different. Nick was happy, yes, but aware that his choices were limited. On his dad's recommendation, Mr Siddley senior had agreed to give him a go. Yes, on that day there was no sense of pride, quite the opposite. His dad walked with a slow reluctance to his gait and a downward cast to his eyes, as if Nick had in some way let him down. Nick never really shook off that feeling and when his dad passed away seven years ago he had stood by his grave with the roof of Siddley's visible in the distance and offered up a silent apology for the fact that he had not quite lived up to his dad's expectations. He knew he had never reached his full potential, a frustration that spilled over into his marriage, and years later when it looked like Kerry might have let him down . . . all he could think about was how much he had given up. It was a burden that he never wanted to put on Oliver's shoulders, even though he understood it more than most. He was proud of his boy for who he was, for what he had gone through and for the future that beckoned, so proud. But he would keep these thoughts to himself.

'It's all well and good looking at what might have been,' Nick responded to Oliver's statement, 'but you can only really deal with what actually is, and I wouldn't have changed a thing about my life up to now, not a thing. And you know, I was thinking about this the other day: we did have you young – some said too young; in fact, most said too young.' He smiled. 'But we never thought so. It always felt right; scary, but right. And knowing what we know now, it meant your mum got to be with you until you were grown up – well, technically grown up – and that's a wonderful thing. She got eighteen years of you and you of her.'

'I miss her.' Oliver sniffed and his lips, pressed tightly together, quivered in the pre-crying pose that his dad recognised as the one his boy had struck since he was a child, when what ailed him was usually a scraped knee or a misplaced toy.

'I miss her too.'

'I talk to her,' Oliver confessed, staring at the mug in his hands.

'I talk to her too, and she answers. Or at least I imagine her answering and it helps.'

'She doesn't answer me, but she smiles at me and crinkles her eyes up like she used to, and it makes me cry again. I try not to think about her when I'm out and about or with my friends, but when I'm on my own I tell myself she's at home.' Oliver sniffed. 'It's easy, really. I picture you at work and her in the kitchen or watching the telly and I think she's there and that I'll see her soon.'

Nick nodded, knowing he had done similar when the loss of her threatened to overwhelm him at work: *she's at the supermarket, parking the car, chatting to her sister, buying our food . . .*

'I don't believe she's gone, Dad, not really. I know it sounds stupid—'

'It doesn't,' Nick interrupted, knowing nothing was stupid and that there was no blueprint for their grief. 'Not at all.'

'I wish I could call her, just once. I want to hear her voice and I'd love to talk to her, just to find out how she's doing. Make sure she's okay.'

'Me too. Although that would be some phone bill, eh?' He tried to lighten the mood and it seemed to work. Oliver smiled and wiped his eyes with his fingers.

'I keep thinking that she was never very good at travelling by herself, you know, like when we were on the way to Filey or she had to catch a bus – she always got in a bit of a panic in case she went in the wrong direction or got lost.'

'And she had a habit of doing both.' Nick chuckled, picturing her wandering off from the car in the wrong direction to where they were heading and him having to call her back: *And where do you think you're going, Missus?*

'It's this way, isn't it?'

'No, Ker, it's not!'

'That's what I mean, Dad, and I keep thinking . . .' He paused. 'I keep thinking that she has had to go on this final journey on her own, all on her own, and I worry about that.'

'You know' – Nick coughed to clear the emotion that bloomed in his throat – 'I *don't* worry about that. I don't know what happens to us when we pass on, Olly, but I am certain that, if at all possible, there would be someone to hold your mum's hand and show her the way.'

'Someone like Grandad?'

He nodded, biting his teeth together hard to control his tears. He didn't want to break down. Not here and not now.

They sat quietly for a second or two as Nick tried to restore his thoughts and beat off the wave of sadness that threatened to knock him from his feet, as it often did. It was Olly that broke the silence.

'I'm sorry I called you in such a state earlier.'

'Don't be sorry. I'm your dad. I want you to be able to call on me any time, and it's been good to see you and to have a cuppa – really good, worth the drive even.' He raised the now empty mug in Oliver's direction as he stood, preparing to leave. 'But I do think we need a code system for days like these and moments like that.'

'What kind of code system?'

'I don't know, Olly, maybe we could say "code green" if everything is fine, "amber" if we are sliding towards danger or you're having a bit of a wobble and need propping up and "code red", which should only be used in extreme emergencies and means get in the car and come down the motorway immediately. You would only need to say "code red" and I'd know that you're actually saying, "Dad, me or my mental health is in mortal danger" or "The house on fire" or "There's a meteorite hurtling towards the Earth" – that kind of thing, okay? That should be a "code red". So I would say with hindsight that today's emergency would at best have been a mild amber.' He ruffled the boy's hair and pulled him into a hug.

'I think you're right, Dad. It was a mild amber.' Oliver placed his arms around his dad's shoulders and Nick inhaled the scent of him, which was changing from that of a boy to that of a man.

A knock at the door made them spring apart and stand in manly poses, hands on hips, chests wide.

'Come in,' Oliver called out in his deepest voice.

Tasha, the girl with the wide, dark spectacles, stood in the door with a big smile.

'Hi, Olly!'

'Hey, Tash, this is my dad, Nick.'

'Oh, Nick. I saw you before.' She said his name as if it were familiar to her and walked forward with her hands knitted at her chest. 'Olly told me about his mum and it made me so sad. How are you doing?'

He found her directness refreshing and mature, despite her rather awkward, childlike stance.

'I think the stock phrase is: I'm doing as well as can be expected.'

She nodded. 'My dad died when I was five. Olly and I have talked about it a lot. My dad was like way, way older than my mum, but it was still rubbish. I didn't think he died; I thought he had become a Teletubby and lived in the Teletubby house and that was why he couldn't come home. And when it came on television I used to sit with my nose pressed to the screen and my mum thought I loved the show; she used to buy me the characters and I even had curtains with them on.' She giggled. 'But it wasn't that – I was looking for little clues that it was my dad inside the costumes. I couldn't decide which one he was, but I think I settled on Dipsy.'

Nick stared at her and felt his mouth move as if forming a response, but the words failed him.

Oliver laughed heartily. 'She comes out with things like that all the time.' He spoke as if the girl weren't standing in front of him, but his tone was one of affection, and in that instant Nick felt like a gooseberry.

'Look, I'd better push off. It's a long drive home.' He smiled at the girl. 'Nice to see you again, Tasha.'

'Sames.' She nodded and it took him a second to interpret her answer. 'We have to get ready anyway; we have a freshers' event tonight in the bar and we need costumes. I'm thinking we should go as cavemen and just scruff up our hair and put on sacks or something and get bones as accessories from the big bin at the back of the canteen.'

'Is that right?' Nick eyed his son, who usually shied away from dressing up. 'I thought you had a load of books to read; hadn't you better make a start?'

'The thing is, Dad, one night is not going to make any difference. I need to not get in a flap about it, put it in perspective, and tonight I think beer is more important than reading.'

Nick smiled at his boy and fished in his pocket for his car keys before making his way down the stairs and out into the cold afternoon air. He smiled up at the window as Oliver waved goodbye from his room with Tasha by his side.

He was tired when he got home. Without the fear and adrenaline that fanned his journey there, the drive seemed to take twice as long. And the fact that he was sustained by no more than a cup of tea and three gingersnap biscuits didn't help.

It had been a long and emotionally draining series of events and the evening had truly pulled its blind on the day. He pulled the car up on to the drive in darkness and pictured climbing the stairs with the usual dilemma. He longed to fall on to the soft mattress and plant his face in the pillow, but at the same time felt the stab of loneliness when he considered her empty side of the bed. The house was eerily quiet and he flicked on the kitchen light before filling the kettle and looking at the dirty dishes from yesterday, and possibly the day before that, still stacked in the sink. He'd do them tomorrow.

The front doorbell ringing took him by surprise. He opened it to find Diane, his sister-in-law, standing on the step with Treacle. He painted on a smile.

'Di! Hello, Treacle.' He unclipped her collar and watched her run inside.

'I bumped into Eric earlier, who was out over the Rec with her.' She pointed at the dog. 'He said you'd had to go and see Olly? What was that all about? Is he okay?'

He looked away from the crease of concern that sat at the top of her nose; the same one Kerry too had inherited from their mum. Tonight any resemblance was more than he could stand.

'Come in, Di.'

She followed him into the kitchen and he had to remind himself to be welcoming and pleasant, wanting nothing less than visitors at this time of night, when his mood was a little low. And the only thing he wanted less than company was the company of his sister-in-law.

'Yes, I went down to see Olly, but he's fine, went into a bit of a tailspin earlier, but I think he just needed reassurance. I've literally just got back. Thirty quid poorer after filling up, and knackered, but actually just glad he's okay. He misses his mum – that's what it boils down to.'

'Course he does. We all do.' Diane looked down, not bothering to wipe the tears that fell. He understood; everything was still so raw, so painful.

'Anyway . . .' She sniffed. 'I told Eric I'd take Treacle, and here we are.' She wiped her nose with a soggy bit of kitchen roll. She managed to make her act of kindness sound like a huge imposition, her undertone of martyrdom ringing loud and clear.

'Do you want a cup of tea, Di? I'm just making.' He pointed at the kettle.

She stared at him with narrowed eyes and bit her lip. 'It's funny, isn't it? How many times have I sat in this kitchen, talking to my sister?'

He blew out. 'I don't know, thousands.' He imagined the laughter that used to explode from the kitchen, the two of them together – it used to make him smile and irritate him in equal measure, the interruption when he was trying to catch up on the news or watch football.

'Yes, thousands, and I never once had a cup of tea. I don't drink it, Nick, can't stand the stuff. I don't drink coffee either.'

'Is that right?' He stared at her, reminded in that second that Kerry was the conduit between him and her family, in fact between him and their friends. She was the glue, the one who remembered birthdays and anniversaries, the names of newborns, dates of christenings, who was dating who, whose marriage was on the rocks, who had a new job and where, how people had done in exams, who was wearing new glasses, had got their hair cut and who did or did not drink tea.

'I said to Mum earlier, you must feel lost, Nick. I think it's bad for us – I miss my sister . . .' She paused to try to control the catch in her throat. 'I guess I sometimes forget that I'm not the only one hurting.'

'I do feel lost.' It was a rare admission. 'Adrift. It's like I've left the house and forgotten something but I can't think what. Like I need to be somewhere but have no idea where. Anyway' – he took a deep breath – 'I'm rambling. Thanks for bringing Treacle home.'

'Any time. You know where we are, Nick.'

'I do. Thanks, Di.' He nodded, keen to get her out of the door before his sadness, urged on by fatigue, overwhelmed him. Diane patted Treacle and made her way along the hallway. He closed the front door and sank down on to the welcome mat on the exact same spot where Oliver had crumpled, and he let his tears fall.

'I don't like being on my own! I miss having my family around me.' He spoke through gritted teeth. 'I don't like it, Kerry.'

1992

The knocking on the front door was urgent. Nick quickly tied his trainer laces and finished the last bite of his toast and peanut butter, eaten illegally in his bed. His dad, the custodian of standards in the house, was already at work and his mum had given it to him with a wink. It made him love her more. Today was the day they had decided to go hunting for the things they needed to build Half Bike and they had drawn up a list:

saddle
lights
pump
wheels
inner tube
tyres
water bottle holder
water bottle
stickers for frame

Nick heard his mum's sing-song greeting and the sound of feet thundering up the stairs. Alex pushed open the bedroom door, his face red, his tone a little panicked, as he began gabbling.

'He's not at home! I can't find him! His dad opened the door when I knocked and he looked really mad and he was a bit smelly, and he said if I see him then I had to tell him to go straight back. I didn't know what to do, so I came straight here!' He sat on the bed, a little out of puff. It was obvious he was talking about Eric, as he was the only one missing.

'What do you mean, you can't find him?' Nick had to admit it was a curious state of affairs that Eric was not around. Eric was always ready to leave his house of a morning or was knocking for Alex, if not already on Nick's doorstep bright and early.

'I mean' – Alex gulped – 'his dad said he didn't know where he was and I thought he might be here, but your mum said he's not.'

Nick considered this.

'Do you think he's in trouble?'

Alex nodded vigorously. 'I do. I think something has happened with his dad, maybe he told him off and that was why he looked so mad.'

Nick nodded; this sounded plausible.

'We should go and look for him,' he decided. 'We're out looking for bike bits anyway; we can look for him and the stuff we need at the same time.'

The boys headed down the stairs. 'Mum?' Nick called. 'We're going to look for bike stuff and Eric.' It didn't occur to either boy that a water bottle and discarded saddle might not be lurking in the same spot as their missing friend.

'Okay, lads, you know the rules, stay together and come back when you're hungry.' She smiled, clearly not sharing their concern for their missing mate.

Nick ran down the path and past his sister, who had set up a deck-chair in the front garden and now sat with a copy of *Look-In* open and lifted to her chest.

'Where you off to, dweebs?' she asked casually.

'We've lost Eric,' Alex explained over his shoulder as they trotted along the pavement.

'Lost him how?' Jen sat forward in the chair and her magazine fell to the floor.

'He's gone missing.'

'Do you want me to come and help you find him? I could . . . I could maybe join your gang for one day?'

Alex laughed and Nick shook his head. 'As if!'

'Well, good.' Jen sat back and reached for her magazine. 'I wouldn't want to join anyway! You're idiots!'

'Your sister scares me,' Alex whispered as they headed towards the Rec. The boys could see after scanning the place that Eric was not here, or if he was he was hidden. They combed the sloping field, looking behind trees and using thick sticks to thresh the long, weed-riddled grass that grew on the east side and where dogs liked to pee, but found nothing – nothing vaguely bike-related that might have been of use and no Eric Pickard.

'Where next?' Alex asked, a little jumpy at the fact that they had been searching for their friend for a whole thirty minutes but had found nothing.

'How about Market Square?'

'Okay!'

The boys ran as the sun began to climb on the bright summer's day, and arrived in the cobbled square with fringes damp from sweat stuck to their foreheads. Three older boys from school sat on the bench. Nick looked at them and then looked away sharply; he knew the rules. He and Alex were about five years away from being able to sprawl like that on the coveted bench unchallenged. He ran his fingers over the comforting outline of the multi-tool in his pocket.

A cursory glance in shop doorways and at the tables and chairs in front of the pub told them this was not where they would find their friend.

'Maybe he's been taken by aliens,' Alex whispered.

Nick stared at him. 'Yes, that's probably it. Or we could go and look up at the Old Dairy Shed?' He suggested the only other place the three ever went.

'Yes!' Alex clicked his fingers as if his friend were a genius.

Surprisingly, the place was a lot scarier during the day. Partly down to the lack of snoggers, which made the space seem echoey and vast, and also because without the darkness to mask its many imperfections the true state of its dilapidation was revealed. The windows that weren't smashed were covered in a dull, green slimy moss and the rafters were covered in pigeon shit. One or two of the birds still roosted there, sitting with chests pushed out and watching as he and Alex crept over rubbish and planks of wood, the remnants of rusted machinery and, most intriguingly, an old fridge freezer which looked to have been dumped there.

'This place is scary,' Alex said softly.

'More or less than my sister?'

Alex considered this. 'About the same.'

It was unmistakable and heart-thumpingly alarming all at the same time, the sound that suddenly floated from behind one of the girders: crying. And not the sweet burble of girls' tears or the kind of crying you heard on the telly, but loud, breathless sobs, as if the person couldn't stop even if they wanted to.

Alex took a step behind Nick and the two walked slowly forward in this pantomime-horse manner.

'Eric?' Nick called out.

'Go away!' his friend screamed.

The two did the opposite and ran towards the voice. And there they found him. Nick looked down at his mate, who sat on the concrete floor with his knees raised and his arms folded on them. His head was bowed on to his forearms and his narrow shoulders shook.

'What's wrong?' Alex asked gently.

'Nowt!' Eric roared, looking up briefly to reveal eyes that were bloodshot, a runny nose and two dirty tracks down his cheeks where tears had carved a sad path over his skin.

The three often found each other's distress comical – when Alex accidentally pinched the skin of his thumb between two links on the bike chain, he and Eric had watched, waiting for the tears that they could then mock. It was just what they did. But not this time. Eric's hurt went way beyond pinched skin.

Nick sat down on the floor and Alex followed suit, and there they sat in silence while their mate sobbed. Nick thought about when he cried and his mum put her arms around him. It made everything feel a little bit better, but there was no way he could hug Eric! An idea came to him. Instead of a full-scale hug that would only embarrass them both, he extended his index finger and the one next to it and pressed his fingers on to his friend's leg. Contact that he hoped might just take the edge off his distress in the way that his mum's hug did for him. Alex copied; extending his two fingers, he pushed them on Eric's other leg and, strangely, it seemed to work. Eventually, with a hiccup to his breathing, Eric extended the two fingers of both hands and laid them on top of his mates'. They were joined and calmed, the three of them, by this odd and well-meant salute.

Eric took a deep breath and wiped his teary lashes with the back of his hand. 'My dad came home from billiards and had a fight with Dave the Milk.'

'A proper fight?' Alex was clearly both intrigued and excited by the prospect.

Eric nodded. 'I was in my bedroom and my mum had told me to stay there, and I was setting up Domino Run when I heard them all shouting. It sounded like something on the telly.' He swallowed. 'I sat at the top of the stairs and my dad and Dave the Milk were thumping each other. They came out into the hallway and I saw my dad punch him in the mouth, and blood flicked up the wall. And my mum came out of the front room in her dressing gown and my dad pushed her back in and then . . .' His tears came again. 'And then my dad chucked Dave the Milk out of the house.'

'Is it because he found out about your mum's secret job?' Alex tried to make sense of it.

'I don't know, but my mum . . .' Eric paused and, with a look of utter despair, whispered, 'My mum went with him. She went with Dave the Milk and I don't know where she is now.'

Nick felt like crying himself. The idea, the very thought of his mum going somewhere and him not knowing where, or worse, the thought of her not coming back! Well, that was really the worst thing he could possibly imagine.

'It'll be all right,' he offered.

'How will it?' Eric asked, without his usual air of sarcasm; he was a kid wanting both answers and reassurance.

'I don't know,' Nick levelled with him, 'but I bet it will.'

The three sat quietly for a while until Alex piped up. 'Do you think because your dad hit him, Dave the Milk might want his handlebars back?'

'I don't think so,' Eric managed.

Nick stood up. 'Come on, we need to go and find stuff; sitting here isn't going to get Half Bike finished, is it?' He wiped the back of his shorts, which were damp from the floor, and was happy that the other two fell into step. He turned to look at Eric, who hadn't lost his sad expression. Nick reached into his pocket.

'Eric, you can be in charge of the multi-tool today. You can keep it in your pocket.'

Eric took it and gripped it tight. Nick was happy to see the small smile form on his friend's face. He ignored Alex's barely audible huff.

'Can I take it home? Just for tonight?'

Nick nodded. 'Yes, you can. Just for tonight.'

FOUR

Winter claimed the landscape of Burstonbridge. Thin frost sat on the grass in the early hours and the ground was hard as iron. The air was sharp with cold and chimneys let out loose plumes of smoke as folk set fires of coal and wood to try to stave off the chill. It was a cold November day with a bright blue sky, three months since they had laid Kerry to rest. Nick's grief, while no less weighted, had changed gear. Gone was the unexpected smack of sadness that hit him at the most random of times and in its place was something slower, a smouldering melancholy that he carried with him like a cloak, one, in truth, he was almost used to wearing. The house was exactly as she had left it, apart from the kitchen that maybe sparkled a little less, the bedroom, which was in need of airing, and he still couldn't get the hang of how to plump and position those damn cushions. Her clothes hung in her wardrobe and her boots and coat were where she had last placed them in the cupboard in the hallway. At first he took comfort from the items, running his fingers over them; they helped him pretend that she was not gone but had just nipped out. Now he didn't notice them as such; they were just part of the fabric of the building that had been her home.

A harsh wind blew up from the moors and cut his skin. Nick pulled his scarf up over his mouth, glad of the warm glow that radiated along his limbs, his exertion providing the fuel for him to climb up the hill to the graveyard. He gripped the stems of the small bouquet which Jean in the florist's had fashioned for him, a neat posy of rust-coloured marigolds and fronds of greenery, along with the obligatory sprig of purple heather, which had been present in every bouquet he had ever given Kerry, both before and after her death. He looked at them now; such a soft, beautiful thing to leave at the cold, hard grave where sad and mournful thoughts lingered. He wished it were not the case that he had given his wife more bouquets in death than he had in life. He wished a lot of things . . .

Standing now at the brow of the hill, Nick caught his breath, looking out over the wide bowl of Burstonbridge below and the russet-and-gold tapestry of farmland beyond. Beautiful.

'I can see everything. It feels like we are on top of the world up here . . .'

'That's how I always feel when I'm with you, Kerry, like I'm on top of the world, like I can do anything.'

'Oh, shut up, Nick, you old softie!'

'Do you reckon we'll bring this baby up here?'

Nick had looked at the bulge of her stomach beneath her coat, her pregnant state alien, petrifying and yet at the same time so familiar, the impending birth fearful and exciting in equal measure. 'I reckon we might . . .'

Walking slowly along the ridge, he made his way to the plot where Kerry had been laid to rest alongside her dad, and he bent low, placing the bunch of flowers on the grave, where the fresh words of remembrance and the cruel, short dates of her time on Earth had been added to her father's headstone. He tried not to look at the vast floral display left by her mum in a fancy silver-coloured urn, where wire held each flower proudly in place, and he tried not to feel the paw of inadequacy bat his conscience at the thought that Kerry's mum and Diane came here more regularly, left more extravagant blooms and no doubt cried harder.

It's not a competition . . .

He heard her words and gave a snort of uncomfortable laughter. 'I know it isn't, but I feel it nonetheless, the feeling that your mum and family don't think I'm doing enough, not doing things right.' He paused, looking behind him and all around to make sure there was no one around before he carried on the conversation.

'You know I've always felt a bit like that with them, and the truth is, Ker, I don't know how to be. I feel sad most of the time, but you already know this, and then when I do feel the gloom lift a little bit, I feel guilty, as though that's not allowed – I don't know what is allowed. And I don't know what to do about Olly; how much should I contact him? Interfere? I think if I haven't heard from him then things must be going all right, but then I read about kids away from home who are lonely or struggling and I feel worried sick about him.' He took a deep breath. 'The house is so quiet. I can't tell you how much I hate coming home to a dark house without the hall light on. I'm still lost, Kerry. Still lost, and I wish—'

'Now then, Nick!'

He turned sharply at the shout in time to see Diane walking along the ridge.

Bloody brilliant . . .

'Di.'

'Ah, you brought flowers.' Her tone hinted that this gesture was long overdue. She bent down and instantly started clearing weeds from the plot, balling them and popping them into a carrier bag she unfurled from her pocket. 'I like to get rid of these; they strangle the flowers and plants. Mum and I take it in turns.'

He was at a loss as to how to respond, aware for the first time of this rota in which he wasn't included. His next thought was that if they had asked him to participate he would not have had the time – or worse, the inclination . . .

'How's Oliver? Mum said she misses him.'

'I bet she does, Di. I do too.'

'Yes, but you've probably had some contact, unlike her. I mean, it's hard enough losing her daughter, but the thought of losing contact with her grandson too . . .'

He could only picture his mother-in-law sobbing and clinging to him and was ashamed of the shiver of unease he felt, as if her sadness were cloying and he wanted nothing less than to be coated with it. 'That's not going to happen.' He shook his head as if to emphasise the point. 'And the way I look at it is, if he's too busy at Uni, too preoccupied with life to call his gran, then that probably means he's having a good time. I know we all miss him, but I know more than that we all just want him to be fine, happy.'

'Oh God! Yes of course! But they do have phones in Birmingham?'

He held her gaze and bit his bottom lip – better than giving voice to the words that queued up on his tongue. *He's eighteen, lost his mum, is away from home, finding his feet; give him a bloody break . . .*

'I hear what you're saying, Di, and when I do finally speak to him, I'll mention it would be good to call his gran.'

She nodded and gave a small, satisfied hum. They both turned to look at the headstone.

'Can't believe it's been nearly four months. Some days it feels like yesterday and others a lifetime.' He made the observation more out of the want of small talk than anything else.

'Three months, nine days and six hours . . .' Di tilted her chin. Again, she had won, knowing more accurately how long it was since his wife had passed away.

'I'd better get on, Di, I'm on a late shift.' He nodded his head down the hill in the general direction of Siddley's. 'See you around.'

'Yep.' She took a sharp intake of breath. 'See you around.'

Nick checked the printed inventory against the batch number on the pallets and gave the thumbs-up to the forklift driver to proceed with loading. He stood back and watched as the forks slid beneath the wooden pallet, stacked high with plastic-wrapped boxes, and slid them with ease into the back of the waiting truck with its door rolled up and the tail lift lowered.

'What you doing tonight, Nick?' Eric shouted across the yard.

'Nothing.' He stared at his mate, as if there might be any other answer.

'Fancy coming to quiz night?'

'Quiz night?'

'Yes, up at the Blue Anchor, all in teams, three pounds each to play and we answer general knowledge questions and the winning team takes the pot. It's a bit of a giggle and we have a pint.'

Nick considered his friend's invitation. 'I'm not very good at general knowledge.'

'You don't have to be, you mardy bastard. It's not about knowing the most; it's about getting you out of the house, about mixing with people and not sitting in watching rubbish telly and talking to Treacle.'

'I like rubbish telly,' Nick said in his defence, unable to deny the lengthy conversations he had with the pooch.

'We all do, Nick, but not every night. Come out, Barbara!'

Nick laughed. 'I don't know . . .' He tried to imagine going to the pub and being sociable and immediately pictured Di clearing weeds from the grave. 'I don't know if I'm up to it.'

'You're never going to be up to it if you don't make the leap. I can't force you, but I think it'll do you good.'

'Thank you, Doctor.' He smiled at his friend.

'Tell you what, come out to the pub and if you don't like it or you're not having fun or you'd rather be at home, then just get up and walk out and no one will think any less of you for it. Even if they do, you'll have already left so you won't know about it.'

'I might do.'

'Good lad.' Eric beamed as if he had given a hard yes.

He gave the invitation little thought until he let himself into his mum's house.

'Only me!' he called, as he wiped his work boots on the mat.

'In't kitchen, love!' came her reply. 'What can I get you to eat?' This before she had even seen him.

'Nowt,' he replied, and made his way along the hall.

'How you doing?' She had an irritating habit of looking at him with her head cocked to one side and her lashes lowered, her expression sympathetic, as if she were on the verge of tears or he were to be pitied. It annoyed him. Emasculated him.

'I'm fine,' he snapped.

'Listen to how sharp you are with me, Nicky. You used to love me being your mum.'

Oh, please not this again . . .

'I still do.'

'Yes, but you used to think I was kind, not a nag; wise, not annoying – and you used to be able to talk to me without sighing or raising your eyebrows.'

'Do I do that?'

'Yes, darlin', you're doing it now.'

He stared at her. 'I don't know what you want me to say.'

'I know.' She pursed her lips as if his phrase only emphasised her point. He knew she spoke the truth. She did irritate him, as if the way she treated him as a boy was perfect, comforting, and yet that same treatment now he was an adult . . . he found it infuriating.

'And how's my Olly?'

'Good, Mum. I bumped into Di earlier and she was moaning that he hasn't phoned Dora, kind of had a go and said he should make more effort with her.'

'Well, she needs to lay off! Firstly, you have enough on your plate and, secondly, that boy is away from home for the first time, having just lost his mum; the last thing he needs is pressure from Dora bloody Forrest. I won't 'ave it, Nick!'

'It's okay, Mum. Calm down. I told Di if he wasn't on the phone to us all every five minutes it probably meant he was having a nice time. I think she agreed.'

His sister, Jen, who had moved back home after her divorce, ran down the stairs. 'Who's having a nice time?' She reached for an apple and bit into it, caring little that the juice ran down her chin. This was home and they were siblings, after all. No need to stand on ceremony in front of the person you had shared everything with from parents to chicken pox.

'Olly. And me too, apparently, if I go to the pub tonight for quiz night – Eric's making me go.'

'Ericisadick,' she mumbled with a mouth full of fruit.

'Yep, you might have already said that once or twice. But you should give him a break.'

'He knows it's only banter,' his sister tutted. 'We've always been like that.'

It bothered him just a little, how scathing she had always been about his friend, who was in his opinion a good bloke, and he had stopped finding her banter funny a long time ago. He bit his lip, trying to quell the rising irritation he felt towards his mother and sister, figuring that as the common denominator it must be him who had the problem and not them.

Tolerance . . . They mean well . . . He heard Kerry's wise words.

'Plus, if you were planning on joining our team, you can think again. We're on a winning streak and I don't want to change our winning formula.' Jen held his gaze.

'I'm more than capable of sorting a team. And I know the Blue Anchor is your hangout, but I'm thirty-five, Jen. I need to leave the house, or what's the alternative, sit and watch rubbish telly and chat to Treacle? No offence, Treacle,' he called towards the sitting room, where he was confident the dog would be asleep on the sofa she was technically barred from sitting on. Nick clicked his fingers, summoning the dog.

He turned and looked at his sister as she devoured her apple.

'And actually, Jen, not having me on your team might be a huge mistake. Far better to be on a team with me on it than against me – remember when you asked me what the capital of Paris was?'

'I got confused! You knew I meant France!'

'But as I said at the time, you answered your own question!' He sighed.

'Tell him, Mum!' Jen pointed at her brother in jest, sounding nothing like a police officer in her late thirties. He laughed, shut the door behind him and with Treacle in tow they set off for home.

Nick was uncertain what to wear to a pub quiz; this was the kind of thing that Kerry would know. He showered and stepped into his jeans and a cleanish shirt, which when ironed, would do for one more wear. His phone rang. It was Oliver.

'How we doing, Olly? I'm sitting down on the bed and so hit me if it's a code red and I can make the necessary arrangements.' He smiled, half admitting to himself that the thought of having to drive to see Oliver for an emergency might actually be preferable to going to a pub quiz with a gut full of nerves and no idea of what to wear.

'Very funny!' Oliver chuckled. 'No code red. I'd say we are all green at the moment.'

'Well, I'm very glad to hear it.' He felt his stomach unbunch.

'Just thought I'd give you a shout and see what you're up to.'

'Funny you should ask.' Nick looked at his reflection in the mirror. 'I'm about to go to the Blue Anchor for a quiz night with Eric and a few people from work and your Auntie Jen, although apparently I'm not allowed to join her team. I think she's still worried I might embarrass her in front of her friends, even after all these years.'

'You're going to the pub?' Oliver's tone was sharp, surprised and, if Nick was hearing it correctly, carried a slight edge of disapproval.

'Well, Eric asked if I fancied it, and I must admit I feel a bit nervous. It's the first time I've been out since . . .' He let this hang.

'You never go to the pub.' Oliver's voice was now quieter, his tone reflective, and Nick felt his pain. And he got it. Oliver was a kid who whilst he wished his dad no ill, didn't want things to be moving on, worried no doubt that they were starting to pick up where they left off before Kerry got sick, fearful that she might in any way be slipping from her position as the first thing he thought about. This Nick understood because these were his worries too. It felt like a disservice.

'I don't know if I'll go, even.' He paused. 'I think Eric was just trying to get me out of the house.'

There was a beat or two of silence before Oliver spoke up. 'You should go, Dad. Eric is right, you should get out of the house.'

'Do you think so?' He held the phone close to his face, wanting at some level to hear Oliver's approval.

'Yes, go, have a nice time.'

'Thank you, son. What have you been up to?'

'Not much.' He yawned. 'Seeing Tasha, working a bit, reading.'

'Ah, reading, good – you're working your way through your overwhelmingly long list?'

'I am, actually.' Oliver laughed.

'And seeing Tasha, you say? Is she . . . Are you . . .?' He wasn't sure how to phrase it, concerned that words like 'dating' and 'going out' might have gone out of fashion a long time since.

'I like her, Dad.' Nick could hear the smile in his son's voice and it made him smile in return.

'Well, that's good, and for the record, I thought she seemed really nice, what I saw of her.'

'Did you like Mum instantly?'

The question caught him a little off guard. 'Yes, yes, I did. I mean I was aware of her for a while, as we were in a lot of the same classes at school, but when I did finally speak to her, when we were a little bit older, then that was it for me.' He remembered the first time he became aware of her, feeling drawn to her in a way that wasn't logical. It was no more than the look of her, the way her hair fell across her face and the way she shone to him across the classroom, like she was the only other person in the room. She had filled his thoughts and his torturous nights and the day he finally got to hold her, kiss her, that was the day he felt like he'd won the best prize the world had to offer. To him she was perfect. He hated that the glow of that prize had tarnished over the years. Their imperfections revealed to each other with every year that passed, and Kerry's secrecy; running up debt that nearly crippled them had almost been the hatchet to their marriage. He would not have liked to predict what might have become of them had her illness not bound them with ropes fashioned from duty, kindness and an almost forgotten love.

'That's kind of how it was for me with Tasha. I saw her that first time with you and then I bumped into her a couple of times at fresher events, but now I just can't seem to disconnect from her mentally, it's like she is always in my head. Do you know what I mean, Dad?'

'I do.' It was Nick's turn to be a little surprised. He could only think of Oliver as their little boy, young, riding his bike down the street with a wobble, minus his stabilisers, or jumping into his lap when the house was plunged into darkness during a power cut. He could still remember the feel of his small body in cotton pyjamas curled into his lap and how he had held his boy close, sound asleep, long after the lights had come back on . . . and now here he was, attending fresher events with a girl in his head. It was a jolt to be reminded that when he was Oliver's age, Oliver was a toddler.

'I knew I liked her and so I had to figure out how to take things forward.'

'I see.' He beamed at the boy's confidence and, apparently, initiative. 'So what did you do to move things forward?'

'I snogged her mate.'

'You snogged her mate?' Nick let out a loud burst of laughter, which Oliver echoed. 'Jesus, Olly, I wasn't expecting that. I think things might be a bit different to how they were when I was trying to land your mum. I think snogging her mate would have seen her running for the hills!'

'I was talking to Joe, who's on my corridor, and he said the best way to get a girl to like you is to make her jealous, and so I snogged her mate, and then I told Tasha I was drunk, which I was, very, and that I didn't really like her mate, and then Tasha posted a picture on Insta of her about to go out and I liked it with smiling cat-eye emojis and that was that.'

'Olly' – Nick gathered his thoughts – 'I have no idea what you're talking about.'

It was Oliver's turn to laugh out loud.

'I'm glad you and Tasha have . . . become friends, but I think if I had to give you one piece of advice—'

'Oh God,' Oliver sighed. 'Not advice.' He elongated the word like it was something toxic.

Nick ignored him. 'If I had to give you one piece of advice, it would be don't play games with people or their emotions. That wasn't the nicest thing to do to Tasha's mate. People aren't disposable. Be straight, always tell them how you feel and remember that we all bruise in the same way. Be kind, respectful.' He assumed that Oliver's silence meant he was contemplating his words. He hoped so.

'So did Mum like you instantly?'

'I don't think so. I don't know.'

The two men sat in silence across the miles, each sliding into the dark void of loss they could never fill with knowledge, as the only person they could ask was no longer here.

'I'd better go, Dad.'

'Sure, thanks for calling, Olly.'

'No worries.'

And just like that the call ended. Nick sat on the edge of the bed and thought about his boy, a boy taking giant leaps into adulthood.

Snogged her mate . . . He laughed again, shaking his head.

The front doorbell rang and Treacle barked accordingly.

'Shush, Treacle!' he yelled as he raced down the stairs and opened the door to Eric.

'You ready, Judith?' His friend rubbed his hands to stave off the cold.

'I thought I was meeting you there?' Nick left his mate in the hall and went to grab his trainers from the kitchen.

'You were, but I know you and thought, left to your own devices, you might bottle it.'

'And you might have been right,' Nick confessed as he shut Treacle in and closed the front door. 'Just spoke to Olly. He's got a girlfriend.'

Eric stopped walking and stood on the pavement. 'Jesus H Christ! Don't tell me that! How in the world can Olly have a girlfriend; he's only six! And I'm a grown-up and I don't have one!'

'Ah, apparently you might have been going about it all wrong. The answer is to find someone you like and snog her mate.'

Eric looked skyward, as if taking the suggestion seriously. 'I'm trying to think of which of Jen's mates I could snog.'

Nick shook his head. 'Give it up with the Jen thing. It ain't never going to happen or it would have by now.'

Eric tapped his nose and walked briskly. 'I've told you before, it's a waiting game. We have a connection.'

'You do not have a connection!'

'We do! There is much more to us than you know about.' Eric looked into the distance.

'Is that right?' Nick looked at him quizzically.

'Just you wait and see.' Eric smiled, undefeated.

The pub was busy with the right hum of chatter and the nostalgic scent of beer and cologne, which he hadn't smelled for a while. It took him back to underage drinking in the pub with Kerry, the two of them supping illegal pints and walking home hand in hand, feeling like the grown-ups they were desperate to become, hurtling towards adulthood and all the responsibilities of which they were unaware at a million miles an hour. He looked around and spotted familiar faces: from work, old friends from school, Barney who worked at the petrol pumps up at Mackie's, and Jen and Beverly sitting at the bar, laughing, doubled over with glasses of wine in their hands.

'Pint?' Eric made a beeline for Jen and Nick saw Beverly nudge her in the ribs with a warning dig, supposedly to let her know that Eric was incoming. Jen spun around on the stool, facing the bar, and he felt for his mate, who surreptitiously brushed his hair with his fingers, still, after all these years, trying to make the very best impression. He followed Eric.

'Evening, ladies.' Eric smiled. 'Can I get you a drink?' he asked casually, the swallow of his Adam's apple suggesting that inside he wasn't feeling quite as confident as he presented. It made Nick feel less self-conscious about the nerves that swirled in his gut.

'No, but thanks, Eric, we just got them.' Beverly lifted her glass in proof. 'Whose team you on, Nick?' she asked, before sipping her drink.

'Eric's, I suppose.'

Jen turned to her brother and kept her voice low, speaking from the side of her mouth. 'You okay, Broth?'

He nodded.

'We just need to keep things as normal as possible. You'll be fine. But I have my eye on you. And so does Eric. I know coming out tonight is a big deal and if you're not okay' – her tone was sincere, her eyes searching his – 'just give me the nod and I'll have you home on that couch chatting to Treacle quicker than you know.'

'Thanks, Jen.' He smiled at her. Her support was as reassuring as it was welcome. 'That means a lot.'

'Oh, don't get mushy.' She shuddered, turning to Beverly and raising her voice. 'I reckon a definite win for us tonight, then, Bev, if dweeb and dweeb junior are teaming up.'

'You can come on our team if you like, Jen?' Eric ignored her jibe and asked with boyish enthusiasm in response, to which Jen rolled her eyes.

'Ladies and gentlemen!' Big Brian from the British Legion, a barrel-chested man with an impressive moustache, who spent six months planning the Remembrance Day parade in the town and the following six months recounting it to anyone he bumped into, now called out across the bar and everyone fell silent. 'This is your ten-minute warning for all those here for the pub quiz: get registered, pay up, dump your phones in the box and take your seats!'

Eric handed him a pint. Nick sipped the foamy head and savoured the hoppy, bitter, wheaty taste on his lips. He hadn't drunk a proper pint in the pub for a long, long time. He had to stop himself from necking it.

'Right, I'll go pay and ditch our phones.' He took Nick's device from his hand. 'You go sit with Alex and Ellie.' He pointed across the room to their old mate and his wife, who might have been the best-looking girl in the youth club, but whom they had quickly learnt was a fun sucker. And it wasn't only her own fun she sucked, but sadly Alex's too. Alex, who had very much been an active shareholder in Half Bike and a proper laugh throughout his teens, had very quickly after he and Ellie waltzed up the aisle turned into a shadow of his former self. He was a man obsessed with paint colour charts and spent his Sundays at the garden centre. His natural and ready laugh had been replaced with a self-conscious smile that was always quickly followed by a glance in Ellie's direction, as if approval or, worse, permission were needed for this show of happiness. He worked in administration for a small insurance company in Northallerton and was someone who always looked like he had lost a coin and found a button. Nick watched Alex finger the collar of his polo shirt, pushing the tips flat against his breastbone, and knew it was most unlikely that he would ever own a Harley Davidson and ride it around Market Square. Nick tried to imagine Ellie's face if he did.

'It's nice to see you out, Nick,' Ellie offered with kindness, and he felt mean for having thought about her 'fun sucker' status.

'Thanks, Ellie. Feels odd,' he confessed.

She made a 'humph' noise and adjusted her bra strap before speaking with her jaw jutting. 'I don't doubt that if it was me who'd popped me clogs, he'd be out on the town before the sandwiches at me wake were curled.' She nodded her head in Alex's direction, tight-lipped and with her hands clutched in her lap. Nick smiled, and his flash of guilt disappeared as quickly as it had risen.

Alex looked at him with an expression of resignation and Nick pictured the boy who used to be the life and soul. He couldn't imagine spending time with someone who made you feel the way Ellie seemed to, the very opposite of supportive. He thought of how Kerry and he had nearly always liked each other's company. At least that was the case until the winter of 2008, when Kerry had had a moment of crisis, flirting with a man who wasn't him and racking up a monstrous debt on store and credit cards, all of which came as a massive shock to him. Her actions had threatened to derail them, leaving long shadows over their marriage that her sickness had largely erased – largely, but not completely. And it was in this shaded grey area of hurt that his thoughts sometimes strayed during the early hours when he stared at the ceiling, trying to make sense of it all. He had liked it in the beginning of their marriage when Kerry had felt like a safe harbour. He looked around the bar and felt her absence keenly. It had been decades since he had been in a social situation as a single man.

The tables quickly filled, the noise level rose and spectators either too chicken to play or too tight to cough up the three-quid subscription clustered around the bar. Big Brian took up his seat between two stony-faced adjudicators and tapped the tabletop microphone in front of him. This was serious business. Eric sidled next to him and raised his shoulders in excited anticipation in the way he always had, like when they were small and standing in the queue waiting for the ice-cream van.

Nick noted some of the teams had five and even six members.

'We've only got four, does that matter?' He looked at Eric.

'We don't need six; we're the cleverest here.' Eric tapped his temple.

'Clever or lucky?' he asked.

'Both, mate.' Eric raised his pint to him. 'Both.'

Ellie tutted and Alex chuckled. Big Brian, however, looked up sharply. 'There will be no talking between questions or during tie breaks.' Nick felt his cheeks flame, as if the man had addressed him directly. Big Brian wasn't done. 'There will be no conferring outside of the team, and anyone caught using a mobile phone or any Internet device to gain an advantage will be banned not only from this quiz but all future quizzes. Phones can be collected after the results.' Brian cast his beady eye over those assembled. Nick looked over towards Jen's table and Beverly pulled a face at him; she too apparently found Brian's manner most amusing.

'The winning pot for tonight is' – Big Brian paused – 'seventy-two pounds in cash, plus a voucher from Orient Rendezvous to the value of twenty pounds.'

Several people whooped out loud. It made Nick smile – the seventy-two-pound prize didn't garner much of a reaction, but the prospect of twenty quids' worth of free noodles or chips from the local takeaway was quite a different matter.

'Pens ready, and we will begin.' Big Brian took a deep breath and Nick looked at Eric, who sat with the answer sheet flat on the table and his pen poised.

'Question One: what is the capital of Switzerland?'

'Geneva,' Alex whispered from behind his cupped palm.

'Isn't it Zurich?' Nick piped up, trying to picture the open page of a map.

'It's Bern, isn't it?' Eric threw the question out there. As soon as he said it Nick knew this was the answer.

'Yes, mate, Bern – that's the one.'

Nick looked around at the other teams, all beaming, nodding and sitting tall in their chairs, seemingly confident that they knew the answer. He was surprised by the competitive streak that fired through him and caught Jen's eye. She gave him a superior look and a slight shake of her head as she mouthed the word 'dweeb'. He ignored her.

'Question Two.' Big Brian coughed. 'According to the Society of Motor Manufacturers and Traders, UK, as of October 2018, what was the best-selling car in the UK?'

'Golf,' Eric opened with confidence.

'Yep, Golf,' Ellie agreed. 'I have a Golf and my sister does too, and Nicola, a girl at work. So I'd say Golf.'

Eric bit his cheek; no doubt to stifle the many sarcastic retorts he wanted to fire at her logic.

'What about a Ford?' Alex piped up.

'Yes, good shout, Alex, Focus? Fiesta?' Nick agreed with his friend.

'Fiesta.' Alex held his gaze.

'I still think Golf.' Eric overrode him and, encouraged by Ellie's vigorous nodding in between sips of her vodka and tonic, he wrote 'VW Golf' as their answer.

This was how the evening continued. The questions were sometimes tough, sometimes not so much, but always fuelled fierce debate. Much to his surprise, Nick actually enjoyed himself, getting lost in the process of dredging his thoughts, trying to dig for facts in the murky silt of grief, searching for answers that included: 'Rocky Marciano', 'Mahogany', '*Toy Story 2*' and 'Beluga caviar'. He felt an unfamiliar flickering of pride when he knew an answer, a nice and rare moment when he felt smart, a sharp, almost painful, reminder of how he had felt at school, like he got it while others foundered . . . a kid who was going places. He remembered his conversation with Oliver.

'*Would you have liked to have gone to university?*' and the response he buried:

'*You bet your bottom dollar I would!*'

A recess was called while Big Brian and his team of two solemnly gathered the answer papers from the tables and went to the back room, home of the skittle alley, to mark them. Jen walked over to their table.

'You can leave now if you want, Nick, save the embarrassment of having your butt whipped!'

'I'll stay put, thanks.'

'What did you put for the car one? It's Fiesta, right?' Jen probed.

'That's what I thought,' Alex said loudly, splaying his upward palms as if used to being overridden; his expression screaming *what can you do?* Ellie gave him a sharp stare.

Nick sipped the last of his pint and stood to go and get his round in.

'Same again, everyone?'

'Please.'

'Cheers.'

'Just half.'

'Oh, I'll have white wine, please.' Jen smiled sweetly.

'You can whistle!' He pushed past her and made his way to the bar. Beverly was waiting with a tenner in her hand, trying to get the attention of Ruby behind the bar.

'Your sister is quite possibly the most competitive person I've ever met.' She grimaced.

'Tell me about it. When we were kids we used to play Monopoly as a family, at Christmas and the like, and she would never let us finish the game early if we got bored. We'd have to slog it out, sometimes for hours, because she couldn't stand to lose and couldn't stand it if things weren't done by the rules. If she needed to go the toilet, she'd take the dice so we couldn't carry on or cheat without her there. I remember my mum looking close to tears and my dad yawning, but that was apparently better than having to sit through one of Jen's tantrums. Sometimes I'd steal money and put it in her bank, just so she could win and I could go outside and play football!'

'You're the only person I've ever heard of nicking from the Monopoly bank to let someone else win!' She pushed her short blonde hair behind her ears and Nick noticed the shape of her cheek and chin: small, elfin, pretty. He felt the punch of disloyalty in his gut and coughed, as if this might expel the taste of guilt that sat on his tongue and in his throat.

'I had to; we might still be there now!'

Beverly let out a loud laugh and Nick looked over her shoulder to see if anyone was watching, relieved to see they weren't.

'What you having, Nick?' She waved her tenner towards the bar.

'Oh, no, nothing. I'm . . . I'm getting a round in, so, but no, thank you . . .' He took a step backwards, pulled back his shoulders and looked towards Eric, who was chatting to Jen, willing him to come over and provide a much-needed barrier. He felt awkward, embarrassed, and glanced at the front door, wondering if it would be terrible to make a run for it. As he considered this he felt Eric, as if having heard his plea, place his hand on his shoulder, and Nick felt instant and sweet relief.

'We're dying of thirst over there!' he laughed, before the smile fell from his face. 'Oh, mate, I just meant—'

'It's okay.' Nick ran his palm over his face, wondering if this was how it was going to be: him embarrassed to talk to a female and his best mate turning puce over using the word 'dying' . . . He hoped not, because it took the fun out of the evening. It took the fun out of *everything*. He looked over at Alex and Ellie, who both stared into space with miserable faces, and wondered why, about to spend money on drinks he didn't really want and couldn't really afford, he had bothered coming at all.

'You all right?' He watched Eric scanning his face, looking for clues that his mouth might deny.

'I think I might—' He gestured his thumb towards the exit and had been about to say 'call it a night' when Big Brian boomed into his microphone, interrupting him.

'Ladies and gentlemen! We have a tie! This means we go to a tie break! And it's between the Vixens and the Four Amigos!'

'That's us!' Eric darted to the table and Nick followed, laughing at the team name. They had always been the three amigos and he liked the way Eric had incorporated Ellie, doing his bit to keep the peace, no doubt. Jen, Beverly and their two friends looked daggers across the room at them.

Perfect.

'And for those of you who don't know, this is how it works.' Brian paused. 'I read out the questions one at a time to each team in turn and we keep going until one team gets a question wrong and it's the other team that wins. Here we go, Vixens.'

Nick noted the thin, set line of determination on his sister's mouth, reminding him of her tenacity during the great Monopoly weekend of 1994.

'Vixens: who was President Trump's running mate in the 2016 US Presidential Election?'

Jen rose in her chair and shouted without conferring, 'Mike Pence!' Her conviction was such that he doubted even Big Brian would have had the courage to tell her she was wrong. He saw Beverly pull a face and laugh with her teammates. Jen was in a league of her own.

Big Brian nodded. 'Correct!' Jen did a fist pump. 'Next question, for the Four Amigos: what chemical element is diamond made of?'

'Carbon!' Alex shouted, and Eric thumped the tabletop.

'Correct!' Things were heating up, the atmosphere charged. 'Vixens, question two: what is the official language of Brazil?'

Jen stared at Beverly and the girls. 'I know it's not Brazilian.' She sucked air through her teeth and tapped her chin as if this might help her concentrate. 'Portuguese!' she suddenly shrieked.

'Correct!' Big Brian cracked a rare smile. Nick could feel the tension in the air, and it was exciting. He wanted to beat Jen just for the fun of it and he wanted a slice of that seventy-two quid!

'Four Amigos, question two: the inhabitants of Albania, Lebanon and Malta can all paddle in the same sea, but which sea is it?'

Nick pictured the map and knew the answer. 'The Middleterrainean!' The moment it left his mouth he knew he'd messed up.

'He meant Mediterranean!' Eric yelled, standing and trying to clarify.

'Obviously I did,' Nick offered, feeling his face colour, embarrassed and aware of Jen's look of glee in his peripheral vision.

'I am sorry,' Big Brian said slowly, his smug smile suggesting he was anything but. 'As the rules state, I can only accept the team's first answer and the correct answer is the Mediterranean. Which means tonight's victors and the winners of the pot and the twenty-pound voucher for the Orient Rendezvous is' – he paused, irritatingly building up his part – 'the Vixens!'

'Yes! Yes!' Jen leapt from her chair and ran around the room like she'd won the bloody Super Bowl and not a free noodle. Nick wasn't sure what was worse, his sister's gloating or the look of disappointment on the faces of the other amigos.

'Middleterrainean?' Ellie asked with her arms folded across her chest, looking at him like he was an idiot, and for a second he knew what it felt like to be Alex. 'What were you thinking?'

'He wasn't.' Alex sided with his wife.

'Middleterrainean?' Beverly stood at the end of the table, shaking her head, as she put her arms into her coat.

Nick tried again to explain. 'It came out wrong.'

She laughed. 'You lot coming for chips?'

'Is Jen going?'

'Yes, Eric.' She held his eye line.

Nick liked the soft tut and crinkle-eyed smile of sympathy she gave his mate.

The two teams made their way along the pavements, where fog loitered and the cast-iron street lamps, the same ones they had swung around as kids, lit the way.

'You did good, Nick.' Jen punched his arm. 'I'm proud of you.'

'Thanks, Sis.' He rubbed the spot where her knuckles had landed.

The frontage of the Orient Rendezvous was lit up like a Christmas tree with red paper lanterns adorned with gold tassels hanging in the window.

'Right' – Jen smacked the voucher on to the countertop – 'can we have eight packets of chips, please, all with salt and vinegar.'

'No vinegar for me,' Ellie called from the back.

'And no salt for me.' Nick only said it to irritate his sister, who sighed. Beverly again laughed loudly and Nick had to admit he liked the way it felt, being able to make someone laugh in this way. He noticed Eric staring at him with a smile on his face.

'What?' Nick asked, a little more aggressively than he had intended.

'Nothing, mate. Nothing.' Eric squeezed next to Jen at the counter. 'I thought you were brilliant tonight. You're so smart.'

Jen smiled broadly at him and Nick was pleased that she didn't shoot him down.

'Here you go, Human Dustbin.' Jen handed him the first bag of chips.

'Cheers, I'm bloody starving!'

1992

His mum pulled the bed-in-a-bag from the bottom of the airing cupboard and dragged it across the hallway to Nick's bedroom floor.

'So how long is Eric staying?' he asked with excitement.

'A couple of days. And it'll be a couple of days every week.' She unfurled the base and duvet and smoothed the creases from the duvet top. 'His dad is on a late shift some nights and it wouldn't do to have Eric home alone so late and so he's coming here. Like a sleepover.' She kissed her fingertips and touched them to his cheek.

'Where's his mum?' He knew she wasn't home but beyond that had very little to go on.

'She's gone away for a bit.' Her tone was clipped.

'With Dave the Milk?'

'Goodness, Master Bairstow, have you been listening at keyholes?' She coughed and he noticed her cheeks had gone a little bit pink.

'Is it because of her secret job?'

'What secret job, darling?' She stopped fluffing the pillows and gave him her full attention.

'Eric told us she had a secret job and she was working with Dave the Milk when his dad was at billiards.'

His mum sat back on her haunches and looked out the window, as if considering this.

'You know, Nicky, sometimes grown-ups tell lies. And I think that was a lie. I don't think she had a secret job. But you don't need to say that to Eric; he has enough on his plate right now.'

'Do you think she would tell Eric a lie even though she's his mum?' He was aghast at the possibility. Nick knew his sister lied to him all the time: *I have rigged it so that if you look at my diary it will explode with green dye that never ever, ever washes off and you will spend the rest of your life looking like The Grinch!*

His mates too: *I saw it with my own eyes, a robber! And Batman just came swooping down and kicked him in the face! Kapow! Bam!*

Even his teacher: *We are going to have fun! Maths can be fun!*

And the worst culprit of all was Dr Hughes: *This isn't going to hurt a bit.*

But the idea of his mum or dad, the people he trusted most in the whole wide world, telling him a proper lie – the thought left him feeling a little winded.

'Yes.' His mum nodded. 'Sometimes even the people who love you the most might tell you a lie, and it might be for a million different reasons and those reasons are not always easy to understand.'

'So . . .' Nicky considered this. 'If she wasn't doing a job, why did she lock herself in the front room with the milkman when Eric's dad was at billiards?'

'Maybe they were watching telly?' she suggested lightly, and finished preparing Eric's bed. There was something in the way she spoke and avoided his eye that raised his suspicion.

'Is that a lie, Mum?'

'Yes, darling.' She smiled at him as she stepped over the bed and planted a kiss on his forehead. 'Yes, it is.'

The front doorbell rang.

Nick leapt over the bed-in-a-bag, raced down the stairs and opened the door to Eric, who stood with a large bag stuffed full with clothes and goodness knows what behind him. Alex stood a little back on the pavement with his hands in his pockets, his posture awkward.

'Come on in, Eric!' His mum stood back so he could pass and ruffled his hair as he did so. 'And what are you up to, Alex?' she asked, with her arms folded across her chest.

'Nowt. Just walked Eric here and now I'll head back home.' He pointed down the street.

'Or' – Nick's mum said slowly – 'I could give your mum a call and see if you can stay too? As long as you don't mind going top-to-toe with Nicky?'

'I don't mind!' Alex ran up the path and the three boys pogoed up and down in narrow hallway. Nick's mum winked at him and reached for the telephone on the wall.

Nick felt a burst of love for this woman, his mum, who he knew would never leave the house to go anywhere with Dave the Milk; she had too much to do here.

The three boys dived beneath the covers with chocolate biscuits in their sticky mitts intended as a midnight snack, but all involved knew these biscuits would be unlikely to survive for five minutes, especially with Eric, the Human Dustbin, around.

Eric farted. Alex threw his shoe at Eric's head and then he farted. The boys collapsed into heaps of side-splitting laughter on the duvets. Farting was one of their funniest things.

'It wasn't me!' Eric protested, as Nick lobbed his pillow at his friend on the floor and then he farted too.

The bedroom door opened and there stood Jen.

'What is all that racket . . .' she yelled before standing still, her nose twitching. 'Oh! You disgusting pigs! This room stinks! Mu-um!'

she called over her shoulder. 'They are farting! It's disgusting! The smell will come through my bedroom wall, I know it!' she yelled.

Nick looked from Alex to Eric, as each tried to contain the laughter that bubbled beneath the surface. Apparently their laughter wasn't the only thing bubbling beneath the surface, as Eric let rip an almighty fart.

'I hate you all!' Jen screeched, and slammed the door.

The three boys couldn't stand for the hysterics that robbed them of all strength.

'Eric!' Alex yelled. 'She's right, you're disgusting!'

In response to which Eric stood on his bed, clenched his fists, pulled his elbows into his waist and farted again.

FIVE

Despite the cool chill of the winter day, Nick opened the window to let the breeze in. Then he dusted the surfaces of the lounge, removing the ornaments and replacing them one by one before running the vacuum cleaner over the carpet. Next he hesitantly lifted the cushions, patting and thumping one or two before placing them randomly along the back of the sofa and repositioning them again. And again, before admitting defeat. The dog stared at him from the rug in front of the electric fire. 'Don't look at me like that. I know they look rubbish. I can't do the cushions! Okay? I admit it. Bloody things.'

Treacle laid her head on her paws and snorted her indifference.

'All this fuss for Olly, eh? It's not like he hasn't walked into this room a million times before.'

The words were easy, but Nick knew this was not like any other visit; it was to be his son's first back to a house where his mum no longer lived, and their first Christmas without her. Oliver was due back tomorrow, four days before Christmas Eve, and whilst Nick couldn't wait to see him, he felt an unfamiliar and unwelcome nervousness about his smart boy coming back from university. He imagined the life of learning to be a refined one where humour might be sophisticated; dining more elegant and conversation intelligent – or maybe this was just how it was in the movies. But it was certainly how he as a teenager pictured university life when he considered his future application.

It wasn't only the potential changes in Oliver that concerned him, but also the fact that his son was coming home to a house that felt different, as if its beating heart had fled. He stared at the boxed Christmas tree that sat on the floor along with the box of baubles, which had seen better days. On the side in Kerry's neat handwriting the words 'Xmas Decs' had been written in a thick black marker. He had little inclination for the task, knowing that in a similar vein to his cushion arranging, his efforts would be embarrassing. The intention had been to get the place ready and festive before Oliver's arrival, but he had run out of time, and as his mum had pointed out, it might be nice to get Oliver to do it – not only as a distraction for him, but also to make him feel at home, a reminder that whilst things had changed, a lot would stay the same, and they needed to carry on.

Nick thought about last year: the house bursting at the seams with relatives, the loud laughter only one decibel away from hysteria, and that same laughter turning to tears at the slightest provocation, all present more than aware of the fact that this was to be the last Christmas they shared with their daughter/sister/niece/cousin/aunt. The whole charade had left both Nick and Kerry quite exhausted, and he had been glad when the last of the revellers had left, paper hats askew, as they trotted down the front path. He and Kerry had collapsed on to this very sofa and held each other quietly, savouring the peace while she lay wrapped in his arms. A precious moment that right now felt like a thousand years ago.

The doorbell rang, pulling him from the memory. His sister-in-law stood on the step with a scarf wrapped around her neck and a stack of presents in her arms.

'Look at you all loaded up, are you one of Santa's little helpers? Come in, Di.'

'Something like that. God, it's bloody freezing in here.' She visibly shivered.

'Is it?' He made out he hadn't noticed rather than admit to leaving the heating off to conserve money, having decided to only put it on when Oliver was home. The chill was nothing that a thick jersey, a vest, a decent pair of socks and a bit of running on the spot couldn't combat. Plus, he was at work more than he was at home, and with Treacle deposited at his mum's house on these days, there was no need to heat the empty rooms.

Di bent down and dumped the gifts in a pile on the floor in the hallway.

'These are just some bits for Olly from me and his cousins, being as we won't be seeing him this Christmas.' She let this trail with a tight-lipped sigh of disapproval.

Nick felt the familiar rise of irritation at her manner and not for the first time he drew breath and let his pulse settle, chanting the silent reminder: *She is Kerry's sister . . . She is grieving . . . It's Christmas . . . and she has bought Olly presents . . .*

'It's not that you won't be seeing him at all, Di, just not on Christmas Day, that's all. I asked him what he wanted to do and told him we'd been invited to my mum's, your mum's or that everyone could come here, if he'd prefer' – he gently gave the reminder – 'but he said he wanted it to be just the two of us. He's dreading it, I think, and so I want to do what makes him most comfortable. And that's what he wants.' He let his arms rise and fall as if it was a fait accompli. 'It's all about Olly right now.'

'Well' – Diane adjusted her scarf – 'there we go, then. Just ask him if he wouldn't mind popping in to see his Gran if he gets a mo.'

'Of course he will. And it's only one day out of the holidays – he's home for a couple of weeks. Don't worry, you'll be sick of the sight of him.' He tried for humour, feeling the instant flicker of self-consciousness as he laughed alone.

Di looked over his shoulder into the middle distance. 'This time last year Kerry and I were shopping and baking and getting excited . . .' She bit her bottom lip, which trembled. 'Truth is, I don't feel like celebrating either, but you have to keep going, don't you?'

'That's it, Di, you do.'

She turned towards the front door. 'And as I said, if you want any help cooking the turkey or the—'

He shook his head – *how many more times!* 'I know, and I'm grateful for the offer, but we can manage, Di. Thank you. And if we can't, I'll shout.'

Closing the door firmly, he walked to the kitchen and, in an act that was rare for him, took a can of lager from the fridge, pulled the ring top and took a long, satisfying glug. It felt good – after all, it was a Saturday, he had no shift at the factory to get to and the day was his own. And here he was drinking beer! The doorbell rang again.

Bloody hell, Di! What now?

He opened the door with a fixed smile, hoping the whole exchange would be over as quickly as possible.

'All right, Nick?' Beverly smiled up at him with her hands shoved into her jacket pockets and her hair stuck flat to her face with the residue of rain. It was a surprise to see her, but a pleasant one. He wished he weren't in his socks and that he had shaved that morning, not sure why these two things were important. He ran his fingers through his hair, pushing it from his face in lieu of a comb.

'Not bad, Bev. You?' He looked along the street, glad that there was no sign of his sister-in-law.

'Yep. What are you doing?' She rocked on the heels of her walking boots and looked at him as if this were the most natural question to ask.

'Erm, I was drinking, actually. Something I never do during the day, but today felt like a good time to start.' He pinched the top of his nose. 'And before that I was wondering how to arrange cushions, you know, standard Saturday.'

'I see. Well, I'd offer to help but I'm rubbish at cushion arranging and all that stuff. I call them sofa parasites, hate the bloody things.'

'I know exactly what you mean.'

'Shall I come in, then?' She nodded down the hallway.

'Oh.' He stood back, still considering the request. 'Sure.'

He closed the door and watched as Beverly made her way along the hall and into the kitchen, as though she had been here many times. Unsurprising, really, it was after all a standard three-bedroomed semi, the same as countless others in this and every other town in the country. She pulled off her coat and laid it on the countertop, rubbing her hands together and flexing her fingers. It felt odd and yet surprisingly natural to have her standing here in the kitchen. Beverly, he noted, was slender, neat and of small build. Her movements were fast and fluid. He had grown used to Kerry's lumbering manner as her illness robbed her of coordination and speed, her motor skills, both fine and gross, deteriorating with the pain in her limbs, the weakness in her muscles and the fog of the painkilling sedation. It had been distressing to watch. To see this woman now standing in Kerry's kitchen, her hands moving quickly and her movements precise, was a reminder of just how much his wife had gone downhill. His heart flexed for all she had endured.

'I'm bloody freezing.' She exaggerated the tremble to her chin, forcing a chattering of her teeth.

'I know – it's turned right cold. If I had the money I think I'd skip Christmas altogether and go and sit in the sunshine.'

'Yes.' She nodded. 'You could head off to the Middleterrainean.'

'Oh, very funny!' He chuckled. 'Am I never going to be allowed to forget that? I still don't think Ellie is talking to me.'

'Well, there you go. They say every cloud has a silver lining.'

He liked her manner. 'Would you . . . Would you like a cup of tea or a cold beer?'

She eyed his can. 'Cold beer, please.' She rubbed the tops of her arms and laughed, as if this choice was actually the very last thing she wanted.

He walked to the fridge, conscious of the dirty breakfast bowl and mug in the sink and the bag of rubbish tied to the door handle with empty dog food tins in it that were giving off a slightly unpleasant smell. He felt embarrassed and was also a little confused on two counts: firstly, why it should matter to him that his house was less than pristine and, secondly, why on earth Beverly was visiting?

It was as if she read his thoughts: 'I thought I'd come and say hi, see how you are. I know how shitty it can be to be on your own around Christmas. My dad passed away a couple of years ago and it was rough, especially the first.'

He knew her mum had left when she was still at school, moved up to Hawick after she had an affair. Word had it that her husband found out and left all her boxed belongings in Market Square. Nothing was a secret in a town this size. He nodded and handed her the can. She popped the lid and took a swig.

'To be honest, it's kind of crept up on me; work's been so busy I've been taking extra shifts,' he explained.

'I know.' She smiled. 'I do the payroll.'

'Course you do.' He swallowed, feeling foolish. 'And my family and Kerry's family have been popping in and out.' He noted the way he spoke about the two families as separate entities, realising that his wife had been the conduit that made them one. 'It seems I can't do right for doing wrong where they are all concerned.'

'How come?' She leant against the sink, the beer in her hand.

'Oh.' He sighed. 'Kerry's mum and sister want to see more of my boy, who is still finding his feet, and my mum doesn't think I can peel a spud without advice, and the truth is we just need to be left alone to get on with it.'

Beverly stared at him. 'Do you want me to go?' She angled her body towards the front door.

'No! No, I didn't mean that.' He didn't want her to go. It was a relief to have someone to talk to who wasn't making a demand of some kind or who treated him like a grieving widower. 'I just wish there was a rulebook on how to behave and the correct timing of everything. Christ, I remember my mum going off at me when I tried to leave the house the day after Kerry died; she said it wasn't the done thing to go outside. Who knew? I wouldn't have minded, but I wasn't going up the bookie's; I was off to buy a pint of milk for breakfast.' He shook his head. 'It's like there are a million rules that I don't know about and so I go around inadvertently breaking them.'

'Well, I don't know you that well, but you seem to be doing just fine, and if your son's happy then surely that's the main thing?'

'You'd think so, wouldn't you? But apparently there are rotas for getting rid of weeds on a grave, the correct size of bouquet to *leave* on the grave, and a minimum number of phone calls a grandson should be making to his gran.'

'Holy moly!' Beverly took a large gulp of beer. 'I can see why you're drinking on a Saturday afternoon.'

'Yep.' He took a sip.

'So when's your boy coming back?'

'Olly.'

'Yes, I knew that, Olly,' she repeated.

'Tomorrow at some point. I'm looking forward to having him home. The house has been quiet without him.'

'I know what that feels like.' She looked at the floor and he tried to imagine not having any family around and wondered if she ever saw or spoke to the mum who had done a runner.

'I'm looking forward to it, but also a bit nervous.' He found it easy to talk to Beverly, unafraid of being judged.

'Nervous how?'

117

He took his time in forming a response. 'It's the strangest thing; I never thought I'd feel anxious about him coming home, but I do. And I suppose . . .'

'You suppose what?'

'I wonder if he has left me behind, even a little bit. Or worse: I wonder if I might embarrass him in some way. I think I always had a fixed idea of what Uni might be like if I went, posh kids who knew stuff that I didn't.'

'You were going to go to Uni?' she asked with slight surprise.

'I thought so, yes.' He felt his cheeks colour. 'Or more specifically my dad thought so. I mean, I had the grades and I think I might have even sent off for a prospectus, can't really remember.' He made it sound casual, recalling the day it had arrived and how he spent the hours before bed reading about the halls of residence and the lecture theatres . . .

'Where for?' She drank again.

'Exeter.'

'Exeter? Could you have picked a place further than Burston?' She laughed.

'Not really, but anyway' – he coughed – 'life had other plans.'

'It usually does.' Beverly rattled the can, which she was emptying at pace. 'It'll be fine with Olly. You shouldn't worry.'

'I guess not. It's just that he's becoming an educated man and I'm a very ordinary one. He's broadening his horizons.' He spoke freely. 'Even the idea of it makes me feel sick. I suppose I don't want him to outgrow me.'

'But you're his dad. That can't happen.'

'I know, I know . . . And he's a great kid, he really is . . . and it's only been one term, but ever since I left him last I wonder how he might have changed? How I might have changed?' He ran his palm over his face, embarrassed. 'I'm not explaining it very well. I suppose I'm just conscious that our lives are so very different from the way they were this time last year and it's . . .'

'Scary.' She filled in the blank.

'Yep. It is.'

'I suppose that's the good thing about not knowing the rules – you can make up your own. Do things your way and at your pace. This is your journey, no one else's.'

'I guess so.' He considered this and felt a little less apprehensive about seeing his boy; in fact, he felt a bit less apprehensive about everything. Her words, offered plainly and without agenda, had a calming effect on him, but of course that might have been the beer.

'Anyway' – she swallowed – 'reason I came by is to say that I'm having a bit of a do on New Year's Eve at my place, not a fancy party exactly, but more a chance to use up any leftovers and the last dregs of wine in the bottles, and so if you're at a loose end, come along. You know where I live?'

'Yes. I do.' Nick pictured her terraced two up, two down in Appledore, a side street off Market Square. Beverly's house, like the others on that road, was an old farm worker's cottage that fronted the cobbled street. He considered her invitation and felt a mixture of relief and disappointment that there was a purpose to her visit, and that she hadn't just popped in.

'I'll see what Olly is up to, but that might be good.'

'Everyone congregates there. It's become a bit of a tradition. People I don't even know pitch up at midnight, but I don't mind, I kind of like the idea of my little house being a beacon, a place where folk gather to see in the New Year. It's good. Bring beer, if there's any left!' She took a large swig and, finishing the can, placed it on the sideboard before reaching for her coat. 'Try to come; it'll be good. There's a few from work coming, and Eric and Jen, and I promise not a Monopoly board in sight.'

'Thanks, Bev.'

'What for?' She paused in the hallway and looked back at him.

'I dunno, just . . .' He searched for the words. 'Thanks for thinking about me.'

'That's all right, Nick. I think about you a lot,' she added almost matter-of-factly before letting herself out of the front door and closing it behind her.

He sat on the bottom stair and felt a flush of warmth and the rush of something that could have been happiness – but he wasn't sure; it had been a long time since he had felt that – and again, it might have been the beer.

I was at school with Beverly. She's a nice girl . . . He heard Kerry's voice and closed his eyes tightly.

Nick woke early, washed and showered and was in the bathroom when he heard a key in the door. For a muddle-headed split second he thought it might be Kerry and his heart jumped before Oliver shouted out, 'Hell-o-o?'

He dried his hands on his jeans and raced down the stairs. 'Hello, son!' He put out his hand and widened his other arm, leaving it up to his son which he might prefer, a hug or a handshake. Oliver stepped into his arms and held him fast. Nick closed his eyes briefly in thanks. There was no time to feel nervous or to second-guess how his boy might be feeling. He was home, safe and sound, and that was all that mattered. Oliver pulled away and Nick studied him; he looked wonderful, even with his unshaven top lip, a poor, wispy attempt at a moustache that Nick would rib him about later, and with the dark bruises under his eyes of someone who was not getting enough sleep.

'You look tired.'

'I'm knackered. I feel like we kind of went from freshers' events into Christmas events. I don't think I've been to bed before three a.m. for weeks.'

'Well, you're back in boring old Burston and there'll be plenty of nap time, as there's not much else going on.'

'I think some of my school mates are home so I said we'd go to the pub later.'

'Jesus, Olly! Tonight? You've only just arrived. You've still got your coat on and already you're planning to go out!' he shouted, half in jest.

'Well, okay, not tonight.' Oliver rolled his eyes. 'But tomorrow, maybe.'

Treacle came trotting out to the hallway and Oliver dropped to his knees, scooping up their hound to hold her close to his chest and run his face over her warm fur. 'I've missed you, girl,' he said with obvious affection.

'Cup of tea?'

'Please, Dad. It's nice to be home.'

These simple words, spoken with the hint of a sigh, removed all trace of worry. Nick saw Oliver scan the walls, the staircase, furniture and pictures, as if reacquainting himself with the fabric of the place. He watched as Oliver walked slowly into the kitchen. Nick remembered the words he spoke during his 'code red' visit, when he had sat on the bed in his student room.

I tell myself she's at home . . . I picture her in the kitchen . . . I think she's there and that I'll see her soon and it helps . . .

'So what's your news?' he fished, as he filled the kettle. 'How's Tasha?'

'Good, yeah, good. She went home yesterday.'

'And home for her is?'

'St Albans. Hertfordshire. She didn't want to go back – she doesn't get on that well with her mum and stepdad – so I told her she could come and stay here if it got too much.'

'Of course she can.' Nick felt chuffed that Oliver was comfortable inviting his friends back here. He thought how much Kerry would have loved to make a fuss of his mates, traipsing up and down the stairs with endless bacon sandwiches and cups of tea.

'Bacon sandwich?'

'Please, Dad, if you're making. Can I put my laundry on?'

'Course.' He smiled as he reached into the fridge for the bacon, noting that only a term ago Oliver would either have left his dirty clothes on the floor of his bedroom or heaped them into the laundry basket, waiting for them to magically appear clean, dried and folded at the bottom of his bed. He was growing up. Nick placed the rashers under the grill and poured hot water on to the tea bags before adding a splash of milk.

'This is the hardest room for me to be in.' Oliver took the mug from his dad.

'I thought it might be. I remember you saying as much before.'

Oliver nodded. 'It was her space, wasn't it?' He swallowed. 'She loved cooking for us and she liked to potter out here with the radio on.'

Nick looked towards the sink and pictured her bopping in her rubber gloves to the sounds of Absolute 90s on the radio.

'She did.'

'And she loved Christmas. She'd have had this place groaning under the weight of decorations by now.'

'Ah, well, I did get the boxes down from the loft, but Nanny Mags thought you might like to do it, or help me do it.'

'Did she now? What am I, six?' Oliver scoffed, sipping his tea.

'Well, in that case, I will set to this afternoon and transform the place into something more grotto-like.' He reached for the grill pan and rested it on the stovetop, turning the bacon with a fork and putting it back under the gas-flamed grill for its final crisping. 'And talking of nans, I've had your Auntie Di chewing my ear off about seeing you.'

'She does go on.'

'She does, son, but only because she cares.'

'I guess so.' Oliver pulled dirty clothes from his bag and sorted them on the floor into whites and mixed colours.

'They've all missed you and so I'm afraid you're going to have to do the rounds.'

'I'm looking forward to seeing everyone, actually. It's weird, Dad. I was never that fussed about spending time with them all when I was at home, but now I'm away, I think about them all a lot more. I guess because Mum's not here any more it kind of makes Gran and Auntie Di – in fact, everyone – more important somehow.'

'I guess it does.'

Nick breathed a sigh of relief. This would make everything easier.

'Bacon!' Oliver shouted and pointed at the grill, where flames leapt. Nick grabbed the pan with the bacon alight and shoved it into the sink, where it hissed on contact with the suds-filled water. He shook his head at his dad and sighed. 'I think I'll go straight to Nan's; at least she can cook me a decent breakfast.'

'Think I might come with you.' Nick looked at the bacon sinking under the foam of washing-up liquid and rubbed his eyes; he was going to have to sharpen his skills for the Christmas dinner, if this was any example.

The two sauntered along the street with Treacle on her lead and Nick realised now with Oliver by his side how in recent months loneliness had begun to creep into his bones. It was one thing walking around town knowing his wife and son were at home, or out and about, but quite another to picture the quiet, empty rooms that would greet him upon his return. He stared at his boy and felt the joyful punch of reunion in his gut.

'What's that on your top lip?' He ran his finger over his own.

'Do you like it?' Oliver beamed.

'Like what? I thought a caterpillar had landed there.'

'I knew you'd laugh at it.' Oliver kicked the pavement. 'I said as much to my mates.'

'Olly, however much I laugh is nothing compared to how much Eric will tease you.'

'I know that too. I grew it for Movember – raising money for men's charities – cancer, mental health, stuff like that.'

He felt proud of his son's efforts. 'Good for you.' He squeezed his shoulder. 'I'll sponsor you, if it's not too late.'

'Thanks. Anyway, Tasha kind of liked it so . . .' He let this hang.

Nick laughed. 'I remember your mum trying to get me to grow my hair into a centre parting with two curtains either side of my face. Like one of the Backstreet Boys.'

'One of the what?' Oliver looked at him with a blank expression.

'Never mind, but it was a haircut fashionable at the time.'

'Did you do it?'

'Did I 'eck as like! I told her it was against factory regulations on the shop floor and got a buzz cut all over – she never made a hair suggestion to me again.'

'That was mean!' Oliver laughed.

'Well, the laugh was on me after all – it exposed the beginning of my bald spot, been a bit thin ever since.'

'See, you could have grown it long and had a comb-over.'

'I could that. Still might.' Nick touched his fingers to the thin hair of his pate, which hadn't spread, leaving him with a full-looking head of hair from any angle other than looking down at him from above. He glanced up towards the heavens and smiled.

Oliver knocked on his nan's front door.

'Aaaaagh!' Nick heard her scream as she spied them through the glass pane at the top of the door. 'It's Olly! Olly's home!' His mum opened the door and grabbed her grandson. With a dishcloth in her hand, she pulled him to her whilst standing on the doorstep, putting them at equal height. 'You're home!' She reached for the handkerchief secreted up her sleeve and blew her nose.

'I am.' Oliver smiled and let her muss his hair and kiss his face. 'Any chance of breakfast, Nan?'

'Oh, darlin', every chance! Come in, come in! Oh, Olly, how we've missed you!' She squeezed Nick's arm as he walked past. 'He's grown!'

'Yep.' He winked at his son, who rolled his eyes. Nick's mum had said this every time she had laid eyes on Oliver since he was a baby.

'I didn't know if you would come here straight away, but I got a few bits in anyway. Now, sit down, love, and let me get you breakfast. Bacon? Sausage? Egg? Fried bread? Beans?'

'Yes, please.' Oliver sat at the table.

Nick stood by the kitchen sink and looked at the boy, remembering his own dad leaning in this exact same spot in his work boots and shorts during that hot, hot summer.

Finish your tea, lad. I've got something for you . . .

1992

Eric stayed for two nights and Alex for one and it was agreed that for the next few weeks this would be the arrangement. His friend was an easy houseguest, apart from the farting, which wound up his sister and therefore became a positive thing. He ate anything and everything Nick's mum put on the table in front of him and even showed enthusiasm for his dad's boring stories, which Nick had heard about a million times before. His dad seemed to like telling them, happy for a new audience. The weather was even warmer and the grass turned brown. They lived with all the windows in the house open, trying to encourage a breeze to take the edge off the uncomfortable closeness, and his mum started preparing salad for every meal, as if even the thought of hot food was too much when the surface of the tarmac shimmered under the heat. After tea they were given orange-juice ice pops that his mum froze in special plastic pods that had sat at the back of the cupboard for as long as he could remember. The hot weather, free distribution of ice pops and his friend staying on a semi-regular basis made the place feel like a holiday resort and not their very average house where, during term time, his life was one of predictable monotony.

His mum and dad even let them inflate and fill the paddling pool in the back garden, and when they weren't in the shed, tinkering on parts with the multi-tool, the three boys languished in the water, which always looked a murky shade of grey, largely because it didn't occur to them to wipe or clean their dirty feet before scampering in and out of the shin-high water. No matter that space was at a premium, they developed an impressive range of games inside the five-foot circular pool. Their favourite was throwing a ball in the air and trying to catch it; the rule was that at least some of their body had to be submerged and they had to remain inside the circle; this game they called 'Petunia'. They didn't know how the word had been settled upon, but the shouting of it and the subsequent melee was enough to once again reduce them to hysterics. Nick often caught his mum watching them out of the kitchen window with a smile on her face, happy that he was happy, and this made him even happier. He couldn't imagine what it would be like to have Eric's mum, who was no longer at home, or to have a dad like Eric's, who had fist fights with the milkman.

By week three of the project Half Bike was in fairly good shape. They settled on a garish shade of green paint, not so much out of choice, but that was the paint Alex's grandad donated to the cause, Alex having apparently filled him in on the great restoration and rebuild during their caravan break in Blackpool. Eric and Nick had stared at the half-full tin of paint, which looked almost neon in certain lights.

'Did someone put Kermit in a blender?' Nick turned his nose up at the offending goo.

'I'm more worried about the fact that there's only half a tin; what did he use the other half on?' Eric raised a good point.

'Something to do with parking spaces at the community centre, I think,' Alex explained a little sheepishly, not best pleased to have his contribution so mocked. Not that he was in any position to grumble, with Nick having given the frame and Eric the handlebars from Dave the Milk; half a tin of paint was quite measly in comparison. But still, a deal was a deal, and Alex still owned a half of a half of Half Bike.

It had been an exhausting day. When they hadn't been painting, concentrating on catching the lime-green runs with the gummed-up bristles of the paintbrush as they each daubed paint where they could reach, the boys had decided to sprint up to the Rec and then over to the Old Dairy Shed, timing themselves to see how quickly they could complete the task. The combination of overzealous competition, the heat of the afternoon sun and inappropriate footwear meant they arrived back at Nick's house panting like dogs and rather floppy. The grey-water pool was the most inviting option and there they flopped, a tangle of arms and legs, until Nick's mum called them in for salad.

Nick looked down at Eric, who had once again settled into his temporary bed on the floor. Gone was the frisson of excitement that had crackled in the air when he first came to stay; things were now a lot calmer. He wondered if this was what it might feel like if he had a brother, instead of his horrible sister. It felt nice. They had agreed that overnight the multi-tool would rest in a gap on the floor between the two beds and in the event of an intruder, whoever managed to grab it first would perform the all-important Batman-style kick whilst aiming the two little prongs at the throat of the assailant. They had spent hours practising for such an occurrence, taking it in turns to be both the Batman-style defender and the baddy. His mum had even been called upon to watch as they demonstrated their skills.

'It's like Kung Fu,' Nick explained, as he took up position on the bed and Eric stood poised with a badass expression in the doorway.

'Righto.' His mum had watched and nodded approvingly as they took it in turns to kick the other in the chest and hold the multi-tool to each other's throats.

She clapped. 'Very nice. Very well done, lads!' It wasn't quite the reaction Nick had hoped for, but at least he had had a chance to show off his moves.

Nick twisted on to his side and spoke into the dimming mauve light of the summer night: 'Do you miss your mum?'

Eric was slow in responding. 'A bit.'

'Do you know where she is?'

Again, Eric took his time in answering. 'I'm not supposed to, but I do. I heard my dad on the phone to my Auntie Nesta and he called my mum a bitch and said she'd gone away with Dave the Milk.'

'Where did they go?'

'Derby.'

'Where's Derby?' Nick knew the names of most of the towns and villages local to them, but he had never heard of Derby.

'I don't know, but it's a long way away. You can't get a bus – I asked the bus driver when I saw him in the Co-Op.'

'I expect she'll come home soon.' Nick wondered if, as he didn't believe this statement, he was also a liar, but it didn't feel like lying; it felt like being nice.

'Maybe.' Eric put his skinny arms beneath his head to form a cradle and took a deep breath. 'I like staying here. Your mum's really kind and she never shouts at you and she cooks your tea every night. My mum isn't like that, not really. She's busy and she likes to watch the telly and . . .'

Nick heard him swallow.

'Our house is cold. It's even cold now, when everywhere else is melting.'

Nick didn't know what to say, so he said nothing.

'When I grow up I want to go and live in a hot country so it's like this all the time, warm and sunny, and I can sleep with the windows open and have a paddling pool in the garden, just like yours. And you can come and visit me if you like.'

'I might.' Nick thought about it. 'If I can have a holiday from my office job.'

'The one where you drive a big car and someone brings you Fanta at the touch of a button.'

'That's the one.' Nick smiled; he liked the thought of this very much.

'If I had a brother, Nick, I'd like him to be just like you.'

'If I had a brother, Eric, I'd like him to be just like you.'

'Shall we get up early and play Petunia before Alex arrives? We'd have more room in the pool with just the two of us.'

'Sure.' Nick thought this sounded like a plan.

'Night, night, Nick.'

'Night, night, Eric.'

SIX

It was Christmas Eve.

The tree was sparsely decked and sat a little forlornly in the corner of the room. On his sister's advice, Nick had cooked the turkey and left it to cool on the countertop. The plan was that he could then slice and heat it the next day and serve it with all the trimmings and thick gravy, cooked fresh in their rather small oven. He didn't know how Kerry used to manage. Oliver was at the pub with a couple of mates from school and, as Nick sat down on the sofa, his text alert beeped.

Happy Christmas Nick

It was from Beverly. He broke into a smile.

Happy Christmas Bev, he replied. He felt his eyes start to close and gave in to the warm feeling of well-being that flooded him . . .

Kerry was kneeling under the Christmas tree. She was wearing her jeans and Christmas jumper, the one made of sparkly wool that meant it shone when she stood by the lights. Her face was pretty, without the distorting bloat of illness, and her cheeks rosy.

The radio was playing Slade's 'Merry Christmas Everybody', and she hummed along as she rummaged in the decorations box, pulling out a rather battered cardboard star sploshed with red paint and threaded with a loop of discoloured string.

'He made this at nursery, do you remember?' She held it towards him and chuckled that soft laugh as she tossed her shiny, chestnut-coloured hair over her shoulder.

Such beautiful hair . . .

'I do,' he remembered. 'He was so chuffed with it, and when he'd gone to bed we laughed at how rubbish it was, knowing he'd inherited our lack of arts-and-crafts skills, and yet every year we put it on top of the tree.'

'It's a tradition now.' She held it up towards the light and admired it.

'I'm afraid the tree looks a bit crap.' He sighed. 'I did my best.'

She pulled a face. 'You forgot the fairy lights, that's why! A rookie mistake.' She smiled at him. 'You know, Nick, there isn't a place dark enough or thoughts depressing enough that can't be transformed by the sticking up of a few fairy lights. That's what I think, anyway.'

'You're right, I forgot. I just wanted it to look nice for Olly.'

'Olly is doing just fine. He is so amazing.'

'He is,' he agreed. 'A credit to you.'

'A credit to *us*,' she corrected. 'And don't worry, you will have a memorable Christmas.'

'I've cooked the bird already.'

'So I saw. Mr Organised.'

'Hardly. I still feel like I'm in a crazy panic, trying to remember what I need to do, how to put one foot in front of the other . . . and if I'm being honest, worried about who I might be offending . . . and grinding out the hours at work.'

'It'll get easier, my love. You'll see.' She turned to face him and twisted the shiny gold wedding band on the ring finger of her left hand. 'This is going to be your year. I'm sure of it.'

'Oh, Kerry, I miss you. Especially because it's Christmas.' He damned the catch to his voice, wanting in this precious moment not to bring sadness into it.

'I know, but you don't have to, you know.'

'Don't have to what?' He was a little confused.

Kerry stood and walked slowly towards him. 'You don't have to miss me, not as much as you do. You mustn't keep it all so tightly packed down. You need to loosen the lid a bit and let it float away.'

Reaching out, she took his hands into hers and pulled him upright, and she was real! The touch of her fingers, warm and solid against his palm, was the most wonderful thing and she looked . . . she looked beautiful, happy and healthy. She slipped against him and the song on the radio changed to the soft, golden tone of Nat King Cole.

'That's more like it,' she whispered with her head on his chest.

He inhaled the scent of her, her favourite perfume still sitting in a bottle in her bedside cabinet, the scent quite earthy. He loved it. Gone was the medicinal, slightly chemical-scented sweat that had accompanied her during and following her chemotherapy. This was the old Kerry, before that bloody illness claimed her as its own. They swayed in the dance they had been practising since the days of the school disco. He closed his eyes and savoured the feel of her in his arms.

'I mean it, Nick. You need to stop missing me so much and start living. Things weren't always perfect between us, were they?'

'No.' He sighed. 'They weren't.'

'So don't glorify it and don't forget – we didn't both die. Only me. I know you love me. I know you always will, but you're young and you need to go on and find happiness; you have your whole life ahead of you. And it'll all be wonderful . . .'

'I love you.' He kissed her face.

'I love you too. Always. My Nick . . . Nick . . .'

'Nick . . . Dad! Nick!' This voice was different, louder, harsher and male. He quickly sat up straight and looked towards the tree, which itself was a little depressing compared to the one he had imagined. There was no radio playing. And Kerry was gone. With the arrow of sorrow piercing his chest and the strong desire to get back to her arms, he rubbed his eyes and stared at his son, who stood in the doorway. He felt a wave of sadness to have been pulled so sharply from his beautiful dream.

'I was shouting at you for ages.' Oliver sighed. 'I just got back from the pub – Treacle got the turkey! She's eaten the whole thing and has shit all over the kitchen floor!'

Nick didn't know why he laughed, but suspected it was that or cry. 'Happy Christmas, son.'

Oliver laughed too. 'Happy Christmas, Dad.'

'I tell you what.' He stood and let his pulse settle. 'I'll go clear up the kitchen and you dig out the tin of fairy lights from the cupboard under the stairs.'

'Fairy lights?'

'Yes, Oliver, they are a thing, you know all the best rooms have them,' he mocked, thinking about the strings that adorned his student room. 'Besides, as your mum used to say, there isn't a place dark enough or thoughts depressing enough that can't be transformed by the sticking up of a few fairy lights.'

Kerry was right. The fairy lights gave the room a pleasant festive glow that warmed their spirits as Nick and Oliver sat back on the sofa. The turkey remnants had been disposed of. Treacle and the floor were cleaned up and the clock ticked softly towards midnight.

'Bedtime?' Nick asked, turning his head to see that Oliver was already dozing, his head resting on one of the cushions. *Sofa parasites . . .* Nick liked that. He smiled and pictured the pretty blonde woman who had stood in his kitchen, necked beer and invited him to a party.

◆　◆　◆

It was the Christmas Day they had wanted, leisurely, fairly quiet and one where they ate sausages with all the trimmings of a traditional lunch whilst the replete Treacle lay sprawled in her basket, sleeping off her turkey hangover with a look of joy and a fat tum. They watched *Return of the Jedi* on the TV and polished off a tub of Quality Street. Their phones beeped with loving messages from friends and family, well received, but still a little irritating, until they muted the speakers and tossed their phones on to the free seat of the sofa. Nick didn't feel too guilty, knowing they would see everyone tomorrow on Boxing Day with a lunch at his mum's and then tea with Kerry's family. But today was *their* day and it went better than they could have expected.

Oliver now slept with his hands clasped across his stomach, and his feet, as tradition dictated, clad in new socks, resting on the coffee table. Nick smiled at his boy. 'We did it, son – we survived,' he whispered.

'More than can be said for the poor turkey,' Oliver mumbled with one eye open, and they both laughed.

'I think I preferred you asleep!' Nick lobbed a cushion at him.

'I need to wake up. I promised to call Tasha. Find out whether she liked her present. She said she'd wait until today to open it.'

'What did you get her?'

'A sandwich toaster.'

'A sandwich toaster? Right.' He couldn't decide whether this was a great present or a terrible one. 'Did she ask for one?'

'No, but she's allergic to cheese – all dairy, in fact – and the girls on our floor share a sandwich toaster but leave cheese residue, so she can't use it. So it's her very own one to keep in her room, cheese free.'

'Nice. And there's me thinking perfume and chocolates were still in fashion.'

'Not on my student budget!'

'Don't start with that. You have a princely sum compared to me when I was your age. In fact, thinking about it, the first Christmas present I got your mum was a baby-changing mat. How's that for romantic?'

'Not very, but practical.' Oliver looked at the lit tree and Nick wondered if, like him, he pictured his mum in front of it. The cardboard star Oliver had made at nursery suddenly tumbled from the top of the tree and landed on the rug. Oliver jumped up to retrieve it and placed it back on the top branch.

'Have you had a nice Christmas Day, Olly?'

'It's been memorable, Dad, hasn't it?'

Nick nodded.

Memorable . . .

Ironing was never his forte, but Nick did his best with the denim shirt his sister had bought him for Christmas.

'So you're actually going to a party?' Oliver laughed and shook his head as he devoured the fried-egg sandwich laced with ketchup that was apparently going to provide a beer cushion for the evening ahead.

'Yes, what's so funny about that?' Nick held the iron still and stared at his son.

'I don't know.' Oliver shrugged. 'I suppose it's just the idea of old people having a party. I mean, what's the point?'

Nick stared at him, a little taken aback as well as lost for words. 'Old people?' He snorted. 'I'm thirty-five! I'm in my prime!'

'Hardly.' Oliver wiped ketchup from his mouth with his fingertips.

Nick sighed in mock-offence. 'I used to think thirty-five was old, but then I got here quicker than I could ever have imagined and I find it's not old, not at all.'

'Mum got short-changed, didn't she?'

'She did.' He liked that they could talk about Kerry with such ease, and yet whilst he would never admit it, tonight, getting dressed to go to a party, something he had not done in more years than he could remember, he didn't want to talk about her, didn't want the reminder of the sadness that bookended his every waking thought.

'So what will you do at your party?'

'Oh, I don't know, Oliver, probably have a game of whist and then a nice cup of milky tea, and if we are lucky someone might have brought along a gramophone and we can listen to some Big Band sounds. But rest assured, after a cup of hot cocoa and with my slippers lined up on the floor, I'll be in bed by ten o'clock. I do need the rest. At my age.'

'Ha ha, but you know what I mean – do you dance? Drink?'

'I don't know, Olly!' He put the iron down and pulled the plug. 'The truth is I'm absolutely bricking it. I can't remember the last time I went to a party, but I'm pretty sure I didn't enjoy it. But I also know your mum is right; I'm young and I have a whole life ahead of me. No matter that this isn't a life I would choose, one without her.'

Oliver stared at him. 'What do you mean, Mum is right?'

'I mean . . .' He sought out words that didn't make him sound like he was losing his marbles. 'I dream a lot about your mum, and I talk to her and she gave me advice and it made me feel better.'

There was a beat or two of silence.

'I can't imagine . . .'

'What?' Nick buttoned up his shirt, concerned by Oliver's expression of confusion, his happy demeanour faded.

'Nothing.'

'No, go on, Olly. Talk to me.'

'I can't imagine you with someone else. I can't imagine someone else being in this kitchen. Mum's kitchen.'

Nick shook his head and caught his breath. 'You don't have to worry about that. You don't. I can't imagine it either.'

Oliver's shoulders seemed to relax a little and both were quiet again for a second or two as the uncomfortable topic fizzed around them.

'So who you going to the pub with?'

'Ned and Jason, and I think some of the girls from my year and a couple of Jason's mates from Uni who have come down. It'll be good.'

'It will.' Nick reached into his back pocket and took out his wallet. He pulled a ten-pound note out and handed it to his son.

'I'm okay, Dad, I've got money. Granny Dora and Nanny Mags both gave me some for Christmas.'

'I know, but a bit more won't go amiss, I'm sure.'

Oliver took the note and smiled at him. 'Thank you.'

'And anyway, you should be saving your Christmas money for something nice, not using it as beer tokens.'

'Like a baby-changing mat?' Oliver asked, wide eyed and with a smile on his face.

'Don't even joke!' Nick felt a hot flash of something that seemed a lot like fear and wondered if this was how his dad felt when he broke the news . . .

'Kerry's having a baby . . . so I'm going to get a job and stay here . . . We're getting married . . .'

'But! But . . . what about college, going to university? All your plans?'

'Plans change, Dad. Plans change.'

'Oh my god, Dad! I even scare myself saying that. I mean, not that I don't love Tasha, I do, but a baby?' He shuddered. 'Not for, like, a million years.'

The front doorbell rang and Oliver let Eric in. He strolled into the kitchen.

'What are you feeding this kid? He's nearly taller than me.'

'And me!' Nick piped up.

'In fairness, Dad, that's not that difficult,' Oliver quipped.

'Oh, I see, one term at university and you think you're too old for a thick ear!' Eric made out to swipe in his direction.

'Lucky you, I can't even reach his ear,' Nick added.

Oliver chuckled. 'He can't reach, and you're too weakened by age!'

'What is this?' Eric asked with mock-hurt. 'I come here to pick up my friend for a night on the town and all I get is abuse? And for your information my height is the one aspect of life in which I'm way above average.'

'I used to be tall,' Nick added.

'You have never been tall, mate.' Eric laughed.

'I was!' Nick scoffed. 'I was way taller than you and Alex when we were little.'

'True, but I think the definition of tall is where you end up, not how tall you are while you're growing. I know I was at least a head and shoulders taller than you that summer,' Eric pointed out.

'What summer? Sounds ominous!' Oliver laughed.

'The summer we built the bike.' Eric's eyes creased at the memory.

'Oh, *that* summer!' Oliver enunciated.

'So you know about that, then?' Eric held his gaze.

'I do. In great detail.' Oliver gave a mock-yawn.

Eric smiled at Nick. 'In some ways it was the best time ever, but it was also the worst.'

'Because you had to share a crappy green bike?' Oliver interjected.

'No, and it was anything but crappy to us,' Eric offered. 'Because my mum left us. I guess I'm just saying I know what it feels like.'

Nick looked to his mate; this kind of revelation was rare.

'But she came back?' Oliver looked a little confused, aware as he was of Eric's mum, who lived in the bungalows by the main road.

'Yes, she came back and then, two years later, she went again, and left little David with me and my dad, and then she came back and . . . You get the idea.'

'That doesn't sound like the best time ever at all.'

Nick rubbed his hands and exchanged a knowing look with Eric. It would be too hard to explain to this young man just what that summer had meant, how their experiences had laid the solid foundation of trust on which their friendship was built.

'I don't know if I should give you this now, you cheeky beggar.' Eric removed a slender wrapped gift from his pocket and handed it to Oliver.

'Oh, thanks.' Oliver pulled the paper off to reveal a fountain pen in a fancy box. 'Thanks, Eric! That's awesome.'

'Well, I figured you'd have more use of it than me; it's been gathering dust in a drawer and I'd rather it was used. It was that or a razor – speaking of which, what is that thing on your lip, son?'

'Oh, don't you start.' Oliver groomed his facial fuzz with his thumb and forefinger.

Nick packed away the ironing board and placed it in the gap between the kitchen cabinet and the window. He was touched by Eric's gift.

'Right, then.' He picked up his jacket and patted his jeans pocket to feel the reassuring shapes of house keys, phone and wallet, before grabbing his box of bottled lager. 'I shall see you next year!'

Oliver groaned. Nick said this every New Year's Eve and had done so since Oliver was small, when Nick would tuck him up in bed and whisper, *See you next year* . . . from the doorway.

'Yes, Dad, I shall see you next year. And don't do anything I wouldn't!' Oliver called down the path after them. 'Like fall and break your hip or lose your bus pass!'

Eric laughed. 'He's in good form.'

'Tell me about it.'

'How's it been?' His friend's tone now was a little more subdued.

'A lot, lot better than I was expecting. Actually, it's been good. Apart from Treacle necking the whole turkey!'

'She never!' Eric roared with laughter.

'She did! We had sausages with all the trimmings.'

'The little beggar!'

'Yep.' Nick was able to see the funny side now Christmas had passed without a hitch. 'I had this weird dream about Kerry . . .' He paused, wondering how much to share.

'Weird how?'

He smiled just to think of it. 'She looked wonderful, really healthy, and she told me that I needed to let go a bit and carry on living – told me that this was going to be my year.'

139

Eric smiled. 'And that's what she would say. She was a top lass. And don't take this the wrong way, but I'm proud of you, Nicky, lad. You're doing great and I think Kerry is right; this is going to be your year. Might be mine too if I get it right.'

'What are you thinking?'

'I'm thinking of spreading my wings and going off to find some sunshine.'

'Well, you work hard. A holiday would do you good.' Nick smiled and the two walked to Market Square in silence. He took a deep breath as they approached the end of Beverly's street.

'Don't forget, you can leave at any time.'

'Yes, Mum,' Nick tutted at his friend, trying to hide the slight swell of embarrassment he felt at his kindness, but also hoping the fake bravado might carry him into the house when he was, as he had stated earlier, absolutely bricking it.

There were more people inside the house than he had been expecting. It seemed like half the back office was here, and a handful of people he hadn't seen for a while. He swallowed, nodding and waving to acquaintances as he made his way through the crowds to the kitchen, where he dumped his box of beer bottles and took one for himself. Beverly was nowhere to be seen and it felt a little strange being inside her house without having said hello, impolite almost. He downed the beer and reached for his second.

Go easy . . . He heard Kerry's voice.

Dutch courage, he replied in his mind.

'Nick! Nick, mate!' He turned towards the shout and saw Mikey Sturridge walking towards him. He was a big lad, a rugby player, who now strode with his arms raised, as if it were water he waded through and not a throng of smaller people. 'Now then!' He grabbed him in a bear hug and Nick smelled the beer fumes on his breath. 'I haven't seen you for a long time! How's tricks?'

'Not bad, Mikey, not bad.'

'It's good to see ya! You still at Siddley's?'

'Yes.' He nodded with a dry laugh, as if there might be any other option in Burstonbridge for someone like him.

'I'm only home for a few days, come to see our lad and my mum and dad, but then straight back to France, where I'm playing my rugby now.'

'I heard you were living it up out there. Sounds like nice work if you can get it.'

'It is, mate, it is. Good weather, good food, good life!' He raised his arms over his head, as if his vast frame were not already taking up enough space.

'Well, I envy you. Best we can hope for is a quick thaw to a cold frost and a dodgy pie from the chippy, but it's home.'

Nick looked over Mikey's head and spied Beverly in the hallway. It was the first time he had seen her dolled up, in a glittery top and with fancy put-up hair and lipstick. She looked lovely. And he felt the long-dormant pulse of attraction fire through him. She looked up and into his face and her mouth broke into a smile that he felt was just for him and his gut jumped accordingly. Nick looked around, furtively, wary of anyone recognising the flicker of desire that rippled through his veins. He was after all a man in mourning, a man who came home to a dark house with no one to flick on the light and await him.

Mikey bent close and the booze and garlic danced from his mouth in a pungent brew. 'You should come over and see me, come to France! I mean it. Kerry would love it; I'm not far from the beach, and there's good shopping! She can top up her tan while we visit a few bars; a mate of mine runs a vineyard, I'm not shitting you! A vineyard! He flogs the cheap stuff to the tourists but the really good wine he keeps back and honestly, Nick, you should taste it. Ask Kerry if she fancies it – where is she, anyway?' Mikey looked around from his vantage height, trying to spot Nick's wife.

Nick stared at him, his mouth dry. He felt his legs sway a little and didn't know how to answer, didn't know what to say. It was inconceivable to him that there might be someone in Burston that didn't know about Kerry, and yet here he was, the kind, sweet buffoon Mikey Sturridge, who had been away, playing rugby and drinking good wine . . .

'She's . . .' He swallowed, but try as he might the words couldn't find their way to his mouth.

'Oh no! I've not put my foot in it, have I? Don't tell me you two lovebirds have had a tiff?' He nudged Nick in the ribs. 'You'll work it out, no doubt, made for each other you two! I remember when she got up the duff and everyone said it wouldn't last and yet here we are. Is she off sulking?'

'No, no she . . .' Nick realised in that instant that there was something nice about living in this small town where he had grown up and where everyone knew his business. It meant that he had not had to have this conversation, as gossiping tongues all over the place had verbally paved the way with his news, meaning all encounters were pre-loaded with the terrible, terrible facts. There was also something inexplicably joyful to him that Mikey lived in a world where Kerry and he were just fine, plodding on as usual. He certainly didn't envy the man his fancy life in the south of France, but he envied him that.

'Sturridge, y'bastad!' Rob Bowman, one of his old rugby contemporaries, yelled from the hallway.

'Got to go, Nick, see you around. And think about what I said!' Mikey thumped him on the arm before making his way towards the hall. He passed Beverly and used his big hand to scoot her out of the way, almost pushing her into the kitchen and into Nick's path.

'I didn't see you arrive.' She bopped on the spot in front of him.

'I've been here hours.' He smiled and drank his lager.

'Cheers!' She raised her glass of wine and knocked it against his bottle. 'Good Christmas? Jen said you hid away until Boxing Day.'

'We weren't hiding exactly – well, only from her.' He pulled a face.

'Ah, fearful she might reach for the Monopoly?'

'Something like that.' He laughed. 'What about you? Did you have a nice time?'

'No. No I didn't, actually.' She shook her head and drank her wine. 'I hate Christmas. It's a bad time of year for me. I always feel really lonely and every advert and programme is a reminder of what I'm missing. And that's why I have a New Year's party – first, it gives me something to look forward to, and, second, it means that whilst Christmas might be shite, the end of the year is always epic!'

He liked her candour. Most folks would try to sugar-coat or enhance their experience, attempting to convince you that their life really was as good as their Instagram life, but not Beverly; she told it as it was and he liked it.

'Well, here's to a less shite New Year!' He raised his bottle and drank it quickly, wishing that he too had thought about a fried-egg beer cushion to line his gut. Eric danced into the kitchen, knocking people out of the way with his pointy elbows and jolting their arms so that drinks spilled. It made Nick wince, thinking of the clean-up.

'Oi, Daphne!' Eric called to him, laughing. 'I just danced with Jen! Actually danced with her! This is the best party ever!'

Nick shook his head and said to Beverly as Eric grabbed two beers and left the room, 'Oh God, I'll never hear the end of it. I hope she doesn't mess him around. They had a thing a few years back; a short-lived thing that looked like it might have legs. But after one weekend away they travelled back separately and normal service was resumed. It's a shame; he'd be so good for her.'

'And she for him.'

'Yes, probably,' he had to admit.

'He's pretty smitten, isn't he?' Beverly chuckled.

'He always has been.'

'Well, Nick, when you know, you know.'

'Yep.' He reached for another bottle of beer. His foot began tapping to the strains of Sheryl Crow's 'If It Makes You Happy' – this was turning into a good party. 'When you know you know.'

It was approaching midnight and Nick was drunk.

It had been a long time since he had felt like this. In fact, he could pinpoint the last time, a night after Kerry's initial diagnosis when Eric and Alex had taken him to the pub and, unaware of how best to help their friend, they got him sloshed. He had woken the next morning with his head in a bucket on the bathroom floor and Kerry sitting on the edge of the bed, crying. This felt a little similar: he was out of his depth, not in full control of the situation and hoping that he might be able to slip home without anyone noticing just how drunk he was.

The music of his youth pumped in his veins as he danced with abandon in the tiny sitting room with his arm around Eric's shoulders and his shirt collar unbuttoned. Each song contained a memory, a moment from his short-lived teens, the time of his life when one minute he was excited about the future, planning to go to college, where he would study hard before claiming his fancy office job, where he would sit behind a desk, and the next he was holding a crying baby in the early hours, pacing the floor while simultaneously fretting about where they were going to find the money for rent. And it had happened with frightening speed, as if he were on a spinning roundabout and it was all he could do to hang on.

'Do you ever wonder,' he shouted at Eric above the din, 'about what your life would have been like if you'd made different choices, done different things?'

'No!' Eric yelled his reply. 'Do you?'

'Stometimes,' he slurred. 'I do, recently. I think I could be living in France or driving a Porsche, or just dancing. But I didn't. I stuck around and it all kept spinning. It was bloody hard. It is bloody hard!'

'I have no idea what you're talking about, my drunken friend!' Eric laughed and they carried on dancing.

Time was skewed and he felt a bit woozy, when suddenly there were loud shouts, counting down, 'Ten . . . Nine . . . Eight . . .' He felt someone grab his hand and saw it was Beverly who gripped his fingers tightly, her little hand in his, pulling him from the lounge, where the crowd counted backwards, walking headlong into another time, a new age and a new year in which Kerry had never lived.

The start of a new chapter.

He wasn't sure how he felt about it – he was too drunk to properly order his ideas. Instead, he took Kerry's advice and loosened the lid on his thoughts a bit, letting some of his sadness float away and at the same time mentally lassoing the spikes of joy that fired through him at no more than this: the touch of a woman, this woman, who for whatever reason was drawn to him as he was to her.

Beverly opened the door to the downstairs toilet and pushed him inside. He leant against the sink and took a deep breath as the room spun. She reached up and pushed his fringe from his forehead. The touch of her finger on his face was like a jolt, an electric shock of a sensation, something new and a feeling he had quite forgotten.

He heard the count reach its crescendo. 'Two . . . One! Happy New Year!' voices screamed and claps were interspersed with whoops, hollers and whistles.

He bent down and kissed her gently on the mouth.

It felt strange and at the same time wonderful. It was the first time he had kissed another woman since he had first held Kerry Forrest's hand on a day trip to Drayfield Moor when he had been all of sixteen and without a clue as to how life would turn out. In truth, he felt very similar now as fireworks of longing exploded inside him and his body folded with sweet desire for this pretty girl who, unbelievably, appeared to want him too. He reached up and twined his fingers in her hair, pulling her to him as he leant in for a longer kiss.

And it was in that moment – as their lips touched and her hands roamed the skin beneath the fabric of his new denim shirt, as he felt his guard slip and his body yield to the joy of another human touch – that all hell broke loose.

1992

'What are you two looking so glum about this morning?' his dad asked as he sipped his tea and ate his toast at the table before work. 'If I had the whole day stretching out in front of me with nothing to do and the sun was out, I'd be a bit happier. Look at you both! You look like you've lost a sixpence and found a shilling.'

Nick and Eric exchanged a look; they had absolutely no idea what a sixpence or a shilling was.

'Mags, have you seen the mardy faces on these two?' His dad now spoke to his mum, who came into the kitchen with an armful of dirty laundry.

'They're fed up because they can't find wheels or a saddle,' she surmised as she dropped to her haunches and fed the dirty clothes into the washing machine.

'Is that right?' His dad sat up and put his mug down. 'Have you tried looking?'

'Ye-es! We've looked everywhere, Dad!' Nick propped his head on his fist. 'We've been to the scrap yard three times and the man there said we are not to go back as we just get in the way and it's dangerous.'

'Plus, he's got a really scary dog,' Eric chipped in.

Nick nodded energetically. This was true. 'And I asked the bin man if he ever saw wheels lying around and he said if he did he'd sell them himself for scrap.'

'That'll be Henry.' His dad raised his eyebrows at his mum.

Eric backed up his friend's story. 'We go to the Rec and up to the Old Dairy Shed every day, in case anyone has dumped any. So far we've found an old fridge and a tractor tyre, and there's always mattresses and stuff on the floor.'

Again, Nick saw his parents exchange a look.

'But we've never seen any wheels,' Eric huffed.

'*And* we went up to the bike shop next to the butcher's,' Nick continued to explain, 'and I asked the man in there if he had any old wheels he didn't want or ever threw any away.'

'What did he say?' His dad leant forward with his forearms on the table. Nick wasn't sure how to phrase it. Eric, however, had no such compulsion.

'He told us to sod off.'

'Right.' His dad took a swig of his tea, but Nick could see him smiling behind the rim of the mug.

'Well, you know what they say, lads; energy and persistence conquer all things. Keep looking.'

'The thing is, Dad, we've only got two weeks of the summer holiday left and if we don't get the wheels soon, we won't even finish the bike before we go back to school, let alone get a chance to ride it!' He cursed the sting of tears that threatened. His words only served to highlight their predicament, and it felt hopeless.

His dad stood and took a deep breath. 'I'd best get going or Mr Siddley'll have my guts for garters. See you later, love,' he addressed his wife. 'And for goodness' sake, you two, cheer up!'

Alex stepped up and down the kerb as they made their daily pilgrimage up to the Rec in search of the elusive wheels.

'Do you think your mum and dad will get divorced?' he asked Eric out of the blue.

Eric shrugged. 'Don't know.' Eric picked up a small round pebble and lobbed it as far as he could. It hit the wall of the church and settled on the pathway.

Nick didn't fully understand what divorce entailed, but he knew that Will Pearce's mum and dad were divorced and didn't live together any more and Will had to have two sets of uniform, one at each house, and last year he had to eat two Christmas dinners as he spent half the day with his mum and half with his dad. It didn't sound so bad.

'Do you think your mum might stay in Derby?' Nick asked.

'Don't know.' Eric shrugged again, preoccupied with pulling the small branches from the stick he had now picked up. What was it with him and sticks? It seemed he always wanted one in his grip to bash, tap or poke his way through the world, like an explorer.

'What does your dad say?' Alex, like Nick, was curious.

'Not much, but I think he's sad. He sits on the sofa and drinks cans of ale like he did when my grandma died, and then he starts singing.'

'What does he sing?' Nick tried to picture the tall, quiet man breaking into song and couldn't.

'"You'll Never Walk Alone".'

The boys were quiet and Nick wondered if the other two, like him, were singing the song in their heads.

'If my mum and dad got divorced, I would go and live wherever Jen wasn't,' Nick asserted.

Alex and he laughed.

'I like your sister,' Eric said softly, looking into the middle distance, as if he were miles away. 'I think she's dead pretty.'

Nick and Alex stopped walking and pulled faces, staring at their mate in horror.

'She's a witch is what she is!' Nick said loudly.

'A scary witch!' Alex added for good measure, with his hands raised and his fingers bent.

'I don't think so.' Eric gave a gentle nod and carried on walking to the accompanying tune of Nick and Alex singing loudly; 'Eric and Jenny, sitting in a tree . . .'

'Well, marvellous!' his dad offered sarcastically, as he stood in the kitchen with his hands on his hips and shaking his head. 'I leave for work with two of you sitting there with long faces, and I get home from work to find the only thing that's changed is that there are now three of you.'

'Hello, Mr Bairstow,' Alex sighed.

'Have you been sat here all day?' His dad washed his hands at the kitchen sink.

'No.' Eric sat up. 'We went round the Rec searching, and then we looked in the bins at the back of the bike shop.'

'What did you find there?' his dad asked.

'Empty egg boxes, a cat-litter tray and some Chinese takeaway boxes with noodles in them.'

'I see.' His dad dried his hands on the tea towel and leant against the sink. 'I don't think you've been looking hard enough.'

Nick hated the feeling of disappointment in his gut, like he had in some way let his dad down. It was the very worst and to be reminded of this in front of his friends felt doubly galling.

'We did, Dad! Honest! We've looked all day! But we can't find wheels or a saddle. The rest of the bike is ready. We've got the paintwork good and the chain and everything is really shiny!'

'And we all put in and bought a can of oil to keep the gears and everything in good shape.' Alex also tried to demonstrate their commitment to Half Bike.

Nick pictured the tussles they had over whose turn it was to administer the oil through the narrow plastic spout with the little red cap on the end.

His dad took a deep breath and reached into his pocket. He pulled out three narrow metal tins and handed them out.

'Wow!' Alex beamed. 'Thank you!'

'Is it for keeps?' Eric asked with a note of disbelief, as if this gift were too good to be true.

'It is, lad. One each.' Nick's dad smiled.

Nick felt his melancholy fade, replaced with something close to happiness, not only to be on the receiving end of a gift, but also that his dad had got the same for his mates.

'Open them up,' his dad instructed.

Each boy used his thumb to pop open the thin metal tin lid with a satisfying thunk and ran his finger over the neatly packed contents.

'This is everything you will ever need to fix a puncture,' his dad explained. Nick pictured riding the moors with the little tin in his pocket, nestling next to his multi-tool. He knew that with his very own transport and these things on his person, he would feel invincible, and even the thought sent a rush of joyous excitement through his veins.

His dad sat in the spare seat at the kitchen table and pointed into Nick's tin.

'You've got a tube of rubber cement – careful, mind, once you've squeezed some out it seeps and it can be murder to get that little black nozzle off next time you need it so clean the top before you put the lid back on.'

The boys nodded.

'There's a piece of chalk for marking any punctures on the inner tube, and those you'll find by holding the inner tube in a washing-up bowl full of water and squeezing it gently all around under the water until you see where the bubbles come up from. There's a square of sand-paper to rough up the surface so that the rubber cement keys to it better and a selection of patches to cover the puncture – round, rectangular and square, and it's important to pick the right one for the right hole.'

Nick and his friends listened intently to the instructions from this grown-up who seemed to know all there was to know about punctures.

'What are these for?' Eric picked up one of two slender pegs of metal with curved lips at either end. He pinged his finger on them.

'They're the metal tyre levers to jemmy the tyre from the rim of the wheel. A bit fiddly at first, but you'll soon get the hang of it, and if it's the difference between getting home easily or pushing your bike miles uphill, you'll be surprised how quickly you'll figure everything out.'

'This is really cool!' Eric beamed.

'Thank you, Dad.' Nick smiled.

'You're welcome, son.'

'We can keep them safe until we get actual wheels,' Alex offered stoically.

His dad stood from the table and looked at them sternly. 'As I said, I don't think you boys have been looking hard enough.'

'But, Dad . . .' Nick began again to explain how they were running out of time and options.

'Don't talk, Nicky, just listen,' his dad began. 'Have you ever thought that maybe you're looking in the wrong places?'

The boys looked from one to another.

'I mean, I know you like to circle the Rec and wander over the Old Dairy Shed, but when's the last time you took a good long look at your bike?' His dad gave him a subtle wink.

Nick thought quickly. It had been a day or so since they had actually been into the garage, too preoccupied with playing Petunia and wandering their routes, searching. Eric and Alex too looked at each other. His dad opened the back door, and without being told the boys jumped up from their seats and ran across the dry grass to the garage. Nick threw open the side door, quickly followed by his mates. He pulled on the overhead light and screamed.

Eric jumped up and down on the spot, whereas Alex dropped to his knees with his hands over his mouth.

There it was in all its neon-green glory; Half Bike! Only it was no longer half a bike, but a *whole* bike with a neat, narrow racing saddle and two perfect, shiny chrome wheels.

'Dad!' Nick rushed over to the big man and threw his arms around his waist, burying his head against his dad's chest in an act so instinctive, a reaction visceral and unconsidered, but entirely appropriate for the sight that greeted him. Eric bundled over and clung to Nick's back and Alex stood and joined the hug.

'I guess they're pleased, then,' his mum called from the open doorway.

'Looks like it,' his dad chuckled, while the boys clung to him like pups.

Eric and Alex took turns in running their fingers over the spokes and squeezing the brakes on to the rims.

His dad bent down and spoke directly to his face.

'Here's the thing, Nick: this is what life will be like for you if you do it right. You have put all you can into this project, you've set goals, made a plan and put in the hours and the universe has come up trumps and helped you over the finish line. That's how it works, and if you go to university and set your goals and work hard, then the world will help you achieve whatever you set your mind to. It'll help you get over the finish line. I believe that.'

'Thank you, Dad.' Nick didn't know what else to say, but knew that the moment felt like a big one.

'Who's going to ride it first?' his mum asked.

'I think Nick,' Alex suggested.

'I think Nick too,' Eric agreed.

Nick wheeled the bike to the front of the house and patted the puncture repair kit and multi-tool in his pocket. He might have only been going to the bottom of the cul-de-sac, but why take any chances? A small crowd of his parents, his sister, who hung back and was a little quiet, and his mates gathered on the pavement. He felt lucky. *Lucky* . . .

'Eric!' Nick stood, proud of the bike, and let his friend take the handlebars. 'I think you should ride it first.'

'Me?' Eric's face split with joy.

'Yep. You should ride her first and then I'll go next.'

'Why me?' Eric asked, as he rushed forward to stand astride the green machine.

'Because you're the oldest,' he lied, hiding the real reason: that he felt sad that Eric's mum had gone to Derby and that his dad drank ale and sang on the sofa because he was unhappy. 'And because I don't want you to remember this as a bad or sad summer.'

'A bad or sad summer?' Eric looked at him briefly as he placed his feet on the pedals and pushed off down the hill, gripping Dave the Milk's handlebars. 'This is the summer of absolutely brilliant!' he screamed. 'THE SUMMER OF ABSOLUTELY BRILLIANT!'

SEVEN

'Where is he, Eric?' Nick stood with his fingers in his hair. He was sobering up fast, having run all the way home and with worry syphoning the alcohol and all joy from his veins; he looked up and down the street outside their house. 'I thought he'd be in his room.'

'He'll turn up. It's Burston; you can't hide here, even if you want to,' Eric sighed.

Nick again punched a text into his phone and fired it off: Please Olly call me NOW! Let me know where you are!

And again he was left wanting for a reply.

'Have you tried your mum?'

'Yep, didn't want to worry her, so kept it vague but he's not there. She'd have said.' He breathed out, hating the acrid tang of his sloshed breath.

'Alex and a couple of the others have been up around the Rec. And Jen put a call in to work, just asking the patrol car to keep an eye out; they'll call if they see him.'

Nick nodded, not really paying too much attention to his friend. 'He was out with his mates from school tonight – Ned, Jason . . . and I can't remember who else. I've texted Ned's dad – he's Carl's lad.'

'Carl from Maintenance?'

'Yep. I don't know Jason's number and I can't remember his surname.'

'He'll turn up, lad,' Eric repeated, placing his hands on his hips and looking skyward, and Nick felt guilty that this was how his evening had turned out.

'I know, I know. I don't think he's in danger.' He blinked away his concerns over suicide and self-harm. Peter, the counsellor at St Vincent's, had warned him about them. 'But I know he's still fragile and I just want to talk to him! I'm such a fucking idiot!' Nick closed his eyes, took a deep breath and felt a wave of nausea.

'You're not.'

'I am, though! This Christmas is supposed to be all about Olly! About making it a little bit less shit for him, and I've messed it up! I've messed it up big-time.' He balled his fists in frustration.

'What happened exactly?'

Nick held his friend's gaze. 'I was in the loo with . . . with Beverly. She . . . She kind of steered me in there at midnight and we' – he swallowed – 'we were kissing.'

'Flamin' Nora!' Eric made no attempt to hide his wide-eyed shock; Nick noticed the small smile of approval on his mouth. He looked away without comment; this was not the time for that.

Yep, flamin' Nora, indeed. He felt the rise of guilt, briefly recalling the high he had been on and the happiness he had felt. 'And the next thing I know, the loo door opens and Olly is standing there, and he was looking back over his shoulder, laughing. He seemed happy, like he was having fun, and I was pleased to see him before remembering the situation I was in. Then he turned, looked up, saw it was me and realised what was . . .' He paused. 'What was happening. And his face . . .' He swallowed the emotion that threatened, knowing he would not forget the way Oliver's face had crumpled, his eyebrows knitting in confusion and a look of pure sorrow wiping away his smile. His shoulders had fallen forward, as if the air had been knocked from his lungs, and he flashed his dad a sneer that looked a lot like hatred. And then he ran while Nick, losing precious seconds, clumsily extricated himself from Beverly's grip and ran after him. 'I called out, "Olly, come back! Olly, I need to talk to you!" But he'd legged it.'

And here we are.

'Wow.'

'Yep, wow.' Nick again looked up and down the street as if, if he stared hard enough, Oliver might appear.

Eric spoke with more confidence than Nick felt. 'He'll be mulling things over. He'll have gone to one of his friends' houses and he'll be trying to figure it all out. He'd probably had a drink too, and that clouds everything, but it'll all be okay. You'll see. Olly will find his way home.'

Nick went back into the house and began to pace the hallway, occasionally looking up and down the street and checking his phone, while trying to think of friends Oliver might have called on. He wished he had Tasha's number, knowing there was a high chance he would make contact with her. As he tried to think of how to get in touch with the girl who he knew lived in St Albans, but very little else, a text came in from his mother-in-law, Dora.

He's at Di's

'Oh thank God!' He felt a flood of gratitude towards his mother-in-law. 'He's at Di's; I'll head over.' He set off, leaving the front door wide open.

'Do you want me to stay here?' Eric pointed at the abandoned house.

'Yes, mate, thanks, and can you call Jen and tell her I've found him, and thank Alex, everyone?' he called out as he made his way along the front path.

'Sure you don't want me to come with you?' Eric asked, yawning as the night's events caught up with them.

'No, I'm good, but thanks, mate. I'll bring Olly home.' The relief he felt was a physical thing; the idea of running across town didn't faze him, quite the opposite.

'Nick.'

'What?' He turned to face his friend, keen to get going.

'Don't beat yourself up. Kerry was right, you know.'

'About what?'

'You need to let go a bit; you need to carry on living.'

Nick didn't know what to say. So many emotions fought for space in his mind that had only recently shaken off the fog of boozy confusion. He raised his hand and jogged out of the cul-de-sac, towards town.

In his haste to get to his boy, he forgot to feel the quiver of dread at what his sister-in-law might have to say about the whole matter, intent as he was on only scooping Oliver up and bringing him home. He pictured them sitting at either end of the sofa, talking rationally over a cup of tea about what had happened and why. And in truth he dreaded the prospect as much as he welcomed it. He wasn't sure how to play it or what to say that might help. He waited to see if Kerry's voice might come to him now when he most needed words of advice.

Nothing.

Light came from the hallway of Diane's modern house on a small red-brick development around the back of the leisure centre. Nick coughed and ran his fingers through his hair, trying not to think about how it felt when Beverly had done similar, earlier. He rapped cautiously on the door with his knuckles, trying unsuccessfully to strike a balance between gaining entry and not waking up anyone who might be sleeping.

Diane opened the door and stood with her hands folded across the front of her bulky pink dressing gown.

'Hi, Di.'

'Well, how lovely to see you. Happy New Year, Nick.' Her words dripped with sarcasm.

He ignored her tone and cut to the chase. 'Is Olly here?'

'My bloody mother!' She looked over his head out across the roof-tops to where her mum lived and spoke through gritted teeth. It would be only later that Nick would reflect on these words, suggesting that, left up to her, she would not have told him Oliver was under her roof. He could only imagine the kind of night he would have spent then. 'He doesn't want to see you.'

'What?' He stood back and almost laughed. 'What do you mean, he doesn't want to see me?'

'Just as it sounds, I can't put it any plainer than that! He came in and was very upset, we had a little chat, and he went up to the spare room. It's been quite a night for him.' She narrowed her eyes at him. 'Oliver was very specific. He said, "If my dad comes over, I don't want to see him." And that's that.'

Nick took a step back on the path and was a little lost for words. 'I don't . . . I don't know what to say.'

'I bet you don't,' she muttered.

'Olly!' he called out, 'Olly, I know you can hear me and I just wanted to say that we need to talk!'

'I'll thank you to keep your voice down in my street,' Di hissed at him.

'Di, I'm very grateful to you for putting Olly up—'

'Why wouldn't I? I'm his auntie.' She cut him short, seemingly keen to assert her position.

'As I say, I'm very grateful to you and glad that Olly felt he could come here, but I need to talk to my son!' He hoped his words might float up the stairs to the spare room, which he knew was at the top of the landing.

'I don't want to talk to you, Dad!' Despite his words, it was a relief to hear his son's voice. 'I don't want to talk to anyone!'

Nick heard the emotion in Oliver's voice and it killed him. 'Okay, Olly, okay, I understand. I don't like it, but I understand. And just so you know, if you're not home by breakfast, I will be straight back round here to drag you home. We need to talk – we need to talk about a lot of stuff – but it's been a long night and maybe you need to cool off and I need to think. So I will see you in the morning.' He turned to walk from the house.

'You make me sick! How could you? Selfish bastard!' his sister-in-law whispered, her mouth contorted, as she gripped the front door and closed it behind him.

Nick turned and took two or three steps down the path before a force hitherto unfelt stirred something inside of him. He took a breath and, with his pulse racing, he walked back to the front door and knocked on it, caring less this time who he woke.

Diane opened it with a look of surprise.

'Do not talk to me like that, Di! Don't ever talk to me like that!' He pointed at her with a trembling finger. 'I'm many things, but I'm not self-ish and you have no right to judge me, none!' He kept his voice steady.

'Have you lost your bloody mind?' She trod down the step and met him on the front path. 'Do you know what you've done? My sister is not cold in her grave and you're already messing around.'

Four and a half months . . . It's been four and a half sad and lonely months . . . both the blink of an eye and a lifetime.

Di continued. 'How could you – do you not give a shit? Do you not care that folk will talk or what this might feel like for Olly?'

Her words were like a slap across his face.

'Is that what you think? That I don't give a shit? That I don't put Olly's feelings at the front of *every* decision I make?' He drew breath. 'Jesus Christ, I'm working myself stupid to buy him all the extras he needs at Uni. I'm doing my level best to keep everything afloat and I'm barely managing, barely!'

'Well, it seems you were managing fairly well tonight, according to half of Burston, who saw you snogging the face off Beverly bloody Clark!'

'You have no idea, Di.' He shook his head, hurt that she had not the slightest understanding of how things were for him.

'You say you loved my sister and yet—'

'Don't you dare!' His voice shook. 'Don't you dare! I loved my wife. I loved her!' He raised his voice. 'And I always will. Always. But be under no illusion that the last year of her life was thoroughly shit. Just awful, and I never left her side, not once, and before you jump in, I don't want a medal and I don't want thanks – I would do it a thousand times over, a hundred thousand times over! But I started to say goodbye to her on the day she got her last results, when they said there was nothing they could . . .' He let this trail. 'And I've been grieving for her ever since then, because for me she didn't die suddenly, on the fifteenth of August at a quarter to eight in the evening.' He shook his head. 'She died a little bit every day from that point until she finally closed her eyes. A year, Di. A whole year of absolute hell. And I held her hand all the way through until the very end. So it might have only been four months or so since we laid her to rest, but I lost her a long time before that.' Nick thought about the gentle erosion – physically, mentally, emotionally – of the woman he loved, until the pale husk that lay attached to a tube resembled her little. So much so that by the time her passing came, his sadness had become cocooned in unspeakable, shameful relief.

'I know all that, don't you think we've suffered too?' she railed. 'You need to put it in context, Nick, you need to—'

'No, Di! This is not some competition about who has suffered the most. We are all hurt, all of us. But this thing between me and Olly and what happened tonight is nothing to do with you, and as for context . . .' He stopped and took a breath, tried to control the quaver to his voice as anger brimmed and threatened to spill the harsh words he knew they would both regret. That was not his way. 'The context is that I was married to Kerry for eighteen years. Eighteen years! We went through some rough times, but we were friends, good friends, and we talked, we talked about everything, and I know what she said and I know what she wanted—'

'What, she wanted you to hang around with Beverly Clark, snogging her in a loo and upsetting my mum and Olly, did she?' It was like she couldn't help herself, jumping in with her venom poised.

'No.' He shook his head, feeling suddenly weary, as if the whole evening's events were catching up with him. 'But I know she wanted me to be happy when she was alive and I know she wants me to be happy now she isn't. It's that simple. We always wanted each other to be happy and I am trying, but it's not easy – in fact, there have been times when, if it wasn't for Oliver, I would have given up.' He cursed the tears that threatened. 'Does that make you feel better? Is that how you would like me to live? So sad, so alone, that I can't stand the thought of getting up each day? Because that's the alternative for me, a very real alternative!'

Diane looked at the floor and her tears matched his. 'No, Nick, that's not what I want, but I . . .'

'But what, Di? Spit it out.' He waited for the next verbal assault and steeled himself, his feet firmly planted, his fists coiled.

'I miss her,' she squeaked.

'Well, that makes two of us, but missing her isn't going to bring her back and it's not going to help Olly and it's not going to help me. Life goes on, it has to. Tell Oliver I will see him at home in the morning.'

He turned and walked down the path and he saw Kerry's face in his mind. And she was smiling.

◆ ◆ ◆

Nick hardly slept, despite his fatigue; his hangover was brutal, leaving him with the throb of a headache as well as the discomfort that came with dehydration and an uncomfortable desire to vomit. When he lay down the room spun. He thought it best to sit up and wait for his symptoms to pass, hoping that would be sooner rather than later.

'Never again.' He looked at Eric across the breakfast table. His friend, who had spent the night on the couch, was, in comparison, sprightly, drinking tea and eating toast and honey. Noisily.

'I'll push off; I expect Olly'll be home soon. You okay?' Eric asked, as he folded the last of his toast into his mouth and drained his mug of tea.

'Not really. I don't know what to say to him.' Nick scratched his stubbled chin.

'Don't overthink it and just tell him the truth.'

Eric made it sound so easy.

'I know when things have hurt me . . .'

He wondered if Eric was talking about that summer when his mum had abandoned him.

'Knowing where I stood, the truth, would have made everything more bearable. The confusion, the worry, was as bad as what happened.'

Nick nodded.

Treacle barked at the back door and, as he let her out, he heard the front door open and close.

Eric winked at his mate and sidled out along the hallway past Oliver, squeezing the boy briefly on the shoulder and giving them the space they needed.

Nick watched as Oliver stood in the kitchen doorway, leaning on the frame. He was beyond relieved that he had come back as requested, unsure what his next move might have been had he not shown up.

'Cup of tea?' He pointed at the kettle.

'No.' Oliver shook his head, hardly able to look Nick in the eye.

'Sit down, Olly.'

'No. I don't want to. I came to get my stuff and to tell you I'm going back to Uni early. Today, in fact. I don't want to be here.'

'No! Please don't do that! I think that would be a mistake. I know you're hurt and I understand why, but leaving without giving us the chance to patch things up, without talking it through is, I think, the wrong thing to do.'

'I don't really care what you think!' The wobble to his voice and the mist in his eyes suggested the very opposite.

'I thought I would apologise to you about last night, but I've been thinking about it and I don't think it's about apologising.'

'Well, you'd be wrong!' Oliver fired; his fists inside his jacket pockets jabbed forward.

Nick kept his calm. 'What I mean is, I want to say I'm sorry for putting you in that position, but I don't want to apologise for my actions, because life goes on, Olly.'

'I was with my mates!' His son continued to rant as if he hadn't heard Nick's words. Maybe he hadn't, too wrapped up in his own thoughts and the words that were battering his lips to escape. 'Someone said there was a party and we all just piled in and we were having a laugh and then I opened the door and there you were!' He jerked his head like someone shaking a snow globe, trying to reset the image.

Nick again replayed the moment Oliver had realised it was him and the look of absolute sadness on his face. He hated it and wished he could erase the memory.

'I can imagine how—'

'No! No, you can't imagine, Dad, not even a little bit! I miss my mum.' His bottom lip trembled. 'I miss her so much and Christmas has been shit. Treacle ate the bloody turkey and you can't do the decorations and it's all been rubbish!'

Nick felt his spirits sink even lower. Not only did he not know how to fix this, but the things Oliver referred to, sources of humour before New Year's Eve, were now in this new light further failures with which his boy could taunt him, reminders that, despite his words, he was still getting things very wrong.

'I know you miss her,' he said softly.

'Is *that woman* your girlfriend?' Oliver spat, ignoring his dad's words, driven by his own agenda.

Nick looked away. 'No.'

'So, what, that was the first time you'd met her?' he asked with a back note of sarcasm.

'No.' Nick now held his son's eye line. 'We work together and have done for years. She knew your mum, of course, and she has been very kind to me. I'd say we are friends and last night was—'

'Don't tell me last night was a mistake, just because you were drunk.' Oliver sneered.

'No, Olly, I was going to say that last night was a bit like a beginning.'

'So you *want* her to be your girlfriend?'

Nick swallowed, his mouth sticky dry with nerves; he remembered Eric's advice about honesty. 'I don't know. I honestly don't know. I've never been in this position before and I'm trying to figure it all out as I go along. I know that it felt nice to be wanted and nice that there is the smallest possibility that I can be happy again.'

'But . . .' Oliver walked forward and leant on the table, as if this might help his point, 'but . . .' He shook his head, as if the words just wouldn't come.

'I know it's a lot . . .'

'No, Dad, you don't know! You keep saying you *know* how it is for me, but you don't. You think you do, but you really don't!'

'So tell me.'

'I'm . . . I'm not ready.'

'Not ready to tell me?'

Oliver shook his head. 'No. I'm not ready for you to move on like that.'

Nick felt his heart flex for the words so bravely spoken.

'Okay. Okay, Olly. I understand. But there is nothing you need to be ready for. Beverly and I are friends, and *if* and when anything else happens it'll be a slow process so that by the time we have to think about it or talk about it then things will feel differently. Even if, right now, it feels like they never will.'

Oliver seemed to consider this and his tone when he spoke was a little softer. 'I don't want another woman to be in Mum's kitchen. In Mum's house.' He shook his head. 'That's the thing I don't want the most.'

'And I understand that too.'

'Has she been here?' Again his eyes seemed to glint at the terrible possibility.

'Once, maybe, but only briefly. She popped in.'

He watched Oliver's jaw muscles tighten. 'I want to go and see Tasha.'

'Please don't go, Olly – stay here and let the dust settle. I don't want you leaving while things feel awkward. I'm your dad and you're my boy. At the end of the day, I've got your back. It's you and me against the world, the Bairstow Boys!' He smiled. 'We need to go kick a ball at the Rec, take Treacle to walk off some of that turkey, go see some football, all the things we have always done, and some of them hard to do when your mum was so sick. Please don't go, Olly; stay here and let me burn you some bacon.'

Oliver allowed a small smile to form at the edges of his mouth. 'You could save time and just dump it straight in the sink.'

'I could that.' He smiled at his son.

The front door rattled; Eric must have left it ajar. Nick sighed, expecting to see his mum walk into the kitchen with the obligatory loaf of bread and pint of milk she always felt he needed, along with a running commentary on the weather, as if he lived on a different continent with a different climate, and a comment on how much Oliver had grown since she saw him two days ago. He felt more than a flicker of irritation. What he and Oliver needed right now was time alone.

'Hello!' the voice called. 'Oh, is this a bad time?'

Nick stared at Beverly, who walked slowly in and stood by Oliver's side, her manner hesitant.

'You are fucking kidding me!' Oliver turned on his heel and raced up the stairs.

'Oliver!' Nick called after him, wanting to tell him it was not okay to talk to Beverly like that and to try to smother the relit flames of his rage.

'Should I . . .' Beverly stood awkwardly, her face pale, eyes averted, as she pointed to the front door through which she had just walked.

'I think so.' Nick more or less ignored her, preoccupied as he was with his son, who thumped around overhead in his bedroom, no doubt packing and preparing to run from the house in which he did not want another woman to tread, whilst the woman who had trod the path to the gate now walked away as quickly as she had arrived.

'I don't know what I'm supposed to do,' Nick said to the ether, pacing as Treacle barked at the back door to be let in.

◆　◆　◆

Dora, he noted, had aged. He thought this every time he saw her. The bungalow was, to the untrained eye, full of clutter, the windowsills, shelves and surfaces jam packed with trinkets, ornaments and knick-knacks. But it wasn't clutter, not to her or those in the know, those aware that each item was a thing most precious to her, chosen specifically from a much bigger collection, salvaged, if you like, when she and her husband downsized from the Victorian villa that overlooked the Rec. The villa had been Dora's parents' home and one where she and Bill had raised their two daughters and built memories over thirty years of marriage, leaving only when Bill's Alzheimer's and failing health meant the stairs were a danger and the proximity to the main road a constant concern for a wife whose husband liked to wander off. Not to mention how his care had stretched their finances almost to breaking point. Ironically, within weeks of moving into their new home, Bill had slipped away after a ferocious bout of pneumonia, which Dora had at the time referred to as God's gift, loving him too much to watch him decline further. No one mentioned how the upheaval of the move was all now a little unnecessary; hindsight, he knew, was a wonderful thing and sometimes a cruel mirror.

'Come in, Nick. How's Olly?'

He exhaled his air-filled cheeks. *Where to start . . .*

'He's gone back to Uni in a bit of a strop. Left earlier today and wouldn't even let me run him to the coach station.' He spoke lightly, hoping to mask the utter desolation he felt when he recalled how his son had spoken to him and the hurried manner in which he had left. He looked at her and shook his head, as if unsure what to add to this.

'Come and have a cup of tea.'

He welcomed the thought of this cure-all and followed her into the tiny but functional kitchen.

'He's got a lot on his plate, Nick. Even if he smiles and tells you everything is great. He hides his hurt and it's not surprising that it comes to the surface every now and then; trouble is, when it does, it erupts with all the other hurts that lie beneath it, backed up for God knows how long, and it seems you, as the person he loves the most, get both barrels.'

'Lucky me.'

'Yes, lucky you.' She looked him in the eye without a trace of humour. 'He's a wonderful boy and this will pass. Everything does,' she added matter-of-factly.

'I just wanted to say thank you for letting me know he was at Diane's last night. I was going out of my mind. I knew, the longer I didn't see him, the worse that interaction would be, or that's what I thought anyway. Right now I don't think things could be much worse.' He huffed.

'Oh, trust me, they could, love.' She smiled at him briefly, a sad smile that didn't quite reach her eyes, and he was reminded that the very worst thing had happened to her: she had lost her daughter. He let her words settle.

'I'm sorry if I dropped you in it with Di; she didn't seem happy to see me.'

Dora gave a snort of ironic laughter. 'She's not happy to see anyone.'

'So I shouldn't take it personally?' he asked lightly, ridiculously relieved at the thought that this might be the case.

'Oh, you should most definitely take it personally! You're at the top of her list.'

'I'm guessing it's not a list of her favourite things?'

Dora plopped the teabags in the mugs and stood with her arms crossed over her jumper. 'God knows I love her, I do. She's my daughter, but I find her hard to fathom. I think she likes trouble; it gives her something to focus on, like casting a stone that puts a ripple in the boredom. She's angry.'

'I had noticed.'

'Not just with you, Nick, with the whole world.'

'What's she so angry about?'

Dora sighed and looked up at the ceiling, as if sorting her mental list into some kind of order. 'The fact that her dad got sick, the fact that her sister died, the fact I sold her childhood home. Plus, she feels that life has passed her by, she's jealous of all the good things that happen to other people; she is overweight and doesn't do anything to change it; and now she's angry with you about the whole Beverly thing.'

He felt his face colour. These words from Kerry's mum! The woman who had made their wedding cake when he was no more than a teen, and she knew he had snogged Beverly Clark. He felt the stranglehold of mortification.

'What . . . What do you think about that?' He tapped his fingers lightly on the pine tabletop and his leg jumped beneath the table.

Again, Dora sighed, as if these thoughts were another burden to bear.

'Truthfully? I think life can be hard, too hard sometimes. And I think you're young. Only in your early thirties, with a whole lot of living ahead of you – God willing,' she added the caveat, 'and I think you have to make a life yourself. You didn't put a foot wrong with our Kerry. And I know that your relationship, like many others, had its ups and downs.' She held his eye, this enough to tell him she was, like him, thinking of the time he had sat in front of her several years ago and poured out his heart.

'It's not only the money, Dora, money we haven't got! But there are rumours she's been seeing Rod Newberry, hanging out with him. I don't know . . . I don't know what to do . . .'

'You'll get through this, love. If you want to' had been her sage advice.

Her words again drew his attention. 'You cared for her for a long, long time and it was tough, and you loved her and I will forever be grateful for that.' She swallowed the crack in her voice. 'I wish . . .' She paused. 'I wish we weren't having this conversation. I wish it was Kerry sitting there mithering me about something. I wish a lot of things . . . But this is where we are and this is what life is: a series of hurdles, some harder to get over than others, with pockets of joy in between. I look at Bill and how he arrived at old age in the blink of an eye, and that's how it works. I've seen it. And I wake every day and have to remind myself that it wasn't just some horrible dream; he and Kerry have really gone.' Dora drew breath. 'You have to make the most of every day, every month, every year. You, more than most, are aware that we never know what is around the corner. I know you do right by Olly and I know you always will. You were a good husband and you're a bloody good dad, and for the record, Beverly Clark is a good lass.'

Nick felt a tingling in his nose and the prick of tears, a sensation that was becoming less familiar, but right now this emotion felt more than appropriate. Dora placed the mug of tea in front of him and handed him a piece of kitchen roll.

'Now, what are we going to do about that grandson of mine?' She sat down opposite him and sipped her tea.

1992

Alex knelt on the concrete floor of the garage and dipped the old flannel into the bucket of water, which foamed with a dash of Fairy Liquid. Nick watched as he pulled a section taut over his finger and began rubbing it over the frame of Half Bike, paying particular attention to the front forks, where mud liked to gather. Cleaning the bike was as much a preoccupation as riding it, but not nearly half as thrilling.

'How fast do you think I went down Cobb Lane last night?' Nick pictured himself hurtling along, recalling the feel of the light bike beneath him, slightly skittish as the narrow wheels glanced the road surface, rushing along the lane, a steep hill with trees and water ditches either side that led to the Old Dairy Shed. It had been exhilarating and scary in equal measure. He might have sat steadily in the saddle, but his heart had raced at the fact that he was ever so slightly out of control.

''Bout ten miles an hour?' Alex suggested.

Nick put down the bicycle pump he had been toying with, firing jets of air from close range at a paper cup to make it move along his dad's workbench. His tone was offended. 'Ten miles an hour? No way! Loads more than that! I think nearer twenty or thirty!'

'Really?' Alex stopped cleaning and looked at his friend.

'Yes! Really! I was zooming.'

'You were zooming, but thirty miles an hour is a lot.'

'I know it's a lot, Alex, it was me that was on Half Bike, thinking that, if I fell off, I'd be dead as a dodo!'

Alex shrugged and turned his attention back to wiping down the frame. Like anyone who spent a lot of time together, the boys knew when an argument was worth pursuing and when it would go round and round in circles, ending only when one of them caved in. This was one of those times.

'Now then.' Eric sloped into the garage. Instead of going immediately to Half Bike and getting stuck in, as was his way, he slumped down in the corner, sitting on one of the canvas fishing stools with his back against the tatty doorless dresser where Nick's dad kept old bottles of methylated spirits, turpentine, a green rusted oil can with a thumb lever, small tin buckets with various paint brushes poking out of the top, a funnel or two and empty Lyle's Golden Syrup pots, some with rusted seams, all holding a variety of screws, odds and ends, and in one, picture wire coiled into lengths.

'What's up?' Nick put the pump down, bored now of the 'trying to make the paper cup move' game.

Eric leant forward and rested his elbows on his knees.

'I saw my mum.'

'No way! Is she back?' This was big news.

'No.' Eric looked at his mate. 'Not really. Not for good. But she was there when I got home last night. She didn't stay long.'

'Was Dave the Milk with her?' Alex asked with a glint in his eyes, no doubt, like Nick, imagining the argy-bargy that might have taken place between Eric's dad and the milkman.

Eric shook his head.

'Oh.' Alex sounded more than a little disappointed.

'She only stayed about an hour and she sat on the sofa like a visitor. She seemed different. It was horrible. She kept looking at the clock on the fireplace, like she had to be getting on, and I didn't know what to say to her, even though I have lots I want to say. I couldn't think of anything. I thought of it all after she'd gone. I told her about Half Bike, though, and she said be careful on the roads.'

Nick tried to imagine his mum like a guest in the lounge, unable to potter in the kitchen and instead sitting on the sofa with her knees together and her bag on the floor like his Auntie Margaret when she visited. He couldn't imagine it, not at all, and even the thought was enough to make him feel sad.

'What did your dad say?' Alex sounded concerned, as if the fight he hadn't witnessed was the worry for him.

'Not much. He stayed in the kitchen, staring out the back window. When I got in he told me to go in the lounge, but he didn't look at me, just stood there. So I went in and there was my mum. And when she'd gone I went back into the kitchen and he was in the same spot. Hadn't moved.'

'What did your mum say?' Alex whispered.

Eric took his time responding. 'She asked me to go to Derby to go and stay with her and Dave the Milk, although he's not on the milk round any more; he's working as a delivery driver, so I guess we should just call him Dave.'

Nick and Alex nodded; this made sense.

'Does she want you to go and stay for the rest of the holiday?' Nick couldn't hide his note of disapproval, selfishly aware that it was when the three of them were together that they had the most fun. One of them rode Half Bike while the other two ran to catch up, or they chatted as they idled their way to the rendezvous point. If there were only two of them, then it would mean one of them on Half Bike and one running to catch up alone. No fun at all.

Eric shook his head. 'No, she means go and *stay* with her. Go for good. Move there.'

Nick's stomach flipped with unease and he stared at Eric, trying to process this concept. 'Move there?'

'Yep. And go to a new school – there's one not far from where they live now.'

'A new school,' Nick repeated, trying to picture walking into Burstonbridge Middle School and sitting in a classroom with an Eric Pickard-shaped hole in it. 'You'd have to get new mates.'

'Yep. I suppose so.' Eric kept his eyes on the floor. 'So would you,' he countered.

'Well, no, cos I'd still have Alex.'

Alex nodded from the floor at this indisputable fact. 'What did your dad say about you going to Derby?'

Eric looked at him. 'He said nothing while she was there, but when she'd gone he said it was up to me, but he'd rather I stayed in Burston with him.' He swallowed.

'So what are you going to do?' Nick wanted to be put out of his agony.

Eric shrugged in the way he did. 'I don't know. My mum said if I went to stay with her and Dave the . . . just Dave, then they'd get me a Sega Mega Drive and a *Sonic the Hedgehog* game for it and she said I could have it in my room so I could play it whenever I wanted.'

Nick silently cursed Eric's mum. This was a very tempting offer.

'Well, you'd have to give up your half of the half of Half Bike,' he stated.

'Do I get his half of a half?' Alex asked excitedly.

'Yep.' Nick spoke clearly, wanting in some way to punish his best friend, who he felt was abandoning him. His stance was confident, hoping his tone might belie the utter desolation he felt at the prospect of Eric leaving Burstonbridge – unable to imagine a life at school, at home – anywhere, in fact, without his lanky mate close by. 'Or we could let someone else have his share.' He addressed Alex directly.

'Like who?' Eric asked indignantly.

'I don't know.' Nick mentally scanned all the boys in his class. 'Someone like Will Pearce . . .'

'Will Pearce?' Eric snorted. 'Don't be ridiculous! He's a wimp! He wet himself in nursery – you'd have to put a plastic bag on't seat every time he rode it in case he did it again.'

'So? What would you care? You'd be in Derby. Which I've heard is rubbish!' Nick hated the wobble to his voice.

'How do you know it's rubbish? You don't even know where it is!' Eric retorted.

'So!'

'So!' Eric stood opposite his mate and the two stared at each other with chests barrelled, two little boys imitating the men they would become, trying to contain the swirl of emotions that fought for control. Nick felt the inexplicable urge to cry and screwed his face up to defeat the tears.

It was Alex who broke the silence. 'I don't think Will's wet himself for a while now. He goes to football with my next-door neighbour and he has never said that he's seen Will wet himself on the pitch. And I think he would have told me. I mean, that's something people would definitely talk about.'

Nick started to laugh.

'Listen to yourself, Marjorie!' Eric chortled, and laughter provided the balm to soothe the stinging cut of hurt left by his revelation, the news that he might be leaving.

'What shall we do now?' Nick asked, wanting to do anything other than stay in the garage and feel this way, staring at the walls, where Eric's words bounced around like cluster bombs, ready to explode the world, as they knew it, wide open.

'We could go and see if your mum's got any breakfast?' Eric suggested.

The boys tried to put the impending loss of Eric to Derby, wherever that might be, to the back of their minds. But it wasn't easy. Even taking turns to hurtle down Cobb Lane on Half Bike lost some of its magic, with Nick aware of the fact that they were on a countdown; this might be the hundredth last time they did this as a trio, the ninety-ninth, the ninety-eighth . . .

Eric climbed into the makeshift bed on the floor of Nick's bedroom and Nick settled into his bed, pulling his duvet up over his shoulders. The end of August was fast approaching and the weather had taken a bit of a downturn. It was a little too chilly to sit in the paddling pool and his mum had tipped the murky water over her flowerbed. The pool itself had been upended and now rested on its sagging rim against the side of the shed, trying to dry out before it got deflated and stuffed back inside the cardboard box in which it hibernated during the winter months. Nick found the dark, damp circle on the lawn where the grass had all but disappeared quite depressing. A reminder that once they went back to school, this was all that would remain, a fading circle of summer that had at its high point been absolutely brilliant.

Nick clicked off the bedside lamp. It was easier to talk in the dark.

'You reckon you'll go to Derby, then?'

'I suppose so.'

'Do you think you'll get a new best friend?' he asked quietly, his fingers coiled beneath the cover.

Eric sighed. 'I don't think you can plan things like best friends. I think they just happen; you start off with an okay friend and they turn out to be a best one.'

Nick nodded, despite the darkness; yes, this was kind of how it had happened with them.

'Half Bike has been the best thing this summer, hasn't it, Eric?'

His friend took his time in replying. 'Half Bike has been ace, but I think the best thing has been staying at your house.'

'Really?' Nick was surprised, knowing the situation would not have occurred had his mum not gone off with Dave the . . . just Dave.

'Yep. I like it here. Your house is always warm and your mum always cooks your tea and gets you breakfast. It's nice.'

Nick considered for the first time that this might not be the case in Eric's house and he wondered what it would be like for his mate in Derby if his dad weren't there to make things better.

'I saw a film once about these two boys who were best friends—'.

'Like us,' Nick interrupted.

'Yes, like us, and they became blood brothers.'

'What's blood brothers?'

Eric sat up. 'It's where you both make a cut on your finger or your thumb and you push the cuts together so you get each other's blood and then, even if you're separated, you're still brothers, because you have each other's blood.'

Both boys let the idea permeate and the air crackled with anticipation.

'Do you think we should do that, then?' Nick tried to make it sound casual.

'We could!' Eric jumped up and switched on the overhead light.

'Do you know how to do it?'

'How hard can it be? You just make the cuts and hold them together.' Eric spoke with enthusiasm and Nick felt the first quiver of nausea at the thought of having to deliberately cut himself.

'Does it hurt?'

'I don't know!' Eric laughed. 'I've never done it, but it only needs to be a little pinprick, just a little dot of blood.'

'Okay.' Nick felt a little relieved. 'Ooh, I know.' He reached into the drawer of the bedside cabinet and pulled out the multi-tool. There was a little edge, a small, sharp, almost invisible curl of steel on the rim of one of the spanner holes that when it snagged his skin caused a small prick of blood to appear. 'We can use this!'

The boys knelt on the floor and Eric went first, putting his index finger into the spanner hole and dragging it over the raised edge.

'Ouch!' He pulled his finger out of the hole and, with a look of determination, squeezed at the base of his finger until a shiny scarlet bauble of blood formed on the pad of his finger. 'Your turn.'

Nick lifted the multi-tool and felt the room sway a little.

'You all right?' Eric stared at him. 'You've gone a funny colour.'

Nick exhaled, trying to focus on the tool in his hand. 'Yeah, I just . . .' He didn't manage to finish the sentence, as he vomited. The action bent him double.

Eric yelled and ran to the door, smearing the white paintwork with his blood in the process. 'Mrs Bairstow! Nick's being sick! In his bed!' he shouted down the stairs.

Nick lay on the floor with his head on Eric's pillow. The room spun and he felt clammy. He heard his mum's footsteps coming up the stairs.

'Nicky! What on earth! You poor love, is it something you ate, do you think?'

'I think it was the thought of the blood,' Eric added unhelpfully.

'What blood? What?' His mum bent down and ran her hand over his sticky forehead.

'We were going to be blood brothers and I cut my finger and he was about to cut his when he threw up.'

It was then that Nick heard the laughter from the landing as Jen made her presence known. 'Oh my God, you absolute dweebs!' she chuckled, before retiring to her room. Nick got the feeling that this would not be the last time she mentioned his wimpy shame.

EIGHT

Nick stepped into his steel-toe-capped boots and pulled on his high-vis jacket. Going back to work after a few days off was never easy, but never harder than when his mind was on other things, namely Oliver, who, when he did deign to answer the texts Nick sent, did so with one-word, curt responses. Although, in truth, Nick was just happy he was answering. He was also more than a little nervous about having to endure the winks and comments from the workforce; he was in no doubt all knew that he had snogged Beverly in the loo on New Year's Eve. He cringed to think of conversations where he was the topic. It had been hard enough knowing they were talking about him when he lost Kerry, but this? He wished the gossip could have been something a little more dignified, the circumstances not quite so bloody awful.

And as for Beverly, she hadn't answered his texts even with one-word answers – nothing. He knew that this relationship, not that it was ever such a thing, had foundered before it had even begun. He felt saddened by the thought, but if ever he would accept his phone calls, at least he could tell Oliver with certainty that he really did have nothing to worry about. No one else was about to take up position in his mum's kitchen any time soon.

Shame, though . . .

He heard Kerry's voice for the first time in a long while and smiled.

'Yep. Shame.' He parked the car and ran to catch up with Eric, who had cycled in and now dismounted, steering his mountain bike towards the factory gates.

'I hate my job,' Eric sighed, his whole demeanour downcast.

'No, you don't; you just hate going back to work, and we all feel like that.'

'Just let me moan, will you?'

Nick laughed. 'Sure, the floor's all yours.'

Eric stopped walking and, with his hand on the saddle of his bike, stared up at the large white side of the Siddley factory. 'Do you ever wonder if this is it? If coming here to this bloody place every day is the sum total of our lives?'

'No, because I *know* that this is it.'

I thought I might have more, thought I would go to university, but then I thought I'd do the right thing, was happy to do the right thing, marry my girl, become a dad . . . and then I thought things would work out and that an opportunity would present itself for me to better this life . . . I thought a lot of things. But now the one thing I do know is that I didn't know jack shit . . .

Eric looked at his mate. 'I keep thinking about my dad, about your dad, and the hours they gave to this place. Born in Burston to mining families who couldn't mine any more or farming families who never owned the land they worked and us, relegated to bloody Siddley's; packing up and shipping off lights so that people with more money than us can attend events, have parties, drinking champagne, no doubt, and eating them canopies, or whatever they are called.'

Nick chose not to point out that you didn't need to be a champagne drinker to shove up a set of fairy lights; at least this much he knew. Again he thought of Oliver. He didn't interrupt his friend, seeing his need to get whatever ailed him off his chest, and hoping that by doing so his mood might improve; otherwise, it was going to be a very long day for both of them.

'I could stand it, you know. I could stand it all – the shit wages, no prospects, crap weather, all of it – I wouldn't notice all the bad stuff if I had someone like Jen to come home to.'

Nick felt the familiar stab of responsibility: his best mate and his sister . . . He had always felt like he should be the conduit, the link that might bring these two together, but what could he do if Jen just wasn't interested?

'As I've told you before, she has her faults. She's messy and she can't cook and she's so competitive.' He laughed. 'And being in a relationship with a serving police officer is no picnic. There's the shifts, the unsociable hours, the dangerous job – for which I think she might carry a multi-tool.' He tried, as he often did, to defuse the moment with humour.

'No, Nick! This isn't funny. None of it is funny any more.'

Nick stopped laughing. It was rare to hear Eric so serious, and it unnerved him.

'I've tried everything over the years, you know I have; I've been patient, attentive, direct. I've bought her gifts, praised her, followed her! I'd have gone to the ends of the Earth just for a chance.'

Nick knew all of this to be true.

'But I'm done.' Eric kicked the wheel of his bike. 'I can't do it any more. It's time I pulled my head out of the clouds and faced facts.'

Nick chose not to comment that it had taken his friend the best part of two decades to face these facts. He felt the stirring of relief, knowing Eric deserved someone nice, and knowing how much he had loved being part of a couple with Kerry, despite the rows and the moments when he felt like he was walking on a cliff edge. Eric was right: it made all the bad stuff worth it when you had someone you loved to come home to. He pictured the empty lounge and cold kitchen where warmth used to live, where Oliver's music used to shake the floorboards and Kerry's singing would drive him to distraction, and he felt a bolt of longing fire right through him. Life had been a rollercoaster, often a worry and sometimes a chore, but he had never felt lonely and that, he knew, had made all the difference. The house had been a home.

Eric wasn't done. 'There comes a point when you realise that you have been banging your head on a locked door, thinking of how wonderful it'll be when it eventually opens, thinking about all the treasures that might lie inside, but I now realise that it's never going to open and I've got a bloody headache.' He rubbed his temples, suggesting his words weren't only metaphorical. 'As I say, I'm done.'

'Well, for what it's worth' – Nick looked his lanky friend in the eye – 'I think it's Jen's loss. I always have.'

'Thanks, mate,' Eric answered with a hardened edge to his voice. There was no funny quip, no smile, and Nick missed the humour that had peppered their chats for as long as he could remember, realising that it might just be true: the man who had always said it was a waiting game and that he was prepared to wait for as long as it took . . . was not prepared to wait any longer.

'It'll all be okay.'

'It will.' Eric nodded. 'Because I'm going to make it all okay.'

'Good for you!' Nick liked his spirit.

'I thought about it a lot over Christmas, and I told you I was thinking of spreading my wings, getting some sunshine. I'm going to make a plan, change things. I'm not going to waste another year hanging around Burston and working hard so that Julian Siddley can upgrade his Range Rover while I ride a bloody bike!'

'It's a good idea. A holiday will reset you. Where are you thinking?'

'I'm thinking Australia.' And then he smiled, his expression back to the one Nick knew.

'*Australia?* Flippin' 'eck! That'll be some holiday!'

Eric shook his head. 'Not a holiday – I've applied for a six-month visa and I'm going to go and work in the sunshine, where I might meet twenty women, all nicer to me than Jen has ever been, and I won't have to drive a shitty forklift truck in this shitty factory. And after six months, I'll try to figure out a way to make it permanent.'

Nick stared at him and felt his stomach drop. He didn't know what to say, but the prospect of his oldest friend being on the other side of the world was almost inconceivable. Eric was one of the fixtures in his life, always had been. Oliver's words came to him now and he clamped his lips together so as not to let them escape.

I'm . . . I'm not ready . . . I'm not ready for you to move on like that . . . He remembered standing in the garage that summer as kids when Eric had announced he was going to stay with his mum in Derby; this felt the same, like he wanted to punch something or shout out that he did not want him to leave. Of course he did neither, and now he stared at his mate.

Australia . . .

'Mr Siddley wants to see you in his office, Nick.'

As he tried to summon a response, Nick turned to see Beverly walk past, her head held high, a little aloof, having issued the statement in a neutral fashion.

'Oh dear.' Eric sighed.

'Yep,' Nick could only agree. 'Oh dear. I'll see you later?'

'Course you will, Doreen. I'm not going today, am I?'

Nick placed his lunchbox and keys in his locker and made his way to the big office, where his boss spent in his days sitting in the red leather captain's chair. He combed his hair with his fingers before knocking and entering to find Beverly standing by the desk. He was a little taken aback. It felt strange to see her in this environment when their last proper encounter had been so very different. He felt his pulse quicken at the memory. He wished she had answered his texts, thus avoiding this awkward reunion that brought their personal life into the workplace.

'Julian wanted to see me?' He wished he had coughed and made his voice deeper. Nerves gave his words a slight warble.

'No, *I* wanted to see you, but didn't want to say so in front of your blabbermouth mate. I figure there's enough people discussing my business right now.'

'Where's Julian?' He looked around the office as if he might be hiding.

'Not here, and will you just forget about him for a second!' She raised her voice. 'I want to talk to you.'

'Oh.' He felt the bite of nerves. 'I tried to call you and I texted—'

She cut him short. 'Yes, yes, I know you did, but we are not kids, Nick. I didn't want a text chat or a late-night phone call. I wanted you to come and knock on my door and sit and talk to me like a grown-up. Face-to-face, a confident man who knows what he wants.'

'I thought about it, but wasn't sure if you wanted me to come to your house or . . .' He ran out of ideas.

She shook her head dismissively. 'You were very rude to me and I didn't like it.' She bit her lip. 'I didn't like it one bit.'

'I know, I'm sorry. But when you pitched up at the house, it was the worst possible timing—'

'Not *just* then!' she interrupted. 'On New Year's Eve you just pulled away and ran – literally ran – out of my house without so much as a goodbye or a wave. Like I didn't count. Like it was no big deal. I stood there like an idiot and I felt so small. It wasn't only you who felt exposed that night, Nick. You were selfish and you made me look like a fool, and I don't like it. I've guarded my reputation carefully over the years. I'm not that kind of woman.'

This he knew; there was not a sniff of scandal or a whisper of gossip about her. She was seen as solid, dependable, smart and kind, *a good lass* . . .

'I don't let people get that close to me, Nick. I don't like people generally, I'm picky, but I took a risk on you and you made me feel stupid.'

'I never wanted to do that.'

'Well, y'did!'

He took a step toward her, imagining for the first time what it might have been like for her and feeling embarrassed that it hadn't properly occurred to him before.

She was right – selfish. Bloody selfish.

The two stood enveloped in strained silence for a beat or two, until the atmosphere calmed and Beverly spoke.

'There's something about you. I feel . . .' It was apparently her turn to run out of words.

'Connected?' The word suddenly came easily.

'Yes.' She nodded, quite sternly. 'I feel connected to you.'

'I feel connected to you too,' he said softly.

'And that's all well and good, but I think your situation might be too complicated for me. It might be that I want more than you can give me and that's not your fault, it's just how it is.'

He felt the second punch to his gut of the day, first at the thought of Eric leaving and now the fact that he and Beverly had seemingly failed before they had even started, and it was only at the very real prospect of this chance slipping through his fingers that he realised he wanted to hold it tight.

'I see.' He put his hands on his hips and glanced at the clock on the wall, thinking about the start of his shift and putting on a hardened air. Hiding his disappointment, he shifted into self-preservation mode.

'No, you don't see.' She took a deep breath and he pushed his toes against the tip of his boots, steeling himself for what else she might have to say. 'I don't regret what happened on New Year's Eve, apart from how it ended – I do regret that, but not the first bit. In fact, I kind of planned it. I thought long and hard about how I could move things forward. It was all I could think about and it was . . . lovely.'

He smiled at her now, because she spoke the truth: it *was* lovely.

'I didn't know Kerry that well, and I don't know Oliver at all and so they felt like nothing to do with me.' She spoke with typical candour. 'I thought I could just have feelings for you and hoped you might have feelings for me and we could see where it went – naïve, really. I can see now that it's a whole lot more involved than that. You have a position in the town as someone who is grieving, your family lurks around every corner, and your boy has lost his mum.' She took a breath. 'I remember you saying that it felt like there were a million rules that you didn't know about and so you went around inadvertently breaking them – and I guess I now know exactly what you mean.' She gazed at him. 'I don't *know* what's appropriate and I don't understand the boundaries I should be observing – maybe I need to read one of them books about the right timing of everything too – but I do know it's not as simple as snogging you and hoping it all works out.'

'I wish it were that simple,' he admitted.

She nodded.

'So what do we do now?' He asked the genuine question, hoping she had the answers.

'Morning!' Julian Siddley marched into the room with a big grin, a bounce in his step and the glow of a man who had spent the holidays somewhere the sun shone. Nick and Beverly both stood tall, trying to make their stances more officious. Nick hated how the man asserted himself in the space; making it clear they were in his office and whether they were mid-conversation or whatever else was of little regard to him.

'Happy New Year!'

'Happy New Year, Julian.' Nick nodded at him.

'How's you, Beverly? Good Christmas?'

'As good as can be expected,' she offered curtly, glancing briefly at Nick and gathering up some papers from the desk.

'I'd better get on.' Nick coughed and turned to leave the room.

'Oh, Nick, while you're here . . .'

'Yes, Julian?' he asked, as the man sank down into the red leather chair behind the desk.

'I know you've got a lot on, but the lock on the men's bathroom door is playing up.'

Nick was about to suggest he get Carl from Maintenance to have a look at it when Julian looked from him to Beverly.

'And you know how much trouble it can cause when doors get flung open in toilets at inopportune moments!'

'Very funny.' Nick felt his face flush and ground his teeth in anger and embarrassment, as Beverly covered hers with a file. 'Very funny,' he reiterated, leaving the room with the echo of Julian Siddley's laughter bouncing off the walls.

◆ ◆ ◆

It had been over a week of little or no contact from Oliver, and Nick had decided enough was enough. No matter that his son was going through a tough time, he was still his dad and Oliver's behaviour was, frankly, rude. He sat back on the sofa with Treacle by his side, resting her muzzle on his leg and snoring gently and regally like the duchess she was.

To his surprise and delight, the call was answered quickly.

'Olly!' He beamed, taking the speed of response as an olive branch at the very least.

'No, sorry, Mr Bairstow, it's only me, Tasha.'

'Call me Nick, love.'

'Okay, Nick.' He could tell she was smiling.

'Is Olly there?' Nick figured it likely, as his son was never more than inches from his phone.

'Erm . . .' He heard her breathing. 'He is, but he said he didn't want to answer the call and I picked up the phone to hand it to him and answered it by accident.'

He liked her honesty and rubbed his eyes at the absurdity of the situation.

'Well, that's fine, tell Oliver he doesn't have to talk to me.'

'Your dad says you don't have to talk to him.' She took the request literally and relayed the words.

He heard Olly shout, 'Good!' And the childishness in his voice made him smile.

'No, that's absolutely fine, Tasha. I'll talk to you instead.'

'Okay,' she answered cautiously.

'Can you ask Olly if he remembers our first caravan holiday in Blackpool?'

'Your dad says, do you remember your first caravan holiday in Blackpool?'

Nick sat back on the sofa and heard a kerfuffle before Oliver grabbed the phone and spoke: 'Not funny!'

'Oh, Olly, please put Tasha back on – I was just getting to the bit where you were too scared to get up and go to the loo in the middle of the night and so weed in your cowboy hat and tried to hide it under the table!'

'I was a little kid!'

'Yes.' He paused. 'And to me you still are, and so forgive me if I don't always know how to handle things, how to treat you. Your mum used to steer me on stuff like this and I'm honestly trying to figure it all out as I go along, flying by the seat of my pants, as they say.'

'So I noticed.'

'You can't ignore me, Olly. It's not fair and it's not healthy. I need to know you're okay and I need our communication. That's all I've got . . .' He paused. 'I made a promise and that was to make sure you were okay, and I can't do that if you don't talk to me.'

'I guess.' He spoke quietly, with a suggestion of relief that pleased Nick. He couldn't stand the idea of them not talking and Oliver being fine with it, knowing that was a path to a whole other place, one he didn't want to visit, where words like 'estranged' and 'alienated' were commonplace. The thought was more than he could stand.

'Good.' Nick beamed. 'I mean, it would be terrible if I had to jump in the car and come to Birmingham with photos of you actually in the cowboy hat.'

'You wouldn't dare!' Oliver fired.

'Try me . . .'

◆　◆　◆

Nick put the lead on Treacle and closed the front door. The sky was indigo, clear, and the bare spikes of trees stood dramatically against the backdrop like cut-out props. The moon was big and bright and he felt a flare of optimism for whatever came next. Oliver had softened towards him a little, and knowing his son was all right made everything feel good in his world. He remembered Eric's words earlier and his optimism faded as he tried to imagine life in Burston without his mate. Eric had always been around the corner, in the background, only a stroll or a phone call away, and the thought of it being any different . . .

'I reckon he's bluffing, Treacle, what do you think?' Treacle ignored him, sniffing at the base of a wall, where a dog had recently peed.

Nick let himself into his mum's house. 'Only me! And Treacle.'

At the mention of the pup his mum let out a wail of delight.

'Aaah, Nanny has missed her little doggy today!' She rushed into the hallway and dropped to her knees to pet the dog, who closed her eyes in a state of bliss as his mum ruffled her fur. He noted how in Oliver's absence she seemed to have transferred the affection and attention she usually lavished on him to the dog. 'We're just having tea; do you want some? Baked ham and mashed potato? There's plenty.'

Of course there is.

No matter that his dad had passed away and Nick had lived away from home longer than he had ever lived *at* home, his mum still cooked for a family of four.

'No, but thanks, Mum. I had a sandwich when I got in.'

'And a sandwich for your lunch, I don't mind betting. You can't be eating sandwiches all day, Nicky! You're a working man! Good Lord, let me drop you off a casserole tomorrow and then I won't worry.' She bustled back to the kitchen, where Jen sat with a plate piled high, tucking in, her vast appetite and love of stodge belied by her athletic frame.

'I don't know where you put it,' he commented as he flicked on the kettle.

'I know where you do!' Jen spoke with her mouth full, patting her own flat tum. Nick breathed in, conscious, as ever, of his slight paunch. 'Anyway, I'm on a late shift; that's why I'm rushing.'

'That explains the speed, but not the volume,' he quipped.

'Sod off, Nick.'

'Language, please!' his mum yelled.

'Anyway, I thought you and Eric were going to get fit? I seem to remember him telling me that was your New Year's resolution.'

'It's always our New Year's resolution, and I'm working on it, but it looks like I might be getting fit on my own; have you heard Eric's news?'

Jen rolled her eyes. 'What news? Has he finally taken the stabilisers off his bike? Or found the *Wolverine* Blu Ray DVD he thought had been taken by a poltergeist, or managed to go through the night without wetting the bed?' She laughed at her own ridiculous suggestions, demonstrating her low opinion of the man whose friendship he treasured.

'Actually, no.' He paused, finding it hard to not lay the blame for his friend leaving at her door in some small way. 'He's leaving Burston. Going away.'

He watched the smile fade a little from her face and she struggled to swallow her mouthful of food. 'Going away? Where?' This too she asked with the suggestion of a laugh, as if it were unthinkable that lanky Eric might go anywhere.

'Australia.'

He watched the colour drain from her cheeks and she placed her fork on her plate.

'Australia?' Her eyes narrowed in disbelief, as if waiting for the punchline, and she looked at the food on her plate with something close to revulsion.

'Yes. He's applied for a visa, wants to work for six months and then, when he's there, he's going to try to find a way to make it permanent. That's what he said.'

'Shit.' Jen stared at him.

'Yes, shit.' He echoed the sentiment.

'I can't imagine . . .' his sister began, speaking slowly.

'Can't imagine what?' he asked.

Jen shrugged. 'Don't know, just can't imagine him not here. Can't imagine him anywhere else.'

'Yes, you'll have to find someone else to take the mick out of.' His tone was sharp.

'You don't know anything, Nick! Absolutely nothing!'

'Funny, I was only thinking the same myself quite recently.'

'I mean about me and Eric,' she clarified.

'There is no you and Eric! One weekend away doesn't constitute a relationship of any importance.'

He looked up and was aghast to see what looked like the bloom of tears in his sister's eyes, although it was a bit late for guilt now; her ribbing of him had been predictable and consistent.

His mum sighed. 'Australia is a very long way away.'

'It is that, Mum,' he acknowledged. 'A very long way away.'

'Do you want jam roly-poly, Jen?'

Jen shook her head. Apparently the news had dented her appetite.

Nick finished his cup of tea and Jen stood quietly and got ready to leave for work.

'See you, Jen.'

He watched as she raised her hand in a brief wave – most unlike her not to fire a verbal barb in his direction while she had the chance.

'So, have you heard from Olly?' His mum tried to keep her tone casual while she washed up the dinner plates.

'Yes. We spoke briefly. It's a start.'

'Give him time.'

He nodded, knowing there was little point in asking her how much time did she think, the woman who still cooked for a dead husband and a largely absent son.

'I spoke to Dora – we met for a coffee in the Morrisons café.' She paused, indicating that what might follow had significance. He cringed at the idea of the collaboration and stared at her, waiting to see what opinion/advice/idea or judgement his mother and mother-in-law had come up with that might improve his life or help him out.

'She asked me if it was serious and I said I didn't reckon it was because, if it was, you would have told me about her, that Beverly. She seemed to know a lot more than I did, said you'd asked her advice.'

'Hardly advice, but we did mention it, yes.' He hated that he had to justify himself to his mum too. Suddenly the thought of living in Australia, away from Burston and everyone in it, didn't seem such a ridiculous idea. 'Well, I'm a big boy now, Mum, and believe it or not I can have a friend without your approval or inviting them over to tea. And "that Beverly" and I are friends, and that's all there is to report right now.'

'Well, you seem a bit tetchy over something that means so little.'

'I didn't say that.'

'No, you didn't. And I might be an interfering old bag, but I know you, Nicky, and I can always tell how you're feeling.'

'Can you tell that I'm feeling mightily pissed off by you sticking your nose in?' he offered with a smile, softening the pointed message with humour.

'I can, actually, and can you tell that I couldn't give a fig and will continue to stick my nose in so long as there is breath in my body?'

'I can' – *touché* – 'and on that note, I will continue on my walk with Treacle.'

◆ ◆ ◆

Nick hadn't planned the route, not at a conscious level, but the earlier conversation with Beverly sat at the fore of his mind, now that worrying about Oliver had been relegated to second place. He walked over the cobbles of Market Square, past the war memorial, and turned into Appledore. It was quiet, difficult now to imagine the street where revellers had gathered, dancing in and out of the narrow cottage with paper streamers around their necks and the flash of disco lights in the front room. Nick took a deep breath and looked down at Treacle, who looked up at him. 'Don't look at me like that; I'm thinking.'

He was aware that to cross the threshold in a sober state, to walk into her home armed with the knowledge that they shared a connection was a big step; it spoke of his intentions, his desire that they might be something more than friends. It was the kind of grown-up face-to-face interaction that someone who knew what he wanted might have. And he felt petrified.

He walked casually towards the front door, thinking that if he lost his confidence he could walk straight past and go around the block and no one would be any wiser. But he didn't lose his confidence. Instead, powerfully drawn by the light that shone from the hallway, he pulled back his shoulders, sucked in his stomach and rang the doorbell.

'Oh, hello, cutie!'

'Nick'll do,' he quipped as Beverly sighed despite her smile and dropped down to greet Treacle.

'Coffee or tea?' she asked, walking back down the hallway towards the kitchen, which was surprisingly spacious without people filling it wall to wall and the likes of Mikey Sturridge, the man mountain, lumbering through the place. Nick kept his eyes averted from the downstairs bathroom door, not wanting Oliver's distressed face to hijack the moment. He liked the way she hadn't asked if he would like a drink or did he want to come in; it was assumed, direct in the way he had come to expect from her, and it reassured him that he had done the right thing in stopping by.

'Tea, please. Is it okay to bring Treacle in?'

'Depends.' She held his eye. 'Is she going to stay here comfortably in a relaxed way, happy to be here with me, or is she going to leg it if someone knocks on the door or get spooked by anyone walking past the window?'

Treacle lay on the floor with her head on her paws, already in a semi-dozing state. 'I think she's happy to be here with you.'

'Well, all right, then.' She reached for the tea bags and made the tea, smiling at him over her shoulder.

◆ ◆ ◆

Nick was awake a tad before the alarm roused him and he woke with a smile on his face. He whistled as he showered, and upon the discovery that he had run out of milk simply settled on toast instead of cereal. It seemed that nothing could dampen his mood. He felt excited with the stir of something a lot like happiness in his gut. He tried to remember the last time he had felt this way and realised it was when he started courting Kerry and suddenly getting up in the rain to walk to school for another day of monotonous instruction didn't seem too bad, not when he got to see Kerry, be with Kerry, stand next to Kerry, share lunch with Kerry . . .

He and Beverly had kissed goodbye after their cup of tea – not the frenzied, booze-fuelled, clothes-tugging, skin-mauling make-out that had occurred on New Year's. No, this was something more sedate, con-sidered, and in truth it had lit this flame of happiness that warmed him.

He parked the car and saw Eric dismount from his bike. He tried to imagine arriving for work and not seeing his friend ahead of him on his bike. It was unthinkable. Nick walked alongside him.

'Morning, lad.'

'Morning.' Eric eyed him suspiciously. 'You're full of beans this morning.'

'Something like that.' He decided not to elaborate; it was one thing not to hide away, but quite another to set the wheels of gossip in motion before he absolutely had to. Plus, he was still unsure of what to say to Oliver, and when. *Timing* . . . 'I told Jen you were thinking of going to Australia last night and she—'

Eric held up his hand. 'Do you know what, mate?' He looked into the middle distance and spoke sincerely. 'I don't want to talk about her, not any more. Okay?'

'Okay. But I just wanted to ask you one thing.'

'What?'

'What happened when you and Jen had that weekend away? It felt like there was a possibility of something more, and then it seemed to . . .' He shrugged, unsure of how to phrase it.

Eric took a deep breath. 'Short story.' He licked his lips. 'I told her I loved her and she burst into tears before running out of the room and coming home. That's it.'

'That's it?'

'Yep. That's it.'

'I see,' he said, even though he didn't, not really.

'But as I say, mate, I don't want to talk about Jen.'

The two walked on in silence and Nick tried to think of a time when his sister had not been the first choice in topic of conversation for his friend. He couldn't. 'Are you still seriously thinking about going?' he asked as they made their way across the yard and into the warehouse.

'Did you not think I was serious?' Eric asked, again with his new air of solemnity, which was more than a little unnerving. Nick watched him park his bike and lock it.

'No, I did think you were serious.' He took his time forming his answer. 'I guess I just hoped you weren't.' It was as close as he could get to telling his friend just how much he would miss him and how he feared a little for a life in Burston without Eric Pickard in it.

'Good, because my visa application is in and I've ordered a book off the Internet – a guide to living and working in Australia.'

'Oh, well, if you've ordered a book.' Nick thumped him playfully on the arm.

'I know you think it's a big joke. I know everyone will, but that just makes me more determined to get on that bloody plane. I'm sick of everyone laughing at me or about me . . .' He zipped up his fleecy top. 'I'm bloody sick of it.'

'Actually, Eric, most people, me included, laugh with you. You're a funny bastard.'

'Well, let's hope I get to be funny in Australia with the sun on my back and budgie smugglers under my work clothes so I can hit the beach after work.'

Nick wanted to laugh at the term 'budgie smugglers' but, aware now of Eric's sensitivity, didn't know if that would inflame the situation. Instead he bit the inside of his cheek and clocked on.

With the mad rush for Christmas and New Year's orders over, work was back to a steady, less hectic pace. Nick oversaw the loading of the lorries and organised the rota for the drivers for the coming month before taking the time sheets up to the office. He knocked on the door and felt a little coy, trying not to look over the desks to where Beverly sat, closest to Julian Siddley's office door. She was on the phone, but still he caught the way her face broke into a smile at the sight of him and it made him feel good that he could conjure this reaction. It might have been his imagination, but it seemed the other women in the office all paid him a little more attention, nodded at his arrival and smiled briefly if he caught their eye, as if they too might be in on the secret. It felt like approval, of sorts.

By lunchtime Nick was pleased to see that Eric's mood had mellowed. They sat at their usual table on the worn benches with the metal trestle legs beneath the strip light that flickered irritatingly with a group of lads from the shop floor who either tucked into sandwiches eaten from small plastic boxes or the meat-and-two-veg option that the canteen rustled up for a subsidised fee each day. Kath Watson and her team had an average age of seventy and had been running the canteen forever and ever. Their banter was warm, the atmosphere they created homey, but as for the cooking? As Eric had pointed out on more than one occasion, *MasterChef* wasn't going to be sending an application form their way any time soon.

'What *is* that?' Eric pointed at the brown sludge that filled Roy's plate.

'Stew.' He lifted his spoonful and paused briefly before taking a mouthful. His expression said it all and he immediately reached for the salt and pepper.

'It's what's been stewed that bothers me!' Eric chortled.

'So, come on, Nick.' Roy paused from his stew consumption and placed the spoon on the side of the plate. 'What's the deal with you and Bev?'

He felt his face colour and kicked his boots against the concrete floor, keeping his eyes trained on his corned beef and pickle between two slices of white.

'There is no deal.' He took a bite.

'No?' Roy continued. 'It's just that a little bird told me she'd seen you coming out of Bev's house last night. And it was dark, she couldn't be sure of the time, but said it was probably nearer bedtime than not.'

'Would that little bird happen to be your sister, Ellen – who lives three doors down?' Eric asked.

'Might have been.' Roy chuckled.

'Well, in that case it was a big bird!' Eric quipped. Roy and his sister both shared a rather solid frame.

Even Roy laughed at that.

'Stop changing the subject.' Roy pointed at Eric. 'Come on, Nick, you seem to be spending a bit of time with Beverly and I'm just asking what's happening.'

'There's nothing happening. Nothing.' He felt his leg jump beneath the table and wished the subject would change. It wasn't that he minded so much talking about it with the lads, despite his embarrassment, but he knew that these conversations were conveyor belts on to which words would hop and be carried right to the door of his sister-in-law and, ultimately, all the way to Birmingham University . . .

'So there's nothing happening?' Roy pressed.

Nick shook his head. 'Nope.'

'Well, in that case, you won't mind if I ask her out for a pie and a pint, will you? I've been thinking about it for a while, and as there's nothing happening with you two . . .'

Nick stared at Roy, holding his sandwich in mid-air, at a loss for words. 'I . . . I . . . I mean . . .' he stuttered.

It was Eric who laughed first, loudly, quickly followed by all the lads at the table. He sat back and watched as Eric reached over and high-fived Roy, who picked up the spoon and tucked into his stew.

'Your face!' Eric doubled over, pointing at his friend.

'He got you good,' one of the younger packers piped up.

Nick stood and grabbed his sandwich box. 'You're bastards, all of you . . .' He decided to take his lunch box to the car, where he could have five minutes' peace – that, and he hoped his puce face might calm in the cold. But he also knew it was time to think about the conversation he needed to have with Oliver, and he wasn't looking forward to it, not one bit. The car was chilly yet preferable. He finished his sandwich and his phone rang. It was Jen.

'What's up?' he asked without preamble; she only called him when something was wrong or something needed doing.

'Nothing!' she fired.

'Nice. That's just what I want on my lunch break, you calling up to yell at me. Can't I get a moment to myself?' He went quiet. Their silence was unusual in that the air between them crackled. He could hear her breathing, and she swallowed once. This was not the manner of the boisterous, aggressive older sister who had taunted, harassed, teased and loved him for as long as he could remember.

'You okay, Jen?' he asked, softer now.

'I . . . I don't know.'

'What do you mean, you don't know? Are you hurt? In danger?' He thought for the first time that it might be a good idea to roll out his code-red emergency drill to the whole family.

'No, nothing like that. I just keep thinking about what you said.' She paused.

'About what?'

'God, Nick! About Eric,' she spat.

Ah, there she is . . . 'What about him?'

'I guess . . . I guess I don't like the thought of him going away.'

He sat forward and rested his arms on the steering wheel. 'I would have thought you'd be having a party and popping champagne corks. You've been going on for years about how much he annoys you, and he'll finally be out of your hair.'

'Shows what you know.' Again that pause; seemingly it was a struggle for her to get the words out. 'I don't want him to go.'

'Why not?'

Her response, when it came, was whispered. 'Because . . . Because I love him.'

He didn't laugh. Didn't mock. Instead he sat back in the driver's seat and let her words permeate.

'You love him?' He knew it wasn't the time or place to point out that her behaviour towards Eric was not that of someone traditionally in love.

'Yep.' She sounded like she might be crying.

'So why have you never done anything about it?' He was curious.

'Because I'm just scary old Jen! Jen who can't join the boys' club that Dad created in our own bloody garage! I even asked once, and you just laughed at me. Jen who annoys everyone, Jen who becomes a police-woman just to show she's as good as any of the boys . . . I was always just a joke to you lot, and I know he would get fed up of me eventually and I couldn't stand to see that happen. It would hurt too much, Nick, so better to keep him close as my friend, like when we were kids. That routine I can keep up forever . . .'

'Jesus!' There was so much about her speech that bothered him he didn't know where to start. 'Dad was proud of you. You didn't let him down, don't forget. I did. He was so disappointed in me.'

'True, he was,' she offered, without humour. 'But he was wrong. You did the right thing by Kerry and that should have made him proud. But he was never proud of me. It was always about the Bairstow Boys, and therein lay the problem – I couldn't compete.'

'Jen, you can't let any issues you might have had with Dad affect your life with Eric.'

'God, I wish it were that simple!' She laughed dryly. 'I never feel like I'm good enough, never feel that anyone is going to want me, not in the long run, and I don't know how to be any different, and now he's going away.'

Nick closed his eyes and took a breath. Her timing could not have been worse.

'You need to tell him,' he offered gently. 'Tell him or you might regret it.'

'I don't know what to say to him.' She rounded the sentence with a small laugh, admitting that for a woman in her late thirties this was the most ridiculous state of affairs. 'As you can tell, I'm not very good at all this stuff. Colin used to say I was cold, hard, but I'm not really, only on the outside.'

It was a rare admission, and even rarer that she had mentioned her ex-husband.

'Well, he was a dickhead.'

'Correction, he is a dickhead.'

'Good point.' He smiled.

'I thought I had more time,' she began. 'Eric has always been there and I've never thought about him *not* being there until yesterday, when you said about Australia.'

'The thing is, Jen, you're my sister, and I hear what you're saying.' This was his way of telling her she was loved. 'But he's my best mate and I don't want him to be messed around. I don't want him to go, of course I don't, but I would hate you to get his hopes up or lead him on – he doesn't deserve that. So if you really feel like you say you do, say something, but if this is another Marvellous Montague moment . . .'

He could sense her smiling as he mentioned the snake she had begged for, cried for, stamped her feet over, until their dad had relented and presented her with a tank containing a small yellow python, which she instantly christened Marvellous Montague. It was a mere twenty minutes after being introduced that she came down the stairs screaming and declared how much she hated snakes. With his daughter near hysteria, her dad had had to take Marvellous Montague immediately back to the pet shop, where he was politely informed that there was no refund for a 'change of heart'.

Jen seemed to be considering this. 'I need to think about it, Nick. I know it's not fair to mess him around and I don't know if I have the courage to be that honest with him. I don't know if I could tell him how I feel. You're right.'

'Sorry, Jen, I didn't hear that, could you repeat it?'

'I said you're right!' she shouted.

'I thought so.' He smiled; it was rare she gave him any credence.
'Dickhead.' She ended the call.

◆ ◆ ◆

Nick lit a candle in the sitting room and sniffed at the odour of dust
that filled the room. It wasn't quite what he had been hoping for, but
he knew the candle had been sitting around for years, its scent long
faded. He blew it out immediately. Treacle, lying on the rug in front of
the fire, looked up at him.

'I know, I'm overthinking it. I'm nervous, Treacle, that's for sure.'

He looked at the picture on the mantelpiece of Kerry holding
Oliver when he was a newborn and felt the familiar tremor of uncer-
tainty through his veins. Truthfully, he knew he liked Beverly, but he
couldn't decide if it was worth this level of anxiety. As he pondered the
thought, the front doorbell rang. He closed his eyes, took a deep breath
and opened the front door.

'I bought wine,' Beverly announced as she walked in, handing him
the bottle.

'Smashing. I'll go and find some glasses.' He hoped he had two
that matched.

'Is something burning?' She sniffed the air at the unmistakable
residue of candle smoke as she shrugged her arms from her jacket and
hung it on the newel post.

'Don't think so.' He walked to the kitchen and opened the mug
cupboard, where four wineglasses sat on the top shelf. Matching, but
rather dusty. He ran them under the tap and dried them with the tea
towel.

'Ooh, you've washed up – not on my account, I hope.' She looked
at the empty sink.

'I did wash up on your account, actually. I also ran the Hoover
over.'

'Well, I never – special treatment. I'm honoured.' She took the glass of wine from his outstretched hand and the two went into the lounge. Beverly took up the spot in the corner of the sofa where his wife had sat night after night with a mug of tea in her hands and watched the soaps on television. It felt a little odd and he was glad Oliver wasn't there, this thought instantly followed by a jolt of guilt that this woman was sitting in Oliver's mum's seat and just how the boy might react.

Let it go, Nick! For God's sake, let it go!

'So, I hear the lads were teasing you yesterday at lunch?' She smiled over the rim of the wineglass.

'Flippin' 'eck, is nothing secret around here!'

'Welcome to Burston!' She raised her glass in a toast. He noticed the shape of her teeth against her bottom lip, painted with a pale pink colour, and the poker-straight hair around her face. She had gone to some effort and the thought that it might be for him made his gut jump with joy.

'I sometimes wish I could fly away, escape.' He took a sip.

'So why don't you?' she asked in a way that suggested it might be possible.

He gave a short burst of laughter. 'Money, family, commitment, finances, cowardice – take your pick.'

'It's funny, isn't it, how some people just have the courage, they go and do great things, different things, and then there's people like me who want to be near the pub where I'm comfortable, the shop where I know where everything is, my little house, my little job, it's enough.'

'I've always been the same. I say I'd like to leave Burston at times, but then I can't think of where I'd go that's better. I think I blew my chance of escape a long time ago. Besides, there's a lot to be said for staying close to home.'

'Is Oliver enjoying Birmingham?'

'Yes, seems to be. He had a wobble when he first got there, felt a bit overwhelmed, but he has a nice girlfriend – well, I've only met her once, but she seems nice and he's smitten. Tasha her name is.'

'I don't want to keep bringing it up, but that was terrible on New Year's Eve, not the snogging bit, as we've already ascertained.' She sipped her wine. 'But the bit that came after. I felt for you and Oliver, and I was *mortified*.'

'I know.' He flexed his toes inside his socks, a little embarrassed whilst at the same time his chest boomed with the compliment that the snogging had been quite nice . . . 'It's hard to see things from his perspective sometimes. And it's hard to know what he needs. He's at that horrible half-man/half-child stage and I often feel like I'm treading on eggshells.'

Beverly nodded. 'I suppose what he needs is to know that his dad is at the end of a phone if he needs him and that you aren't going to disappear like his mum did.'

He found the ease with which she spoke about Kerry as reassuring as it was alarming.

'He needs to know that you're the kind of man who is going to stay close to home, and I get it.' She took another sip. 'I always took great comfort from knowing my dad was at home and wasn't about to go gallivanting off. No matter where I was or what I was getting up to, the thought of my dad at home, giving me a base, a safe haven should I need it, meant the world.'

'Talking of gallivanting – and please keep this to yourself – but Eric is thinking of getting away, going to Australia.'

'Australia? What, for a holiday?'

'No, for good, to work. At least, that's what he says.'

'God, I can't imagine that. I always think of him as part of the furniture.' She held the wineglass on her lap.

'And I think that's the problem. He's sick of being taken for granted.'

'Do you think it's anything to do with Jen?' she asked, without any hint of the self-consciousness some might have felt when discussing his sister in this way.

'I think it's a whole lot to do with her. He's finally given up, and I don't blame him. But the irony is, I think she might actually have feelings for him.'

'Jeez, she hides it well!'

'She's a complicated character, and I don't know if I know her as well as I should.' He thought about their conversation. 'I think a lot of her spikiness is a defence against getting hurt.'

'Like a hedgehog?'

'Yes, something like that. A Monopoly-playing hedgehog.' They both laughed.

'Eric's a good sort.' She smiled and sat back in the chair, relaxed, and this was infectious. He felt his bones soften and his breathing calm.

'He is that.'

'You'll miss him, but you can always visit.'

Nick laughed. 'Yes, if I win the lottery! And as I don't even do the lottery, the chances of that are pretty slim.'

'Well, you'd have to find a way. He's your best mate.'

'I know.' He drained his glass, liking the cool tang of the dry white against his tongue. 'It'd be nice if you could fly off, wouldn't it? Just for a trip, a few days, a change of scenery and then come home. It'd make anything bearable if you could escape.'

'What, like a pilot with your own plane?' She smiled.

'I'm thinking more like a bird,' he suggested. 'One of them tropical birds who gets to sit on the branch of a palm tree on a deserted beach, just sitting in the sun, thinking . . . and then if the fancy took me, I'd soar, high in the perfect blue sky where there wasn't a whiff of a cloud, and take in the view. Flying out over the sea, high above the chaos of the world and the noise and the chatter. I'd ride the warm current and swoop down to the crystal-clear water for a spot of seafood for lunch and then back up as high as I could go with the warmth of the sun on my back. I think it would be the most amazing feeling to have wings that could take me wherever I wanted to go, whenever I wanted to go. Imagine – no discussion, no planning, no justification; all I'd need to do was look in the direction I wanted to head and take off. I wouldn't even need to look back or say goodbye . . . freedom.' He looked up, remembering that Beverly was sitting on the other side of the sofa. He gave a short burst of self-conscious laughter. 'Mind you, knowing my luck, I'd wish to be a bird and end up as one of those wonky-legged pigeons that lives on the railway, or worse, my mother-in-law's budgerigar! Christ, imagine being trapped in that cage and having to listen to the visiting Diane drone on about what a disappointment I am each and every day, with the telly blaring and Dora drying her tights in front of the fire while the cat licks his arse. That'd be my luck!'

Beverly laughed loudly and her hair fell forward over her face as she struggled not to lose the wine that filled her cheeks.

'You are funny, Nick.'

'I don't think so.' He shook his head. 'I've forgotten how to be funny.'

'No, you haven't.' She cupped the glass in her hand. 'You're just out of practice.'

'I suppose I am. It's hard to be funny or find anything funny when you have the weight of the world on your shoulders and you're wading through quicksand. And that's what the last year or so has felt like. Kerry's last months were hard, the last the hardest of all.'

There was a moment or two of uncomfortable silence. These were uncharted waters, discussing his wife with the woman he'd kissed. It felt both odd and yet necessary.

'It must have been.' She looked down and sat forward, the relaxed air all but gone. 'But when you properly come out the other side, you will laugh more. And I'm no expert, but maybe as you haven't been able to laugh and live freely without worry for so long, life might be sweeter. Not that you will ever get over the loss.' She floundered as if, like him, she was wary of besmirching Kerry's memory. It was the verbal equivalent of handling a hot coal, flinging the words and the sentiment from palm to palm, trying not to feel pain or cause pain and at a loss how to safely lay them down to rest. He looked forward to a time when this anxiety would ease, not that he could or would say this out loud. He tried to remember the last time he had been able to laugh, properly laugh with Kerry, and it was difficult to picture.

'I hope so,' he conceded. 'I feel like I've been in a cage – her too, and not a cage she would have chosen, one fashioned from her illness.'

'I guess her passing was . . . in some ways . . . a relief. Is that the right thing to say?' She faltered and two spots of colour appeared on her cheeks.

'I don't know if it's the right thing to say, but there's truth in it.'

Beverly toyed with the stem of her wineglass.

There was a beat or two of silence.

'I should probably think about heading off. It's getting late for a school night.' She spoke with certainty and shuffled forward on the cushion.

'Well, that was a quick visit; there's more left in the bottle.' He pointed towards the kitchen.

'Yes' – she swallowed – 'but I have an early start tomorrow and I don't think Julian Siddley would thank me for falling asleep at my desk on account of too much wine.'

'No, probably not.'

'Thanks, Nick, for . . .' She let this trail, embarrassment robbing them both of the pleasant goodbye the evening had promised. She jumped into action, placing the glass hard down on the tabletop and simultaneously grabbing her bag, which lay on the floor by the sofa. Nick looked up, a little dazed, and realised that by mentioning his grief and his wife it had whipped the possibility of romance from under them. Talking about Kerry placed her as firmly in the room as if she were sitting on the chair in the corner.

He part skipped, part ran to the hallway and opened the front door, waiting like a security guard trying to usher the last of the customers out of the shop door at closing time, keen now to halt the rising embarrassment levels that threatened to drown them. Beverly grabbed her jacket from the newel post and more or less barged past him, head down, looking at the gate at the end of the pathway as if planning her escape.

'Cheers, then, Nick.'

She spoke quickly; in the brusque manner you might address a friend when in a hurry, and was gone.

Nick sighed and looked at his reflection in the hall mirror. He looked tired. He *was* tired. He gathered the glasses from the coffee table and took them to the kitchen, where he rinsed them under the tap. He placed them upside down on the draining board and stared out into the darkness of the garden. The house felt deathly quiet. He felt a little flat. The evening, which had started with such promise, had not ended remotely how he had envisaged. There was the distinct gnaw of dissatisfaction in his gut and he wished he could do a re-run, where he would steer the conversation into safer waters, or at the very least, try again to be funny.

He heard the hammering on the front door. It sounded urgent and he dashed along the hallway, wiping his damp hands on his jeans as he went; his heart thudded at what might be the matter. Treacle cowered by his leg, offering moral support but little else, the most rubbish guard dog in the world.

'Beverly!' He immediately tried to think of what it was she might have forgotten. She looked a little harassed, her breath quickening, her face flushed. She pushed the door and came in, closing it behind her.

'It can't be like that!' She stared at him.

'What can't? What?' He was trying to keep up.

She pulled her handbag close to her chest and spoke with conviction, her eyes bright. 'It can't be that if you mention Kerry in a certain way I feel the need to scuttle away like something scolded. She can't be a no-go area for us verbally. That would be impossible, and wrong. I've tried to initiate conversations about her to show you I'm fine, mature, open, but it's actually a lot harder than I thought. But here it is, Nick: you were married to her for a very long time and she is Oliver's mum and this is her house.'

'Yes.' He swallowed. 'Yes.'

'And nothing we can do or say will change those facts, not that we would want to, not at all. We *need* to be able to talk about her, of course we do. And it's my belief that if we want to explore this . . . this . . .'

He helped her out. 'Connection.'

'Yes, thank you.' She smiled. 'This connection, then we need to be able to talk about the stuff that is awkward, the stuff that makes us think or embarrasses us, because that's often the important stuff and it's certainly the stuff that will help us move forward.'

Nick stared at her, a little at a loss for words but in absolute agreement. He knew she was right, not that it made the thought of being so open any easier. Kerry and he had grown up together, open books, and yet despite their longevity the nature of her demise had meant they had become expert liars, the keepers of secrets too unpalatable to voice.

'How are you feeling today, love?'

'I feel good, fine, maybe a little better even . . .' She had barely been able to lift her grey-skinned face from the pillow.

'What did the doctor say to you, Nick?'

'Oh, he said you're doing really well. Really well, and that maybe you might be able to come home for Christmas . . .' He examined his fingernails, unable to look her in the eye.

'Okay?' Beverly asked, holding his gaze and taking a step closer to him.

'Okay.' He smiled and reached out, pulling her towards him. He kissed her on the mouth and she stood on tiptoe while they held each other in a brief, tight hug that fired bolts of joy right through him.

'I know folk will say this is too soon, that I'm overstepping a mark making a move, whatever, but who makes those rules? How soon is too soon? The truth is, this has happened and I feel happy,' she whispered into his hair.

'I feel happy too,' he admitted, burying the thought that this happiness came with a large side helping of guilt.

'Right, glad we got that sorted. I really am leaving now.' She hitched her bag on to her shoulder. 'But how about I come over on Friday and bring another bottle and we can try this again?'

'Yes. I'll see you then.'

'Well, actually, I'll see you tomorrow at work, Nick, but I know what you mean.' She smiled at him and let herself out.

Nick closed the door and slumped down on the bottom stair with his heart hammering. 'Jesus!' He ran his hands over his face and felt the pull of fatigue, unsure of what had just happened but conscious of a tiny shift in his world, the smallest ripple that was frightening but at the same time just the teeniest bit exciting. Friday, three days away, a day that now loomed in his mind. He felt the flutter of nerves.

He trod the stairs and whistled for Treacle, who ran up ahead and curled on the bottom of the duvet, where she now, illegally, slept.

He decided to call Oliver before he went to sleep, partly to rid himself of the thinly veiled guilt he felt at the fact that Beverly had spent an hour or so sitting in his mum's chair, but also because he missed the boy, pure and simple.

'Are you all right, Dad?' His son answered the call, his concern touching.

'Fine, son. Just thought I'd phone and say night, night.' Nick winced. The phrase sounded childish; he was now addressing his eighteen-year-old boy, a man, to all intents and purposes.

'You off to bed?' Oliver laughed. 'It's early!'

Nick glanced at the bedside clock. It was nearly half past ten. 'I suppose it is for you, but for me it's plenty late enough.'

'I'm just about to start getting ready; I'm going out.'

'You're going out?' Nick tried to hide the surprise in his voice.

'Yes. Going to collect a few mates from their halls and then we're going to a club, but we won't get there till one at least.'

'I don't know, Olly. It's another world. Even when I was your age a late night meant staying out till last orders. If I went to a club I'd be asleep in the corner.'

'Then we'd probably shave your eyebrows, or at the very least pin a note on you saying, "Free to a good home".'

Nick laughed at the idea of this fun. It was a stark reminder of how he had gone from riding his bike and hanging out with Eric and Alex to pushing a pram and searching for extra shifts. 'How's your reading list coming along?'

'Not bad.' He heard his son move. 'Sorry, Dad, Tasha's lying on my arm and it's gone to sleep – hang on a minute.'

Nick listened with a bloom of embarrassment at the unmistakable sound of the duvet ruffling and the click and knock of someone in bed changing their position. Suddenly the call felt like an intrusion and he looked at the empty pillow next to him. He felt the weight of expectation when he thought about Friday night and what might happen between him and Beverly. Not that he wanted to make assumptions, but it was a simple fact that he had only ever slept with Kerry, and hadn't done that for the best part of a year. When his world and routine coasted on chaos and worry had been his master, sex had been the very last thing on his mind.

'I spoke to Gran and Nanny, called them both and had the exact same conversation twice.'

Nick smiled, glad his boy had had the forethought to do this, one small act that he knew made both women so happy, and had the added bonus of keeping Diane off his back.

'They both wanted to know what I was eating and whether I was warm enough, and Nanny said I should get a flu jab just in case and Gran said not to walk home alone after a night out.'

'All good advice.' He laughed, happy that seemingly neither conversation had contained anything that might unnerve Oliver; after all, they were still, after New Year's Eve, building bridges.

'Have you been up to anything, Dad?' Oliver asked casually.

'No, not really – work, the usual.' He closed his eyes and he remembered Beverly's words of earlier: *We need to be able to talk about the stuff that is awkward, or embarrasses us, because that's often the important stuff* . . . He drew breath, thinking of how he should begin to introduce the topic of Beverly and the fact that they were becoming friends. In truth, not only did he feel too weary to have the conversation, but he didn't want to burst the bubble of ease within which they now chatted.

'So how's Treacle?' Oliver said, removing the tension from the moment and changing the course of Nick's thoughts.

'She's great, snoring like a good 'un!'

Oliver laughed. 'You're letting her sleep on the bed, aren't you!'

'What me? No, never,' he lied.

'Dad, I'd better . . .'

'Yes, of course, you go and get ready. Speak soon, Olly. And say hello to Tasha for me.'

'Will do. Night, night, Dad.'

His son's parting words brought a lump to Nick's throat. This six-foot man with his girlfriend and his reading list, living at his fancy university and about to hit the town, a man finding his place in the world, and yet with these words Nick understood that he was still his little boy.

You and me against the world – the Bairstow Boys . . .
Always.

1992

'Morning! Do you want something to eat, love? I've got bacon, eggs, Coco Pops?' his mum asked Eric as he came in through the back door and into the kitchen.

'No, thank you.'

'No, thank you?' his mum yelled. She rushed over and placed her hand on his forehead. 'Where's Eric, and what have you done with him?'

'I don't feel like breakfast today.' The tremble to his bottom lip was unmistakable.

'Oh, lovey, are you feeling a bit sad?' Nick watched as his mum bent down and placed her arm across Eric's narrow back. 'It's understandable; you've got a lot going on.' She smiled at him. 'Don't worry about breakfast, but you tell me when you're peckish and I'll rustle you up something nice, okay?'

'Okay,' Eric managed.

'Why don't you two go off to the garage?' His mum winked at Nick, and he got the hint, knowing that Eric would probably talk more freely when it was just the two of them. 'I'll send Alex your way when he rocks up.'

Nick abandoned his egg on toast and followed his friend into the garage. Half Bike gleamed in the corner; they hadn't ridden it yesterday, what with the weather being so grim.

Eric began to cry. A big cry where his nose ran and he didn't bother wiping his face.

'What's wrong?' Nick felt a little embarrassed on his friend's behalf and wasn't sure of what to do or say next. He sat on one of the fishing stools and Eric followed suit.

'Nothing!' he barked through his tears.

'You always say that. But it has to be something or you wouldn't be crying,' he offered softly and without judgement, and waited as the moments ticked by, the silence broken only by his friend's sniffing. It felt like an age.

'It's my mum . . .' Eric started.

'She's not coming to get you straightaway, is she?' This was the worst thing Nick could envisage, as he clung on to their final two weeks together, trying not to think about the day they had to say goodbye.

Eric shook his head. 'No. But my dad told me last night that she's . . . she's having a baby . . . That's why she left with Dave, and that's why my dad is so mad.'

Nick wrinkled his nose and looked up. He wasn't sure about the mechanics of it all but knew for certain you had to be married to have a baby, and Eric's mum was married, so he couldn't really see why it was such a shocker. He also knew that babies could be a pain, a noisy pain, and wondered if it might not be a good thing that Eric's dad didn't have to live with the baby, who was going to grow up in Derby.

'It might be nice having a baby brother; a sister, not so much.' He pictured Jen with her superior nature, who usually only said mean things to him and his friends. A brother, he decided, was a better option.

'But I don't, I don't want her to have a baby!' Eric hiccupped.

'Why not?'

'Because . . .'

'Because what?' Nick asked gently.

'Because I don't want her to love anyone but me.' Eric's voice was small.

Nick stared at his friend, genuinely at a loss for words. 'Love' wasn't a word they used readily. They sat awkwardly in silence, bar Eric's snivelling. Eventually Nick thought of a good distraction.

'Do you want to play Petunia, but on the grass, as my mum's collapsed the pool?'

'Sure.' Eric wiped his eyes with the back of his hand, stopped crying, and the boys made their way to the brown circle of grass where they lay, as if still in the pool, and threw the ball high in the air. By the time

Alex arrived the weather had again taken a turn for the worse. It was a grey, windy day and one they were resolved to spend in the garage. His mum kept them fed with a ready supply of cheese-and-ham sandwiches and packets of Jammie Dodgers, while the boys took Half Bike to bits and cleaned it thoroughly.

'I think, when I grow up, I might like to work in the bike shop,' Eric announced, using the oil can to grease the brakes.

'The bike shop in Burston?' Alex checked.

'Yes. I won't stay in Derby forever, will I, Vera? I'll stay there until I'm old enough to work and then I'll come back and buy one of the big houses by the Rec and get a job in the bike shop. Then I could do this every day.'

'I could work there too,' Alex suggested. 'Then we could muck about every day!'

Eric laughed at the prospect. 'Or if I don't work in the bike shop, I might be an inventor and invent a machine that kills milkmen.'

Nick and Alex pulled faces at each other.

'Well, if I don't work in the bike shop, I might be a professional footballer and play for Man U,' Alex said.

'But you're a rubbish footballer,' Nick pointed out. 'You aren't even on the school team!'

'I know I'm rubbish *now*,' Alex conceded, 'but if I play for Man U then I can train and get good – my dad says they are, like, the best in the whole wide world, and then imagine, we would be able to sit on the bench in Market Square whenever we wanted! No one would throw a Man U player off the bench, would they?'

'No, they wouldn't,' Nick agreed. It sounded like a plan.

'What about you, Nick?' Eric asked.

'I still think I want to go to university.'

'Oh yes, that's right, you're going to learn ballet, aren't you, Mavis?' He and Alex laughed loudly.

Nick was about to respond when his dad came into the garage.

'Right then, lads.' His dad clapped his hands together and winked at Eric. Nick guessed his mum had filled him in on the crying. 'I know that Eric leaving Burston is going to be a bit of a blow to you all and isn't something any of you could probably have imagined.'

Nick shook his head. It sure wasn't.

'So I've spoken to your dads and we have a bit of a surprise for you all.'

Eric looked up from his tinkering and Alex paused, mid Jammie Dodger.

'We are going to let you go camping up near Drayfield Moor, just for one night.'

'Yes!' Nick screamed, jumping up and down.

'Brilliant!' Alex beamed, wiggling with excitement.

'We haven't got a tent,' Eric pointed out.

'Ah, don't you worry about that. By the time we drop you up there you'll have a tent, sleeping bags and a cooking stove. You'll have to fend for yourselves, mind, for one whole night, and then one of us will collect you the next morning.'

'What will we cook?' Eric asked.

Nick laughed; he might have guessed that grub would be at the forefront of his mate's mind.

'I don't know, lad, whatever the missus has knocking about the fridge, I suppose; sausages and the like.'

Eric beamed, placated.

'Is it true?' Jen yelled as she marched into the garage.

'Is what true, pet?' his dad asked.

'That you're letting this lot go camping by themselves and I'm not even allowed to have a sleepover with Scarlett and Georgia?' Her brows knitted in an expression of mild fury.

'It's different.' Nick's dad smiled, as if he hoped this might be enough to calm her.

'Different how?' Jen pushed. 'Different why? Because they're boys? Because that's just not fair! Girls can do anything boys can – anything! And me and my mates want to go camping! I've always wanted to go camping!'

'Well . . .' His dad swallowed. 'You're right, girls can do anything boys can do, and I will seriously think about you girls all going camping when the boys come home.'

'But I don't want you to think about it, Dad! I want you to say we can go for definite! Otherwise it's not fair!' Jen ranted.

'I'm not sure girls can do everything that boys can,' Eric said calmly, and all eyes turned to him. Nick wasn't sure whether speaking up like this in the wake of Jen's rage made him brave or stupid.

'Yeah?' She jabbed her finger towards him. 'Name me one thing that you can do that I can't.' Jen stood to her full height and crossed her arms over her chest.

'Pee standing up,' Eric answered, and as Nick, Alex and his dad began to chuckle, Jen turned on her heel and shouted as she went.

'God, I hate you, dweebs! You're idiots! All of you!'

NINE

Nick changed the bedlinen and opened the bedroom window. He closed the wardrobe doors and scooted down the stairs before tidying the kitchen and hoovering again. He laid out clean pants, jeans and his new shirt, all ironed, and placed the bottle of deodorant/body spray that Oliver had rejected and gifted to him, thinking a little spritz might not do any harm. He checked the bottle of white wine that was already chilled in the fridge and eyed the big bag of crisps he had bought to put in a bowl on the coffee table. He dropped Treacle at his mum's on the way to work; she was only too pleased to have the pooch overnight. Nick felt the smallest smidge of guilt at how vague he had been about the reasons why. He figured that with Beverly popping over it would be less than ideal if he had to take Treacle out for a shit halfway through the evening. It was Friday and as Nick drove into the Siddley's car park he noticed he wasn't the only one with a spring in his step.

'I got it!' Eric yelled at him across the bumpy tarmac as he parked his bike.

'Got what?' Nick locked the car and put his sandwich box under his arm, catching up with his mate.

'My visa! That's it, buddy! That's what I've been waiting for. I'm off to Oz!'

Nick didn't know what to say. He was pleased to see Eric so chuffed, but at the same time this made it seem very real. Up until that point the idea of his best mate going to Australia had seemed like a threat rather than a plan.

'Wow.'

'Yes, wow!' Eric bounced on the spot like the excited kid he was a mere blink ago.

'That was quick.'

'Not really, four weeks, and who cares – I've got it! I can see it now, me on Bondi Beach in the bloody sunshine while you lot are picking and packing lights. I shall think of you, Nicky boy, as I put another steak on the barbie and reach for a chilled beer.' He clapped his hands in anticipation.

'When do you think you'll go?'

Eric shrugged. 'Not sure. I have to leave within the next twelve months or my visa runs out, but that shouldn't be a problem; it's not like I have any pressing engagements keeping me here.'

'Have you spoken to Jen yet?'

'No.'

'Maybe you should?' He didn't want to interfere, and it wasn't entirely without self-interest that he made the suggestion.

'She knows where I am.' Eric looked straight ahead and it was only the tension in his jaw that suggested the thought of leaving her behind might be a wrench.

Beverly ran down the steps from the top of the warehouse and marched across the floor.

'You okay?' he asked. Her expression suggested that something was up, and his low level of self-confidence meant the first thing he thought was that she had changed her mind about coming over that night, maybe changed her mind about him altogether. His second thought was that if this *was* the case, then he had got up an hour early needlessly, wasted good sleeping time cleaning and had bought a big bag of crisps for nothing.

'I . . .' She searched his face and glanced towards Eric, her top lip peppered with nervous sweat.

'What's up?' He mirrored her anxiety.

Beverly shook her head. 'Nothing. Nothing, I've just heard . . .'

'Just heard what?' he pushed, his heart booming.

'Nothing. Nothing. Forget it.' She gave a false smile and shook her head. 'I can't say anything.' She tucked in her lips, as if this might prevent her from breaking whatever confidence she held.

'Can't say anything about what?' He gave a gentle, nervous laugh.

'I have to go, Nick.' She let her eyes linger on his face before racing across the floor, heading in the direction of Mr Siddley's office.

'What on earth was that all about?' Eric looked at him as if he might have the answers.

'I wish I knew!' He laughed it off, trying to hide the swell of anxiety in his gut.

◆ ◆ ◆

Four hours.

That was how long he had to wait to find out what the hell was going on.

He took his seat at their preferred bench with the lads. Roy, as ever, had a generously heaped plate of canteen food in front of him on the table; some kind of grey meat with mixed vegetables that looked as if they had been boiling since last July. Nick unpacked his rather unglamorous cheese sandwich; conscious of wanting fresh breath later, he had forgone the pickle and onion. By the expression on Roy's face Nick was rather glad of his boring lunch.

'Looks nice, Roy.' Eric nudged his friend.

'It's not as bad as it looks, actually.' He took a mouthful and his expression suggested this was a lie. They all laughed.

'Not that I care.' Eric folded his arms across his chest. 'Today I don't care about much.' He smiled at Nick, who felt the stir of melancholy that his friend was keen to go, whereas he could view his impending departure only with a sense of loss, just like his sister, apparently.

There was an unexpected kerfuffle at the swing door; heads turned in that direction. In walked the boss, with a mini entourage. All eyes fell on him, no one sure if they should stop eating and pay attention or carry on with their lunch. Not only was this a most unusual occurrence, but also the clock kept ticking and it was a known fact that the hour they had for lunch passed quicker than any other hour in the day.

'Can I have your attention, please, ladies and gentlemen!' Julian Siddley shouted out, pulling a chair from under a nearby table, the scrape of the legs across the concrete floor scratchy and unpleasant. He stood on it in front of the noticeboard. It was an extraordinary display from a man who usually ate his lunch in his big office or sloped off to the golf club, where a 'meeting' would prevent him returning for the rest of the afternoon. Not that Nick judged him for that; he was the boss, after all. Nick looked up and saw that Mr Aubrey Siddley and Julian's wife, Caitlyn, were also there, standing either side of the chair with downcast expressions and hands clasped in front of them. Aubrey had aged, of course. Nick remembered the first time he had met him on that day so long ago, the first and last time he was to travel in such a fancy car. His mouth lifted at the memory.

'How fast can it go?'

'Faster than I'm allowed to.'

Caitlyn, he noticed, moved her feet a little awkwardly, as if she couldn't find a comfortable position, and with lips thin and set shook her glossy hair from her face as though it were long and not short. Nervous.

'Oh no,' Nick muttered under his breath; he figured that this show of family unity could mean only one thing: Joseph Siddley must have died . . . He felt a wave of nostalgia for the elderly man who had been the chairman during his dad's tenure; he had even come to his dad's funeral. Nick decided there and then that as well as making a point of shaking Julian's hand after this, he would write to the family, to tell them in a more formal way how genuinely sorry he was for their loss and just how much he and his dad had thought of old Mr Siddley. As he was trying to mentally calculate how old Joseph must have been, Julian began talking and, for the first time Nick could remember, the canteen fell silent.

He had never truly thought about the phrase 'so quiet you could hear a pin drop', but in the next minutes he understood it completely. The atmosphere was eerie, haunting, reminding him of the cavernous, echoey dairy shed of their youth, as if the place were derelict and not crammed full with men and women, old and young, all midway through eating their lunch on what had started out like any other day.

'This is a very sad day for me, for all of us,' Julian began. 'Siddley's has, as you know, been here on this site, proudly employing the good people of Burstonbridge since 1946.' He paused and let his eyes sweep the room. 'I know that some of you, like me, are the second or third generation to work here.'

Nick thought about walking through the factory gates with his dad at an age younger than Oliver, and cursed the emotion that threatened, a reminder that he might be getting better, healing a little bit every single day, but that his grief was still only sitting under the surface, ready to hijack his thoughts at any given moment.

Julian took a deep breath and gripped his hands behind his back, the buttons on his double-cuffed shirt straining a little across his ample stomach. His high forehead was shiny.

'There is no easy way to say what I need to say and so I will simply cut to the chase.' He coughed.

Oh no . . . oh no, no, no! Please God, no! Nick, like many who stared at the man, sensed what was coming next, and held his breath, hoping, praying he might be wrong, because if what he suspected was true, they would not be mourning the death of Joseph Siddley but be feeling a nail in the coffin of them all.

'Siddley's of Burstonbridge . . . is closing down.'

There was a collective, horrified gasp, again followed by silence, broken only by the soft stutter of the few that whimpered. No doubt they, like he, were picturing what a life without a regular wage might mean. He closed his eyes briefly. The atmosphere was horrible. It dragged his guts to his boots and left him feeling icy cold.

Julian and Aubrey stared at the floor, their expressions hard to read.

'Now, I can only imagine what an announcement like this means to you.' Julian paused and raised his palms, as if trying to hold back the swell of protest he might have expected, but folks were too numb for that. 'I will not be going into too much detail today, but we will of course be talking to all of you individually over the next few days to answer any and all questions you might have.'

'Fuck!' Roy laid his spoon on the table and put his head in his hands. 'I'm fifty-eight. I haven't finished paying for Christmas yet – what am I going to do?'

'My daughter's getting married next year.' Nick heard the woman on the table next to him speak, before she too began to cry.

All Nick could picture was the day he and Oliver had walked around Ikea with him counting the pennies and fretting over the cost of the mis-bought single duvet, and that was while he had money coming in. How were they going to manage? He had only in recent years shaken off the burden of Kerry's debt, only recently managed to sleep through the night without waking in a cold sweat as he tried to make the numbers add up . . . and now this. It felt in that moment like he couldn't catch a break.

'When? When's it closing down?' one of the younger handlers shouted from the back, his voice a rasp of distress tinged with anger. The lad shoved his hands deep inside his thick jacket, his face thunderous. Nick knew it wasn't his place, but he wanted to try to calm him, lay his hand on the man's shoulder and tell him that this wasn't something the Siddleys would have chosen to do lightly. He wasn't Julian's biggest fan, that was true, but he was aware that the family fortunes were as bound to this business as their own. Although he had to admit there had been no warning, no indication, and this made the news even harder to bear. He heard Kerry's voice loud and clear for the first time in a long time, and he was glad of it.

Life throws curveballs and you've got to either catch them and throw them back or dodge them. That's it . . .

'Three to six months.' Julian held the man's eye line, his voice steady.

Three to six months . . .

No time at all . . .

Three wage packets . . .

You are kidding me . . .

The whispers rippled around the room and bounced up to the metal rafters, where the dust of celebrations and happier times still lingered: the day they won the Queen's Award for Enterprise for international trade, and they sipped fizzy wine after hours and clapped loudly at their own achievement; Kath had waltzed with old Mr Siddley. Also the party held in this very room to celebrate sixty years of business, when nearly everyone had contributed to the veritable spread laid out on the tables and they had watched Julian cut into a three-tiered cake and fired party poppers over each other's heads.

Kerry had bought a new dress, black with a glittery band of beads around the neck. She looked lovely, we slow-danced in the kitchen when we got home then had toast and honey before bed . . .

'Will there be redundancy?' One of Kath's 'girls' shouted from behind the counter.

'There will be remuneration packages available that I will discuss with everyone in their one-to-one sessions,' Julian answered calmly, rehearsed.

At least that's something . . . Nick latched on to this one positive: *Keep the wolf from the door . . .*

'I thought the business was doing well! We haven't lost orders and we were so busy over Christmas!' one of the men shouted in disbelief from the side of the room.

He watched Julian Siddley falter and again tried to read his face. It was then that he saw Beverly sat on a table to the right of him. She was staring straight at their boss and her face was nothing short of thunderous.

For a day that had started with so much promise, it turned into something very different. The atmosphere was charged. Some, he noted, worked twice as hard, whether trying to stave off the inevitable or as a distraction from it, he wasn't sure. Others loitered by the perimeter fence, staring out over the undulating expanse of green, this beautiful slice of God's own country that they had made their home. They took to their phones, some shouting their anger for all to hear, a protest. Others whispered the news to loved ones, who no doubt would be thinking of just what the closure might mean for them, mentally erasing next year's Christmas gifts, potential holidays and seeing the red underlined demands for bills they might not be able to meet.

Eric joined him in the canteen mid-afternoon and handed him a cup of tea.

'So what d'you think?' He sipped his own hot brew.

Unsurprisingly, it was the only topic on everyone's lips. Nick exhaled, a new and lingering ache in his chest delivered by this latest blow.

'I don't know what to think. I keep trying to imagine waking up on a weekday and not coming here.' He let his eyes sweep the room, where Julian's words still echoed. 'But I can't. It's all I've ever known, you too. And our dads.'

Eric nodded. 'True that.'

Nick tried to envisage life without a regular wage and felt a cold sweat prickle his skin. 'It doesn't seem real. I've only been financially straight for the last few months, because of . . .' He let this hang.

'I know.' Eric nodded, one of the only people who did know about the financial liability that Nick had borne, battling to keep debt collectors at bay and all through no fault of his own. The memory of the bruiser on the doorstep with a legal notice in his hand and sunglasses on his head still made him shiver.

'Not that I'm flush, I just about manage if I'm careful, but this . . .' He shook his head and looked up at the people who walked around with a stunned stumble to their gait and expressions of either disbelief or fury. He wondered if, like him, they were already trying to think of ways to cut back.

No heating on, ever.

Tins of beans for tea.

Fill up with cheap porridge in the mornings.

Get rid of the car. It's not worth much, but it'll mean less outgoings.

'Jobs are hard enough to come by in Burston, and there's about to be a couple of hundred of us, all walking into the same places with the same CVs.' He rubbed his chin before reaching for his tea. 'At least *you* don't have to worry – as you said, you'll be on Bondi Beach and reaching for a chilled beer.'

Eric put his tea on the table. 'It's messed up my plans, to be honest. I mean, I'll still go, but I was hoping to save for the next couple of months to have spending money, just to tide me over until I can apply for a work visa, find a sponsor or whatever. If they go bust, will I even get redundancy? I mean, they are talking about remuneration, but if the coffers are empty . . .'

'I don't know,' he answered truthfully. This was all new ground. 'You have some money saved, though?'

'Yes, but that's for rent and stuff. I need more,' Eric huffed.

'Don't we all?' He gave a wry laugh.

'I'm just waiting to see what Julian offers. So what's happened, do you reckon? I mean, business doesn't seem to have slowed. It doesn't make sense.'

'I don't know, mate. But I wouldn't be surprised if the Siddleys hid any dip in orders from us, probably hoping they could find a way out without this.' He considered how rough this must be for them, seeing their business slip from their fingers. 'As much as I dislike him, I feel a bit sorry for Julian. I do. It can't be good, can it? I mean, his dad and his grandad made the business rocket and he's been in the big chair for less than three years and run it into the ground.'

'Yes, God forbid he might have to sell his Range Rover.' Eric rolled his eyes.

'As I say, I feel sorry for him, and you can't begrudge the man a nice car. If we had his money we'd do the same. I'd love a car that I didn't have to pray over that it was going to make it to the end of the journey.' Nick pictured the shiny, sleek silver Jaguar he had seen on Mackie's forecourt not so long ago. 'Not that it'll be an issue much longer; I'll have to let the car go when tax and insurance are due.' He closed his eyes briefly, picturing the empty driveway.

'Don't do anything too hasty. If there's a job out and about you'll need transport. Some of the lads were saying they're taking on ware-house staff in York.'

'That's a fair old commute.' He thought of the cost of fuel. 'I'll keep my ear to the ground, of course. I'll get Jen to help me with a CV.'

'Have you even got a CV?' Eric asked.

'No.' Nick laughed dryly. 'Never needed one.'

Eric downed his cuppa. 'Me either. Did Bev not say anything to you?'

'No, I think she was as shocked as us.' He pictured the look on her face earlier.

'It's proper shit, mate.' Eric stood, tea break over.

'It is that, proper shit.'

◆　◆　◆

That afternoon he took calls from his mum, Jen and Dora, who had all heard on the grapevine about the closure, of course. Phones buzzed and beeped all over the shop floor. News of this magnitude travelled fast, especially when the ripples were to be felt throughout the town.

'So what did they say?' his mum asked.

'Just what I told you, that it's closing.' He felt irritation at having to repeat the depressing fact.

'Did they say when?'

'Three to six months.'

'Did they say why?'

'No, Mum. You probably know as much as I do. I'm in to see Julian on Monday and then I'll find out the details – what I'm entitled to, that kind of thing.'

'What you going to do?'

He ground his teeth, really not in the mood for her questions, to which he had no satisfying answers.

'I honestly don't know.'

There was a beat or two of silence until his mum spoke, and he felt his irritation fade, replaced with a rush of gratitude towards the woman who had always, since he was very small, tried to find solutions. 'You know you can always come home, you and Olly, of course. If you have to sell the house or rent the house or whatever, do like Jen did. Move back, save up. You'd be more than welcome, but you already know that.' He pictured her rolling out the bed-in-a-bag for Eric on the nights his dad worked a late shift.

He shuddered at the thought of giving up his house, his independence, the home he had created with Kerry and the only address Oliver had ever lived in. Not to mention the worry of how he could possibly supplement Oliver's student loan if he was without a wage. He made the decision there and then: no matter what it took, his son would finish his degree; they would find a way.

'Thank you, Mum. I think we're a long way off that – I *hope* we're a long way off that – but I appreciate the offer. As I say, I'll know more on Monday.'

'Well, I won't tell Treacle, no point in upsetting her.'

'You know she's a dog, right?'

'Yes' – his mum was smiling, he could tell – 'but she's a very clever dog.'

◆ ◆ ◆

Nick showered and pulled on his clean, ironed jeans and shirt, the one his sister had bought him for Christmas. The news of the closure had all but extinguished the small flames of joy he had felt in his stomach when he woke. It was not only a shock for all the individual families affected, but to Burstonbridge as well. Nick was no stranger to shock; he knew better than most that life and everything in it turned on a penny, not that it made it any easier to figure out what to do next.

He tried to put the news out of his mind as he paced the kitchen, feeling the burble of teenage nerves and wishing Beverly would arrive right now and end this excruciating wait. The anticipation was almost unbearable; supposing they had nothing to say to each other? He genuinely considered texting her to cancel, thinking of the instant relief that would bring. He laughed out loud at how ridiculous that was. He checked the wine again and decanted the crisps into a plastic salad bowl and placed it on the coffee table. Sitting on the sofa, he made out to put his hand into the bowl to check he had positioned it in the optimum, reachable spot.

'For God's sake, get a grip, Nick.' He spoke aloud as the front doorbell rang, jumping up.

'Hi.'

'Hi.'

Beverly walked into the hallway, shaking her head, speaking as she crossed the threshold, as if this were no grand, anticipated entrance and she was merely stepping back in after stepping out. All worries about awkward silences slipped from his mind.

'Oh my God, Nick, what a horrible day. One of the worst I've ever had.' She placed her coat on the banister and pulled a bottle of wine from her handbag before lobbing her bag on the floor. 'I have literally spent hours consoling people in the corridors, handing out tissues and trying to reassure everyone that everything is going to be fine. Even when I know it won't. I don't think I've ever hated a day more. I couldn't wait to leave tonight. And Julian is nowhere to be seen. Bloody typical!'

'I'm in shock,' he confessed.

'We all are.' She handed him the bottle of wine. 'I think we need to get this open quickly!' She laughed. 'If ever I needed the medication of alcohol, it's tonight.'

'Way ahead of you.' They walked into the kitchen and Nick popped her bottle in the fridge and removed the one he had had chilling since yesterday.

'I can't believe it. I thought they were going to announce Joseph had died and so when he spoke . . .' Nick shook his head, still with an air of disbelief. 'When did you find out?' he asked, as he poured two generous measures into the glasses.

'First thing this morning.' She picked up a glass – 'Cheers!' – and raised it towards him. 'Here's to the end of the world as we know it!'

'Blimey, that's a bit worrying.' He gave a nervous laugh and raised his glass regardless. 'I said to the lads I feel a bit sorry for Julian – that can't have been easy for him, what he had to do today, and I admire the fact he stood and faced us all. I think that took guts. That's old-fashioned values right there, and it was appreciated. I bet there are some bosses who would have sent an email or got someone else to do it.'

Beverly shot him a look. 'Don't feel sorry for Julian, for any of them. Old-fashioned values? Yeah, right.' She took a deep breath. 'Okay, Nick, what I'm going to tell you *must not* go any further. You can't tell a soul, but I need to tell someone.' She took a glug of wine. 'Promise me you won't say a word to Eric, or anyone. I've signed a contract to say I will keep things confidential, but what are they going to do, fire me?'

'No, but if you've signed something they might sue you.' He spoke earnestly as they made their way to the sofa and sank down as they had before, and this time he didn't think of Kerry. He thought how lovely Beverly looked in her jeans and white lacy top, pretty and relaxed; she smelled good too.

'Good point.' She shrugged. 'Okay, so I know why they are closing Siddley's.'

'Well, I think we can all figure that much out. It must be lack of sales or the cancelling of contracts; why else would they—'

'No, Nick.' She cut him short. 'It's not lack of sales or cancelled contracts; in fact, business is absolutely booming. They're raking it in,' she spat.

'I don't . . . I don't understand.' He stared at her. 'So why, then?'

'Oh, Jesus!' She dropped her shoulders as if the weight of knowing and not telling were more than she could stand before straightening and looking Nick in the eye. 'Julian is selling the land – the whole site, and the acres surrounding it.'

'Selling it to who?' He was trying to keep up.

'Ah, here's the killer bit.' She sat forward. 'He's selling it to Merryvale Homes.'

Nick had of course heard of the national building company, famous for building identikit orange-brick mini towns all over the country, sprawling estates where the roads and cul-de-sacs were given softened names like Meadow View and Lavender Close in an ironic nod to the countryside they ploughed up and destroyed. Mentally he was a few steps behind Beverly, trying to figure out why a new-house builder like Merryvale might want to buy a lighting business in the middle of Yorkshire.

'Why?'

'Because, Nick, the Siddleys not only own the land the business is built on but also all the land around it, and they are selling the whole lot to Merryvale, who are going to build at least a thousand houses on it – up to three thousand!'

'Houses?' He stared at her.

'Yes, houses. Lots and lots of them, so that new folk, out-of-towners, people with jobs who work in Thirsk and the surrounds can come and live in Burston and commute to those jobs, and the people already in Burston, people like us, will have even fewer jobs, because the only bloody place to work is Siddley's, and they're closing the business and selling the land to the people who'll build the houses!' She shook her head at the irony of it all.

'But' – he was trying to get the facts straight in his mind – 'maybe they'll move the business?'

Beverly shook her head. 'No, they won't. Julian and Aubrey made it quite clear that they had no intention of keeping a business open that makes them a fraction of the money they will earn by selling. Julian's the last Siddley we will see – his kids are only little and I think he's planning on taking his millions and retiring to the sunshine. The lazy idiot.'

'But . . .' He faltered again, thinking now not of his own circumstances but of the town. 'How will Burston cope with all those houses? It's hard enough getting out on to the A roads in the morning as it is.'

'Ah, here comes the sweetener: apparently we'll get a new supermarket with a petrol station and possibly a school and a doctor's surgery, all built on the east side of town.'

'Mackie's garage would go down.' Nick thought about the Mackie family, in particular Gina Mackie, whom he had snogged once at a school disco. The family had been pumping gas and selling plastic-wrapped sandwiches and warm Cokes from an inefficient fridge for as long as anyone could remember. He shook his head; he couldn't picture the place Beverly was describing.

'They wouldn't be the only ones – the mini supermarket, the baker, the florist, the butcher. I doubt any could compete with a big supermarket.'

'And they don't know?'

She shook her head. 'No one knows, only the Siddleys and me and you, any local councillors who are in on the negotiations, people like Big Brian, and probably Julian's lawyer bloke and all the other suits I've made tea for in recent weeks. Julian actually tried to tell me it might be a good thing, as there would be new jobs in the businesses that would spring up around the housing estates, like cafés and hairdressers, maybe a new takeaway. I just stared at him. He has no idea.'

'I can't believe I felt so sorry for him today.' Nick confessed, 'I told Eric not to be too hard on the man as it must be tough to see the business fold, and all the time . . .' He flexed his fingers. 'I'd like a quiet word with our Julian.'

'I think there's going to be a lot of folk who are going to want a word with our Julian. It's greed, Nick, pure and simple. Bloody greed! The Siddleys have enough – more than enough, more than most of us could only dream of – and yet they want more, and it's all right for them, they live over in Drayton Moor—'

Nick pictured their vast mansion behind its grand, scrolled-iron gates.

Beverly wasn't done. 'They don't give a toss that they'll be ripping the heart out of our little community. It's a bloody disgrace!'

'Is it a done deal? Are you absolutely sure? Don't they have to get planning permission and stuff like that?'

'They do, and there's a chance they might not get it. But I'm pretty sure money greases palms, and they must know there's a good chance of all or some of it going through. Phase one is buying the land, clearing it and taking a punt. And here's the real kicker: even if they don't get planning permission, apparently it's still worth the risk for Merryvale because if it pays off they win big, and if it doesn't pan out, they walk away, lick their wounds and we get to look at the space where we used to be employed while the weeds grow up through the ground. And the Siddleys, of course, won't care either way.' She paused and snorted her distaste. 'They'll have already cashed that big fat cheque, regardless.'

'I'm shocked. I honestly don't know what to say.'

'Me too. Shocked and bloody furious.'

The two sat quietly, each mulling over the harsh reality of what was about to happen to their sleepy little market town.

'Anyway, that aside . . .' Beverly scooted closer to him on the sofa. 'It's nice to see you, Nick.'

'It's nice to see you.' He reached for her hand and liked the way it felt, nestling inside his.

'I tell you what.' Beverly looked up at him. 'Why don't we make a pact not to talk about Siddley's, not tonight. It's too awful, and I have the feeling we're going to talk about nothing but the bloody place closing for the next few months, so when we're away from work like this, it should be an end-of-the-world-free zone, how about that?'

'That sounds good. And this house needs it; it feels like it's been an end-of-the-world zone for quite a while.'

'I bet.' She stayed silent and he felt that in some way this was a test, putting into practice their agreement to be able to talk freely, without censorship, about everything and anything – and by that they meant Kerry.

'Having you here . . .' He paused. 'I mean, seeing you is . . .' Again he faltered. 'I suppose what I'm trying to say is that you're the first thing that has brought me sunshine in a very long time and I'm thankful for it.'

'And you me,' she replied steadily, flexing her fingers in his palm.

'Things with Kerry were . . .' He chose his words carefully. 'It wasn't . . . It wasn't all perfect. I mean, even before she got sick.'

'It never is.' She spoke with a certainty that encouraged him to open up.

'True, but I think when someone dies it feels like you're expected to wipe out all the negatives and only remember them in glowing terms. It feels a bit like that with Olly too – if I raise my voice or there's any tension, I see the way he looks at me, as if to say, *My mum wouldn't do that.* And I have to remind myself that she did do that. She did shout at him, fall out with him; she wasn't saintly.'

'Have you spoken to Olly about it?'

'No. It's another topic on the list of things too raw to mention. Maybe in time.'

Beverly sipped from her wineglass. 'I don't think any life is perfect; I don't think any person is. I think there's only perfect for you and that's enough, really, isn't it? You find that person who you don't mind falling asleep with and waking up next to and that's enough. And it must have been enough for you and Kerry because you survived for all those years. You always seemed happy together.'

'We were to a point.' He nodded. 'But as I say, it wasn't perfect. She . . . She did something and it, it was hard.'

'Did what? That sounds ominous. Killed a man?' Beverly laughed. 'Sorry, I don't know why I said that, I'm nervous.' She blinked.

'It's okay. I'm nervous too and, for the record, it nearly killed *me.*' He took his time. 'She got into quite a lot of debt.' He paused again, torn at his indiscretion and yet already feeling the wave of relief at the very prospect of talking to someone about it. 'She kept it secret and I still don't really understand why, but she started buying things.'

'What things?' Beverly looked up at him, calm now, and curious.

'Oh God, anything! But nothing we actually needed or was useful – things like several pairs of slippers, pictures she would never hang, nail polish in every colour, beach bags, board games, all sorts. Occasionally I'd notice something new and she would be a bit coy, which was odd, as I never begrudged her a penny – of course I didn't, we were a part-nership. I never cared about who earned what; it was a shared pot. But then things changed when letters started arriving and she tried to hide them.' He took a moment and rubbed the chill from his arms. 'And then one Saturday morning – Olly was about ten – I picked up a brown envelope from the welcome mat and found out that we owed seven thousand pounds.'

'Shit!'

Nick nodded. *Seven thousand pounds . . .* An amount so big the weight of it wrapped in her deceit had nearly sunk them.

'It turned out she had credit cards and store cards I knew nothing about, and it was all a bit of a shocker. I found brand-new clothes, literally still with the tags on, stuffed into boxes in the bottom of the wardrobe. They weren't even her size. I wasn't mad, not really, more worried about why she was doing it and sad that she had felt the need to do it all so secretively. Plus, I was shit scared about how we were going to pay it all off – as I say, one shared pot. It was all around the same time as the Rod Newberry incident—'

'What Rod Newberry incident?' she interrupted.

He gave a snort of laughter and pinched his nose. 'Don't tell me you're the only person in Burstonbridge who wasn't in on that slice of gossip?'

'I must have been washing my hair that day, or maybe I just don't give a shit about what other people gossip about.' She gave him a knowing look. He remembered that her mum's dramatic departure had been gossip fodder for quite a while.

'Maybe you don't.' He took a breath. 'When the coffee shop went bust . . .'

'Oh, yes, I forgot she worked there – carry on.' Beverly sipped her wine.

'Well, she wasn't really herself. Looking back, I think she missed the company she had at work and I guess she was bored without the routine of her job. Anyway, she started hanging around Rob Newberry.'

'The butcher?'

'Yes.'

She shuddered. 'He gives me the creeps. Has always been a bit winky.'

'Winky?'

'Yeah, you know, a bit "talks to your face, but looks at your boobs", and winks.'

'I have to say, as much as I dislike the bloke, that has never been my experience.' He spoke dryly and again she burst into laughter and her reaction made him feel good . . . *funny.*

'Well, Alex mentioned in passing that he'd seen them over the Rec and I didn't think anything of it. We would both bump into everyone up there when walking or taking the shortcut from town home, but there was something in the way he said it, as if he knew something, and it bothered me.'

'Alex likes a gossip.'

'He does, and I factored that in, but when I mentioned it to Kerry her reaction was a little off and it sat like an itch in my head, you know?'

She nodded.

Nick remembered that night, her coy smile and subdued body language . . . 'I forgot about it eventually, but then my sister said something.'

'What?'

'How she'd seen Kerry with Rob at the bus stop, and not like they had bumped into each other, but relaxed, leaning in, like people do when they're interested in each other, like they'd planned to meet there. Anyway, that was about the extent of it. I mulled over what to do and after tea one night I told Kerry that she was free to do whatever she wanted with whoever she wanted, but *if* she wanted us to work as a couple and to stay married, then she had to cut out sneaking around with Rob, or anyone else for that matter. Because it wasn't fair on anyone. Especially me.'

'God, Nick!' There was a moment of silence, until Beverly spoke again. 'What did she say?' She leant in.

'She didn't deny or confirm it, but sobbed and said she was sorry, which I took as admission of something, and then she went very quiet for a week or two, kept her thoughts to herself, but I could hear her crying in the bath.'

'That's really sad.' Her expression was pained, seemingly at the thought of Kerry's distress.

'Yes. It was sad for us all, really. I didn't know if she was crying because she was going to miss him or because she had hurt me.'

'You didn't ask?'

Nick shook his head. 'I don't think I could have coped with the answer. And I think, in truth, a small part of me wanted it to be the thing that finished us.' He felt a little sick at the admission. 'I had to deal with those thoughts and then reconcile the fact that we were going to carry on. It messed with my head; hers too, I'm sure. It put distance between us that faded over time but never really disappeared. It's funny, when we left school I used to feel jealous of her mixing with David McCardle and Matty Peters.'

'Well, David *was* captain of the under-sixteens for their entire unbeaten season. How do I know this, you might ask. Because he is still talking about it!'

Nick pictured him on the shop floor doing just that. 'It's true, though; I thought those good-looking boys – the flash ones with their own cars, while I was still relying on the bus – they were who I'd have to keep an eye out for, thought they might be my competition. But I'd given up being jealous years since. I never for a second thought I needed to worry about her going to pick up our weekly meat order.'

'Maybe she was looking for something because you stopped worrying?'

This truth was a verbal ice pick that struck him squarely between the eyes. He flinched.

'Shit, Nick. I'm sorry. I shouldn't have said that. It was out of order. It's none of my business.' She looked down, embarrassed, and he felt her stiffen by his side.

'No, it's okay, I want it to be your business, and I know you're right to a degree. I think I took her for granted. I think we took each other for granted. It was hard not to when we were both caught in the slog of living, working and falling into bed each night, keeping the wheels turning and trying to make things the best they could be for Olly. The gilding that coated us when we were newly married got worn off by life, the rub of problems, worry, rows – it exposed patches that eventually took over, and I think I realised that being with someone I fancied was not necessarily enough to guarantee happy ever after. And then' – he paused – 'I haven't ever said this out loud before, but . . .' He thought about the phrasing, took his time. 'When Kerry got sick' – he shook his head and smiled, as if what he was about to say was both ridiculous and terrible – 'we had to wipe the slate clean. We had to find a way to come together, support each other, spend time together, and concentrate on each other in ways we hadn't before. It made us close and I think we saw the best of each other in those last months. I didn't know I could care for her like I did, physically, and I didn't know how generous and thoughtful she could be when it came to her death. But she was practical, never dramatic, kind even, and she made it the best it could be for Olly and me. That was remarkable of her, a gift. I'd never stopped loving her, not really, but I guess as a couple we became more functional, practical rather than romantic. And weirdly, at the end, we were romantic. It was nice.'

'I think you were both lucky,' she said with obvious emotion in her voice.

'You do?'

'Yes. That kind of certainty, that kindness blossoming when you both needed it the most, is a wonderful thing.'

'God, Beverly, here we are sharing a bottle of wine and all I'm doing is talking about Kerry and sad stuff. I know we have an agreement, but you must think I'm great company!'

'As I've already said, I think it's good we can talk about stuff. Important.'

'I do too. But I'm out of practice, at talking and lots of other things.' He felt his face colour as he realised this sounded like he was talking about sex, when in actual fact he had been thinking of wining and dining someone, flirting, dancing, and yes, actually, he had to admit, maybe a little bit about sex . . . 'I didn't mean . . .' He floundered.

'You worry too much, Nick. You need to not overthink things and, for the record, I think you're doing just fine.'

'Thank you.' He winked at her.

'Although you can cut that winking thing out!'

They laughed and Nick reached for the bottle of wine.

With two bottles of wine devoured and the alcohol sloshing pleasantly in their veins, the sharp edges of worry had been softened and his body had lost its tension, his muscles no longer corded, his thoughts quieted. It was nice. The evening had a warm glow of comfort about it and he got the impression that she, like him, was happy to be here on the sofa, while real life happened on the other side of the front door.

Beverly tilted her face up and kissed his cheek. This was the moment he had been thinking about and he twisted so he could kiss her on the mouth. It was a comfortable, easy, wonderful thing, the way they slipped against each other on the sofa, taking their time to kiss slowly, getting to know each other, hesitantly, giggling with joy, as if neither had expected this glorious gift of attraction that bound them.

'Shall we go upstairs?' she whispered.

Nick nodded and stood from the sofa. He took her by the hand and led only the second woman in his life up the stairs and towards the bedroom. Beverly hung back and stood in the doorway on the small square landing.

'Are you okay?' he asked. Nerves made his mouth dry and he felt the quake of apprehension in his limbs, this, however, almost overridden by a new and welcome sensation, one he had not felt for some time, and which he recognised as desire. He stood by the bed and wondered whether to go and lead her over to the bed, or maybe he should strip off and get in, or . . . He was so out of practice and truly couldn't remember how these things started. He wanted so badly to get it right.

He watched her eyes dart to the open bathroom door, where he knew a lilac toothbrush sat next to his in the ceramic pot on the sink. She then looked back to the wardrobe, where the door had popped open to reveal a neat row of jumpers, blouses, summer frocks and a pair of jeans, all hung with care. Redundant clothing for a woman who used to live there, a woman who had entered this very room and climbed into the bed thousands of times.

Nick felt paralysed by indecision; he didn't know what to say or what to do.

'I guess,' Beverly began, her voice no more than a whisper, 'I didn't really think what it might be like to be in Kerry's room with her things around us. I don't know what I thought, but I assumed that maybe, her clothes and—'

'Oh!' He walked forward and shut the wardrobe door, as if out of sight out of mind were the best way to deal with this. 'I suppose I should have sorted things, maybe got rid of some of—'

'No!' Beverly almost shouted. 'No, not at all – I would never ask; I was not saying that. God! That's such a personal thing and I would never suggest . . . The time is right when it's right I guess, and only you know when that is.' She gasped, her head hung forward. 'Shit, Nick.' She sighed. 'I'm sorry.'

'No, I'm sorry.' He walked towards her and pulled her to him until the air was less spiky and their pulses less flustered. 'Do you want to go home?'

'No. I don't want to go home.' She shook her head and he felt sweet and instant relief. 'How about we go back to the sofa?' she whispered. 'I think I liked it better there.'

'Me too.' Nick grabbed the faux fur throw from the end of the bed and, hand in hand, they walked back down the stairs.

They lay with their heads on one of those darned cushions and with the throw draped over them for warmth. Beverly was petite and fitted nicely in the space on the edge of the couch, her head resting on his chest. It felt good to be in such close proximity.

'It's funny, Bev,' he began, whispering into the night air.

'What is?'

He took a deep breath and stared at the ceiling. 'I'm skint. My job's going. I'm still torn up over losing Kerry, riddled with guilt over just about everything. I worry about Oliver. And yet right now, lying here with you, I feel happy. It's like I can put all of that bad stuff to the back of my mind when I'm with you, and it feels really nice.' He felt her nod against his chest.

She ran her fingers up under the front of his shirt and he closed his eyes. The touch of her fingers against his skin was a flame to the kindling that had lain dormant for so, so long.

Beverly looked up at him through her long, sooty lashes. 'We don't have to . . . I mean. I want to, but I don't want to rush you. It's that timing thing again.' She smiled.

Nick moved on to his side so he could kiss her properly, pulling her towards him. He smoothed the fringe from her face and hoped his every action told her that she didn't have to worry, the time was right.

The time was now.

1992

Nick wished he had paid more attention to his dad when he had shown him how to pitch the tent. As the taillights of his dad's car disappeared along the trail and over the brow of the hill, he looked at the long slender blue bag in which lived the tent poles and the chunky bag next to it with the canvas neatly folded inside, and knew he didn't have the first clue.

'Right.' Alex crouched by their supplies. 'What's first?'

Nick felt the pressure of his role as assumed leader; his palms began to sweat and he looked again out over the narrowing track, as if staring hard and willing it might make his dad return and help them set up the tent.

'You know what you're doin'?' his dad had asked before leaving, and with an inflated and misplaced sense of pride overriding any practicalities, Nick had laughed. *Sure!* He pictured the tent being unpacked in the front garden during their practice run yesterday, the way the poles had clattered on to the lawn with twangs and thuds, as metal hit metal and made him flinch.

'We have to lay all the poles out and fix them together. The narrow ends slide into the wider ends. They only fit one way so we can't go wrong.' And just like that he remembered the man's instructions, verbatim. It felt good, as if his mates were right to place their faith in his leadership.

'Hello, boys!'

Nick looked up to see Eric walking around with two large bread rolls snaffled from the food bag held up on to his chest. He laughed loudly.

'My name is Veronica!' Eric said in a high-pitched tone, 'and I've got enormous boobies!' Eric waggled the baps up and down. It might have been the giddiness of being out here alone or it might have been that Eric was genuinely funny; either way, the three collapsed in fits of giggles that gripped them so badly Nick had to run away a little and wee into the scrub. He laughed again when he thought of his sister's face when matched by Eric, made all the funnier when he realised he was thinking of it while peeing, standing up.

The tent was up. Kind of. The poles had slotted together easily enough and had gone into the right eyelets, sliding into position.

The canvas had been pulled taut and the flysheet attached with little knots. Their triangular home for the night was vaguely tent shaped and would certainly provide shelter of sorts. The only problem was that somehow, in a way the boys couldn't quite figure, the whole structure was twisted slightly, as if a giant hand had come along and put a kink in the middle. They pulled the guy ropes and secured them with the metal pegs, taking it in turns to wield the solid lump hammer on to the heads, driving them into the hardened, rain-deprived soil of the moors. Apparently the drizzly weather at the latter end of the summer was not enough to compensate for the good baking of the first few weeks. The three piled in through the unzipped door and lay looking at the blue ridge of the roof. It felt like some achievement.

'We can do whatever we want – no grown-ups!' Alex laughed.

'Yeah, like swearing, I can shout out, SHIT!'

Nick took up the verbal baton passed by Eric: 'Yeah, SHIT!' he shouted, a fantastic grown-up word, all the funnier for being yelled into the quiet.

'SHIT!' It was Alex's turn.

'SHIT IT!' Eric embellished.

'SHIT BALLS!' Nick matched him, and they laughed until tears ran.

'SHIT STICKS!' Eric triumphed. 'Shit sticks' was undoubtedly the funniest thing they had ever heard. It took a good few minutes before they all caught their breath and were able to talk.

'I'd quite like to live in a tent.' Eric kicked his foot against the side.

'What, instead of going to Derby?' Alex raised the terrible topic.

'Yep. Then I wouldn't have to live with any stinking baby!'

'What stinking baby?' Alex asked.

Nick liked that he knew about this already. It made him think, not for the first time, that whilst they were a gang of three, he and Eric were bestest best friends. It made the thought of him going even harder, as if being left with Alex were some sort of consolation prize.

'My mum's having a baby.' Eric sighed, as if even having to say the words out loud was a little more than he could cope with.

'Is Dave the dad?'

Nick turned his eyes to Alex. What a ridiculous thing to say! Didn't he know that Eric's mum was married to Eric's dad? How could Dave be the baby's dad? He smirked at his friend's ignorance and rolled his eyes.

'Yes, he is. That's what my dad said.' Eric again kicked the side of the tent.

Nick sat up and looked from one to the other. He was confused and embarrassed in equal measure and wished his mum were close by so he could ask her how this was even possible. He knew the word 'sex' and knew that babies came from your mum's tummy, but he also knew with certainty that babies were made when people were married.

Eric almost whispered now, 'When I have a son . . . I'll never make him go and live in some rubbish place that isn't Burstonbridge.'

Nick joined in: 'I'll never let mine go camping without staying and making sure the tent is properly up.'

Alex sighed. 'I'll never call mine a little poof, just because he put his mum's nightie on to see what it felt like.'

There was a moment or two of silence until laughter again erupted from them.

'God, Moira! What are you like?' Eric shouted.

'MOIRA!' Nick screamed.

Even Alex joined in: 'Holy shit sticks, Batman!' was his contribution. Nick loved to laugh like this and knew that, no matter that Eric was going to move away and his mum was having a stinking baby whose dad might actually, somehow, be Dave, this was and always would be what he remembered about the summer: laughing like this. Laughing so hard he needed to pee.

'Let's get out of here!' He jumped up and burst through the door on to the moors, where adventure awaited.

The three wandered down the slope in their shorts and wellington boots, getting the feel of their surroundings. Each had their precious puncture repair kit in their pocket, though Half Bike had been left at home, and in his other pocket Nick kept the multi-tool. Even though it was still light, Alex carried the bulky torch into which Nick's dad had put new batteries. Eric, of course, brandished a long stick, with which he cleared the path ahead. He worked in the way a jungle explorer might, jabbing into the scrubby heathers looking for venomous snakes, and beating the dried, thirsty fronds of bracken in case they harboured deadly spiders.

'My dad told me that there's a giant black puma that lives around here.' Alex lowered his voice, as if wary that the puma might be within earshot.

'You are kidding, right?' Eric asked, wide-eyed, stick in hand.

Alex shook his head. 'It hunts like a tiger or a lion and takes deer and sheep and stuff when it's hungry, and people find the dead animals with all their guts ripped out!' He demonstrated with his splayed fingers tearing at his own rib cage. Nick swallowed, thinking that he and his mates were not far off the size of deer or a big fat sheep. He was glad they had the torch with them for the night time, confident that no puma would dare approach if they saw that sturdy beam of light.

The boys walked and chatted, devising a series of calls and shouts to be used in an emergency. After much debate and countless deliberations and demonstrations without consensus, it was decided that in an emergency the best call to make was the shout of 'SHIT STICKS!'

'Or we could just shout out, "Help!"'

Nick stared at Alex, who was annoying him; his suggestion was not in the spirit of things.

'We need to have a call that's especially for camping, a call that tells the others that the puma is around. I mean, you can shout out, "Help!" any time.'

Eric picked up the mantle. 'Yeah, like "Help! I've run out of bog roll!"'

This made them laugh.

'Or' – Alex walked backwards, facing them – 'like "Help! My name is Will Pearce and I've wet my pants again!"'

All right, Nick had to concede, that *was* funny.

The boys meandered to the right as the sun began to dip and a cool breeze ran like nature's hand over the tops of the plants and shrubs, causing them to lie flat momentarily as the wind caressed them.

'I'm hungry,' Eric announced.

'You're always hungry!' Alex pointed out.

'Yes, but I'm normally a bit hungry and then there are times during the day when I'm mega hungry and this is one of those times.'

'Let's head back.' Nick turned and looked in the direction from which they had come. In his head he had expected to see the track winding its way back to the top of the hill where the blue tent was pitched. His heart stuttered when he saw clusters of bracken and heathers crowning the undulating landscape, tufts of grass and patches of soil. It all looked remarkably similar and there was no clear or obvious clue as to where they had left the tent.

'Which way?' Eric asked.

Nick felt it was important to be decisive and pointed to the right. 'This way and then round a bit.' His pulse raced as the three began to climb with an increased pace, seeming to sense, although unspoken, that the dark would be coming in and that Eric was hungry. Nick tried to shut the thought of the black puma out of his mind, but was convinced he heard a low growl coming from the undergrowth.

The boys walked for longer than they had when travelling away from their camp and there was no sign of the blue tent or the particular hill next to the car track.

'Where now?' Alex asked, a little breathless.

In his head Nick shouted, *How should I know? Why are you asking me?* He looked up and then around, and rather than admitting to the fact that they were very lost, he tramped on, pointing ahead.

'I'm hungry,' Eric murmured again.

'Shut up, Eric! We know!' Nick snapped.

As they climbed higher, the narrow track turned into a bigger lane and there in the distance was a walled building.

'I think we have to go and ask someone in there if they've seen our tent or can point us in the right direction.'

The boys stood and stared.

'Supposing whoever is in there kidnaps us?' Alex whispered.

'Then we use the call of "SHIT STICKS!" and stab them with the multi-tool.' Nick remembered how they had practised the Batmanesque move in his bedroom. He sounded confident, but his pulse raced just the same.

He wasn't sure if the place was a hotel, a hospital or a block of flats. It sat behind wide metal gates set in high brick pillars, and on top of the brick pillars were two stone lions. Again Nick thought about the puma.

A long sweeping driveway flanked by trees led to a building that looked like a doll's house, but massive.

'Who lives here?' Eric curled his fingers around the railings of the gate and peered up the driveway.

'No idea.' Nick took a deep breath. 'How do we get to knock on the door?'

'I don't think we should.' Alex spoke up. 'I think we should carry on walking.'

'But we don't know where to walk,' Nick pointed out, admitting defeat. 'It's going to get dark and we've left the tent and all our stuff somewhere.' The thought of having to explain to his dad that they'd lost all the camping equipment was more than enough to spur him on. That and the prospect of spending the night wandering in the dark at the mercy of the big, prowling cat and having to listen to Eric's growling stomach. He scoured the brick post and saw the brass sign, which read 'Alston Bank', and there was a button set into a shiny brass panel. Nick pressed it and tried to quell the nerves that made his leg shake.

Eventually a male voice answered, 'Yes?' An authoritative voice that intimidated him.

'Erm, my name's Nick Bairstow and I'm here with my mates and we are lost. We can't find our tent and I wondered if you could give us directions.'

'Did you say Bairstow?'

'Yes.'

'Any relation to Jack Bairstow?'

'He's my dad.' Nick turned to the other two and pulled a face; this was weird.

The man gave a small, throaty chuckle. 'I'm pressing the button now to open the gate; come up to the house,' he instructed, his tone softening. They heard a buzzing noise and the gates whirred slowly open. The gates clunked shut behind them. The three tramped along the gravel drive with unusual quiet, part in awe of the grand place in which they found themselves but partly with naked fear. They were more than a little trapped. Nick put his hand in his pocket and gripped the multi-tool.

As they drew closer to the mansion a boy about their own age came cycling along the drive, appearing from behind an ornate circular fountain at the top of the driveway.

'Hello!' He seemed pleased to see them. 'My name's Julian!' He steered with one hand, a neat trick not lost on the cycling novices. Nick stared at the mountain bike, very different from their beloved cycle. The frame was sturdier, its wheels wider and it was customised with fancy red fire flashes, all right if you liked that kind of thing. Nick pictured Half Bike with its streaky green paint job and felt a flare of affection for the precious item currently nestling in the garage. He looked forward to getting back and cleaning it.

Julian pulled the bike to a stop and jumped off, letting it fall to the ground, where it landed with a crash, lying on its side with the back wheel spinning, while the boy walked alongside them as if they were mates, which they most definitely were not.

Nick kept glancing back at the bike, abandoned. He noted the mud-caked spokes of the wheels and the scuffed ends of the once-shiny chrome pedals. He hated the way Julian had let the frame fall on to the small chips of stone without a care for its welfare. Nick knew that letting the bike fall like that would at best pit the paintwork and at worst scratch it. He didn't like the way the boy treated something so new, shiny and, he assumed, expensive; it seemed ungrateful and it bothered him more than it should.

'Is this a hotel?' Eric asked.

'No! Why would you say that?' Julian laughed. He was a posh lad. 'It's our house!'

'Flippin' 'eck!' Eric gasped, and Nick thought it was the best thing to say, as it was indeed a house of flippin' 'eck proportions. He had never seen anything like it. He knew that there were rich people and poor people, and if he'd had to guess, he'd have said that his family lived somewhere in the middle. This was the first time he had ever been faced with such wealth and the reality that some people had far, far more than they needed while others, like Eric in his cold house where food was often slow in forthcoming, went to bed chilly with an empty tum. The thought was enough to make him miss his mum, not that he would share this thought, of course, knowing that to do so would invite ridicule and being called a name like Marjorie.

'How old are you?' Julian asked.

'I'm ten,' Eric answered sternly, as if he too mistrusted the boy, who was a bit overfriendly.

'Ten,' Nick offered.

'I'm nine.' Alex sighed at the injustice of having a late birthday.

'I'm nine too. What school do you go to?' Julian kept the questions coming.

The boys looked at each other, unaware that there was any other school close by and also loath to think about the fact that Eric would be going to a different one.

'Burstonbridge,' Eric answered proudly.

'I'm at Ashbury House.' Julian said the name as if it should be familiar to them, which it wasn't. 'Do you like rugby?'

'Don't know.' Eric answered for them all. They only played and supported football.

'Do you ride?' the boy asked.

'Yes, we share a bike and it's really fast. Nick got her up to thirty miles an hour on Cobb Lane,' Alex pointed out, and Nick was not only glad of his mate's enthusiasm for poor old Half Bike but also the recognition of his speedy feat.

Julian threw his head back and laughed loudly. But this laugh was different from the pee-inducing hilarity they had shared earlier. This was a mocking laugh, the sound of derision, and Nick didn't like it one bit. He felt a flash of dislike for this boy.

'I mean horses, of course! Do you ride *horses*? We have stables, and I have a new pony called Ruskin but we call him Rusky. Do you want to see him?'

Nick and his mates were staring at the boy, wondering how to answer, when a man's voice called out.

'Now then, lads!' The boys looked up at the man who came from the front door of the house. He looked a bit like Julian but had an accent closer to their own. It was odd to Nick how much this put him at ease.

'Which one of you is Jack Bairstow's lad?'

'Me.' He raised his hand.

'Nick?'

'Yes!' This was amazing to him – there they were up on Drayfield Moor in the middle of nowhere in this man's massive garden and he knew Nick's name!

'I'm Aubrey Siddley; I work with your dad.'

'My dad works at Siddley's!' Nick beamed at this connection.

'Yes.' The man laughed. 'That's right, he does.'

'My dad works at Siddley's too,' Eric piped up.

'Does he now? Who is your dad?' the man asked, smiling.

'Gary Pickard.'

'Ah, Gary, yes.' The man let his eyes wrinkle at the edges, as if he felt a little bit sorry for Eric, and Nick wondered if he had heard about the whole Derby thing and the stinking new baby.

'Does your dad work at Siddley's too?' Mr Siddley asked Alex, who shook his head.

'No, he works for British Gas.'

For some reason this made the man laugh.

'Right, so we are lost, are we?'

'Yes.' Nick stepped forward. 'We're camping for a night, and my dad dropped us off on the track and we set the tent up and then went to explore a bit, and now we can't find the tent.' He looked at the floor, feeling more than a little responsible for their predicament.

'Right, well, if your dad drove in from Burston, I reckon I might know the track you mean. I'll go and fetch the car and we'll get you back to base camp; how about that?'

'Thank you.' Nick remembered his manners, knowing his dad would remind him of them if he were here.

'Can I come, Daddy?' Julian jumped up and down with stiffened arms and legs.

'No, lad. Your mum's got supper on the table.'

Nick saw Eric's eyes glaze over and knew he was imagining the table inside the big house, wondering what food Julian's mum might be preparing.

Mr Siddley disappeared around the side of the property.

'Bye, guys!' Julian called. The boys waved an awkward goodbye to him.

'How many bedrooms do you think there are in that house?' Alex stared up at it.

'About seventeen,' Eric guessed.

Nick thought this number was way too big but with nothing to base his assumption on he kept quiet. It was as he counted the upstairs windows, trying to figure out how many bedrooms there might be, that Alex shouted loudly.

'No way!'

Nick whipped around in time to see Mr Siddley pull around to the front of the house in a gleaming navy-blue Rolls Royce.

The boys ran around the car, admiring the immaculate paintwork and stopping just short of running their fingers over the surface. Nick stared at the large chrome grille that had a silver figure sitting proudly above it. Mr Siddley wound down the window.

'Hop in, then; mind your feet on the seats.'

Nick made his way around the wide vehicle, admiring the shiny chrome wing mirrors and the chrome strips that lined the smear-free windows. It was the most beautiful car he had ever seen. The most beautiful *thing* he had ever seen!

Eric opened the door to the back seat and piled in, followed by Nick and finally Alex, who held the torch on his lap. The first thing he noticed was the smell. Breathing deeply, he inhaled the heady, intoxicating scent of the warm caramel-coloured leather. He knew it was a smell he would never forget. The second thing was the absolute comfort of the seats. They were wide, soft and yet supportive. He sank into it, the rounded edges so nice to feel against his skin. He had a perfect view of the dashboard between the two vast front seats and stared at the enormous number of dials and indicators that sat recessed inside the glossy wooden panel. He wanted to push every button and run his finger over every dial. And it was quiet! So quiet. He would have thought that a vehicle of this size and stature would make quite a racket, but the engine almost purred as it rolled along the long driveway.

'How fast can it go?' Eric asked.

'Faster than I'm allowed to.' Mr Siddley laughed as they stopped at the gates, which seemed to magically whir open. Nick turned and looked back towards the house and spied Julian, watching them from a window above the front door. He felt a little guilty, thinking that maybe he should have invited Julian to come along, but they didn't know him at all and the tent wasn't that big; plus, he wasn't sure he wanted someone in their gang who treated his things so badly. His eyes now settled on the discarded bike and again he felt the flare of fury. Why did that boy think it was okay to treat something so precious this way?

Nick paid little attention to the route they took, and would have been quite happy to be driven around like this all day and all night. Whilst some might have been drawn by the glorious countryside beyond the window, Nick could only concentrate on the fine detail that made this car magnificent: the shiny pop-up door locks, the wood panelling inside the doors, the chunky yet rounded handles with which to open them, and the air vents sitting like mini portholes, edged in the thinnest strips of bright chrome.

'I like your car,' Nick managed, finding his voice.

'She's a beauty all right.' Mr Siddley ran his hand over the top of the wide, wooden steering wheel, which had a caramel-coloured leather triangle in the middle and silver double 'R's entwined on it. 'Do you think you might like a car like this one day?' the man asked in the mirror, looking straight at Nick.

'No.' Nick shook his head. 'I don't think it would fit on our driveway,' he replied honestly, and for some reason this too made the man laugh.

'You're a practical fellow, young Bairstow, and that's a good way to be!'

Nick felt his cheeks colour at the compliment, not entirely sure what it meant to be practical but fearful that it sounded a little dull.

'Now then.' The car slowed. 'I'm guessing this must be your tent, as that is certainly your dad.'

Nick whipped around to see his dad standing a little way from the road on the other side of the track by the side of their tent with his hands on his hips. He hoped he wasn't going to be angry.

'Jack.' Mr Siddley wound the window down and Nick watched his dad walk around to address the man.

'Mr Siddley! How did . . . What's going on? I'm sorry.'

Nick didn't know what he was apologising for and didn't like to see his dad flustered like this, the man whose word was law.

'No need to apologise. Out you hop, lads.'

Alex opened the door and the three climbed reluctantly from the vehicle.

'I think our intrepid explorers might have taken a wrong turn.'

'Yes.' Jack Bairstow shook his head. 'I'm in the car over the brow of the next hill – didn't want them out here entirely alone.'

Nick looked at his mates. He didn't know how to take this news. He was in equal parts furious that the man didn't trust them to make it through one night of camping and relieved that his dad was close by, on hand, listening out for the call of 'SHIT STICKS!' that might mean puma attack – or worse, they couldn't figure out how to cook the sausages.

'Are you camping too?' Eric tried to catch up.

'No, Eric, I'm sleeping in the car with the seat reclined, but with the window open, listening out.'

'The things we do for them, eh, Jack?'

His dad laughed and nodded. 'I watched them put the tent up, turned my back for a minute and they'd gone!'

'They went down and round the lower moor and were trying to come up the wrong side, a bit of a wild-goose chase.' Mr Siddley laughed.

'Is it true there's a big puma around here?' Alex asked with a rasp to his voice.

'Oh, yes.' Mr Siddley nodded solemnly before whispering, 'A big beast he is, by all accounts, only comes out at night, and I've heard he's rather partial to the colour blue.'

The boys looked from one another to their tent. Nick had never been happier that his dad was right there by his side.

TEN

It had been a turbulent night. Sleeping on the sofa meant Nick woke sporadically to find himself either squashed into the corner with his face against the squeaky leather, or about to fall off the rounded edge, depending on the many sleep configurations they tried until dawn broke. And then, as if exhaustion had taken over, he and Beverly fell into a deep sleep. The furry throw covered their nakedness. Their clothes had been removed and flung with abandon over the rug and the coffee table. Nick got up to pee in the night, gingerly climbing over Beverly's sleeping form and trying in vain not to disturb her. He had smiled at the sight of his jeans and shirt heaped on the floor and her underwear, small and floral, odd, delicate things that he was not used to seeing around the house of late. The wineglasses, empty bottles and the half-eaten bowl of crisps littered the surfaces. It looked like there had been a party. The sight of this glorious detritus folded his gut with joy. It was proof of someone living a life that was more than dog walks, early nights and sandwiches for supper. It felt slightly illicit and carefree, frivolous and a little daring, all aspects of life that had been off his radar for a long, long time. He stared at his face in the bathroom mirror and smiled. He looked a little younger, remembering how wonderful sex was, and realising now that he had missed it more than he ever would have dared to admit.

And now they slept.

Nick was vaguely aware of an unfamiliar noise and tried and failed to force his lids, gluey with fatigue, open. His first thought was that Treacle might need letting out, before pulling from the murky depths of his thoughts the fact that the dog had stayed at his mum's. He wondered vaguely if the post had plopped through the door or whether someone walking past had nudged the gate. Not that it mattered. Nothing did. It was the weekend and here he lay with the skin of a naked woman next to his.

Light snuck in through the gaps in the curtain and his brain ticked into semi-alert mode. His thoughts turned to a cup of tea and then immediately wondered if he had any fresh bread and whether Beverly might like some toast. Breakfast was not something he had envisaged or planned for. And then there was another noise; to his horror this was one he did recognise: the sound of the front door closing. His heart boomed in his chest. And before he had a chance to shout out, move or make a plan, he heard Oliver's voice calling from the other side of the door in the hallway.

'Dad? Hel-lo! I'm home! Tash is here too. Dad?' His son's voice echoed along the narrow hallway.

'Shit! Shit!' He tried to jump up and jarred Beverly awake in the process, unceremoniously kneeing her in the back. She now sat up on the sofa and drew the furry throw to her chin, looking a little dazed.

'Olly!' he called out, drawing breath, as his heart continued to hammer. He was about to say, *Just give me a minute*, or *I'll be out in a sec*, or *Don't come in!* Or a million other things that might, just might, have taken the sharp edge off the situation and given all present the smallest window of opportunity to preserve some modesty and limit the damage that was about to be done. And by all present, he meant himself, Beverly, who now sat with a look of part confusion and part terror, Oliver . . . and Tasha. Tasha, the girl his son loved and who was visiting their home for the very first time.

'Oliver!' Nick rushed towards the door and, seeing Tasha standing a fraction behind his son, jumped back into the room to retrieve his jeans from the floor.

'What's going on?' Oliver laughed, looking at Tasha with an expression that was as confused as it was apologetic. Clearly the last thing he would have told her to expect was his half-naked father hopping around on one leg in the lounge trying to step into his jeans.

'Take Tasha into the kitchen and get the kettle on. We'll be out in a sec.' He tried to keep his tone neutral, welcoming, smiling briefly at Tasha and doing his best to make this seem like any other normal arrival home, when it was anything but.

At the use of the word 'we' he saw the penny drop. Oliver's eyes searched his before scanning the floor, where Nick knew he would spot the clothes they had wantonly discarded.

Shit sticks!

He pushed the door until it was almost closed and looked at Beverly, who, hair mussed and eyes heavy from sleep, stared at him.

'What's going on?' she managed.

'Oliver and his girlfriend Tasha have turned up.' He felt his stomach bunch as he watched her close her eyes, bring her knees up under the cover and rest her forehead on them. It looked like she was trying to hide from the situation, or at the very least wake up from the embarrassing nightmare in which she found herself. He understood both. Nick also felt the bolt of guilt, the very idea that he might look upon his son's surprise arrival home with anything other than joy, and yet here he was, wishing Oliver had given some notice.

'What do we do now?' She kept her voice low.

'Get dressed,' he urged. 'I've told them to wait in the kitchen.'

'Oh my God!' she whispered.

'I'm sorry, Bev.'

She gave his apology short shrift; there were more pressing matters at hand, like rummaging around on the floor, trying to retrieve her bra and knickers.

In the face of the emergency, any shyness over their naked state in these new and uncharted waters was lost. There was no time to reach subtly for pants and shirts while the other turned away or, as Nick had planned, to gather up his stuff and dress in the kitchen while the kettle boiled, giving her space and privacy to do likewise. Instead, they encroached on each other's space in the small, square room, tripping over the lumps of shoe that lay beneath cushions and fumbling in the semi-lit room to fasten bra hooks and button up Christmas-gift shirts, bending over, bums in the air to scrabble under the throw, trying to locate socks and, in Beverly's case, a missing camisole.

Nick raised one foot to put his sock on and stumbled forward, landing in a crumpled heap on the armchair that sat in the corner. He twisted to sit in it and looked at Beverly, who was trying not to laugh.

'I know this isn't funny,' she whispered with her palms raised, 'but if it wasn't so embarrassing, it would be a little bit funny.' She smiled at him. 'I have my knickers on inside out.' She pulled a face.

Nick felt a rush of affection for this woman, who could have made the situation so much worse. The fact that she could remain calm and find humour with no idea of what waited for them outside the door was something quite wonderful.

'You're lucky.' He paused. 'My briefs are in my pocket!' He pulled the offending scrunched-up item from his pocket briefly before shoving it back into his jeans.

With their clothing and a little of Nick's dignity restored, he drew the curtains, opened the window and watched as Beverly placed the cushions on the sofa.

'I'm not very good at cushions.' She looked at him soberly and he again stifled his laughter; in light of the situation in which they found themselves, cushions really didn't matter.

'Me either.' He reached out and ran his fingers over her neck. The small touch was enough to remind him of the current of desire that ran through them, joined them. It was no small reassurance when he considered going outside of the room to face Oliver. He tried to remind himself that he was the dad and Oliver was his child and that this was not Oliver's ship to steer, but this momentary blip of reasoning quickly evaporated; he and Kerry had never parented in that way.

'You go ahead.' She twisted her face and kissed his wrist. 'I'll pop to the bathroom and come down in a bit, give you a chance to smooth the path.'

Nick nodded and took a deep breath; he hated the hammer of nerves that beat a rhythm in his stomach. Opening the door with false bravado, embarrassment shading his thoughts and actions, he walked into the kitchen. Oliver and Tasha sat at either side of the kitchen table in silence. The atmosphere could best be described as tense. Tasha's nose twitched under the heavy frame of her glasses and Oliver stared at his hands, which fidgeted on the tabletop.

'So, this is a lovely surprise – good journey? How did you get up here?' He faced the cupboard, glad of the diversion as he hunted down the mugs.

Tasha spoke up, her voice a little smaller than Nick remembered when she was in her own environment, her manner a little more reserved. 'We got the night-time coach that took us to York and then we got the train to Thirsk and then the bus over here. It's been quite an adventure, but it was nice to see the countryside, and we slept on the coach and talked a lot, so it went quickly, really.' She swallowed.

'You should have said you were coming,' Nick offered lightly, and Oliver caught his eye. Nick knew his boy well enough to read his expression: *I wish we had . . .* 'I'd have got a proper breakfast in and whatnot. It's great to see you, Tasha! Welcome to Burston!'

'Thank you.' She looked at Oliver, asserting her loyalty despite Nick's attempt at friendly banter.

'I'll nip out later and do a big shop, get all your favourites in, Olly. Are you still shifting enough cereal on a daily basis to feed an army?'

Oliver again looked at his hands, his face drawn.

'I told him he eats too much cereal. Sometimes he fills up a mixing bowl and eats that in front of his computer; it's, like, at least two billion teaspoons of sugar.' Tasha filled the silent gaps and Nick was strangely grateful, figuring that if she hadn't been there then Oliver would have a lot more to say, a lot that Nick knew he probably didn't want to hear, and possibly delivered in a manner that had the power to wound. Still stunned by the news that he was to lose his livelihood, and now this stomach-bunchingly awkward encounter, he didn't know if he was properly equipped to deal with anything else right now.

'Morning, everyone,' Beverly said softly, walking in slowly, hesitantly, as if testing the water or waiting for an invitation. She hovered before deciding to sit at the table between Tasha and Oliver. Nick resisted the temptation to walk over and place his hand on her back and guide her to the chair, thinking his physical reassurance might help. He chose to ignore the slight curl of Oliver's top lip and the narrowing of his eyes. It didn't bode well.

'Morning, I'm Tasha.' The girl nodded and smiled briefly and Nick wanted to hug her.

'Hi, Tasha. Beverly.' She smiled at the girl. 'And how are you, Oliver?'

Nick noted the nervous edge to her voice and the way she swallowed, clearly feeling more anxious than he realised. He hated that she had been put in this position, especially when last night had been so bloody perfect.

'Imokay,' the boy responded, eliding his words to get the whole interaction over in the shortest possible time.

Nick put the mugs on the countertop and reached for the caddy in which the teabags lived. He had heard the distinct tone to Oliver's voice, the sound of vocal cords pulled taut under the strain of trying not to cry, and his heart ripped. He wanted to take the boy in his arms and hold him tight, tell him that it was all going to be fine, that this was still and always would be his home and that Nick loved him.

You and me against the world . . .

But in the presence of his girlfriend and Beverly, Nick knew it was best to let him be.

'Do you know, Nick, I think I'd better make a move actually.' Beverly pointed towards the front door as she stood from the table. 'Nice to meet you, Tasha, and nice to see you again, Oliver.' She spoke with false brightness as she left the kitchen.

'I'll see you out.' Nick followed her along the hallway and opened the front door. 'Bev,' he began, speaking softly, aware of the audience, his eyes searching, hoping she got the message that he wanted to say more.

She smiled up at him and closed her eyes briefly. 'It's fine. Call me later.' She squeezed his arm and walked up the garden path. He felt a spike of longing as she walked away, wanting to call her back and tell her that he would prefer it if she stayed, but of course that wasn't possible, not today.

Closing the front door, he swallowed at the thought of having to go and face his son and Tasha, feeling curiously like he had lost his ally. Painting on a smile, he clapped his hands and marched ahead.

'Right, who wants toast?'

'No, thanks. I just want a shower.' Oliver avoided eye contact as he stood and reached for Tasha, who followed him up the stairs.

Nick sat alone and put his head in his hands.

'Why does everything have to be so bloody complicated?' he whispered into the ether. 'I need fresh air.'

It was a beautiful day. Nick walked with purpose and glowed with the memory of what it had felt like to lie with Beverly. The sun sat high in the sky and golden rays spread like beams from God's torchlight from behind the wispy clouds that were propelled by the faintest breeze. Nick climbed up the ridge, stopping to take in the view that lay beneath him. His eyes settled on the rusting roof of the Old Dairy Shed, into which he had never invited his sister. He wished he could go back and do just that, make her feel wanted, try to soften the spike of low self-esteem that now lanced her potential relationships. The Old Dairy Shed, like other farm buildings in the area, was dilapidated and unloved, and yet a place for which he felt such affection.

Everything can prosper with a bit of love . . .

He heard Kerry's voice and smiled. He needed to hear that today.

It was rare for him to pause and appreciate the stunning expanse. It seemed he was always in a hurry these days – to get home or to his next shift. Countless were the times he had wished he didn't have to be anywhere. Yet now the prospect of having no shift to clock on for, free to spend his days idling without a wage, filled him with cold dread.

Careful what you wish for, eh, Nick?

He had decided to get a head start and contact employment agencies on Monday, to start putting feelers out. But that was Monday; right now, he was just going to look at the view. He let his eyes sweep the hedgerows binding the narrow lanes and the fields rolling as far as the eye could see in a glorious verdant patchwork until they met the wide twist of the river in the distance. Ancient trees stooped and flourished at the water's edge. In a mirror image on the other side of the river, the fields sloped upwards to the top of the valley and beyond, the crests of the dark, imposing moors made a pale mauve by spreading heather set slightly in shadow. The big sky was blue and, despite the chill of the day, the sun glinted off the water that foamed where it hit boulders and clusters of twigs gathered against the bank. Nick stayed there, watching the light change. And those glorious shafts of golden light firing from the sun as it rose higher, bathing the fields and all it touched in a beautiful glow. Long shadows stretched and yawned across the meadows, alerting every living thing that the day was marching on.

Nick found himself almost reduced to tears, but this time by the sheer beauty of his surroundings. He walked on until he came to the bench by Kerry's grave and sat down hard. The damp wood flexed a little under his weight. He gathered his thoughts, sniffed and looked cautiously at the grey stone beneath which his wife lay. It was an odd thing. He addressed her now for the first time ever having slept with another woman. Whether his sense of betrayal was necessary or justified made little difference, he felt it just the same.

'Hey, love,' he began. 'I don't know what to say. I feel a bit lost, a bit happy and a bit worried that I have no right to feel even the beginnings of happy, but then I think, why not me? Why not? And who's to say when the time is right? How soon is too soon? I wish I knew.' He laid his fingers on his thighs and pictured Kerry when she would turn mid-walk, look him right in the eye and smile or nod, agreeing to something he had shared. Her face, her lovely face, not too different from that of the teenager he had fallen in love with all those years ago, always pretty, always to him that girl sitting in the classroom.

'What a week,' he continued with a dry laugh. 'They're closing Siddley's. I can't believe it. It hasn't sunk in. I keep thinking that there will be an eleventh-hour reprieve – something.' He shook his head and realised he spoke the truth. 'I keep thinking about when Dad said I could get a few shifts – do you remember? We were pleased as punch, thought it was a king's ransom. I can't remember exactly how much I was earning, but I know it was a pittance. Just enough to pay the rent and to keep us in tins of soup and packets of cheap spaghetti, and that was all we worried about, wasn't it? God, we were so young, Kerry, naïve, really, but happy, eh? Happy, then.' He took a deep breath. 'Things are changing and I feel like I'm struggling to keep up. Eric wants to go to bloody Australia! Can you believe that? Australia!' He shook his head. 'I know he's always had a hankering for the sun, but I can't imagine not seeing him every day. But then I can't imagine not seeing you every day, and yet here we are. Beverly stayed last night and . . .'

Nick paused and turned to his right at the sound of someone climbing the ridge. He sat up straight at the sight of his son, who stopped and looked back down the hill, as if deciding whether or not he wanted to be in such close proximity, alone with his dad, before making his way over.

Nick budged up on the soggy bench. Oliver sat as far away from him as was physically possible. It was rare for them both to be here at the same time.

'I just wanted to talk to Mum.' Oliver sat forward with his elbows on his knees.

'Me too.' He spoke calmly, holding his ground.

Nick watched as his son stared at the grave; he suspected Oliver was talking to his mum in his head. It felt a little like an intrusion and so he sat still and quiet. When Oliver sat back and sniffed, Nick spoke.

'Where's Tasha?'

'At Auntie Di's.'

'Auntie Di's? How come?' Nick couldn't help but allow the note of concern to escape, underpinned with surprise.

'We went to get Treacle from Nan's and were walking her back when we bumped into Auntie Di, and she said I should probably come up and see Mum, and Tasha went with her. I think they're going to bake something.'

Just my bloody luck . . .

'Smashing.'

'What? I can't see Auntie Di now?'

'No, Olly, of course you can. Have I ever said anything remotely like that?'

Oliver huffed.

'I don't know if you heard how she spoke to me on New Year's Eve, but it's not nice to be on the receiving end of it.' Nick knew he sounded defensive. 'I've never told you not to see Auntie Di or Gran or anyone. I never would. I think the more people you have holding up your safety net the better – I've always thought that.'

Oliver gave a single shake of his head.

'I don't know if I prefer the silent treatment or your anger. I can't decide.' Nick sighed.

'I came home because Nan texted me and told me Siddley's was going. I thought you'd be fed up and so I came home to surprise you.'

'That was really good of you, Olly. I *am* fed up. It's terrible news for everyone affected and terrible news for Burston.' He looked out over the fields and tried to picture at least a thousand brand-new houses . . .

'I have to say' – his son laughed sarcastically – 'you didn't seem that fed up when I came in, and it was me who got a bit of a surprise.'

'Yes.' Nick twisted on the bench to face him. 'We need to talk about that, don't we.'

'So does she live there now?'

'No!' Nick shook his head vigorously. 'Of course not! That was the first time she stayed over and it wasn't planned.'

Oliver widened his eyes, tilted his head to one side and pulled a face that suggested he did not believe this for one second. Nick ignored it and carried on, more intent on making progress than setting the record straight.

'I'm sensitive to how you feel, Olly, more than you know, but I can't be beholden to you – it's not fair.'

'Not fair?' Oliver swallowed. 'I'm so angry, Dad!'

'And you have every right to be angry about the blows life has dealt you, every right.' He looked at Kerry's headstone. 'But you have no right to be angry at me, not because I've made friends with Beverly; that can't be—'

'It's not only that,' Oliver interrupted. 'I'm angry that Mum's not here to meet Tasha, and I'm angry because there was another woman on her sofa, in her kitchen. And it makes it real, because if *she* is in the kitchen then it means my mum isn't.'

'I understand.'

'No, you don't!' The boy raised his voice. 'You can say that as much as you like, but you don't, Dad, you can't! And you never will. You can only know what it's like for you but never for me.'

Nick turned to face him. 'So what do you want me to do? What exactly do you want me to do, Oliver?'

Oliver shrugged.

Nick didn't try to hide his irritation. 'Don't shrug! That's not an answer. You can't have such strong opinions and *not* have a solution. How do you want things to work? What *would* make you happy?'

'I don't know,' Oliver mumbled, kicking at the grass.

'I think you do know, but you're just not saying.' Nick knew him well enough to figure this was the case.

'Okay, I want you to stop seeing her. I don't want you to see anyone, and I know I can't ask that, but that is what would make me happy because . . . because I'm still not ready.' He whispered the last bit.

Nick took his time in forming his response. This was the difficult stuff to talk about that he and Beverly had mentioned, and he knew she was right; it was exactly this stuff that moved things forward. He kept his tone level, subduing the emotion and anger that threatened to flare. 'Thank you for answering me so honestly. I appreciate that. I do. But the fact is, it's happened, Olly. The genie is out of the bottle. I've spent time with Beverly. She stayed over, and I have to be honest and say that I would like her to stay again. I've got a lot going on right now in my life that is far from good. Like losing my job for one.' He let this hang. 'And she is one part of it that is good. Being with her makes me happy.'

'But you promised me . . .' Oliver looked away, out over the expanse.

'I promised you what?'

'You promised me that it was you and me against the world, the Bairstow Boys – that's what you said!'

'And that hasn't changed! That could never change! Oliver, you're my son. I love you, kid.' Nick paused and bit his lip. 'But there is room in both of our lives for more. You have Tasha and, if things work out, then maybe I might have Bev. But despite what you think, it's still very early days.'

Oliver took a deep breath. 'I'm still getting used to the shape of the two of us without her.' He nodded towards the grave. 'And I can't imagine a new shape with a new person, someone I don't even know, someone in my house. It feels like the end of everything, even more than losing Mum. This feels like a new beginning that I don't have a part in.'

'But that's simply not true. What is true is that you don't know Beverly, not yet, but you have to trust me to make a decision that I think will be good. Just like I always have when you were too little to have a say, I've always guided you, guided *us*, to live the best life we could with what we had.'

Oliver seemed to calm a little. His words when they came were considered, poison-tipped arrows that lanced Nick's breast and stuck in his heart.

'It feels like you've got shot of me and got shot of Mum and you're starting over.' His voice was full of gravel, the rocks of grief crushed and now lining his throat.

Nick didn't have time to order his thoughts or plan what to say; the tears that sprang overtook both considerations. It was an instinctual response, as instantly and without warning he was crying. He bowed his head and let his sorrow drip from his chin as he made sounds of distress, trying to catch his breath before the next bout of tears robbed him of the rhythm.

Oliver shifted a little closer on the bench and Nick felt him place his hand in the middle of his back. It helped. A little. Eventually, as his sadness subsided, Nick straightened and rubbed his face with his hand, wiping his palms on his jeans to rid them of his tears. His eyes felt sore and he didn't doubt they looked it; that kind of crying always left its mark.

'That is' – Nick took a sharp breath – 'categorically not true, and that you even think it hurts me more than I can say.'

'I didn't mean it. Not really. It just came out wrong.' He heard Oliver swallow.

Nick didn't respond to this inadequate, half-hearted apology. It would take a little more than a hand on his back and those mealy-mouthed words to erase the hurt.

'It's just that I—'

Nick ground his teeth. 'Stop talking, Oliver. Stop talking and just listen to what you say and how you say it. Now, I'm no expert – far from it, I'm still feeling my way through this whole bloody process – but the difference between you and me is that I think about you and your needs all the time, every bloody day, but you? You can only think about what is right for Oliver. What Oliver needs, what makes Oliver happy.' He paused and coughed, clearing the snotty residue that had slipped down the back of his throat. 'And you're not a kid, not a baby. I think it's time you started to widen your emotional net. What about me? *My* needs, *my* wants? I'm more than just your dad, Oliver! I'm a person in my own right and I'm lonely and I'm sad.' He took a breath. 'And all the things that you get from being with Tasha – the companionship, the love, the escape, the joy – why do you think I'm not entitled to that? Is it because I'm so *old*? Is that it? Or because you think I should be living in the shade of grief for eternity? *Why?* Tell me. Because it's not fair. It's not bloody fair that I'm made to feel this way. I loved your mum – I love her.' He swallowed the catch to his voice, not wanting to cry again, done with that. It was too exhausting and served nothing other than making him feel like crap. 'I love her, I always will, and I love you. But I'm more than Kerry's widower and more than just your dad.'

Oliver looked at him, and it was a second or two before he spoke. 'But you're not more than that to me.' He drew breath. 'You're just my dad. That's all, and it's everything. My dad. I understand what you're saying, but I want you to be there just for me.'

Nick didn't know what to say. His son's words were gentle, honest and ripped his heart as much as his hurtful ones. He looked towards the plot where Kerry lay and hoped for inspiration. Oliver wasn't done.

'But then I want a lot of things. I want to be seven again and to come home to Mum making my tea and then, while I'm eating it, I want you to come in the door and kiss her on the cheek and wink at me and suggest we have a kickabout on the front grass when I've finished. That's what I want. Being adult is hard.'

Nick was relieved at the burst of laughter that spilled from him.

'Being adult?' He continued to laugh and shook his head affectionately. 'You're an eighteen-year-old student, Olly, with the whole wide world at your feet – you have no idea.'

'I don't want an idea, judging by what I've seen so far.'

'Don't write it off just yet; being a grown-up isn't all bad.' Nick ruffled his son's hair.

'What's that?' Oliver nodded to the small posy poking from Nick's pocket.

'It's a little bunch of heather.'

'For Mum?'

'Yes. I gave her a sprig of heather on our first date; we went for a walk up on Drayton Moor and I picked her a bunch and she kept it. It's still in her bedside drawer.'

'Surprised you got a second date if that's where you took her.'

'Me too, son. Trust me, I was punching above my weight and I knew it.' He paused and smiled, remembering the day they'd walked across Market Square hand in hand and he'd felt ten feet tall. 'I was a couple of years younger than you are now, if you can believe that, and I felt like I'd won the lottery.'

Oliver put his hands inside the pockets of his puffy jacket. 'So how can you just . . .' He looked up; the words didn't come easily. 'How can you just get Beverly in?'

'I haven't got her in! That makes her sound like a delivery, but we are friends, more than friends, and I do like her, I do.'

'Do you love her?' Oliver asked with a frankness that demanded a straight answer.

'I don't, but I think I could, and that's something I never thought I would say.' Nick held his eye line.

'Me either.' Oliver dug the heels of his boots into the grass.

Nick took a deep breath and the atmosphere calmed. Their talk and their tears had been somewhat cathartic.

'I know this is hard, all of it, so hard, *too* hard sometimes, but we can do this.'

'Can we, Dad?'

'We have no choice.'

'True that.'

'And for the record' – Nick stood and pulled the posy from his pocket – 'I would love to go back to those evenings coming in from work, knackered and seeing your face over the tea table, so pleased to see me, and your mum humming as she dished up supper. Staying in every night and saving up for our little jaunts to Filey in the summer, those were the best times. I miss her, Olly.'

'I miss her too.'

'I know, and no matter what comes next I think I always will, but life goes on, son. Life goes on.'

'Even if you don't want it to sometimes,' Oliver whispered.

'Look around you, these headstones – markers for people who were just like you and me, Burston people who have probably walked in this very spot. They would love a day up here, sitting in the fresh air with the people they love – what wouldn't they give for just one more day?

Life is a gift and we have to live it the best we can. Both of us. We owe it to everyone who no longer has a life.'

'People like Mum.' Oliver watched as Nick walked over and placed his little posy on the grave of his beloved.

'Yes. People like Mum.'

◆ ◆ ◆

Nick dropped Oliver in Market Square, where Tasha waited for him on the bench. He liked the way her face broke into a smile at the sight of Oliver and he liked the way she treated him. Now he pulled the car up outside his sister-in-law's house and rang the bell, and stood on the path, rocking on his heels. Diane's smile dropped when she saw it was him.

'Nick.'

He almost forgot how she made him feel, like a bad smell that lurked in the drains.

'Diane. Have you had a nice time with Tasha? She's great, isn't she?' Diane nodded. 'Kerry would have loved her.'

'She would that. I said as much earlier.' There was a pause where he thought she might invite him in and he loaded up the reasons on his tongue why he had to get on. He needn't have worried. No invite was forthcoming. 'Anyway' – he clapped his hands – 'I believe you've got Treacle.' As he spoke the dog ran from the kitchen to meet him, tail wagging. 'Hello, girl.' He bent down and patted her side.

'She's been a bit upset,' Diane offered, her mouth set in a thin line.

'Upset?' He ran his hand along Treacle's flank. His first thought was concern that she might be ill, his second was how much it might cost to put right. 'What's up, little mate? You not feeling a hundred per cent?' Treacle turned her head and pushed her nose towards him in greeting, her tail still wagging. 'Has she been sick? She seems grand.'

'Well . . .' Diane hesitated. 'Maybe not so much ill as unsettled.'

'Unsettled?' He was trying to pick the bones from her vague diagnosis, whilst studying the mutt, who looked to be in fine health.

'Mmmnn . . .' She paused and gave an almost imperceptible tut. Nick straightened and held her eye line with a feeling that what came next he might not necessarily want to hear. Diane drew breath and her chest heaved. 'Pets, dogs especially, can be sensitive to change, upheaval, especially if it involves new people . . .'

And then the penny dropped with a heavy clank in his brain.

Here we go again . . .

'Is that right?' he asked with as much of a clueless tone as he could muster.

'Yes, Nick, that's right.' She changed tack and folded her arms with barely disguised hostility, her words dripping with disapproval. He stared at her, deciding not to make this easy, not to apply any verbal salve or justification for what she might be thinking. He would let her do the work, dig the hole and then he hoped she might jump straight into it. Her face coloured and the bloom spread along her neck and chest as she finally spat it out. 'I heard you've been hanging around with Beverly Clark again.'

'You heard that, did you?'

'Hard not to, Nick, when the whole bloody town is talking about it!'

'The whole town? Or just the people in your house?'

'What are you suggesting?' she spat. 'I've got nothing to feel ashamed about!' She tightened her arms across her chest, her lips pressed so tight they looked bloodless.

He kept his calm. 'Are you saying I *have* got something to feel ashamed about?'

'I don't know, Nick, you tell me.'

He saw the glint of tears that gathered in her eyes and he slowly drew breath, reminding himself that, whilst she had no right to judge him, this was Kerry's sister.

'I can't believe that you might think it's okay to go gallivanting around with Beverly while my sister is not long in the ground! What do you think that feels like for me and for Mum?'

He remembered Dora's words, spoken not so long ago, offered generously and kindly.

. . . You, more than most, are aware that we never know what is around the corner. I know you do right by Olly and I know you always will. You were a good husband and you're a bloody good dad, and for the record, Beverly Clark is a good lass . . .

'I would think that, if I had been gallivanting, that would be hard, Di, but the truth is I, like you, am just trying to find my place in a world that has a great big bloody Kerry-shaped hole in it, and I've been talking to Beverly, spending time with Beverly, and it helps, and I would hope that as my sister-in-law you would be happy that I'm finding something, someone, that helps, because I'm sure, as you know, the nights are long and the days cold when the foundation has fallen out of your world.'

Diane looked down at her slippered feet. 'I just don't want tongues wagging. This is a small town and it's hard enough without that too, and it's not fair on me or Mum or Olly or Treacle!'

Treacle looked up at him, and her expression on any other day with any other topic under discussion would have been quite comical. Nick dug deep to find the confidence with which he had addressed Oliver earlier.

He had had enough.

'You know, you're right.' Nick nodded at her as he attached Treacle's lead. 'This is a small town and tongues have always wagged. Do you remember when that rumour swirled about Kerry and Rod Newberry?' He dropped the name almost casually, confident in his belief that she had been at the heart of the rumour-mongering, sticking her oar in and adding fuel to the fire which he guessed warmed her cold and lonely life of a winter's night.

'I do.' She kept her eyes cast downward and scuffed her slippers on the doormat.

'I know Kerry was hurt – *really* hurt – by it all, and she felt it made it hard to take stock, to figure out what to do next, how to respond. And the reason she found it so hard was because not only was her private life – *our* private life – being laid bare, but that persistent gossip surrounding the whole event with its loud background noise made it nearly impossible to think. Do you know what I mean?'

'I do.' Her voice was now little more than a whisper.

'Well, I just hope that in this small town people have the good grace, the kindness, to realise that any background noise right now will not help any of us – not you, not your mum, not me, nor Olly or Treacle.'

Diane gave a stiff nod.

'Thanks for having her.' He lifted his hand in a wave as he and his little dog set off down the path towards home.

1992

Nick woke early and lay in his bed looking at the ceiling. Today was the day he had been dreading – the day Eric moved to Derby. Nick didn't know how to say goodbye, didn't know if he could or indeed if he wanted to. His mum knocked on the bedroom door and entered.

'How did you sleep, pickle?'

'Not good.' This felt bad. If he was this sad at the beginning of the day, he could only imagine how he might feel at the end of it.

She sat on the edge of the mattress. 'You should remember that, no matter how hard it might be for you to say goodbye to your mate, it'll be a hundred times harder for Eric. So try to make it the best it can be for him, Nicky. He is going to a place he has never been before to stay in a strange house and start at a new school. Can you imagine?'

Nick shook his head: no, he couldn't.

'We can reassure him that we will see him very soon and that he can come and stay whenever he wants to, whenever. Which he can, of course. He can come here any weekend or any half-term, next summer, even . . .' She paused and swallowed in the way she did when she saw something sad on the telly.

'Is that a lie, Mum?'

'I hope not, love. I hope not.'

'I think of Eric when I wake up; he's my best best mate. I don't want him to be in rubbish old Derby.'

'I know, my love, I know.' His mum held him close and he closed his eyes, wishing things were different.

'Do you think he'll come over here before he goes?'

There was a familiar knock on the door and Nick smiled.

'I put extra bacon on.' His mum kissed his forehead. 'I think he smelt it all the way over in his house.'

Nick jumped from the bed and ran down the stairs to open the front door.

'I've got to be back by eleven.' Eric's greeting.

'What do you want to do until then?' Nick was drawing up a list of all the possibilities in his mind.

'Well, first you can both come eat breakfast,' his mum announced as she came down the stairs.

'Are you crying, Mrs Bairstow?' Both he and Eric now stared at his mum's face, streaked with tears.

'No. No, I'm not. I just had a little something in my eye.'

Nick pulled a face at his mate. This time he knew his mum was lying.

He watched as Eric forked rasher after rasher of crispy bacon into his mouth, wondering who would feed the Human Dustbin in Derby.

'We could do two games of Petunia,' Eric suggested, mumbling through his mouthful, 'then we could ride Half Bike to Alex's and take it in turns to time each other on Cobb Lane – then we could go up past the Old Dairy Shed and over to the Rec; then you and Alex could drop me back at my dad's and my mum will be there with Dave and the van.'

'Have you packed all your clothes up?' Nick tried to picture this.

Eric nodded.

'And has your mum got you that Sega with *Sonic the Hedgehog* for your bedroom?'

'Not yet.' Eric reloaded his fork. 'But she promised they'll get it soon.'

'You off today, then?' Jen appeared and skulked in the doorway.

Eric nodded.

Jen stared at him. 'Take care.'

'I will. Are you gonna miss me?'

'A bit. Maybe,' his sister conceded.

All were drawn to the sound of his mum at the sink, and this time there was no disguising her tears.

Afterwards, the morning felt like any other. The trio laughed, took turns riding Half Bike and wandered around the Old Dairy Shed while Eric wielded a long stick, poking into corners and flipping over stones.

'Has your mum had that baby yet?' Alex asked.

'Of course not, Deirdre! They take a long time to bake, about a year,' Eric informed him.

'A year?' Alex was shocked, as was Nick, but he tried not to let it show, always feeling a little uncomfortable when something Eric knew with certainty was news to him.

Their mood changed when they walked along Eric's street. Nick felt inconsolable at the thought that when they said goodbye it wouldn't be the same as 'See ya!' which meant just that, that they would be seeing each other tomorrow, but actually a proper goodbye – Eric was being bundled away from this life, his school and his best friends.

'It's not fair,' Nick said out loud.

The other two looked at him and nodded; no need to ask to what he referred.

Eric got to ride Half Bike to his house as Nick and Alex walked alongside slowly, a sad, quiet entourage who dreaded the parting as much as they wanted it to be over and done with. The van was parked in the kerb. Eric climbed from Half Bike and ran his hand lovingly over the frame.

'I mean it, if you let Piss Pants Pearce go on it, put a plastic bag on the saddle.'

'We will,' Alex said, looking at the floor.

'There you are, Eric!' his mum yelled from the front door that used to be hers. 'For God's sake, you always have to push it to the limit! Dave wants to be away by eleven and it's nearly ten to! I told you not to go far! You need to double-check your room and say goodbye to your dad.'

Nick noticed two things: the way Mrs Pickard shouted at Eric with a nastiness in her voice that he knew his mum would never use when talking to him, and also the way she glared at him and Alex, not even saying hello, let alone goodbye. He felt a rare flash of hatred for the woman and didn't care if she caught the look he gave her.

Eric jutted out his bottom lip and sniffed as two fat tears rolled from his eyes. Nick felt a tingling in his nose until his tears fell too. It was only seconds until Alex joined in and all three, standing with Half Bike between them, let their sadness fall from their eyes. Nick pushed out his index finger and the one next to it and pushed the two fingers into his friend's arm. Eric did the same to Alex and Alex to Nick, and there they stood, joined by their salute of comfort when a full hug felt like too much.

'Now, Eric! Get in this bloody minute!' his mum screeched.

Without another word, Eric walked to the house with his head bowed and his feet dragging.

'Eric!' Nick called, running up the path after him. He caught up and pressed the small brown leather pouch into his friend's palm. 'You might need this.'

Eric looked down at the multi-tool in his hand, and had his face not been contorted with tears, Nick knew he would have smiled. And probably called him Barbara.

ELEVEN

Nick yawned as he pulled into the car park and looked up at the building, the only place he had ever worked. It was hard to believe that he had last been here on Friday, three days ago. So much had happened that weekend; it felt like it had been weeks. He had seen Beverly again on Sunday, knocking on her door after dropping Oliver and Tasha at the coach station.

'Hello,' he had said, standing on the doorstep while she stared at him. 'This is me coming to knock on your door like a grown-up. Me, Nick Bairstow, a confident man who knows what he wants.'

Beverly eyed him quizzically and put her hands on her hips. 'Is that right? And what is it you want exactly, Mr Bairstow?' she asked with a smile on her face.

'Two things, please: a cup of tea and sex. And not necessarily in that order.'

Beverly placed her hand over her mouth and turned her head towards the open-plan sitting room. 'I am so sorry you had to hear that, Auntie Mary, Vicar . . .'

Nick felt his face turn puce and his bowel spasm. 'Oh my goodness!' He reached out his hand as if he could take back the words, knowing they would have been overheard. 'I was only joking! It was a dare! I do apologise.'

Beverly turned slowly back to him. 'Well, Mr Bairstow.' She opened the door wide. 'I was only joking too. I don't even have an Auntie Mary, and the vicar left ten minutes ago.' She winked at him.

'You little beggar!' He jumped over the doorstep, grabbing for her hand. 'You had me going!'

Beverly twisted from his grasp and ran up the stairs. He followed her. This time they ran laughing into the bedroom without hesitancy, awkwardness or any concern over etiquette; the two tumbled on to her bed, where they stayed until morning.

Now Nick looked at his watch; he'd just made it in time for his meeting with Julian Siddley. Beverly was following close behind in her car. They didn't want to give the good folk of Burston another thing to talk about.

Nick knocked and entered.

'Come in! Come in!' Julian beckoned from behind the big desk.

'Julian.' He walked over and shook his boss's hand, noting the slight tremor to the man's fingers as they met his own.

'Nick.' Julian gestured to the seat in front of the desk.

He sat.

'So, how *are* things out there this morning?' Julian jerked his head towards the warehouse and the packing floor.

Maybe it was because Nick knew what he did about the reasons for the sale, or maybe it was because, with no need to pretend any more, he could see through the veneer of the man he worked for; either way, he felt a prickling of dislike for Julian's tone and his line of questioning, and felt resentful for all the hours he had put in, for what?

He remembered what Beverly had said: . . . *the Siddleys, of course, won't care either way; they'll have already cashed that big fat cheque regardless.*

'As you'd expect, really,' Nick levelled. 'Folk are worried, disappointed, scared.'

'Of course. Of course.' Julian nodded sagely and touched his fingertips to form a pyramid at his chest while he listened.

'I mean, there's not that many jobs to start with around here, and so to take a couple of hundred families and remove their income is going to have a huge impact. Not only for the people made redundant, but their partners, kids . . .' Nick let this trail, knowing it wasn't really his place to make this comment on the man's decision, but doing it anyway.

Julian breathed in and out through his nose and sat forward to rest his elbows on the desk. 'So, Nick, I know this news is tough, but let's talk it through. I can answer all your questions and we can go from there. Rest assured, I want to be as candid as I can and to make sure that you're supported in every aspect of this transition.'

The words sounded very much like they had been learnt from a script. Nick clasped his hands in his lap and stared at the man, who wore a comfortable layer of fat, the result of good living, and a cushion, Nick was certain, many who worked at Siddley's wished for, knowing it would provide a buffer to the blows that came their way. His boss's expensive, chunky watch nestled snugly on his tanned wrist, and his cologne smelled crisp and lemon-scented. Anyone looking at him would know he had money. Nick felt the familiar cloak of inadequacy wrap around his shoulders. He wondered what it might feel like to wake each day as Julian Siddley, never having to worry about whether he could afford the bills or put petrol in the car or have to choose between food and fuel. Not having to worry about any of that stuff while spending time in his eight-bedroom Georgian house with a swimming pool. It must be nice.

'And, specifically, how are you feeling about it all, Nick?' The way Julian used his first name with a friendly slant told Nick he expected him to be an ally.

He looked over Julian's shoulder to the filing cabinet where the mint imperial jar used to live. 'Just as you'd expect, really.' He again drew on this stock phrase to avoid further commentary. And again Julian trotted out his standard response.

'Of course. Of course.' He paused. 'The good news, if you can call it that' – he gave a small laugh – 'is that you have been with us a long time and your remuneration package is healthy. Just a little shy of seventeen thousand.'

'Is that the final offer?' Nick kept his expression neutral.

Julian smiled briefly, as if this were a question he had been told to expect.

'I can try to push it to twenty.'

'Thank you.' At least that was something, although even he knew that a lump sum could quickly dwindle when there was no more coming in. The trick to making it last was not to think of it as a lump sum but to draw from it just what he needed . . .

'So you would be happy with that?' Julian pushed.

'It is what it is.' Nick nodded.

'Quite, quite.'

Nick sat forward. 'Can I ask you something?'

'Yes, of course, fire away.'

'Why?'

'Why what, Nick?'

'Why is Siddley's closing down?' he asked outright, watching the man's top lip bead with tiny droplets of sweat that matched the ones on his forehead as his cheeks flushed with colour.

'It's complicated . . .'

'Is it?'

'Yes.' Julian tapped his fingertips on the desktop, avoiding his gaze. 'We are flogging a dead horse here, Nick. The market is getting tougher, margins tighter, the economy is uncertain and so we are cutting our losses.'

Nick knew now that the man thought he was stupid, trying to bamboozle the guy who checked rotas and dispatched lorries. Nick also now knew that his boss was a liar and a coward. He figured that whilst it would have been unpleasant to hear the real reason for the sale, that being there was too much money on offer for them to resist, it would have been a darn sight easier than being lied to. He stared at him, and Julian tried to fill the awkward silence with idle chat.

'I know this is a bit off topic, but I'm very glad that you and Beverly are friends; she is one in a million, as are you. I'm happy for you both, really happy.' He gave a wide smile, which Nick didn't return.

'I've known you a long time, Julian—'

'You have.' The man interrupted with a slight nod of his head.

'I trust you.'

'And I you.' Julian blinked a couple of times in quick succession.

'You have always been fair and friendly.'

'I hope so.' Julian smiled.

'But I worry about how you treat things, including people.'

'You worry how?' Julian twitched his shoulder, as if uncomfortable under Nick's scrutiny.

'You should never just drop a bike, let it fall hard to the ground, especially when that ground is gravel. It can flex the frame or scratch the paintwork.'

Julian's eyebrows knitted in confusion, his expression one of bewilderment. 'Sorry, you've lost me. I don't understand . . .'

'No.' Nick stood and let his eyes sweep over the office. 'You don't.'

Having closed the door behind him, he thought for the first time of the twenty-odd thousand pounds that would be his payoff, hoping that if he found work before the money ran out there might be a little bit left over as a nest egg for Oliver and a small treat for his mum.

Eric lumbered up the stairs. 'My turn, Shirley.'

'Good luck.'

'What did he say?' Eric looked jumpy, nervous.

'Not much, just gave me my remuneration figure.'

'How much?' Eric asked in the way only someone who had been his friend since early childhood could.

'Nearly seventeen grand, but I asked if there was any more and he said they'd try to go to twenty.'

Eric whistled. 'I think mine will be about fourteen – not to be sniffed at, lad. But I'll push for a bit more too – it's not like we haven't bloody worked for it.'

'And you'd be right.' Nick nodded; he could see that this was the golden handshake that would send his friend on his merry way to Oz, enough beer tokens to ensure he had the best time.

'Right, better get in.' Eric grinned. 'I might ask him if I can take a couple of boxes of festoon lights as a leaving gift; I can just see them strung up around my barbecue.' He moved his hand in an arc over his head as he nudged his mate with his elbow. 'I mean, what are the Siddleys going to do with all that stock? They'll be glad I'll be taking some off their hands.'

Nick felt his pulse race and his gut bunch. It was a moment he would never forget, one where a thought so pure, clear and obvious rang out in his head like a musical note. He pictured the boxes of stock that lined the corridors, the warehouse piled high with lighting rigs and the lorries all sitting idle in the yard, waiting to make deliveries to shops and the customers who wanted what Siddley's had. He pictured his dad's face when Nick put on his high-vis jacket for the first time, a look that said, *I wanted more for you, son* . . . And it would have been hard to explain how he felt buoyed up and courageous, but he pictured Beverly pulling him by the hand into the bedroom, he remembered what it felt like to stand in front of Kerry's grave with the beautiful moors of North Yorkshire spread out in front of him, the way he had breathed deeply and freely, and he knew, he knew with absolute certainty, that this was his chance! This was the opportunity he had been waiting for! He was ready.

'Eric, you're a bloody genius, mate!' Nick slapped his shoulder.

'Why am I?'

'You just are!' Nick shouted along the corridor as he ran toward the stairs, keen to go and find Beverly. 'A bloody genius!' he yelled over his shoulder.

◆ ◆ ◆

Beverly poured hot water into the teapot as Eric sat opposite him at the table in her kitchen.

'So what's this all about, kids?' Eric asked with enthusiasm.

Nick paused, licking his lips, which were dry with nerves, wanting to get the wording right for what he needed to say. 'The reason I wanted the three of us to get together is because of something you said yesterday.'

'When I showed a streak of genius? Ta, Bev.' Eric reached for the mug of tea she handed him.

'Inadvertently, yes.'

They both stared at him, and the attention they paid gave Nick the confidence to continue.

'Beverly, as you know, works directly for Julian, and there's things about the closure that she knows but isn't allowed to share.'

'I signed a document.' She pulled a face.

'What things?' Eric looked confused.

Nick glanced at Beverly across the kitchen, who gave a subtle nod, permission of sorts.

'This cannot go any further,' he stressed.

'Okay.' Eric's expression was now solemn as he sat tall in the chair; the serious, smart Eric that lurked behind the comic façade was in the room.

'Siddley's is not in trouble, not at all. It's not lost orders; in fact, business is booming.' Nick watched his friend screw up his face as if trying to make sense of why it was closing.

'Right. Go on.'

'They have sold the land, the land where the factory sits and all around it, to Merryvale Homes.'

'To build houses.' Eric was faster on the uptake than he had been.

'Yep, up to three thousand of them.'

'Jesus! The little bas'tads!'

'Exactly. But no matter that the business is strong, the Siddleys are going to just stop trading.'

'It's a tragedy!' Eric caught on. 'All those new houses and not a bloody job to go to.'

'I know, I know.' Nick took a deep breath. 'But here's the thing: you were right about what you said on the stairs yesterday.'

'Which bit?' Eric scratched his head.

'You asked what the Siddleys were going to do with all that stock.' Nick locked eyes with Beverly and then looked back to his mate. 'They have a plan, apparently, to dump it at slashed prices just to cover their costs.' Nick swallowed. 'I want us to buy the stock – in fact, not only the stock, the packing machines, the lorries – everything. I want us to buy it all and keep the business going, and I think we can do it.' His heart raced and his speech quickened as excitement took over. 'Bev has had a look at the stock inventory, the insurance documents on the machinery values, order books, et cetera, and we reckon that the whole lot is worth about two hundred and fifty grand.'

'Oh, is that all?' Eric curled his top lip and made as if to reach into his jeans pocket for his loose change.

'It's a lot, I know.' Nick laid his hands on the tabletop. 'And we'll need more than that to get a premises up and running, and for the rebrand, the computer systems, other equipment, insurance and everything else, but with my redundancy, yours and Bev's, we think we can get enough of a lump sum to go to the bank with a sound business plan and get a loan and do it properly.'

Eric stared at him.

'Say something, Eric,' Nick urged. The suspense was painful.

'I think if anyone can pull this off, you can.' Eric shook his head and sat back, avoiding his mate's eye line. 'But I wasn't joking about going to Australia. I want to be somewhere warm. I want a different life.'

'But being part owner of your own business! That would sure as hell be a different life!' Nick heard the edge to his tone; frustration placed a sliver of anger in his voice.

'Half of a half . . .' Eric smiled wryly.

'Half of a half,' Nick repeated with a lump in his throat.

'I'm no businesswoman, Eric,' Beverly said softly, 'but I know all there is to know about Siddley's from an administrative point of view, and what you and Nick don't know about the process, the packing, the logistics and everything else isn't worth knowing. When Nick suggested it to me I thought it was nuts, a pipe dream. But we spent all last night drawing up figures and thinking of how to make this work, asking whether it *could* work, and we think it can.'

Nick liked the ease with which she used the word 'we'.

Beverly walked over and placed her hand on his shoulder. 'I believe in Nick, and he wants you by his side.'

'I want your redundancy too,' Nick levelled.

'I always knew you were only after me for my money!' Eric joked, the boy who had slept in a cold room and run to Nick's childhood home when breakfast at his own wasn't forthcoming.

'Will you at least think about it?' Nick asked, trying not to sound desperate and put any pressure on his friend's slender shoulders.

'I don't need to think about it. I agree with Beverly; I believe in you too. I always have. You were right; you are cleverer than me, cleverer than us all.'

Nick shook his head. 'Not clever, lad, just lucky . . .' He smiled.

'But I won't be here. I bought my ticket today. I go in eight weeks. Melbourne, to start with.'

Nick stared at him and felt the sick pull in his guts at the thought that his friend would not be here to go on this journey with him. He wondered how Jen would respond to this news – Jen, who was a lot more fragile than any of them had suspected. That, and there was a now a hole in the funds they needed for their business plan.

'I need you to understand,' Eric whispered.

'I do, mate.' Nick sighed. 'I don't have to like it, but I do understand.'

Nick's mum laid out a selection of ties on the sofa. 'He always looked very smart in this one, your dad.' She ran her fingers over the navy and pale blue diagonal stripes. 'He wore it to Jen's wedding. Looked proper smart.'

'Do not mention that day, ever!' Jen fired from the chair in front of the television.

'Don't be like that, love. It was a smashing day! The sun shone, the cake was amazing and you were such a beautiful bride.' His mum sniffed.

'I agree, I was a beautiful bride and that day was smashing. It was the days that came after that were problematic, every one of them. Colin is a knob.'

'Colin is not a knob.' His mum tutted, and he and Jen tittered to hear her use the word. 'He just wasn't for you.'

'Oh, here we go, the idea that he wasn't my "one" but was just a rehearsal for the real deal. Well, I tell you what, it was a bloody long and painful rehearsal, five years of my life I'll never get back.'

'Who do you have in mind for her, Mum? How about Big Brian? I noticed he was very keen to kiss your cheek when he handed over your noodle voucher in the pub,' Nick teased.

'Urgh!' Jen shuddered. 'He's a knob too.'

'Is everyone you know a knob?' her mum asked as she arranged the ties, and again he and his sister laughed as the word left her mouth.

Jen stifled her laughter. 'Practically.'

'Eric – he's for her. I love him, always have. I see her with Eric; she's just too stupid to see it,' his mum offered casually.

He looked at Jen, who stared now at their mum, and her words when they came were considered. 'Actually, I'm not too stupid to see it, Mum.' She paused. 'But it's not that simple.'

His mum paused from sorting her husband's ties and spoke fondly to her daughter. 'But it really is, Jen. You both just need to be honest and grow up.'

'I think . . . I think it's probably harder to let someone love you and let yourself love them and then for it all to go wrong and then have to deal with that,' his sister said quietly.

'That's what a chicken would say. Someone who didn't have the courage to take a chance. And that's what love is; it's taking a big chance! There is no guarantee, ever. But if you don't try, Jen . . .' Mags let this trail.

His wise old mum turned to him and Nick smiled. 'Now, Nick, which tie do you want to borrow? I like the blue or the green, and I think wearing your dad's tie to go and see the bank manager will bring you a bit of luck. Your dad would be so proud; he always was so proud of both of you.' She bit her lip.

Jen looked down as emotion rose.

'I think the blue, thanks, Mum.' He reached out for the tie she handed him and let his fingertips brush the shiny polyester surface. It felt nice holding this item that his dad had worn. It was in these small moments that he both missed him and felt close to him. Clothes, possessions . . . they became important when someone died. He tried to imagine walking into Beverly's bedroom and being surrounded by her previous boyfriend's clothing, his bits and pieces.

'I think maybe I'll go and see Eric, have a chat.' Jen spoke as she shifted in her seat and picked invisible lint from her clothes.

'You'd better do it sooner rather than later. He's bought his ticket for Australia. He's off to Melbourne in eight weeks.' Nick tried to keep the melancholy from his voice.

Jen sat up in the chair. 'Eight weeks?'

'Yep. That's all.'

'You'll really miss him, darling, won't you?' His mum spoke softly.

'I will.'

'I will.'

Both he and Jen answered at the same time and looked at each other without a joke or a smile. Eric was going to the other side of the world and there was nothing remotely funny about it.

◆ ◆ ◆

Nick and Treacle walked home as darkness encroached. He felt the tie in his pocket and thought about his dad.

Bairstow Boys – against the world!

He thought about how it couldn't have been easy for Jen, trying to elbow her way in and finding her entry barred. She had mentioned asking to join their gang and he might have remembered something like that. How had he reacted? Did he laugh? He didn't know how he could put it right. Nick turned the key in the door and headed straight for the kitchen, where he lifted the roll of black bin liners from the cupboard and tore one off. No time like the present. Starting with the closet in the hallway, he slowly lifted Kerry's walking coat from the hook and folded it into the bag; next he popped in her wellington boots before running up the stairs. He carefully took his time, removing her clothes from the hangers and folding them one by one, letting his eyes linger on the fabrics, picturing her in her jumper and jeans, just in from walking Treacle with her cheeks flushed and her hair messy.

'I don't need these bits of cloth and stuff to remember you by, lass. You live in my mind and behind my eyelids.' He smiled at this truth.

Working diligently, he emptied the wardrobe and Kerry's bedside cabinet, ridding it of empty blister packs of painkillers, old bottles of nail varnish and outdated coupons for everything from half-price pizzas to money off a spa day. At the back of the drawer his fingers touched upon the small christening Bible with the tissue-like, gilt-edged pages. Inside the front cover sat the pressed sprig of heather he had given her so long ago. Holding the book to his lips he inhaled the scent of the leather and felt the familiar twist of longing in his heart. He transferred the book and its precious contents into his own bedside drawer, where it would sit alongside the small brown leather pouch containing the multi-tool his dad had given him a long time ago, both items he would treasure always. Next, he worked in the bathroom, gathering up nail-varnish remover, face cleanser, boxes of tampons, hair products and even the lilac toothbrush that sat nestled and gathering dust in the little ceramic pot next to his.

He carried the collection of black bin liners to the front door and separated them into two piles, one pile for the bin lorry and the other for the charity shop in town. Nick opened the top drawer of the unit in the lounge and pulled from it Kerry's watch. He stood by the sofa with the watch in the palm of his hand and ran his hand over the smooth glass of the face and the metal bracelet into which it was set. A relatively inexpensive piece of jewellery and yet one Kerry had loved and worn every day since he had given it to her ten years ago, a make-up gift offered as they tried to glue back the pieces of their marriage. She had only taken it off when it slipped and shifted on her skinny wrist, catching on the narrow plastic tube that delivered her drugs, irritating her as she lay in the bed at St Vincent's.

Sitting now, he called Oliver.

'Hi, Dad.' His son's tone was less than welcoming, but at least he had answered. Nick figured that was better than the silent treatment he had been dealt not so long ago.

'How's things?'

'Good.' Oliver spoke sharply.

'How's Tasha?'

'Good.'

Nick closed his eyes, without the energy tonight to navigate the silent pauses that littered their conversation like rocks in a river. Not only was he tired, but he wanted to go over the business plan one more time before tomorrow.

'I've been sorting some of Mum's things.'

'What things?' Oliver fired, instantly on the attack.

Nick exhaled. 'All of her things, really. Some of her clothes and bits and bobs are going to charity; she had rubbish in drawers and that's going to the tip.'

'Are you getting rid of *everything*?' The boy swallowed.

'Not everything, Olly, no. For example, I've wrapped her dressing gown and put it in a box for the loft; she's had that since she had you. And her wedding dress, that's going into the same box, along with the blouse she wore when she came out of the hospital carrying you – I've got loads of photos of her in it, holding you. Her school report cards, her netball medal, all the cards and pictures you made her at nursery and school and of course all of our photos. They're all being packed and stored in the loft. And anything else I thought might be important or that you might want, some books and bits and pieces.'

'Okay. Good.' This time the words were offered in a whisper.

'That's why I'm calling, really. I'm sitting here with her watch in my hand and I thought you might like it.'

'Oh!'

'Her wedding ring and the little bits of jewellery she got for her twenty-first are yours too, but I'll hang on to it all for you for now.

But the watch . . . I was just thinking, and it's only a suggestion' – he paused – 'that you might like to give it to someone important in your life. I know your mum would like that. And I'm not suggesting Tasha, although that would be fine.' Nick drew breath and rubbed his tired eyes, knowing he wasn't being that clear. 'I guess what I'm saying is that when you find a woman who is going to be a permanent fixture in your life, someone you think worthy of it, then you can give her your mum's watch.' Nick cleared his throat. 'That's all I'm saying. I'll put it in a padded envelope in your room, in your drawer for safekeeping.'

'Thank you, Dad.'

'No worries.' He smiled. 'I'll let you go. I want to go over my business plan one more time before bed.'

'Nanny Mags said you were nervous.'

'Did she?' He exhaled. 'She'd be right, but you don't know if you don't try, eh?'

'Yep. Good luck.'

'Thanks, Olly. Night, night.'

'Night, Dad.'

1992

Will Pearce stood in the garage and stared at Half Bike, shaking his head.

'I don't understand.'

Nick sighed. 'It's not hard to understand, Will.' He tried to explain again. 'Me and Eric and Alex built this bike together, but Eric went to live with his mum a week ago and so we are looking for someone to take his place in our bike gang.'

'More of a bike club than a bike gang,' Alex clarified.

'But what would I have to do?' Will continued to stare at the bike with a look that suggested he was a whole lot less impressed with their bike than they were.

'You don't have to do anything,' Alex explained, exasperated. 'Just come out on bike rides and time whoever is trying to break the record for flying down Cobb Lane and help polish the frame and put oil on the chain and the sprockets. That kind of thing. We have another game called Petunia, but we can show you how to play that later if you want.'

'What's a sprocket?' Will asked eventually.

Nick and Alex exchanged a look. This was hopeless.

'Look,' Nick tried again. 'We are offering you a half of a half of the bike.'

'A half of a half?' Will looked even more confused, if that was possible.

'Yes,' Nick explained. 'I own half the bike and Alex and Eric have the other half split in two, so half of a half.'

Will laughed loudly. 'That's a quarter! Not half of a half! You mean Alex and Eric own a quarter!'

Nick didn't like the way the boy laughed, hated that there were things he was clueless about while others seemed to know them with such ease.

'Well, you might be, like, maths Jesus, but you don't know what a sprocket is, Marjorie!' he yelled.

Will looked as if he might cry then picked up his backpack.

'I don't think I want to ride your bike or play Petunia or be in your bike gang—'

'It's not a gang. It's a club,' Alex interrupted.

Will shook his head. 'Whichever. It's not for me. Thanks, though.' He was opening the side door, seemingly keen to make his escape, when a familiar voice yelled through the door.

'Did someone say Petunia?'

'Eric!'

Neither he nor Alex noticed Will sidle along the path.

'What are you doing here?' Alex bounced on the spot. 'Have you come to visit?'

'Nope.' Eric beamed. 'I moved back. Yesterday!'

'You moved back?' Nick screamed. 'No way! He moved back! He's come back!'

All three boys jumped up and down before running out into the back garden and racing around the edge of the lawn like corks popped from a bottle, flying with their arms outstretched, bundles of pure energy that had to run until they calmed. This was the best news ever, ever!

'Eric's back!' Nick yelled up to the open window through which his mum popped her head.

'So he is.' She blew him a kiss. 'Bacon, Eric?'

'And eggs, please!' he yelled over his shoulder, as he tore around the lawn.

The three boys giggled and chattered as they ate, sitting close together around the kitchen table while Eric filled his face and his stomach.

'Why did you move back?' Alex asked, going to work on a Jammie Dodger.

Eric kept his eyes on his plate. 'I spoke to my dad and he said I could go to Cubs if I wanted and that he'd get me the uniform and everything, so I came back.'

'Oh. Good.' Nick didn't care what the reason was; he was just so very happy to have his best friend back in the fold.

'And you'll be staying here tonight, love; your dad called and he's on a late shift.'

Nick smiled at his mum, feeling a bubble of happy that filled him right up.

'You're back, then? That didn't last long,' Jen sighed from the doorway.

'Yes, I'm back. So you can stop missing me!' Eric laughed.

'I didn't miss you, you dweeb!' Jen yelled angrily before flouncing from the room, but the slight smile on her mouth suggested otherwise.

'What's first?' Eric asked. 'We should definitely go up to the Rec and see what's changed and then go to the Old Dairy Shed and have a poke around . . .'

Nick agreed. It had been a whole week since they had last patrolled these places, and a lot could happen in a week.

That night his mum rolled out the bed-in-a-bag and switched off the big light. 'Now I know you two have a lot to catch up on, but you've got school in a few days, so an early night would be good. No chatting till all hours.'

'Night, night, Mum.'

'Night, night, darling, and night, night, Eric, and welcome home.'

'Night,' Eric whispered. 'I brought the multi-tool back.' Eric reached out and placed it in the gap between their two beds.

Nick was happier to see it than he could have said. He hadn't felt half as comfortable going to sleep without his weapon of choice nestling close to hand just in case.

'I wish this was my home,' Eric whispered.

'You can come over any time you want to; my mum and dad have already said that.'

'Nick . . .'

'What?' He didn't question why they were both suddenly whispering.

'I didn't come back because of the Cubs uniform, although I might still join Cubs. My dad did say I could.'

Nick heard him swallow.

'What did you come back for then?'

Eric took his time responding. 'My mum didn't want me there any more.'

Nick stayed silent; he couldn't think of a single thing to say. Couldn't imagine his mum not wanting him near her.

Eric drew breath. 'It was horrible at their house. They haven't got any carpet anywhere and her and Dave were always rowing or kissing.'

'Yuck!' Nick managed.

'Yes, yuck!' Eric agreed. 'And I wasn't allowed in the lounge because Dave couldn't be disturbed when he was watching telly, and so I just sat in the bedroom, and if I came downstairs he shouted at me or she did and so I went back upstairs, but there was nothing to do and no Sega. And then yesterday she came up to my bedroom and she was smiling and I thought maybe she was going to start being nice to me and I was quite happy, but then she said that it hadn't worked out and it was probably best if I came back here to stay with my dad.'

'What did you say?'

'I didn't say anything. I just got up off the bed, opened up my bag and started to put my clothes in it.'

'I bet your dad's happy to have you home.'

'He is – we went up to the chippy last night and I had two large battered sausages.'

'Nice.' Nick pictured the bubbly batter-covered feast.

'I think my mum is a fucking cow!'

Nick was shocked. This wasn't language they used or heard, although he suspected Eric might have picked it up from Dave or his mum. Even hearing it made his tummy flip.

'I don't think you can say that about your mum,' he whispered.

'She is, though! She only cares about Dave and the stupid new baby. I don't even care, though – you were right, Derby is rubbish! And they can forget it if they think I will ever go back, even if they actually get me that Sega.'

Nick thought it unlikely that they would get him the Sega, thinking that if they had meant it they probably would have had it waiting for him when he arrived, but he didn't say it out loud.

'We should take Half Bike apart tomorrow and give it a really good clean, oil it up and check the chain and the like.' Eric yawned.

'Yes, definitely.'

It was Nick's turn to yawn, and the conversation slowed as fatigue set in.

'I meant what I said, Nick. I wish this was my home, and I think I know a way I can be part of your family.'

Nick felt his stomach roll – not the blood-brothers thing again. Even the thought made his mouth fill with water.

'How?'

'I'm going to marry your sister and then you'll be my brother-in-law and we will be proper family, for always.'

Nick considered this. 'But my sister is horrible, plus, she thinks you're a total dweeb.'

'I don't think she's horrible; I think she's brilliant. And I know she says it, but I don't believe she really thinks I'm a total dweeb.'

TWELVE

Nick parked outside Beverly's house and closed his eyes; he took a deep breath, trying to keep his nerves at bay. He picked up the file from the front seat with a copy of the business case nestling inside.

Beverly must have been looking out of the window waiting, as she appeared on the pavement in her work suit and with her hair set. She looked professional and smart; her appearance gave him a flash of confidence.

'Wow!' She pulled her head back on her shoulders. 'Well, look at you, mister! You scrub up well.'

He blushed; this was the first time she had seen him in a suit. The suit bought for his dad's funeral and also worn to his wife's and now, hopefully, on the day he would impress the bank manager.

'All set?' she asked, as if they were about to head off on a day trip and not to the bank around the corner in Market Square, where someone else, no doubt more used to wearing a suit than he was, held his future in their hands.

'Yep. I've gone over the numbers and practised the pitch.' They walked slowly forward.

'Good.' She took his hand and squeezed it. 'Don't look so glum; this just might be a day we look back and remember as the day our lives changed.'

'Yes.' He lifted her hand and kissed the back of it. 'I'm not glum, just nervous.' He breathed out sharply. 'Are we mad even trying? Maybe it'd be easier to just . . .'

'What, Nick? To not try? Should we fear rejection so badly that we don't even *try*? Is that what you're suggesting?' Her brows knitted. She meant business.

'No.' He shook his head. 'It's just that . . .'

'What?' She spoke quickly, whether irritated by his suggestion or aware of the march of time, he wasn't sure.

'It's just that this is the first time I've ever done anything like this.' He bit his lip, wishing he could talk to his dad, knowing that he was always full of good advice, steering him right. A memory filled his mind, clear and detailed: the summer of 1992 – when he had first seen Half Bike, knowing what he wanted but not sure how to go about achieving it.

You will never know what you are capable of until you try, lad. The trying is good for you and the rewards great if you take the chance. But mark my words, you will succeed. If you want it badly enough . . .

Nick felt his face break into a smile.

'Right. Let's do it.' He quickened his pace, marching her along the cobbles and turning right into Market Square. He spied a group of lads on the bench and smiled in their direction; today, in this suit, with the business plan under his arm, he felt like the kind of man who could ask them to shift if he wanted to. He felt like a bloody footballer!

He and Beverly sat on the padded green chairs outside the little office to the side of the main open-plan foyer and waited. A young woman walked past with a silk scarf in the bank's colours tied in a jaunty bow at her neck.

'Shouldn't be too long now.' She smiled.

'No worries.' Nick raised his hand. 'We have an appointment with Mr Williams, the bank manager.' He rattled the file of papers in her direction, feeling so out of place he tried to justify his presence.

'Oh.' The woman pushed her glasses up on to her nose. 'You're not seeing Mr Williams today – it's our finance manager you're seeing. He handles all new business enquiries.'

'Thanks, Joanne, we're happy to wait.' Beverly winked at her.

'No worries, Bev.' Joanne gave a sweet smile and walked off.

'Joanne?' Nick turned to Beverly.

'Kath Watson's granddaughter.'

'Poor thing,' he whispered out of the side of his mouth. 'Do you think Kath cooks at home too?'

The two giggled as the office door opened. And there stood the rather portly finance manager in a grey suit and with his hair swept to one side in a severe parting.

'You have got to be kidding me!' Nick stepped forward and shook hands with the finance manager, none other than Will 'Piss Pants' Pearce.

'Now then, Nick. Long time no see.'

'Yes, long time, Will.'

'I guessed there couldn't be more than one Nick Bairstow in the area. I've been working in York, but I'm back here now. Come in.' Will pointed at two chairs in front of the narrow desk. Nick saw a copy of their business plan spread out on the desk; the corners were thumbed and it was scattered out of sequence.

'I've had a good look at your business plan.'

And that was it, without any of the preamble he had expected or time to panic; before Will had even sat down, they were straight into it.

'And what did you think?' Nick took a seat, not knowing whether this was an appropriate question or not.

'I think it's sound.' Will pinched the bottom of his nose.

Nick felt joy lick up his throat like flames of happiness. It was all he could do not to whoop and jump up. Will sat down and smoothed his tie down towards his waistband. 'That doesn't mean this is a done deal, not by any stretch,' he said with a brief shake of the head, 'but it's certainly interesting.'

'Right.' Beverly nodded.

'You've never run a business before, Nick. Do you think you'll manage?' Will asked, his expression neutral.

Nick wasn't sure how to respond, having expected the questioning to be about the costs, profit, losses, that kind of thing.

'I haven't, that's true, and I don't think I could run *any* business, but I'm confident I can run this one. It's all I've ever known and I've worked in every department. Plus, I'll have experts working alongside me, people like Beverly' – he nodded at her – 'Dennis Knowles, Roy Maynard, David McCardle and others, they all know what they're doing and I'd employ anyone in that place in a heartbeat. So I won't be doing it alone, although the buck will stop with me, of course.'

'And you're confident you can get the stock and the equipment for the figures stated?' Will ran his eye over the columns of numbers and tapped at the bottom of one page with his index finger.

'Well . . .' Beverly sat forward in the chair. 'We are confident in our costs, but we have yet to have the okay from the Siddleys.'

'I see.' Will let his eyes linger on her, as if making a judgement call. 'And the premises?'

'Again' – Nick swallowed – 'we are yet to secure a premises, but we have a few ideas.'

'Such as?' Will pushed.

'One of the out-of-town business parks near Northallerton or Thirsk, or there's the chance of securing something closer to Burston, like an old farm building. We are in talks with the land agent over the road.' Nick pointed to the window and over the road to where their old schoolfriend Ryan Peters had set up shop, specialising in farm and commercial property.

'Do either of you have any assets or anything you could put up as security against the loan you're after?'

'Like?' Beverly again sat forward in her chair.

'Like a house.' Will spoke bluntly.

'I have a house.' Nick nodded, looking at the green carpet and wondering if what he was doing was wise, messing with Oliver's future inheritance.

'I have a house too,' Beverly added, and Nick smiled at her.

Will nodded. 'Just so you know, I either reject or make recommendations for loan applications like this based on a number of criteria and then my report goes higher up the chain for final sign-off. I know the bank would look a lot more favourably on the investment if you put a house or houses against it. Anything that lowers the risk for them makes the whole thing more attractive, obviously. They just want to know that the investment is a sound one and that they are not going to lose their money.'

'So . . .' Nick was having a little trouble keeping up. 'Where are we here, Will?'

'Where we are is that I think I can pull an offer together for you, but only once you have the final figure in agreement from the Siddleys, a premises identified with an idea of cost, and some kind of asset against which we can offset the loan.'

Beverly looked at him. 'So we still have a bit of work to do.'

'We do.' Nick understood, and whilst his earlier enthusiasm was a little quashed, Will 'Piss Pants' Pearce had not said no. 'We'll get the information and the agreements together and come back and see you.'

'Yes, do that.' Will stood to indicate their meeting was at an end.

'I feel like we can do it, Will, I feel that we can satisfy the bank and make the business work – in fact, I'm confident of it. And that means jobs for Burston people, about half of our school year, in fact.'

Will nodded and shook Nick's hand. 'Well, all that leaves is the loan, and I can help you there. I'm pretty good with numbers.'

'Like that blonde girl on *Countdown*, Rachel what'sername?'

'Yep.' Will smiled at him. 'Or like maths Jesus.'

'Oh! Will, I. . .' Nick felt his face flush.

'Don't say another word, Bairstow.' Will stared him down. 'Not another bloody word!'

◆ ◆ ◆

Nick sat next to Beverly on her sofa and pulled the tie from under his collar. 'I don't know whether to feel elated or deflated.'

'I choose elated!' She bounced. 'He could have said no and we'd have fallen at the first hurdle, but we didn't – he said our business plan was sound and that he'd make an offer; all we need is to do what he said. We need to talk to the Siddleys.'

'And put one of our homes up as a guarantee.'

'I would be happy to put mine up. Nothing ventured nothing gained, and I know we can make this work.'

'I'd do the same.' He held her hand. 'I think it's time I put my money where my mouth is.'

The phone rang in his pocket.

'Now then, Eric?'

Beverly rolled her eyes affectionately. Eric might not be sticking around to be part of this adventure, but he was still as keen as mustard for his friend to succeed.

Eric cut to the chase. 'How did it go?'

'It went okay. We still have some work to do, but if we can pull it off it seems like the bank can help us.'

'That's fantastic!'

'Yep, and you won't believe who the bloody finance manager was.'

'Who?'

'Will Pearce!'

'You are kidding me!' Eric laughed.

'I'm not.'

'Did he have a plastic bag on his seat?'

'Eric, don't! This man might have the veto on whether I get to be my own boss or not. I can't be biting my lip every time I see him in case I call him "Piss Pants!"'

'"Piss Pants!"' Eric echoed, and the two laughed like kids. 'Anyway,' he said finally, 'I've decided to have a little leaving party. That's also why I'm calling.'

'Oh, right, where and when?'

'Two weeks Saturday at your house.'

Nick sat forward. 'My house?'

'Yes, nothing too rowdy, just a handful of us and a crate of beer. Thought we'd get chips in after we've been to the pub.'

Nick smiled at Beverly, who was able to hear the conversation. 'Sounds like I don't have any choice.'

'Don't worry. I'll clear up any mess and pay for any damage.'

'Damage?' Far from reassured, Nick felt his pulse race.

'Don't get your knickers in a twist, Shirley. It'll be grand. Got to go!' Eric ended the call.

'Sounds like you're having a party, then?' Beverly sighed and lay back on the sofa.

'Looks like it.'

'You should ask Oliver.'

'Do you think so?' He was happy and anxious in equal measure that she brought his boy into the equation.

'I do. It might be a good atmosphere for me to build a bit of a bridge, and he needs to say goodbye to Eric; he's like family to him, isn't he?'

'Yes. Yes, he is.' Nick's friend's leaving might be another blow for his son, who, like him, might feel that the safety net he spoke about was dwindling. He also thought of Jen and wondered when she was planning on talking to his best friend.

'I'll call him later; he'll want to know about the bank meeting any-way. Plus, I need to get back and let Treacle out.'

'I think we did really good today.' She rested her head on his chest and he ran his fingers through her hair; it felt nice, comfortable. He pictured the cold, dark hallway that awaited him and for the first time Nick wished he didn't have to go home . . .

Treacle barked to be let back in. Nick opened the door, watching her tootle past to her spot on the sofa as he tapped in Oliver's number.

'Hi, Dad.'

'Hi, Olly, thought I'd call and let you know how we got on today.' He crinkled his eyes, ridiculously aware of how the word 'we' might be antagonising and wanting nothing less right now than to reignite the simmering debate over him and Beverly.

'So how did it go?'

Nick exhaled; seemingly he had got away with it. He looked sky-ward at the utter ridiculousness of it all.

'It went well! Surprisingly, I knew the man at the bank, but I'm not sure if that's a positive or a negative. Anyhow, there's a bit more work to do, but they didn't throw me out laughing, which is what I dreamt the night before last, so yes, good, I think.'

'Of course you knew the bank man; it's Burston! You know everybody.'

'True. How's Tasha?'

'All right.'

'Just all right?' He noted the absence of the enthusiastic note that usually underpinned any mention of her.

'Yeah, I dunno.'

'What does *that* mean?' Nick leant against the sink. He heard Oliver sigh.

'It's just . . . How do you know if you've picked the right person? I mean, how did you know that Mum was the one you wanted to marry, be with, live with . . .'

He considered his response. 'I suppose the correct answer is that you *don't* know. Apart from that feeling, that crackle of intuition that tells you this seems like the right thing to do. But there is no guarantee, no hard and fast rule. It's more about a leap of faith. Nanny Mags was saying the other day it's about being brave, trusting that little voice of instinct. And I guess, in my case, believing that no matter what anyone else thought or said, I had made the right decision. And it *was* right. Not always perfect.' He pictured the wrapped shop-bought items lying untouched in the bottom of Kerry's wardrobe. The attached tags showing amounts that added up to sleepless nights, her actions, which placed a small pebble in the shoe of their relationship and then her terrible diagnosis and the almost inconceivable thought that, as she got sick, they as a couple healed. 'But without doubt the right person. The right choice.' He smiled at this truth and looked over towards the stove, where he saw the back of her, pre-illness, tucking her hair behind her ears, her apron tied behind her back . . .

'I suppose because she was having me too, that must have made it hard to walk away.'

'I never wanted to walk away. Never. I was shocked, certainly, to find out I was going to be a dad – don't think I'd long understood the whole mechanics of making babies, and there I was, having one of my own.'

'Too much information, Dad.'

'Sorry.' He laughed. 'It's true, though: we faced our challenges – everyone does, but I loved your mum and having you was just the best bonus. It changed me. I realised that it wasn't only about what I wanted or needed; it was all about what was right for you. It is still the most remarkable moment of my life – when they handed me you, all wrapped up, tiny and with a squashed red face like a little tomato. I knew I had to be a better person. I knew that you deserved the best life, and I've tried, Olly, always.'

'Yep.' There was a beat of silence while they both mulled over these heartfelt words. 'I've been thinking about what you said about Mum's watch.'

'You have?'

'I wouldn't give it to Tasha. I mean, I know you and Mum were even younger than I am now, but I feel too young to know if it's a long-term thing.'

'Well, I'd say that's the voice of instinct I'm talking about, and it's good you're listening to it.'

'I guess, and I think you're right – it should go to someone impor-tant, a permanent fixture in my life. And so I'm going to hang on to it for now.'

'I think that's wise. How's your course going?'

'Not bad. I've handed my assignment in and I've got another one due about business accounting.'

'I could have done with you today in my meeting.'

'Did Beverly go with you?'

This was a win; Oliver had in the past avoided using her name at all costs, referring to her as 'that woman' or 'she' – Nick smiled, it felt like a breakthrough.

'Yes, in fact she suggested you come to Eric's farewell party in a couple of weeks. He wants a small gathering, just close friends and a cold beer to send him on his way properly to Australia.'

'It's going to be weird. I can't imagine Eric not being around.'

'Me either, son, me either.'

'Night then, Dad.'

'Night, son.'

◆ ◆ ◆

He could tell Beverly was nervous, more so than she had been in the meeting with the bank. She crossed and uncrossed her legs and coughed several times, sitting up and then slouching back, as if unable to get comfortable in the chair. Her hands fidgeted in her lap. It was odd to be sitting in front of Julian Siddley for the purpose of asking if they could, in effect, take over his family company.

'So . . .' Julian paused and tilted back in his chair. 'To clarify, you're asking if we would sell you the current stock, the machinery, transport and our order book? And the figures are all here?' He tapped the proposal on the desk in front of him.

'Yes.' Nick saw no point in beating about the bush; with things moving quickly, time was of the essence.

Julian twisted his jaw and picked up his fountain pen, tapping it on the desk.

'I would need to talk it through with my father, of course, and I've no idea what his reaction will be. I do know one thing, though: I don't think I'd be happy with any future company, yours or anyone else's, using the Siddley name. That would be out of the question without a Siddley at the helm.'

'Agreed.' Nick again nodded. 'So you'll let us know?'

'I will, sooner rather than later.' Julian stood and the two shook hands, and Nick liked the way it felt, like equals.

'I can't decide if you two are brave or nuts,' Julian said affectionately.

Beverly smiled at her boss as they left his office. 'Bit of both, I think.'

1992

Nick lay back against the pillows and watched his dad close the curtains, shutting out the darkening sky on this early September night. It was funny how at the beginning of the summer holidays the weeks had stretched out ahead of him like an eternity, but now, on the night before school, it felt as if they had passed in a blink. His mum had washed and pressed his uniform, which hung on the back of the wardrobe door.

Jen was singing in the bath, much to his annoyance. Her flat sound floated under the bathroom door and right into his room.

His dad sat down at the foot of his bed. 'You don't have to worry, you know.'

'About what?' Nick felt a flutter of worry at the man's words, the word 'worry' instantly causing worry. And what should he worry about? School? His mum?

Jack Bairstow took a deep breath and rubbed the day-old stubble on his chin. 'I guess what I'm trying to say is that just because Eric's family are' – he scratched his nose – 'struggling a bit . . . because his mum has gone to Derby and all that, I don't want you to worry about Mum and me or our family or what might happen to you and Jen.'

'I don't.' He didn't.

'Good. Good.' His dad smiled and pulled the duvet up to Nick's shoulders before running his calloused palm over his son's forehead. It was a rare touch and it felt lovely. 'You need to know your mum and I are solid, we are mates, and that's what you need to look for in the person you end up with. Above all else, you need to be mates. It's important.'

Nick nodded, wondering how on earth it would be possible to be mates with a girl – *yuck!*

'And as I say, you don't need to worry. I know Eric doesn't have the easiest of times, and I think things must be tough for him right now, but he's lucky to have a good friend like you.'

Nick pictured his friend in his cold house and missed him sleeping on the floor. He glanced down at the space where the bed-in-a-bag had lurked on and off during the summer.

His dad rose and switched off the overhead light and gripped the door handle.

'You're going to fly this year; I can feel it.'

'I hope so.'

'And you've had a good summer?'

'The best, Dad.'

The summer of absolutely brilliant . . .

'You got to build your bike.'

'I did – I went down Cobb Lane at about fifty miles an hour!'

'Wow! That must have been scary.'

'It was a bit.' Nick shrugged. 'Good, though!'

'And you went in a Rolls Royce,' his dad reminded him.

'I did. Have you ever been in a Rolls Royce, Dad?'

His dad gave a soft, mournful laugh. 'No.'

'Why don't you ask Mr Siddley if he'll take you out?'

'Hmmm, I'm not sure. People who drive cars like Rolls Royces and own companies like Siddley's . . . they are cut from a special cloth, not the likes of me.'

This made Nick a little sad. He wanted his dad to be cut from the special cloth.

'I'm lucky to have a boy like you, Nicky, lad. I'm proud of you.'

His words danced like fireflies high above their heads, pinging against the ceiling and circling the room, filling the place with warmth and light.

'I think if I have a kid, I want to be a dad just like you . . .'

'To be honest, Nicky, you make it easy. You always seem to know how to do the right thing, not like some around here. I was talking to Kath Watson, a girl who's just started working in the canteen, and she's already got four kids. I'm trying not to judge but she's saddled for life – that's it! Her whole life, mapped out. I want more for you, son. I want you to aim high, work hard, get qualified and make sure you have the very best life you can, 'cos it's the only one you've got.'

'I will, Dad.'

'And don't forget that at the end of the day I've got your back. It's you and me against the world, the Bairstow Boys!'

Nick smiled and sank down into the pillow. He liked being one of the Bairstow Boys.

THIRTEEN

'Don't worry about picking her up early tomorrow; you might have a hangover, and I love having this little doggie here!' His mum kissed Treacle, who lay in her arms like a baby.

'Thanks, but I doubt I'll have a hangover; I'm a bit too past it for that kind of party. I'm out of practice.'

'Not what I heard . . .' His mum let this trail.

'Oh, thanks for reminding me!'

'Things seem a bit more settled, though, love, where Olly is concerned?'

'I'd say so. I mean, it still feels like walking on eggshells when he and Bev are in the same room, and I understand, but . . .'

'But you need to live your life.'

'I do, Mum.'

'He'll come round.'

'Hope so. Anyway, tonight it's only Eric and a handful of us sharing a few beers and scoffing pie and chips after the pub. What's the worst thing that could happen?'

His mum sniffed up her tears as her sadness spilled. 'I can't believe that boy is going to the other side of the world! I'm going to miss him.'

Nick nodded and placed his hand on her arm. He hated to see her cry.

'Mind you' – she sniffed – 'it'll save me a fortune. I've been feeding that lad since he was at junior school – he's eaten me out of house and home. I've never seen an appetite like it, apart from our Jen.' The two sighed. Eric and Jen, to them it seemed obvious.

'See you tomorrow.'

'Yes, love, see you then.'

His mum closed the door and Nick thought about how much Eric would be missed. In truth, he had been so busy working on the business plan, pulling everything together, that his friend's departure had not been at the very front of his mind. He had also concentrated on tonight's gathering, unable to remember the last time the house had held a party, choosing not to linger on the reason why. It was almost unthinkable that his mate would, for the first time ever, no longer be within walking distance. Nick briefly considered calling up Will and asking if he fancied filling the friendship vacancy created by Eric. Again.

He walked into the Blue Anchor and recalled the last time he had done so on pub quiz night, when nerves filled his gut and grief sat heavy on his shoulders. Tonight he felt different, lighter and looking forward to the future, whereas before he could only see a cold, dark loneliness looming ahead. This new-found optimism was, he knew, down to two things: Beverly, of course, who had relit flames of happiness inside him, flames that he thought were long extinguished; and the fact that as all the pieces of the jigsaw came together it was looking increasingly likely that he would, in the near future, sit in the big chair of a company very much like Siddley's. Only it would be better, because Nick knew not to spend his days sitting behind a desk, and that to get his hands dirty, doing any and every job he expected someone else to do, was the way to get respect and to fully understand what was going on.

The price had been agreed on the stock and machinery, and with his house as a guarantee on the loan all they needed now was to find premises.

'Mary!' Eric yelled as Nick walked towards the table, drawing one or two looks from locals who were amused by the name. 'What you having?' Eric rose.

'No, my shout.' Nick worked his way around the table. 'Alex?'

'Pint, please, mate.'

Ellie tutted as if her husband had inadvertently given the wrong answer. Nick caught Bev's eye and they smiled knowingly at each other. *Poor Alex . . .*

'Just a Coke for me.' Ellie lifted her glass, as if doubting Nick could get her order right without this example to follow.

'Jen?'

'Erm.' He noted his sister's body language, her hands clasped in her lap, shoulders dropped. She looked like she was trying to hide. Her voice too was quiet. 'Glass of white wine would be lovely, thanks.'

'I already know what Eric's having.' His mate had drunk cold bottled lager since they were teens. 'And for you, Bev?'

'I'm okay, thanks.' She tapped her full glass of orange juice.

'Cheap round! Marvellous!' Nick clapped as the door opened and in walked Oliver with Tasha in tow; the table broke into a cheer.

'Hey! You made it!'

Nick had not expected him to come all this way, but to see him again was wonderful. He pulled his son into an embrace and held him fast.

'Good to see you, Olly. Welcome home, lad.'

Eric jumped up from the table and took the boy into his arms. 'Welcome home, son.'

'I just wanted to come and say goodbye and good luck.' Oliver sounded so confident, so grown-up, it made Nick's heart swell.

'I'll miss you all.' Eric swallowed. 'But you're all welcome to come and visit any time you like. Just give me a bit of notice and I'll get the barbie fired up!'

As the bell rang for last orders, the troupe made their way along the street to Nick and Oliver's house. Beverly slipped her hand through his arm and Nick immediately looked towards Oliver, noting with relief that he and Tasha were deep in conversation peppered with laughter.

'When you're the big boss' – Alex slurred a little – 'are you going to get a spanking big navy-blue Roller like the one old Siddley had? Do you remember that day?'

'I bloody do!' Eric shouted. 'We were lost on the moors – got chased by a big puma and I nearly starved to death!'

'Eric.' Nick shook his head. 'We didn't actually see the puma and you didn't nearly starve to death. It must have been only an hour between your last snack and your tea.'

'Aye, but I were starving.'

'You're always starving,' Jen joined in.

'Well, hello, Pot.' Beverly laughed. 'You, Jen, have the biggest appetite I've ever known!'

'Yes, but she can eat what she likes; she keeps beautiful by running it off every day, chasing after all them baddies, don't you, Jen?' Eric spoke over their heads and Jen stopped walking.

'You all right?' Nick noted she looked a little pale.

Jen ignored him. 'Do you really think I'm beautiful, Eric?'

'I do.' He smiled at her. 'I always have.'

Jen took a step forward and reached up to kiss Eric on the cheek. He grabbed her around the waist and without hesitation kissed her full on the mouth. Jen reached up and knotted her hands in his hair and there they stood, locked together before breaking apart, breathless and beaming. There was a moment of awkward silence while the rest of the group looked from one to the other, no one quite sure what the situation demanded. Luckily, Alex, who was more than slightly inebriated, was there to break the silence.

'I never thought she was beautiful. I only thought she was bloody scary! I still do.'

And even Ellie laughed.

'It's true!' Alex yelled. 'If it were a toss-up between having to encounter Jen or go alone to the Old Dairy Shed in the middle o'night, then I'd pick that old shed any day. We were drawn to that place like moths – we loved it.'

Kerry's words again came loud and clear to his head and Nick saw an image so clear, so obvious, it left him feeling a little dizzy.

Everything can prosper with a bit of love . . .

'Oh my God! Alex, you beauty, that's it! You've found the missing piece of the jigsaw!'

'He has?' Ellie snorted, back on form.

'The Old Dairy Shed.' Nick stared at Eric, who required no further explanation.

'Yes! Mate, yes! The Old Dairy Shed!' Eric shouted, before releasing Jen and rushing over to lift his friend clean off the floor in a bear hug.

It had hardly been a party, more a gathering in the lounge with all sitting on those darned cushions. Oliver and Tasha had long since retired for the night and Alex and Ellie had left.

Nick managed to extricate himself from Eric's grip after returning the protestations of love that came thick and fast from his mate's drunken mouth. He tried to close the front door on Eric, who was walking Jen home; he waved to his sister, who loitered at the bottom of the path, calling, 'Hurry up, you dweeb!'

Nick fastened the bolt. 'I'd say that was a very good night.'

'It was.' Beverly chewed her lip.

'Are you okay? I noticed you were a bit quiet.' Nick led her into the kitchen and sat her at the table before filling the kettle. Tea at this time of night was always a good idea. 'If you're worried about Olly, I would say that tonight was ground-breaking. He seemed happy, relaxed. I'm certainly happy, relaxed. And Alex's suggestion is the best one! I can't believe we didn't think of it before – the Old Dairy Shed. It's perfect! On the other side of town, plenty of space, been sitting empty for years, good access down Cobb Lane. I used to cycle down it, get up some good speeds with a tailwind and—'

'Nick,' she interrupted, speaking softly. She knitted her hands on the tabletop. 'Come and sit down.'

'Sorry, I'm gabbling, I know, just excited.' He bunched his shoulders and grinned at her. His smile, however, faded when he saw her expression.

'Nick.'

The way she said his name while sitting in such close proximity told him this was a conversation that carried the weight of formality. It reminded him of the chat he had had with the doctor at St Vincent's.

So how long are we talking?

Days, weeks at most . . .

Spend time here, Nick, bring Oliver, say goodbye . . .

Nick swallowed the nerves that gathered in his throat. He wondered what he had done wrong, figuring that her upright posture and tone were the scaffolding to enable her to end whatever this thing was between them. This 'connection'. A wishy-washy term really, and nowhere near as robust as boyfriend and girlfriend, partners, a couple. He minded more than he thought he would. It wasn't only the prospect of not seeing her any more, but also the shock; he had thought they were going places. He liked the time he spent with her, looked forward to their budget nights in around the telly or on the sofa with a bottle of cheap plonk and a big bag of crisps to share. He would miss the distraction of her in his mundane life, miss the chat that nearly always ended in laughter, and he would miss the sex, a whole new adventure and one that had been off limits to him for so very long. He would miss lots of things. This was not how he had seen this fabulous evening ending.

'Nick,' she repeated, and he swallowed, sitting back against the chair and waiting for the words that he didn't want to hear, but he was clearly not in the driving seat. This was her call.

'This is not easy for me and so I need you to . . .' She paused, seemingly the words as hard for her to say as they were for him to hear. 'I need you to bear with me and not rush me and listen and then we can talk and think about what comes next, okay?' She licked her lips.

'Okay.' He nodded, but in truth he thought it was a lot simpler than that. She would feed him something along the lines of, *It's not you; it's me . . . You're not ready . . . I'm not ready . . . The timing is wrong . . . We can still be mates . . . It's been fun . . .* and then he would hold her awkwardly, counting down the embarrassed seconds until he could usher her from the front door and come back to this very spot, where he would sink down and feel sorry for himself. He realised in that second that he would miss her more than he thought, a lot more.

'Okay.' She nodded her agreement and gave a small smile of relief, seemingly delighted they had the semblance of a plan. 'I like you.'

'I like you too,' he levelled.

'It's been a wonderful time for me, but I still don't really know what this . . . thing, is between us.' She rolled her hands in front of her.

'No, I guess we've kept it vague, feeling our way, giving the other a get-out-of-jail-free card, not made too many plans, left the option to bail in place.' He thought he'd make it easy for her. And in hastening her words, a little easier on himself too.

'Yes, I guess so.' She paused and took a breath. 'But things have kind of taken me by surprise.'

'Right.' He coughed, watching as she filled her cheeks with air and blew out slowly, as if a little light-headed. 'For God's sake, just say it, Bev.' He looked her in the eye. 'Just say it.'

And so she did.

'I'm pregnant.'

Nick had heard the words, but it was as if she spoke in a foreign tongue, because surely the words he had heard and what she had meant to say must be two different things.

'You're . . .?' He felt his heart boom in his chest and his palms were a little clammy.

'I'm pregnant.'

Nick bent forward and rested his elbows on his thighs; he felt the ground rush up to meet him. He took slow, steady breaths so he didn't topple from the chair.

'You're pregnant?'

'I am.' She nodded and, whether consciously or not, placed the flat of her palm over her stomach.

Nick continued to breathe slowly and then stood; the room suddenly felt quite airless. He walked to the window and threw it open, letting the breeze suck the net curtains out into the cool evening air.

'It's a shock, I know.'

He turned sharply, almost having forgotten she was there, so preoccupied with his own thoughts, which were a raging torrent of confusion.

'Are you sure, Bev?'

She nodded briskly. 'One hundred per cent.'

He could see that her eyes were searching and thought about what this might be like for her, having to give this information – just as tricky, he suspected, as it was for him to hear it.

'Are you okay?'

She nodded.

'How . . . How pregnant are you?' he managed, coming back now to sit next to her at the table.

'Only just. About ten weeks.'

Nick mentally did the maths. 'That was very early on, when we . . .' He faltered. He might have got this woman pregnant, but still didn't know her well enough to talk about the mechanics of sex without the gauze of embarrassment. It spoke volumes.

'I don't know what to say!' He gave a nervous laugh.

'That makes two of us.' She pulled the sleeves of her jumper over her wrists.

'Have you thought about what you want, about how you might . . .' Again he faltered.

'I'm keeping this baby.' She cut to the chase and for the first time he pictured Oliver and having to tell his son the news. 'I'm thirty, Nick, not a kid. I didn't plan it, didn't consider it; we are so new.'

'We are that.' It was his turn to agree.

'But I do know that this might be my one shot at being a mother and I'm going to take it. I like you, Nick. I might even love you, a bit.'

He took her hand into his, and this one small gesture was enough to make her tears brim.

'But I don't expect you to jump on board and commit to anything you don't want to or feel obligated to. I really mean it. I'm used to being on my own and I've dealt with a lot of shit by myself, and I can do this alone if I have to.'

Her tears were heart-rending and he felt a pull of something in his chest that felt a lot like love.

'But I *am* on board! You're pregnant; how can I *not* feel obligated?'

'Christ, way to make a girl feel special.' She withdrew her hand.

'That's not what I meant; that's just how it came out.' He placed his hand on her arm. 'What I meant was, how can I walk away when you're carrying my baby? My baby! This baby!' he repeated, as if this fact was starting to sink in.

'What baby?'

He and Beverly turned to the voice that had asked the question from the kitchen door; neither had heard Oliver come down the stairs.

'Oliver!'

His son ignored Beverly and addressed him directly. 'I said, what baby, Dad?'

Nick looked from his son to the mother of his unborn child, sitting at the table. 'It's still very early days . . .'

'I have literally just this second told your dad,' Beverly explained, now with her hand over her stomach in protection of sorts.

'Told my dad what?' Oliver leant on the door frame as if he needed the support.

'I'm having a baby,' Beverly almost whispered, and Nick hated that the announcement that should be made with whistles and fanfares was muted and apologetic. It wasn't fair.

'Actually, to say *we* are having a baby would be more accurate.'

Oliver gripped the wall and looked like he might faint, and Nick understood. The news was still sinking in for him too, and with each moment of realisation he had to fight to keep calm.

'Come and sit down, Olly; we need to all talk about this, all of us.'

'There's nothing to talk about.' Oliver's voice was steady, and in that moment Nick knew he would prefer the shouts of anger that were predictable.

'Please, Oliver, come and sit down,' Beverly tried. 'No matter what happens, you and I will always be joined together; this little one is your family.'

Nick stared at her, confident that whilst spoken with the best will in the world, her words were not helpful. Oliver ran back up the stairs and returned only minutes later with Tasha, her hair mussed and her glasses askew, a coat on over her pyjamas and trainers on her feet.

'Where are you going?' Nick shouted.

'To Auntie Di's!' Oliver yelled as he slammed the door behind him.

'Perfect.' Nick slumped down on to the bottom stair. 'Bloody perfect.'

He looked up at Beverly, who stood opposite him now.

'Would you like me to head home?'

'Yes.' He stood and took her hands into his. 'I would like you to head up the stairs home. I would like you to walk through the front door and be home. In short, I want you to be home with me and I want to be home with you.'

Beverly let her head drop to her chest as her tears fell.

'I'm having a baby,' she managed through her tears. 'I cry a lot!'

'Don't cry. You're not going through this alone. *We* are having a baby.' He pulled her close and kissed her scalp. Looking over her head to the lounge, he saw himself and Kerry kneeling at either end of the rug, while Oliver tried and failed to take his first steps. Falling back on to his fat-nappied bottom.

He can't do it alone; he needs you to support him . . .

'And I will, I will support him every step of the way, for always.'

'Or her.' Beverly reached up and kissed his face.

And it was only then that he realised he had spoken the words out loud.

'Do you think I should call Di? Or go after him?'

Beverly shook her head. 'No, I think you should let him have his protest and pour his heart out to his Auntie Di, who will love it. And then in the morning you should go and bring him home. We need to make it right with Oliver. I can't be the reason for any disruption or unhappiness, because if I am then I will always be that person and I won't stand a chance. We can't have a hostile atmosphere, especially not in Oliver's home, his refuge.'

'You're right.' He sighed, wondering how he was going to fix this and thankful that Beverly was willing to try.

'But right now, can we please go to bed?'

Nick waggled his eyebrows in her direction.

'And you can forget that; growing a baby is bloody exhausting.'

Nick walked up the path and knocked on his sister-in-law's door. Having spent the majority of the night staring at the stars through the window, with his thoughts pulled between pure joy and deep concern, he was exhausted.

'Nick.' She stared at him from up high on the front step.

'Di.'

'I suppose you want to talk to your son?'

'I want to talk to him and bring him home, yes.'

She shook her head. 'Well, you've really done it now.'

'Done what?' He looked at her quizzically.

'You think this is a game? A joke?' She paused. 'A baby, Nick? Really? What were you thinking? You've only known her five minutes!'

Nick bit his bottom lip and listened.

'And what is she after? Jumping into Kerry's shoes so quickly. And what about Oliver, that boy deserves more, deserves better. And don't get me started on—'

'Get rid of it . . .' Nick cut her off.

'What?'

'Get rid of it.' He looked up and into his sister-in-law's face. 'That's what you said to Kerry when she told you she was pregnant. You said, get rid of it. You said she was ruining her life. You said that poor little mite didn't stand a chance with me as its dad. That's what you said, and Kerry sobbed when she told me. We were only kids and we needed every ounce of support from wherever we could get it. And support came from many places, but not from you. Never from you. You were furious, judgemental, angry for some reason, and it bothered Kerry, upset her, and it upset me.'

'I love Oliver!' He noted the emotion in her voice.

'I know you do now.'

'I always did!' she shouted. 'From the moment he was born, that lovely baby!'

'Yes, but if Kerry or I had listened to you he would never have *been* born, and make no mistake – he was, and he's the greatest achievement of my life, Di. The very best thing I've ever done, and if this new little one turns out to be half the person Oliver is then I will be the luckiest man alive.'

Nick looked up over Diane's shoulder to see Oliver standing behind her; he didn't know how much he had heard. The boy walked forward with Tasha not far behind.

'Thank you for having me, Auntie Di.'

'Any time, you know that,' she managed through her tears, swiping at her eyes with a balled-up tissue. 'I am always here for you.'

Oliver and Tasha walked slowly by his side. Nick didn't know what to say or how to say it. He suddenly felt rather old and a little tired.

'You two go on home; I'll see you there in a minute. I just need to go and fetch Treacle from Nan's.'

'Okay.' Oliver gave him a small smile.

Nick let himself in and walked into the kitchen, where his mum stood at the stove frying up bacon and eggs.

'Morning, son. Breakfast?'

'No, thanks, Mum.' He turned to the table, where Eric and Jen sat tucking into toast and tea, waiting for their bacon and eggs.

'Morning, Edna!' Eric lifted his mug in a salute.

'God, how can you look and sound so chirpy after the amount you drank last night?' Nick shook his head.

Eric grinned. 'Because I'm happy.'

'And why are you so happy exactly?'

'Because I love your sister and because I think she might love me. We are still ironing out the details.' As if to prove it, he placed his free hand along Jen's shoulders and pulled her to him, and she didn't punch him or push him away; in fact, she looked quite pleased.

'Is this true? You might love my friend?' he asked his sister affectionately, reflecting on their conversation, when she had confessed as much.

'As I said, I'm considering that possibility, yes.' She looked down, her blush spreading.

'I'll say this only once. I've known you a long time, Eric Pickard, but if you hurt my sister I'll break your face. She is one in a bloody million.'

Jen beamed at him. 'Cheers, Nick.'

'Well, I don't know what to make of it all.' His mum flipped the fried egg in the pan. 'Eric stayed over last night but there was no sign of the bed-in-a-bag, if you get my meaning.' Jen and Eric laughed. Nick pulled a face as unwelcome images floated into his mind. His mum continued. 'It seems like these two are finally doing the right thing and he's jetting off to Australia!'

'I know,' he agreed. It was terrible timing.

'Although I'm quite looking forward to waving him off. I need the rest from all the cooking, and at last I can run the fridge down and take it easy a bit . . .'

Nick was perplexed. It was only a short while ago that she had shed tears at the thought of him leaving.

'Looking forward to it? You do know where Australia is, Mum?' He took a breath. 'It's a long way . . .'

'Calm down, you dweeb.' Jen shook her head at her brother. 'He's only going for a month.'

'A month?' Nick laughed with something that felt a lot like relief. 'But I thought you had a plan to start over, a new life . . .' He stared at his best friend.

'Yes, son, but plans change. Plans change. I reckon I'd like to invest in your business and maybe have my own private place to park my bike at the new flash offices – and a fancy title, of course. Plus, Jen said I could go to Cubs if I wanted and that she'd get me the uniform and everything, so I'm staying here.'

Nick felt the swell of happiness in his gut. This was good news; it was, in fact, absolutely brilliant.

'You're a bloody weirdo!' His sister laughed.

'Yes.' Eric took a bite of his toast. 'But I'm your bloody weirdo.'

'We'll see.' Jen sipped her cup of tea. 'We'll see.'

With Treacle on her lead, Nick decided his news could wait. He wanted Jen and Eric to have their moment.

He walked slowly home, laughing to himself at the turn of events. It seemed his friend was right: the waiting game paid off after all. Nick paused in his driveway and looked up at the house. His eyes were drawn to the small rectangular window above the front door, from where the light shone. This light in the hallway was at this moment more than just an aid to ensure a stumble-free trip up the path; it was a beacon, a sign of the life that lay behind the door, the promise of a warm welcome, a cup of tea and company. Music filtered from Oliver's bedroom window, Nick could see him and Tasha dancing in shadow. It was a house full of life and light. It was home.

He put the key in the front door and let Treacle off her lead before walking with some urgency towards the sound of crying.

Oh, no . . . Oh, please, no!

Beverly sat at the kitchen table with her head in her hands, sobbing.

'Oh, God! Oh, no, Bev, what happened? Is it something Oliver said?'

She nodded and gasped for air, her eyes swollen.

'Something he did?' His mind ran riot and he felt the swell of anger. *How dare he reduce her to this? What gives him the right?*

Again she nodded. Reaching up, she grabbed Nick's arm and pulled him down into the seat opposite hers.

'What happened?' he asked softly.

Beverly took a deep breath and reached for the kitchen roll, into which she blew her nose.

'He . . . He came in with Tasha and . . . and went upstairs.' She paused and took another breath and then wiped her eyes. 'Then he came straight back down again and . . . and sat where you're sitting and he . . .'

'He what?' Nick felt the tightening of his jaw.

'He said he wanted me to have this.' She opened up her palm to reveal Kerry's watch, and suddenly it became clear that she was crying happy tears, happy tears of acceptance. 'And he said that his mum would want me to have it too.'

Nick felt his own tears spring. And he nodded at this truth – Oliver, like him, had realised that this woman who was carrying Nick's baby was going to be a permanent fixture in his life, someone he thought worthy.

Oliver's right, she's a good lass . . .

Nick smiled as Kerry's words filled his head, and he nodded.

Thank you, Kerry, thank you, my girl . . .

Summer – two years later

Nick stood by the perimeter fence and looked out over Cobb Lane. He was trying to calculate just how fast he might have gone downhill on Half Bike all those years ago. Age and wisdom told him it couldn't have *actually* been fifty miles an hour, but it sure as hell felt like it.

'Those were the days.'

'Who are you talking to, Bunty?' Eric called from the forklift cab, having just loaded up the last lorry of the day, the side of which was emblazoned with the name Bairstow. Eric might have been a director of the company, but he loved nothing more than driving his beloved forklift.

'Myself!' He chuckled.

Eric laughed. 'Bev told me to say, "You've got visitors."'

'Who? Where?' Nick looked around the loading bay and out towards the car park where his beloved silver Jaguar sat.

'Di, Dora and Olly. I think they're in the canteen.'

'What have I done now?' Nick asked sheepishly, as he made his way across the warehouse to the cavernous café area, where Roy sat at one of the tables, spooning a rather dubious-looking grey stew into his mouth.

'That nice, Roy?' Nick laughed as he waved to Kath, who stood behind the serving hatch.

'It's not as bad as it looks, actually.' Roy went in for another spoonful.

'I'll have to take your word for it. I thought I had visitors?'

'Bev took them up to your office.'

'Ah, cheers, mate.'

Nick jogged up the rather industrial staircase in the renovated Old Dairy Shed. It had filled him with joy to see the old girders repaired, stripped and painted and the walls rebuilt to restore the place to its former glory. The mezzanine deck with its offices and meeting room was a new addition, with a snazzy glass front that meant he could watch over operations at all times. Even Will Pearce had nodded his approval on his last visit, and Nick had thankfully managed to remove the bin liners that Eric had seen fit to place on all the seats in the meeting room just prior to his arrival. Not that he could do much to control his errant best friend; he never had been able to, thinking of the time he had shouted 'Shit sticks!' so loudly he was certain his dad, keeping an eye over the brow of the hill, must have heard. It made him smile even now, thinking about that day and hiding from the big black puma . . . *We were idiots!*

Nick heard the babble of conversation as he approached his office. Beverly was sitting behind his desk, while Dora, Diane and Oliver sat at the round table in the middle of the room.

'Right, Nick,' Diane addressed him the moment he walked through the door. 'Oliver gets two tickets for his graduation, and the question is, who should go?'

He looked over towards Beverly, who glanced at the watch on her wrist. The watch Oliver had given her, a precious thing. She rolled her eyes and sat back, indicating she was keeping well out of it.

'Oh, well, I had just assumed it would be me and Bev, unless Olly has other ideas?' He looked towards his son and again tried not to grimace at the sight of his unkempt beard. He wished he would shave it.

Oliver, however, assured him it was a thing; everyone who was anyone now had a beard. Nick ran his palm over his clean-shaven chin.

'I don't mind.' Oliver's comments were less than helpful.

'Thanks for that, son.' Nick nodded in his direction.

'I just think, as our Kerry can't be there, she would want her sister or her mum there in her place.' Diane folded her arms across her ample chest.

'I don't mind not going; it's a long way is Birmingham and I can't go on a bingo day, in case I didn't get back in time.' Dora winked at him and Nick smiled at his ally, the woman he was so fond of.

'Thinking about it' – Oliver sat forward – 'I think it's best if Dad and Bev come, cos then Bev can help me with my tie and everything, and I know Tasha wants to hang out with you on the day, Bev. And it's a chance for you to meet her mum and her mum's new fella.'

Beverly nodded, and Nick could see she was happy, relieved to have her position asserted so publicly. And today, like every day, he felt thankful that he had listened to that crackle of intuition and had taken a leap of faith. Trusting that little voice of instinct, believing that no matter what anyone else thought or said, he had made the right decision. And it *was* right. He loved her. He absolutely loved her!

Oliver wasn't done. 'Then I thought we could all come back here and have a tea at yours, Gran, all of us together, with one of your amazing cakes, Auntie Di.'

Nick watched his sister-in-law beam and knew that Oliver's new job in sales and marketing would suit him well; he always seemed to know when to speak and just what to say.

Our boy, Kerry . . . BA Honours, can you believe it?

'Here he is!' Dora turned towards the front door as Nick's mum walked in with Archie on her hip, fresh from nursery.

'Hello, darling!' Di yelled, clapping her hands.

'Hey, little one,' Dora added.

There was no doubt this little boy was so loved.

Archie's lip began to tremble; he was a little overwhelmed by all the attention.

'Do you want Olly to take you to the field?' Beverly asked her son. Archie nodded vigorously; being with his big brother in the wide-open stretch of land to the right of the site, which Nick had recently acquired, was one of his favourite things. It was their very own football pitch and, Nick figured, a sound investment for the future – just in case Merryvale or someone like them *were* ever successful in getting a planning application passed to build houses in Burston, Nick wanted to keep as many green spaces around his business as possible.

'I'll walk them down.' Nick smiled at his wife and left the office, walking ahead of Oliver, who carried his little brother with ease. He found there was something profoundly moving about seeing his oldest carrying his youngest, a generation apart and yet brothers, mates.

Nick took a deep, slow breath. It felt good to be outside on this very hot summer's day.

'I honestly don't mind about graduation, Dad, but it should be you and Bev who go.'

'I agree, son. Graduating, eh? Did you ever get round to reading all them books?'

'One or two of them.' Oliver kicked at the ground.

Nick laughed, remembering the 'code red' day when he had nearly given it all up. 'Don't worry about graduation day. I think just let them talk it out. Sometimes Di just likes to get things off her chest.'

'Yep.' Oliver nodded; he put Archie on the ground and watched as he ran straight for the goal. 'He might be a footballer when he grows up.'

'He might be. Alex once considered playing for Man U.'

'Man U? I didn't know Alex played footie!'

'He doesn't, but he figured Man U would teach him how.' Nick laughed at the absurdity of the idea. 'I'm glad you're coming to work here, Olly, but I don't think you should stay forever.'

'Cheers for that!'

'You know what I mean, son. I'm not saying you can't end up in Burstonbridge. I for one wouldn't want to be anywhere else, but I want you to aim high, work hard and make sure you have the very best life you can, 'cos it's the only one you've got.'

'I will. I know that, Dad.'

'You're going to fly this year. I can feel it.'

'I hope so.'

'And you've had a good summer?'

'I have, it's been the best, just hanging out at home and spending time with this little fella.' Oliver ran forward and scooped his little brother into his arms. 'Don't you ever forget, Archie, lad, I've got your back. It's you and me against the world, the Bairstow Boys!'

Nick smiled and turned to go; he had calls to make. It was garden party and outdoor festival season and they were busy – mind you, they were always busy.

'Dad?'

'Yes, Olly?'

'I wanted to ask you, whatever happened to Half Bike?'

'Ah.' He turned to face his boys and felt the lump of emotion rise in his throat. 'It was a couple of years after we built it and one of us in our little gang needed money for a train ticket.'

'A train ticket?'

'Yes, a secret mission so they could head off to Derby and meet their little brother, and that person was so chuffed, so excited to be making the trip, that he slept with the cash in an envelope under his pillow. It was a wrench to see Half Bike go, but worth it really.'

'Which one of you needed to go to Derby? Eric or Alex?' Oliver was curious.

'Ah, that would be telling . . .'

Nick smiled, remembering the moment he had handed the cash over. 'What did you go and do that for, Rosemary?' had been Eric's response, as he tried not to cry.

His phone rang.

'All right, Bev?'

'Yep, Dora and Di and your mum are just leaving. I think I'll drive them home and go and get dinner started.'

He smiled and pictured her in their lovely new kitchen in the Victorian villa overlooking the Rec that they called home.

'Can I get you anything before I go, love?'

Nick looked up at the sign over the gates that bore their family name – his father's name, his sons' name and his sister's name – and he knew that to walk beneath them all those years ago by his dad's side would have been some moment. And yet here he was: he had done it, figured it out, worked hard and the universe had helped him over the finish line.

'Actually, yes, love, could you get me a can of orange Fanta?'

He heard her laughter down the line.

'Can of orange Fanta? Get it your bloody self!'

ABOUT THE AUTHOR

Photo © 2012 Paul Smith of Paul Smith Photography at
www.paulsmithphotography.info

Amanda Prowse likens her own life story to those she writes about in her books. After self-publishing her debut novel, *Poppy Day*, in 2011, she has gone on to author twenty-two novels and six novellas. Her books have been translated into a dozen languages and she regularly tops bestseller charts all over the world. Remaining true to her ethos, Amanda writes stories of ordinary women and their families who find their strength, courage and love tested in ways they never imagined. The most prolific female contemporary fiction writer in the UK, with a legion of loyal readers, she goes from strength to strength. Being crowned 'queen of domestic drama' by the *Daily Mail* was one of her finest moments. Amanda is a regular contributor on TV and radio but her first love is, and will always be, writing.

You can find her online at www.amandaprowse.com, on Twitter or Instagram @MrsAmandaProwse, and on Facebook at www.facebook.com/AmandaProwseAuthor.